VOLUME
ONE

SKYW

IMAGE COMICS, INC.

Robert Kirkman – Chief Operating Officer
Erik Larsen – Chief Financial Officer
Todd McFarlane – President
Marc Silvestri – Chief Executive Officer
Jim Valentino – Vice President
Eric Stephenson – Publisher / Chief Creative Officer
Jeff Boison – Director of Publishing Planning & Book Trade Sales
Chris Ross – Director of Digital Services
Jeff Stang – Director of Direct Market Sales
Kat Salazar – Director of PR & Marketing
Drew Gill – Cover Editor
Heather Doornink – Production Director
Nicole Lapalme – Controller

IMAGECOMICS.COM

SKYWARD, VOL. 1. Fourth printing. March 2020. Published by Image Comics, Inc. Office of publication: 2701 NW Vaughn St.,
780, Portland, OR 97210. Copyright © 2020 Joe Henderson & Lee Garbett. All rights reserved. Contains material originally publi
in single magazine form as SKYWARD #1-5. "SKYWARD," its logos, and the likenesses of all characters herein are trademar
Joe Henderson & Lee Garbett, unless otherwise noted. "Image" and the Image Comics logos are registered trademarks of Image Co
Inc. No part of this publication may be reproduced or transmitted, in any form or by any means (except for short excerpts for journa
or review purposes), without the express written permission of Joe Henderson & Lee Garbett, or Image Comics, Inc. All names, chara
events, and locales in this publication are entirely fictional. Any resemblance to actual persons (living or dead), events, or places, wi
satirical intent, is coincidental. Printed in the USA. For information regarding the CPSIA on this printed material call: 203-595-3
For international rights, contact: foreignlicensing@imagecomics.com. ISBN: 978-1-5343-0833-6

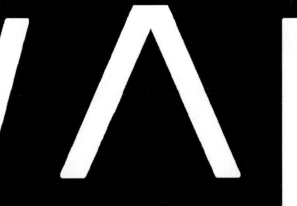

'MY LOW-G LIFE'

WRITER
JOE HENDERSON

ART & COVER
LEE GARBETT

COLORIST
ANTONIO FABELA

LETTERER
SIMON BOWLAND

ART & COVER
LEE GARBETT

EDITOR
RICK LOPEZ Jr.

PRODUCTION
CAREY HALL

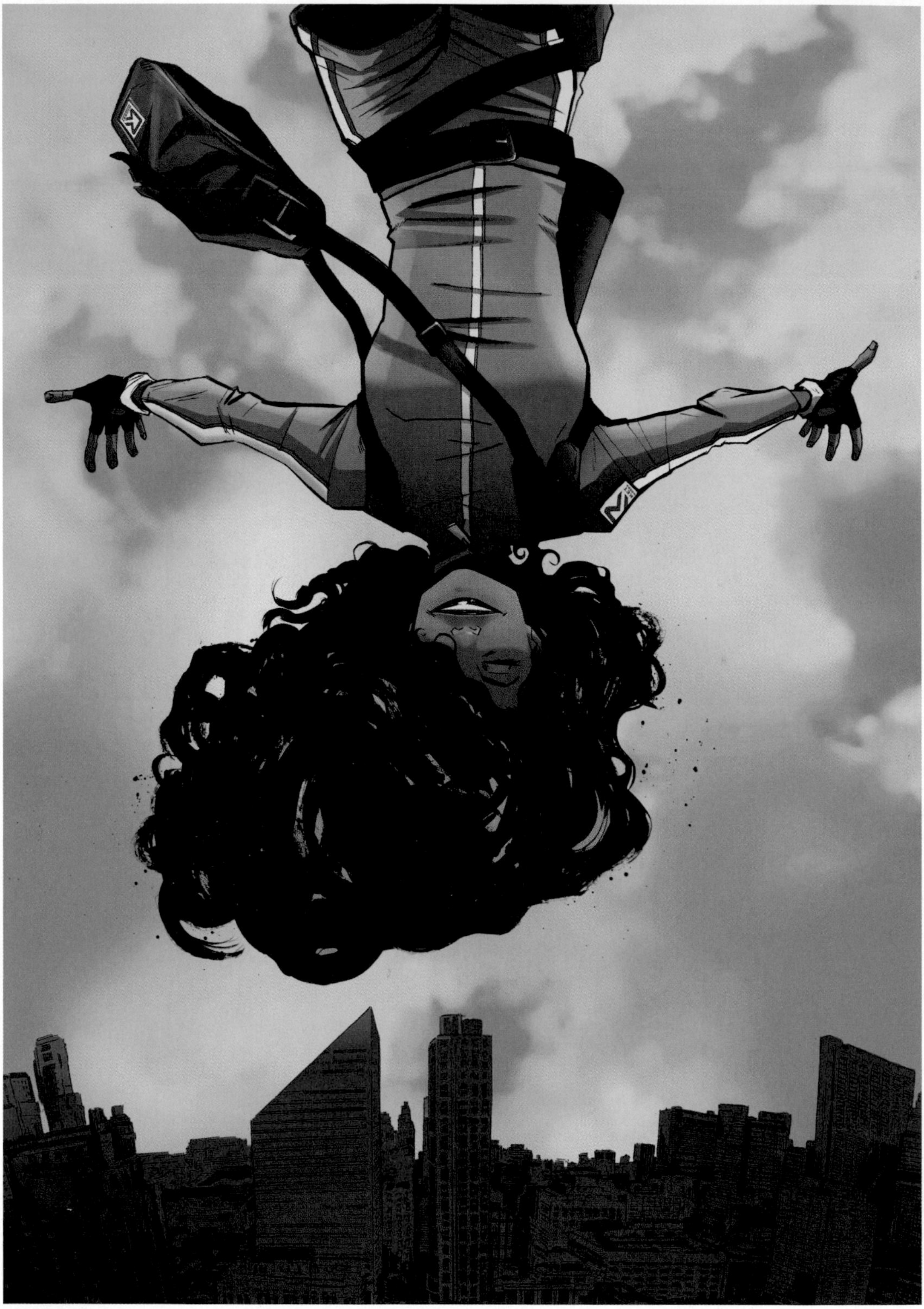

CHAPTER ONE

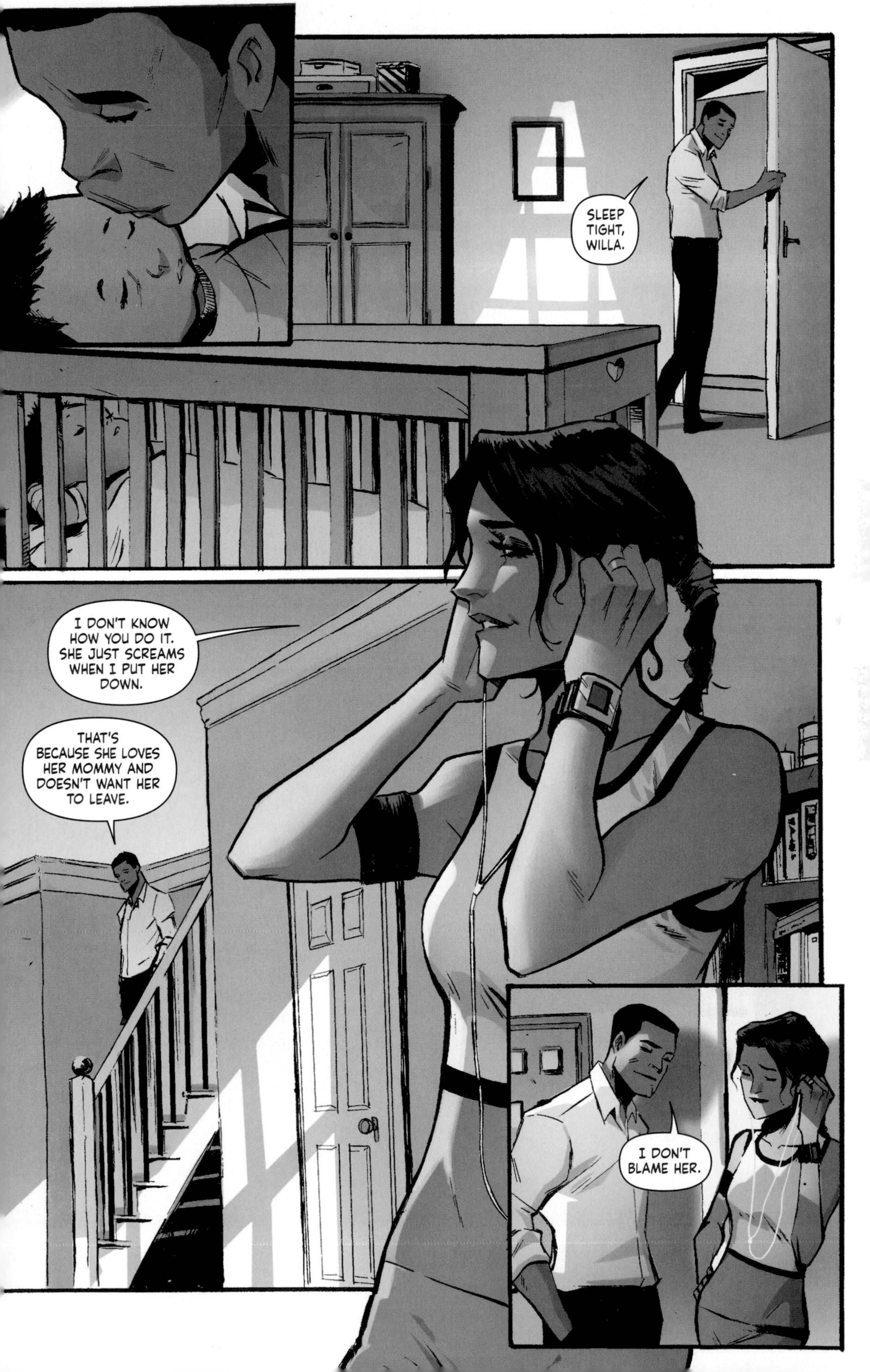
SLEEP TIGHT, WILLA.
I DON'T KNOW HOW YOU DO IT. SHE JUST SCREAMS WHEN I PUT HER DOWN.
THAT'S BECAUSE SHE LOVES HER MOMMY AND DOESN'T WANT HER TO LEAVE.
I DON'T BLAME HER.

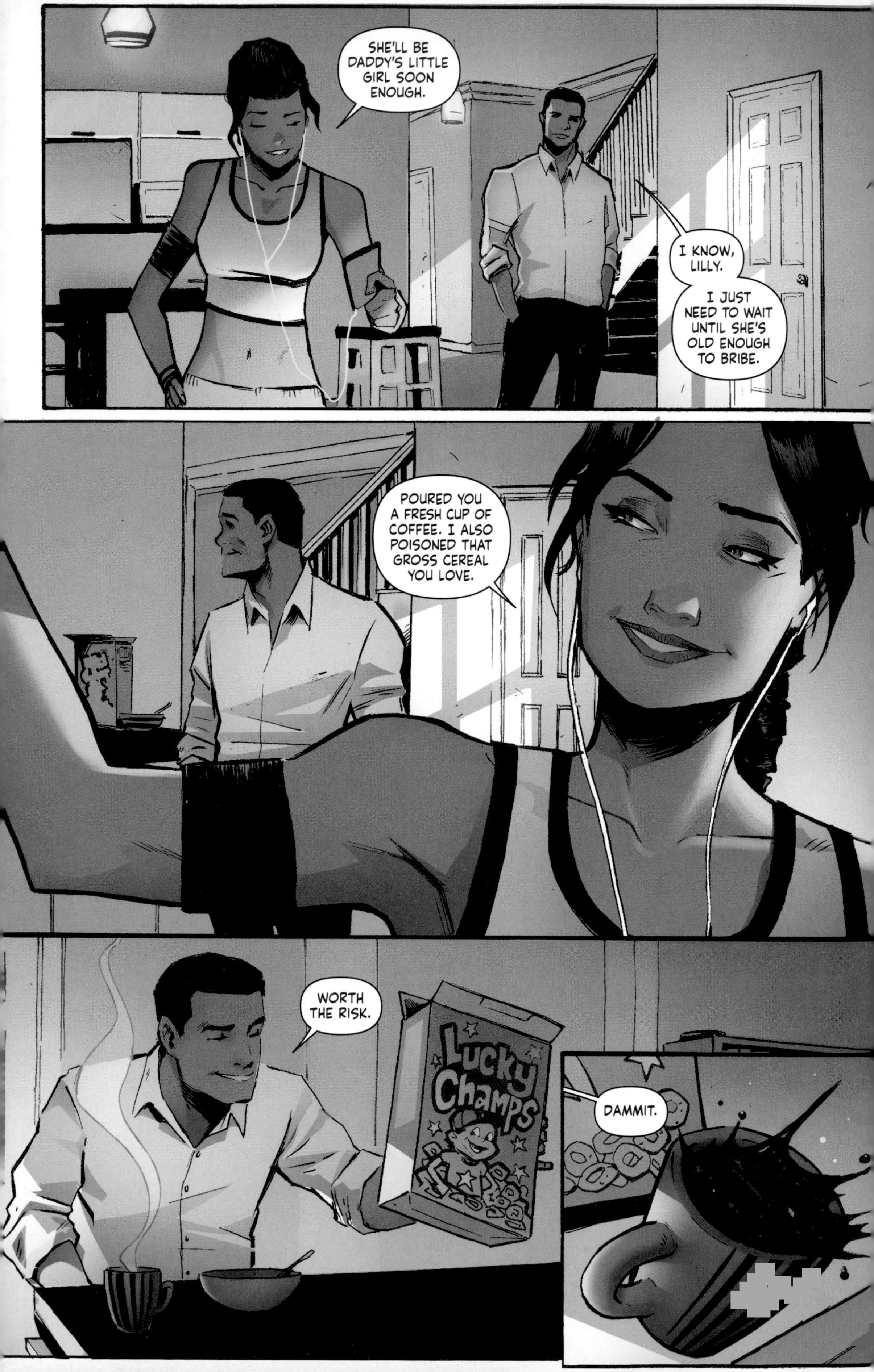
SHE'LL BE DADDY'S LITTLE GIRL SOON ENOUGH.
I KNOW, LILLY.
I JUST NEED TO WAIT UNTIL SHE'S OLD ENOUGH TO BRIBE.
POURED YOU A FRESH CUP OF COFFEE. I ALSO POISONED THAT GROSS CEREAL YOU LOVE.
WORTH THE RISK.
Lucky Champs
DAMMIT.

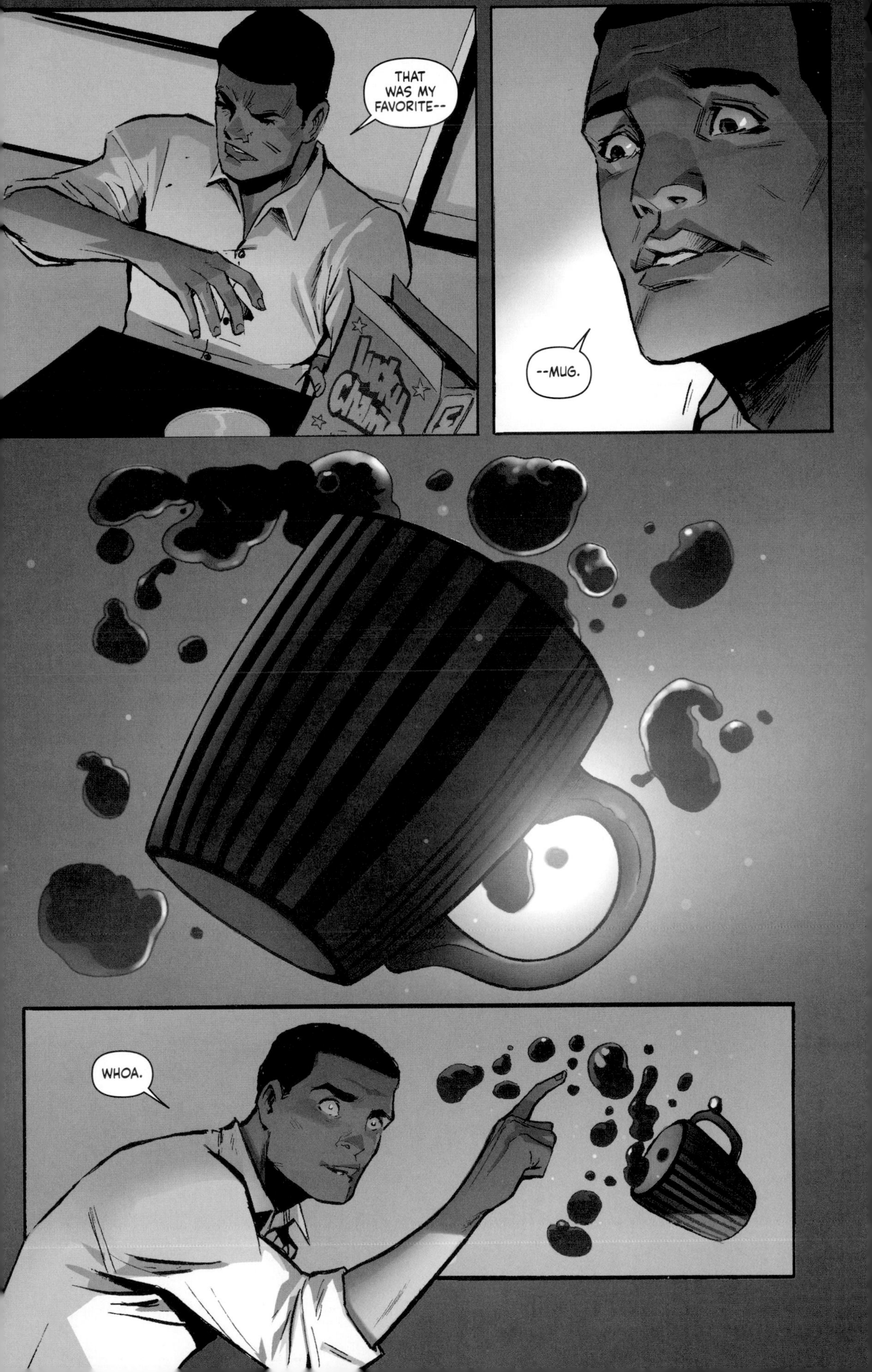
THAT WAS MY FAVORITE--
--MUG.
WHOA.

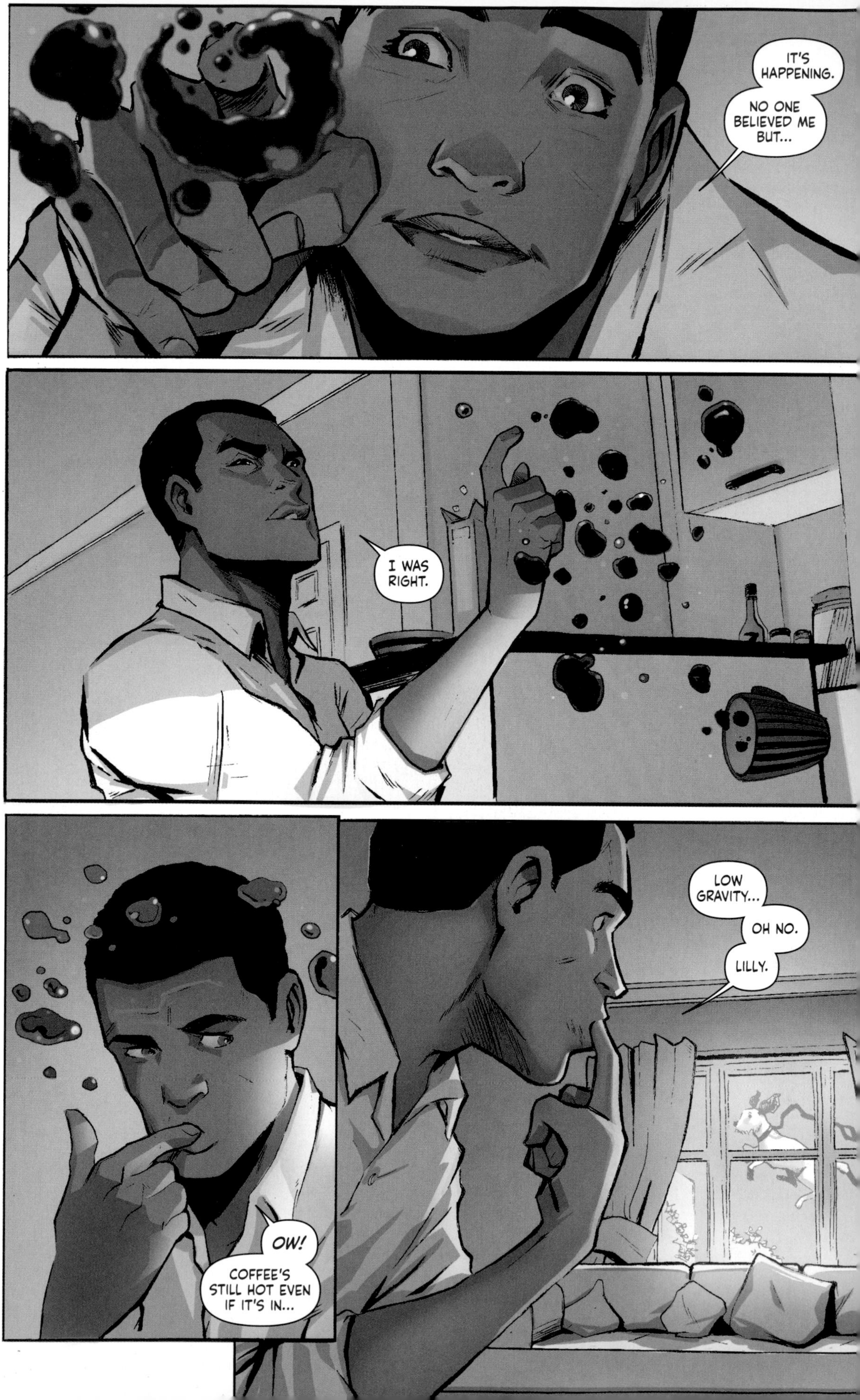
IT'S HAPPENING.
NO ONE BELIEVED ME BUT...
I WAS RIGHT.
OW!
COFFEE'S STILL HOT EVEN IF IT'S IN...
LOW GRAVITY...
OH NO.
LILLY.

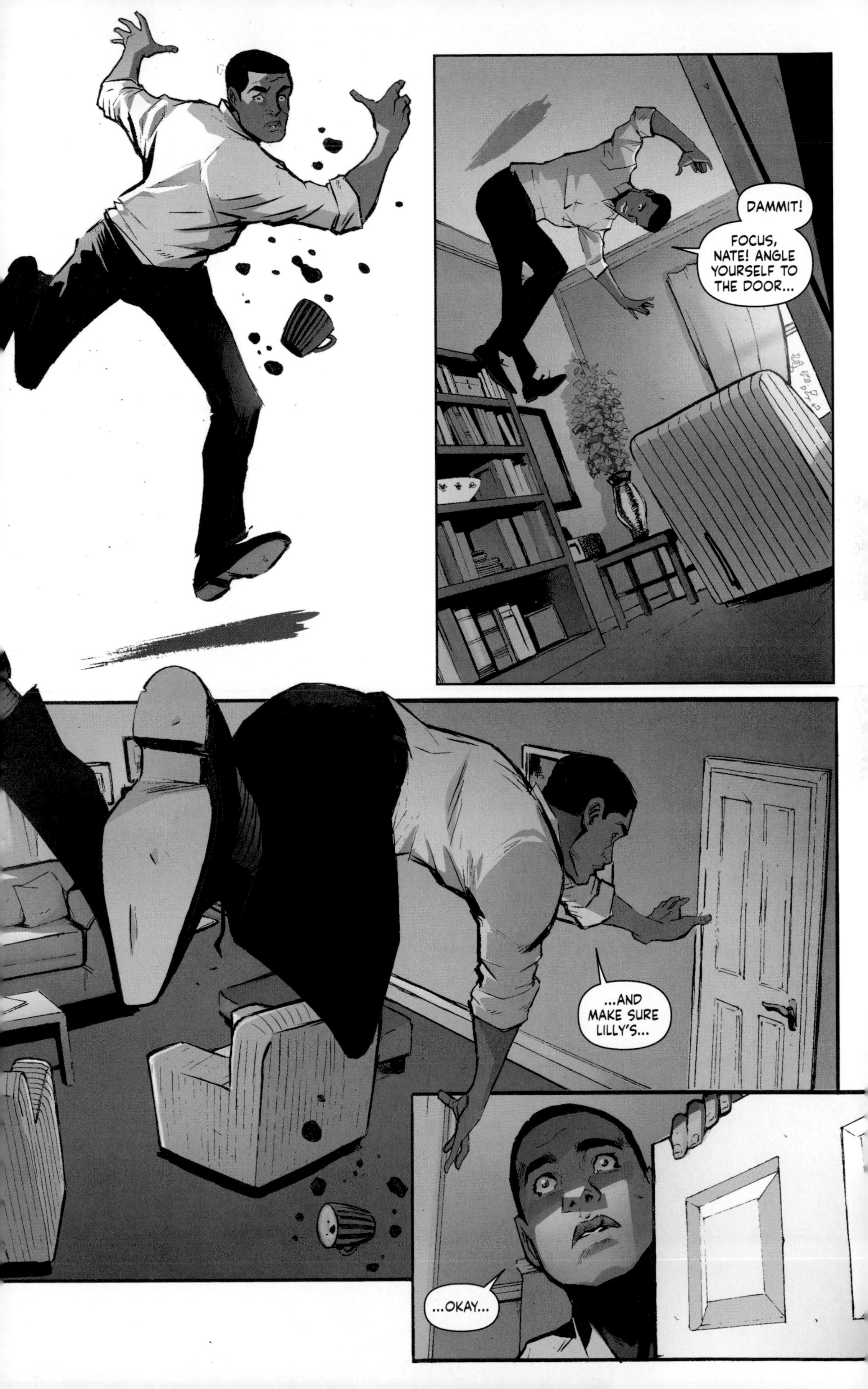
DAMMIT!
FOCUS, NATE! ANGLE YOURSELF TO THE DOOR...
...AND MAKE SURE LILLY'S...
...OKAY...

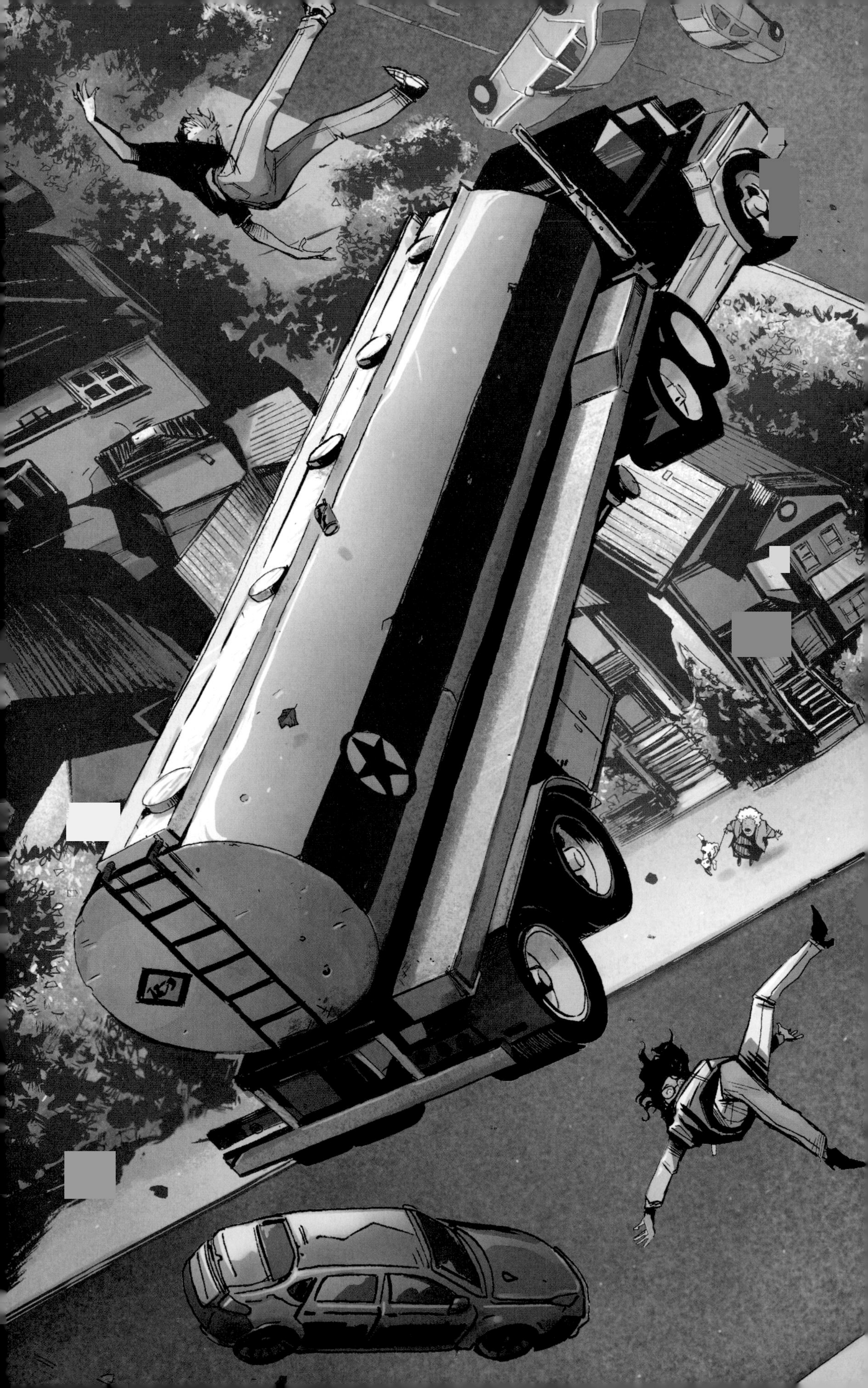

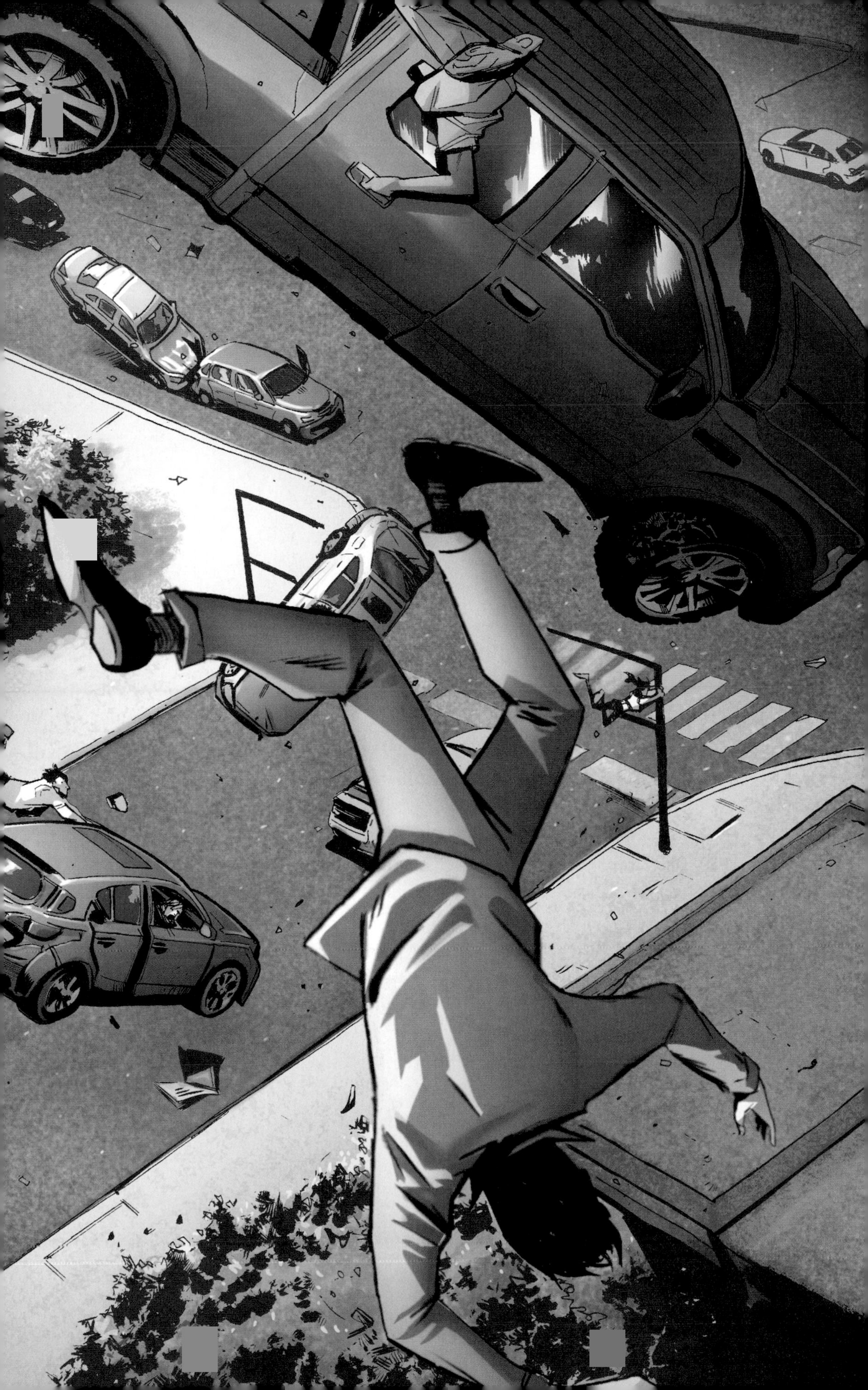

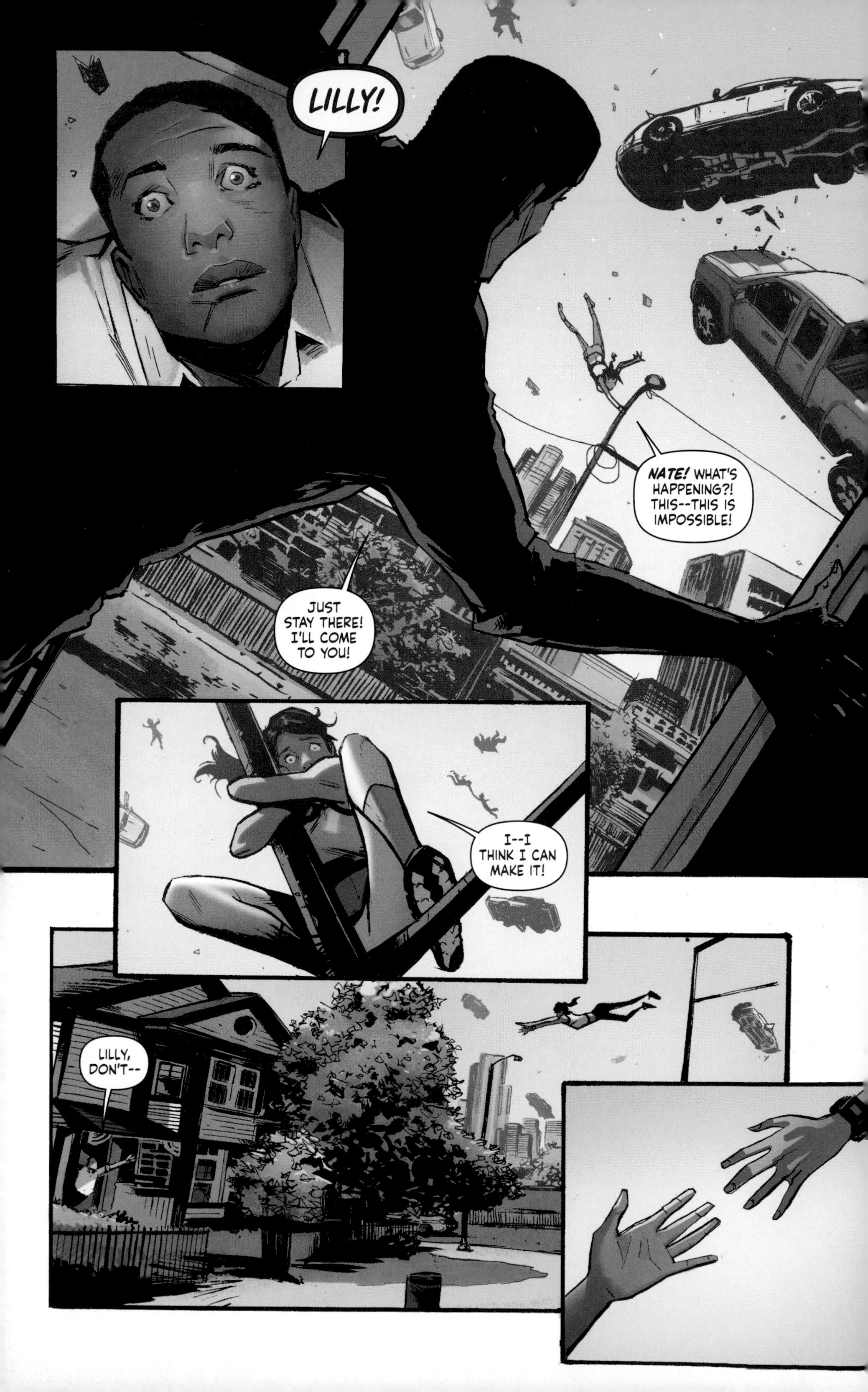
LILLY!
NATE! WHAT'S HAPPENING?! THIS--THIS IS IMPOSSIBLE!
JUST STAY THERE! I'LL COME TO YOU!
I--I THINK I CAN MAKE IT!
LILLY, DON'T--

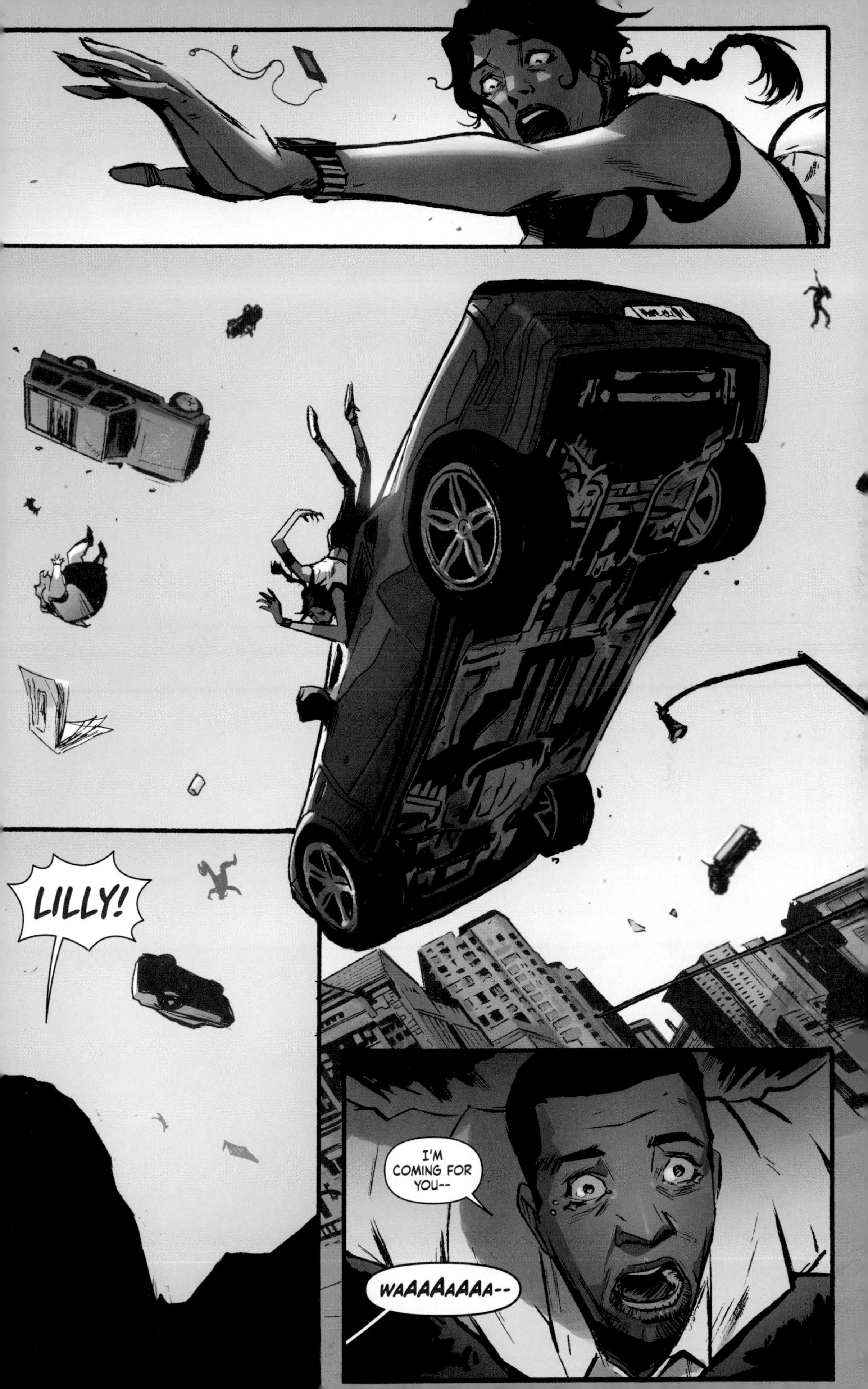
LILLY!
I'M COMING FOR YOU--
WAAAAAAAA--

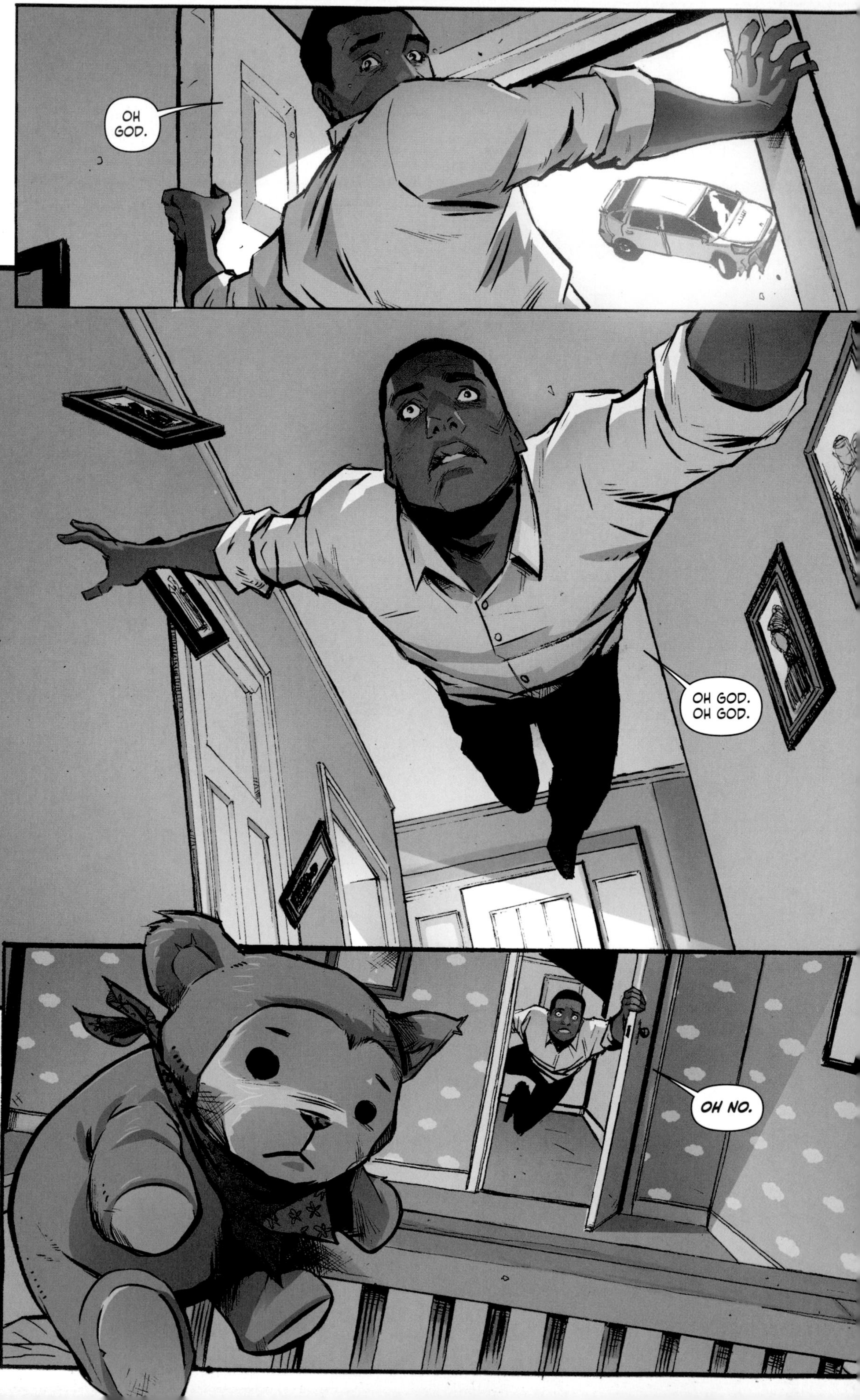
OH GOD.
OH GOD. OH GOD.
OH NO.

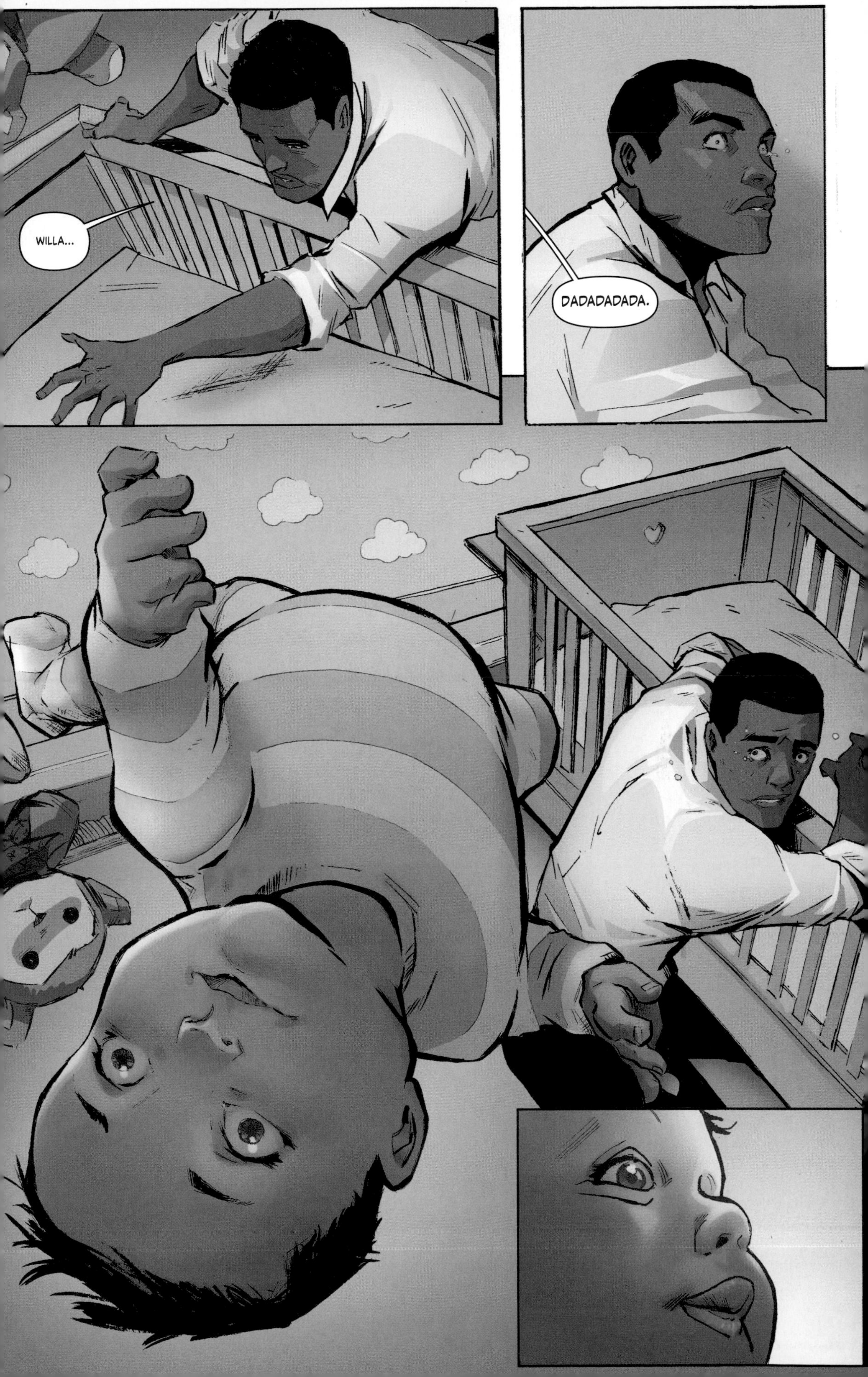
WILLA...
DADADADADA.

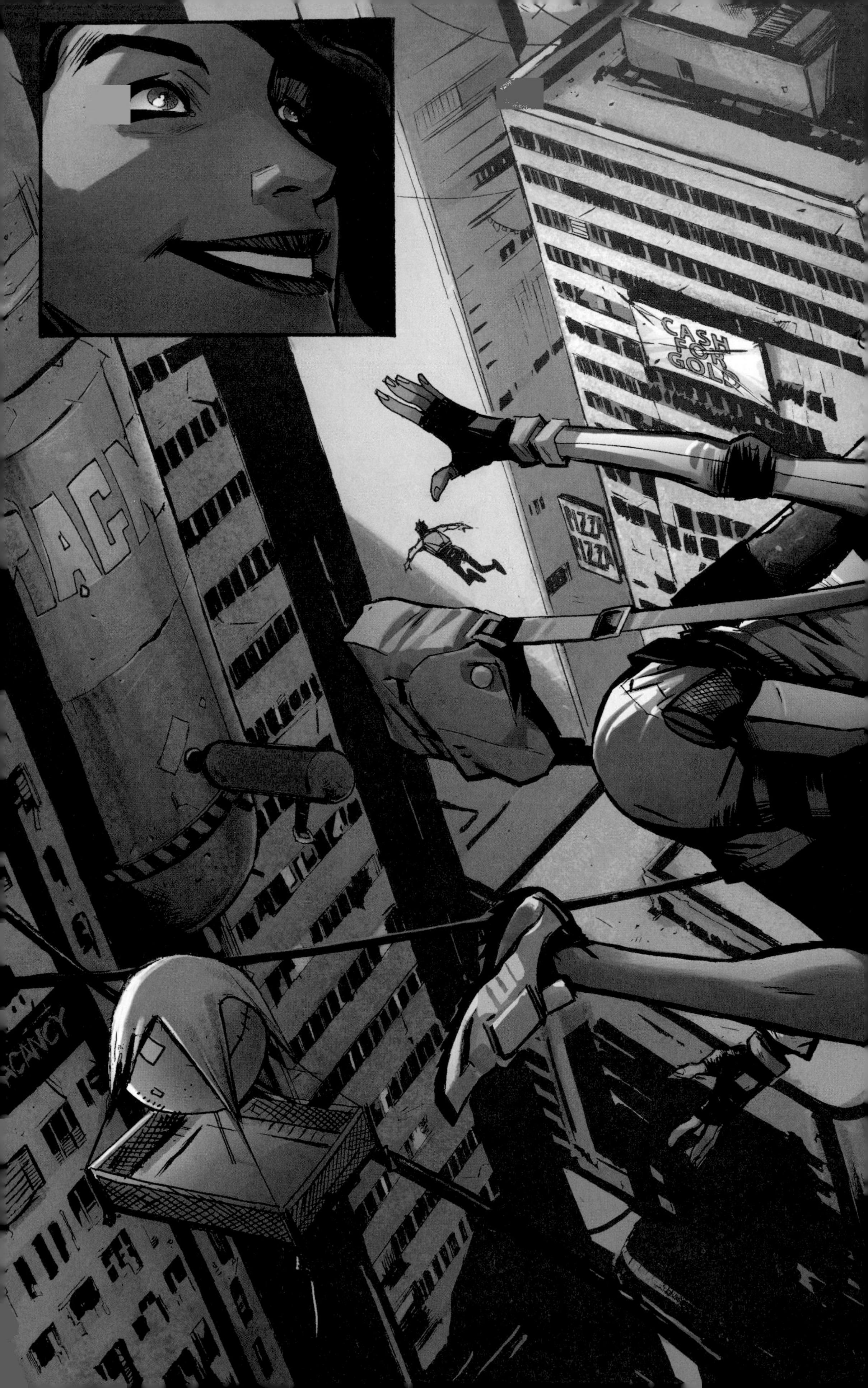
CASH FOR GOLD
PIZZA PIZZA

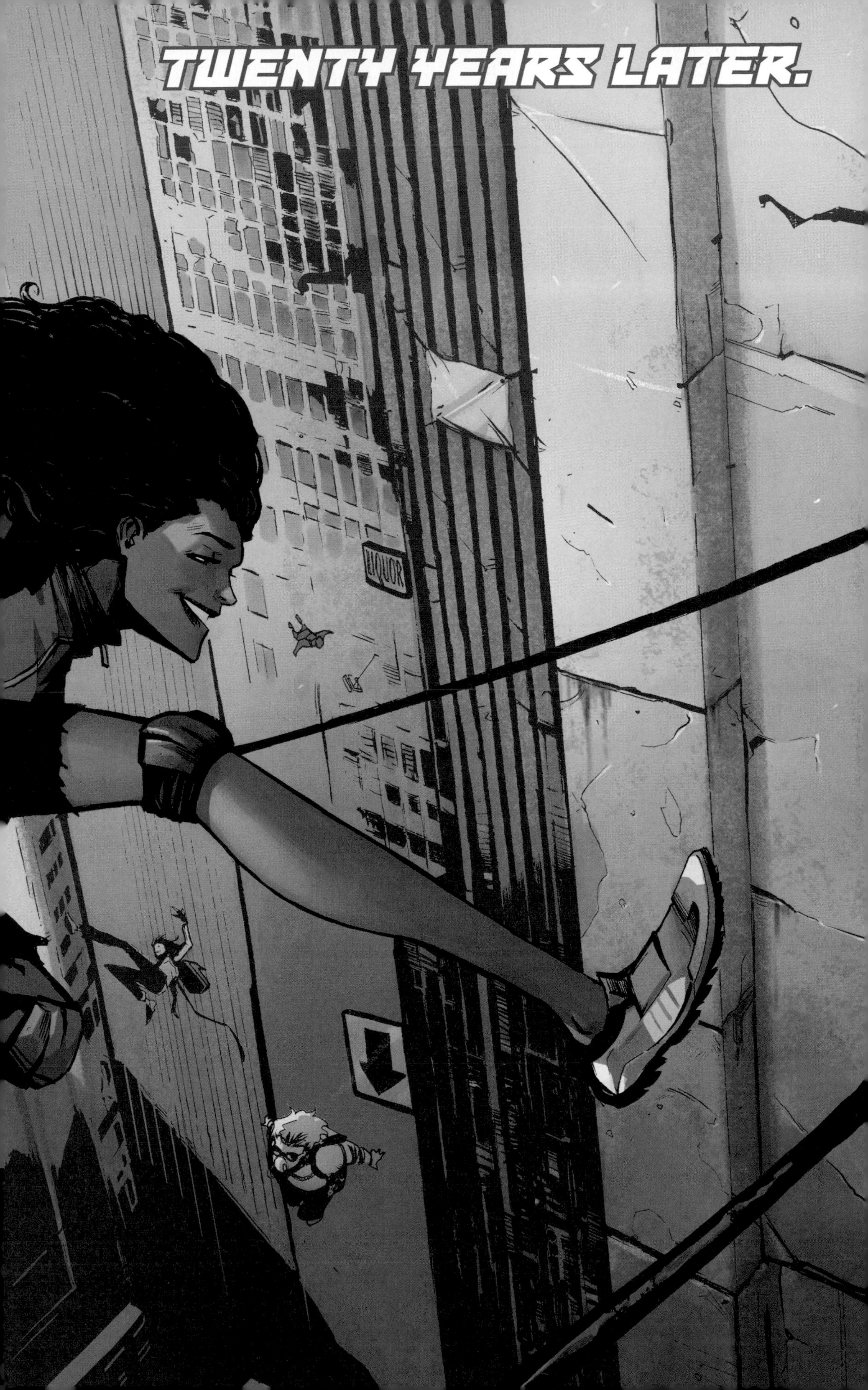

TWENTY YEARS LATER.
LIQUOR

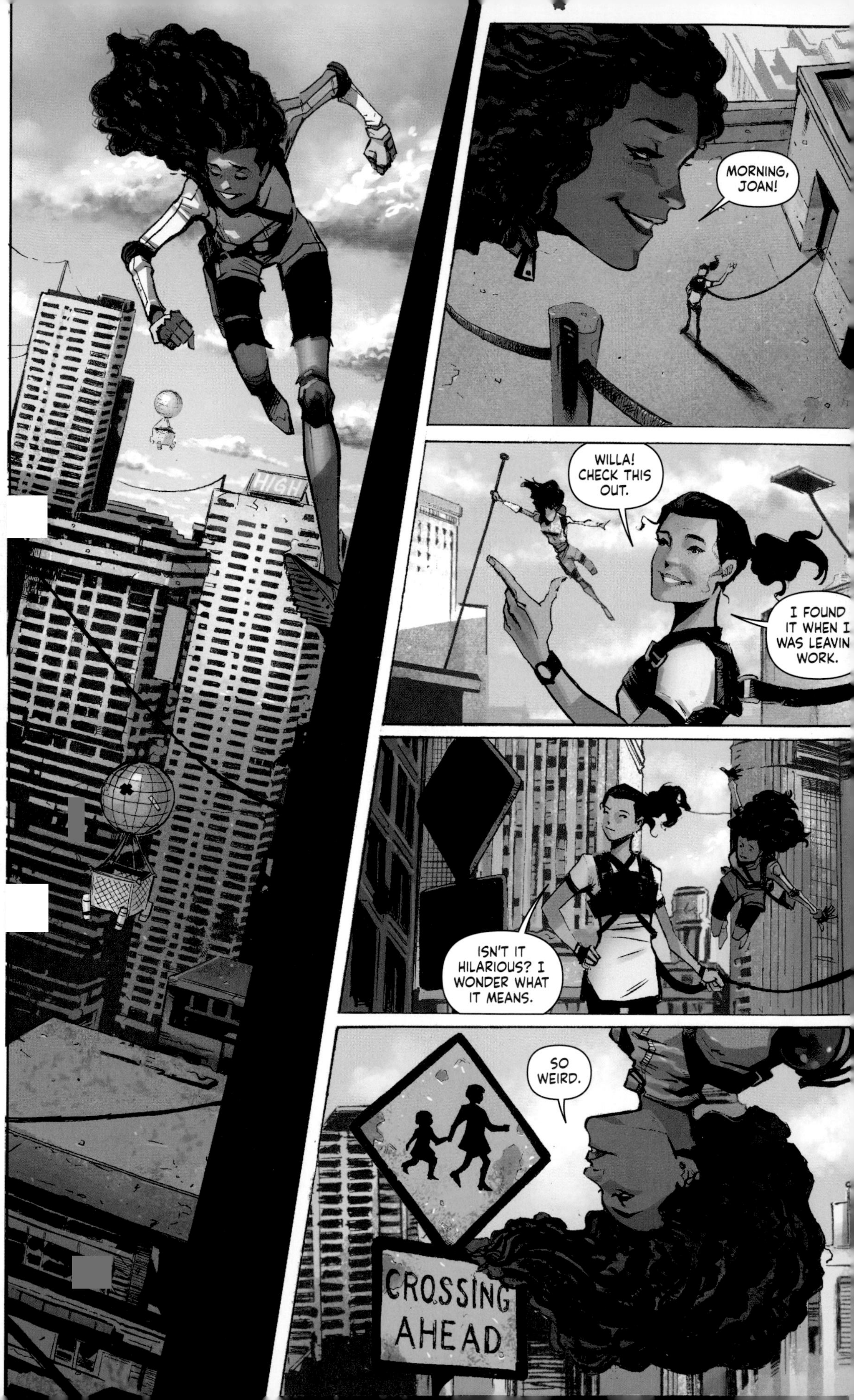
HIGH
MORNING, JOAN!
WILLA! CHECK THIS OUT.
I FOUND IT WHEN I WAS LEAVIN WORK.
ISN'T IT HILARIOUS? I WONDER WHAT IT MEANS.
SO WEIRD.
CROSSING AHEAD

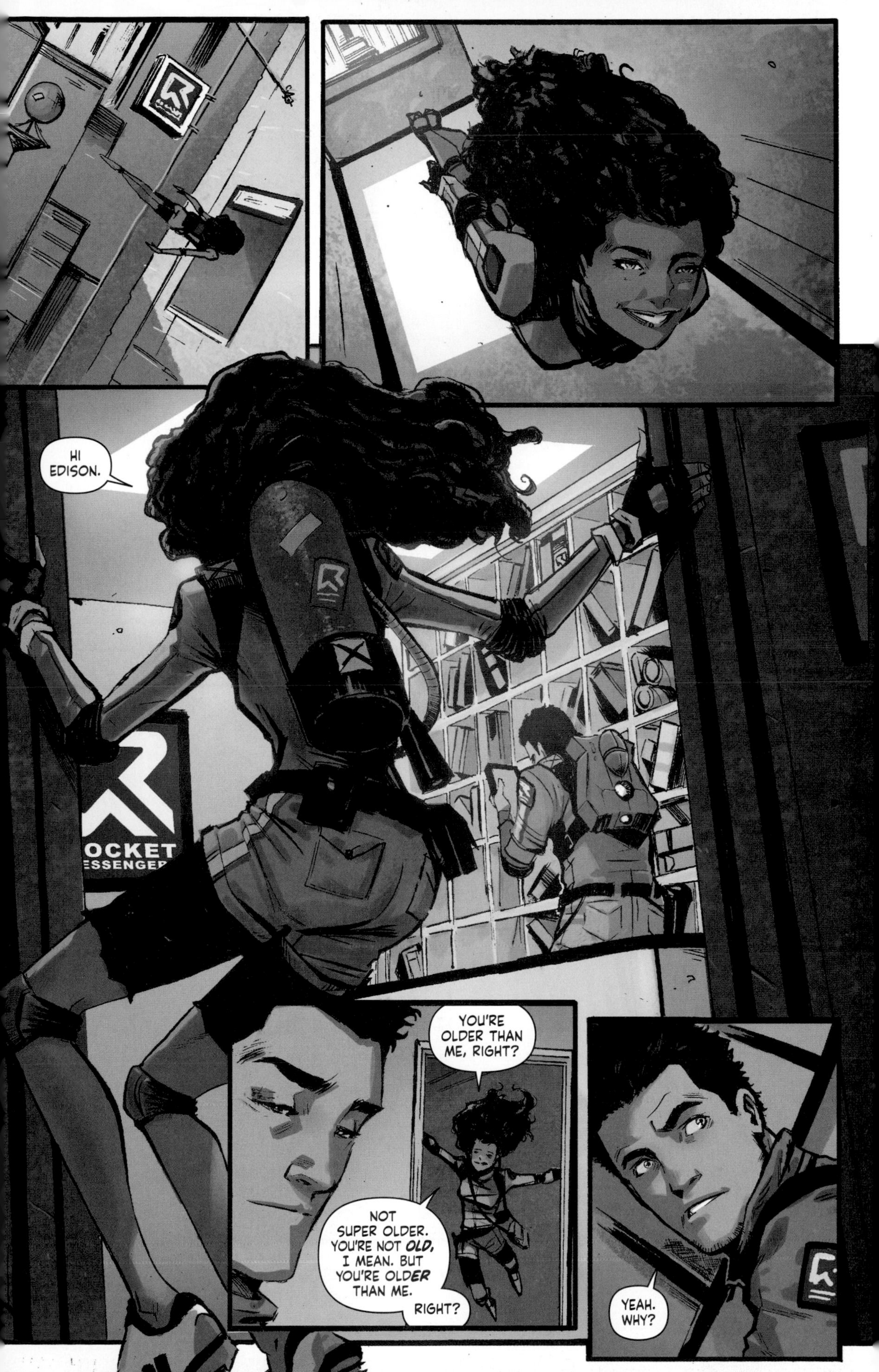

HI EDISON.
ROCKET MESSENGERS
YOU'RE OLDER THAN ME, RIGHT?
NOT SUPER OLDER. YOU'RE NOT *OLD*, I MEAN. BUT YOU'RE OLD*ER* THAN ME.
RIGHT?
YEAH. WHY?

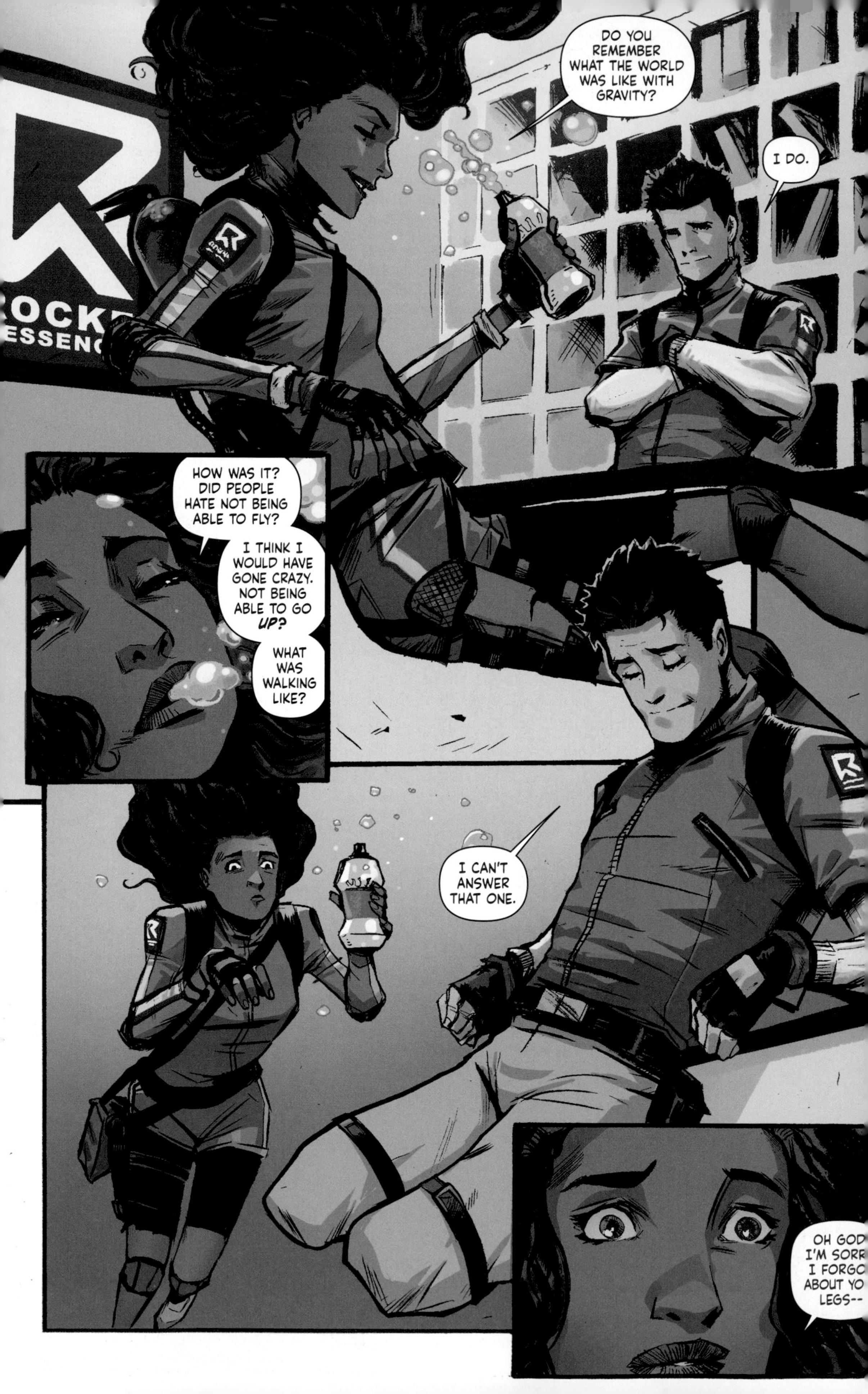
ROCKE
ESSENC
DO YOU REMEMBER WHAT THE WORLD WAS LIKE WITH GRAVITY?
I DO.
HOW WAS IT? DID PEOPLE HATE NOT BEING ABLE TO FLY?
I THINK I WOULD HAVE GONE CRAZY. NOT BEING ABLE TO GO *UP?*
WHAT WAS WALKING LIKE?
I CAN'T ANSWER THAT ONE.
OH GOD I'M SORR I FORGO ABOUT YO LEGS--

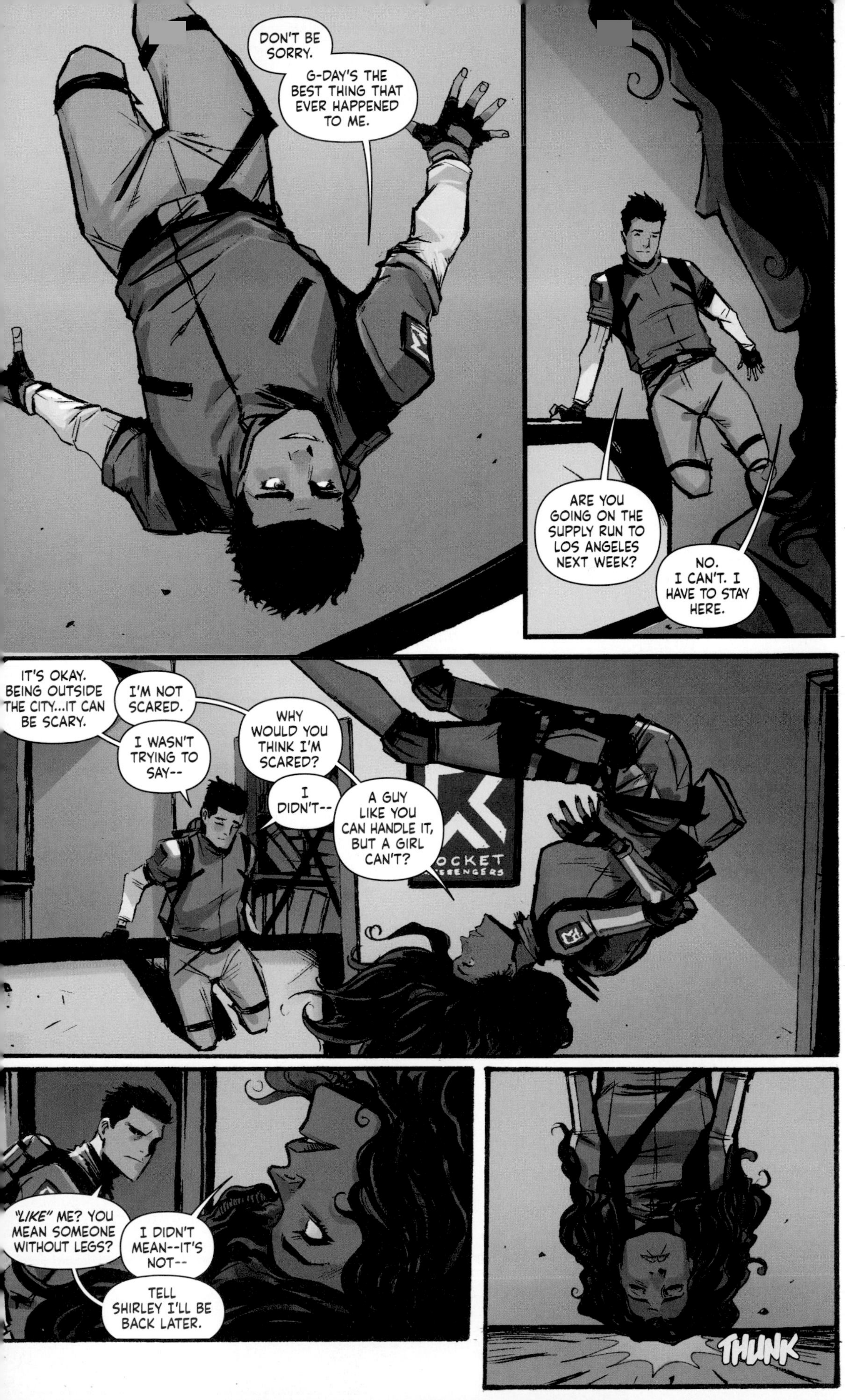
DON'T BE SORRY.
G-DAY'S THE BEST THING THAT EVER HAPPENED TO ME.
ARE YOU GOING ON THE SUPPLY RUN TO LOS ANGELES NEXT WEEK?
NO. I CAN'T. I HAVE TO STAY HERE.
IT'S OKAY. BEING OUTSIDE THE CITY...IT CAN BE SCARY.
I'M NOT SCARED.
I WASN'T TRYING TO SAY--
WHY WOULD YOU THINK I'M SCARED?
I DIDN'T--
A GUY LIKE YOU CAN HANDLE IT, BUT A GIRL CAN'T?
"LIKE" ME? YOU MEAN SOMEONE WITHOUT LEGS?
I DIDN'T MEAN--IT'S NOT--
TELL SHIRLEY I'LL BE BACK LATER.
THUNK

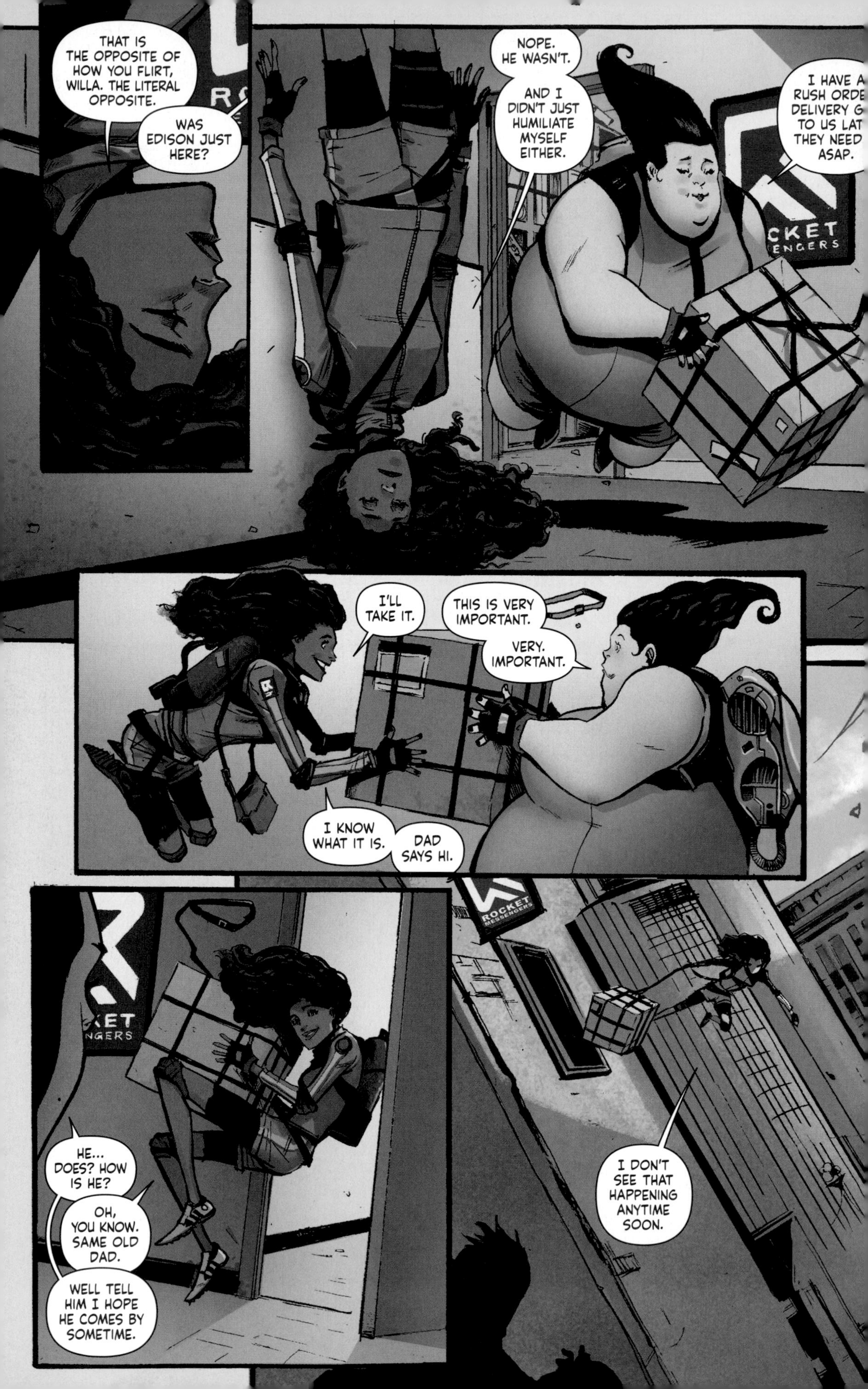

THAT IS THE OPPOSITE OF HOW YOU FLIRT, WILLA. THE LITERAL OPPOSITE.
WAS EDISON JUST HERE?
NOPE. HE WASN'T.
AND I DIDN'T JUST HUMILIATE MYSELF EITHER.
I HAVE A RUSH ORDE DELIVERY G TO US LAT THEY NEED ASAP.
ROCKET MESSENGERS
I'LL TAKE IT.
THIS IS VERY IMPORTANT.
VERY. IMPORTANT.
I KNOW WHAT IT IS.
DAD SAYS HI.
ROCKET MESSENGERS
HE... DOES? HOW IS HE?
OH, YOU KNOW. SAME OLD DAD.
WELL TELL HIM I HOPE HE COMES BY SOMETIME.
I DON'T SEE THAT HAPPENING ANYTIME SOON.

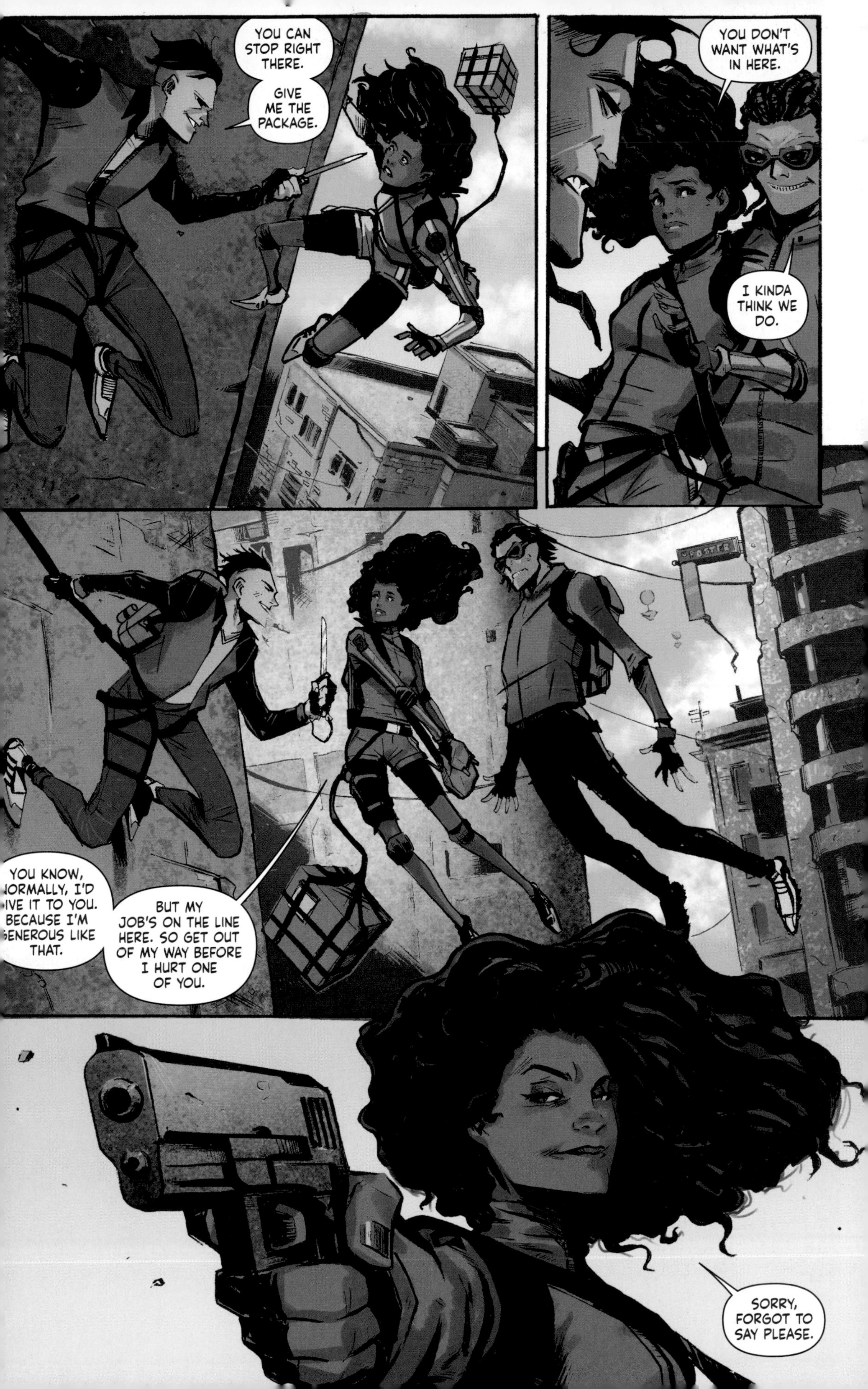

YOU CAN STOP RIGHT THERE.
GIVE ME THE PACKAGE.
YOU DON'T WANT WHAT'S IN HERE.
I KINDA THINK WE DO.
FOSTER
YOU KNOW, ORMALLY, I'D IVE IT TO YOU. BECAUSE I'M ENEROUS LIKE THAT.
BUT MY JOB'S ON THE LINE HERE. SO GET OUT OF MY WAY BEFORE I HURT ONE OF YOU.
SORRY, FORGOT TO SAY PLEASE.

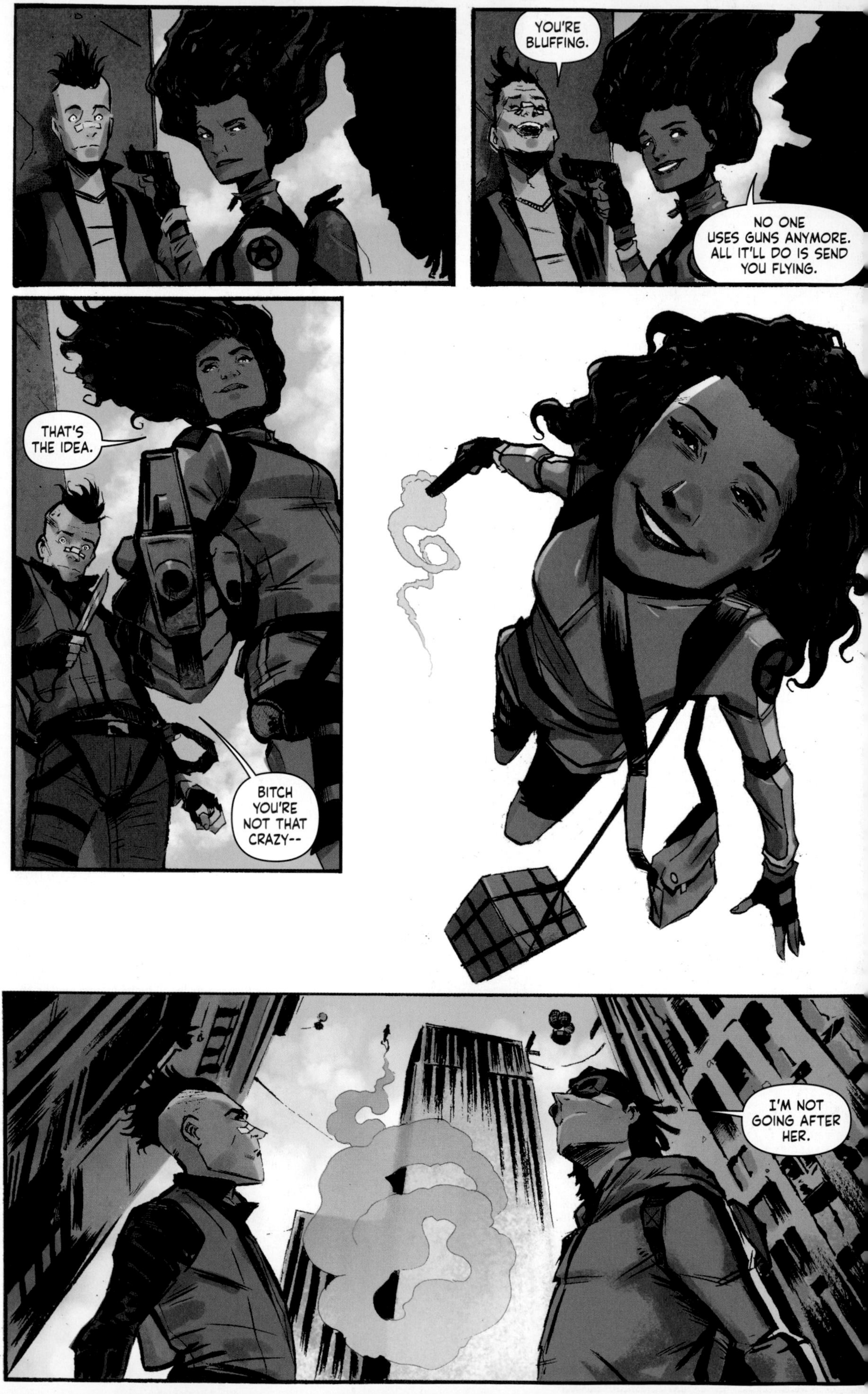
YOU'RE BLUFFING.
NO ONE USES GUNS ANYMORE. ALL IT'LL DO IS SEND YOU FLYING.
THAT'S THE IDEA.
BITCH YOU'RE NOT THAT CRAZY--
I'M NOT GOING AFTER HER.

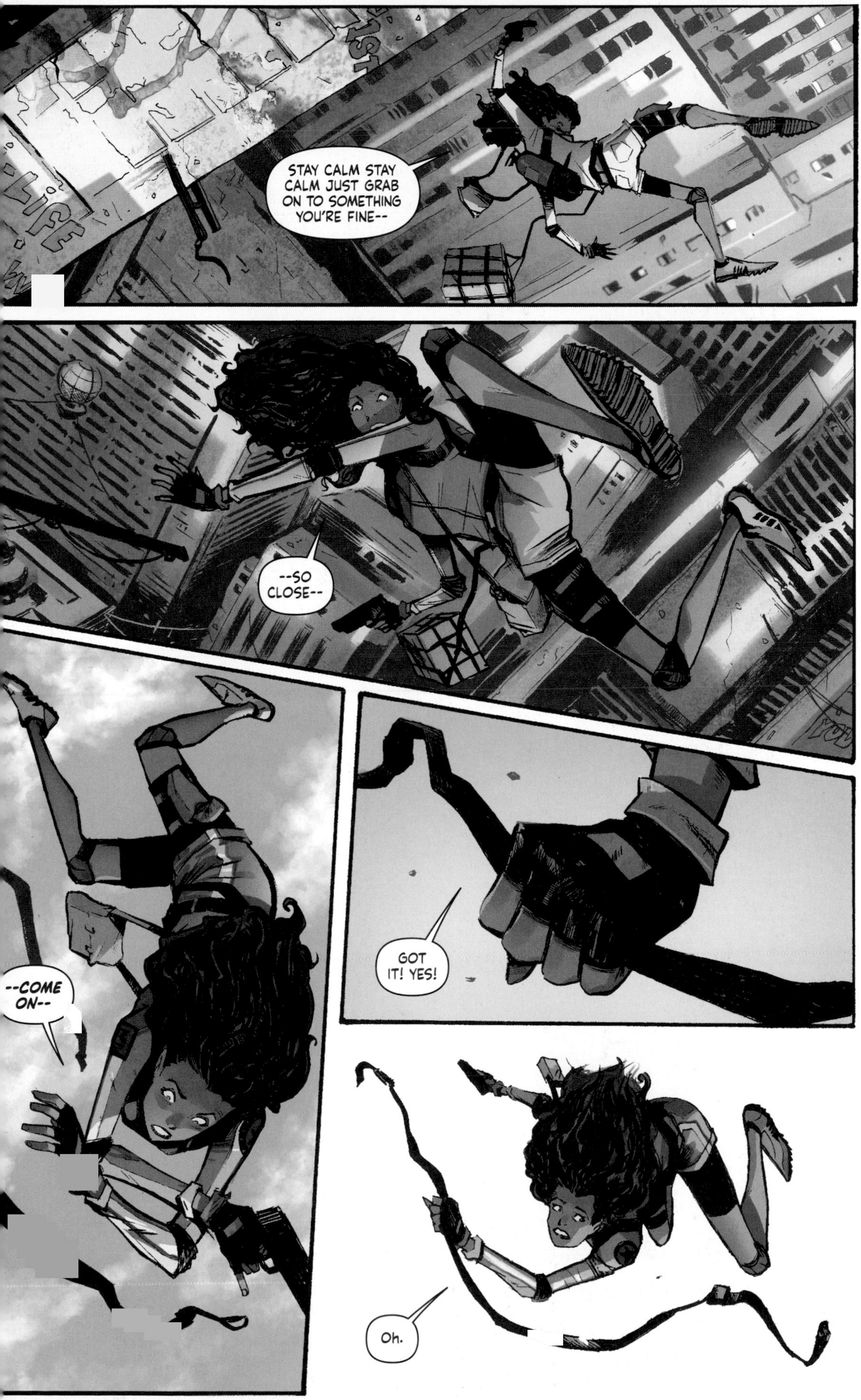
STAY CALM STAY CALM JUST GRAB ON TO SOMETHING YOU'RE FINE--
--SO CLOSE--
--COME ON--
GOT IT! YES!
Oh.

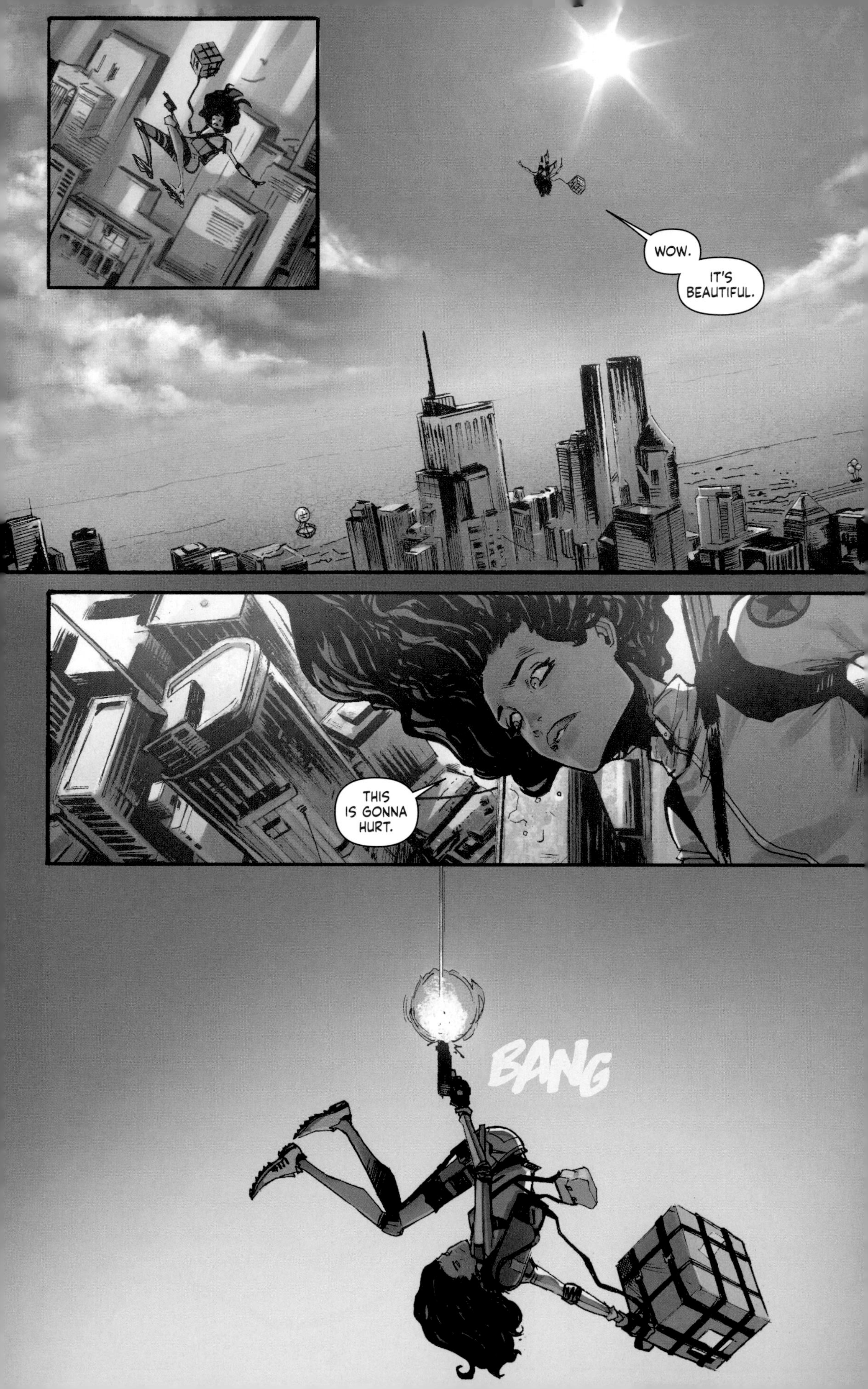
WOW.
IT'S BEAUTIFUL.
THIS IS GONNA HURT.
BANG

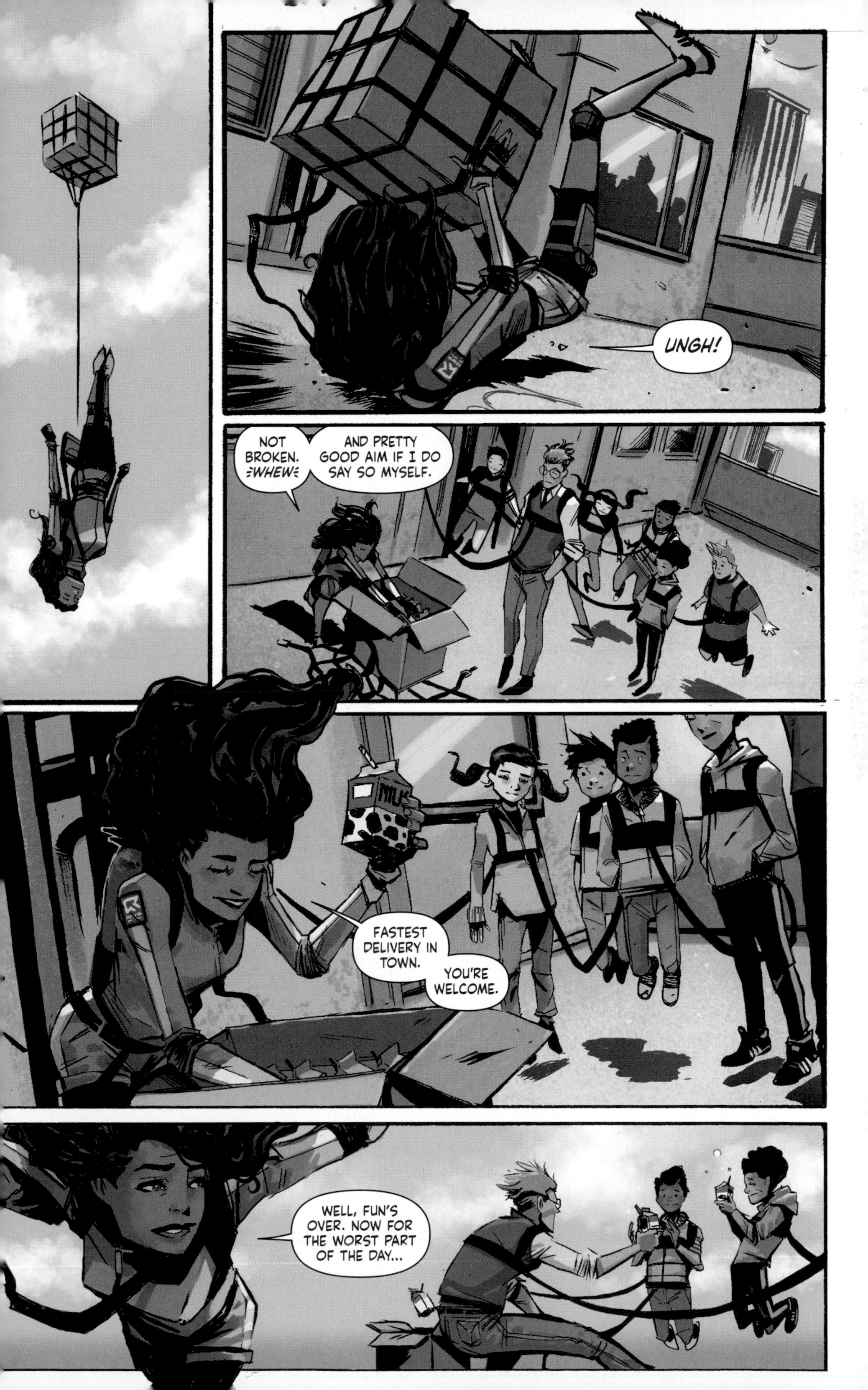
UNGH!
NOT BROKEN. WHEW
AND PRETTY GOOD AIM IF I DO SAY SO MYSELF.
FASTEST DELIVERY IN TOWN.
YOU'RE WELCOME.
WELL, FUN'S OVER. NOW FOR THE WORST PART OF THE DAY...

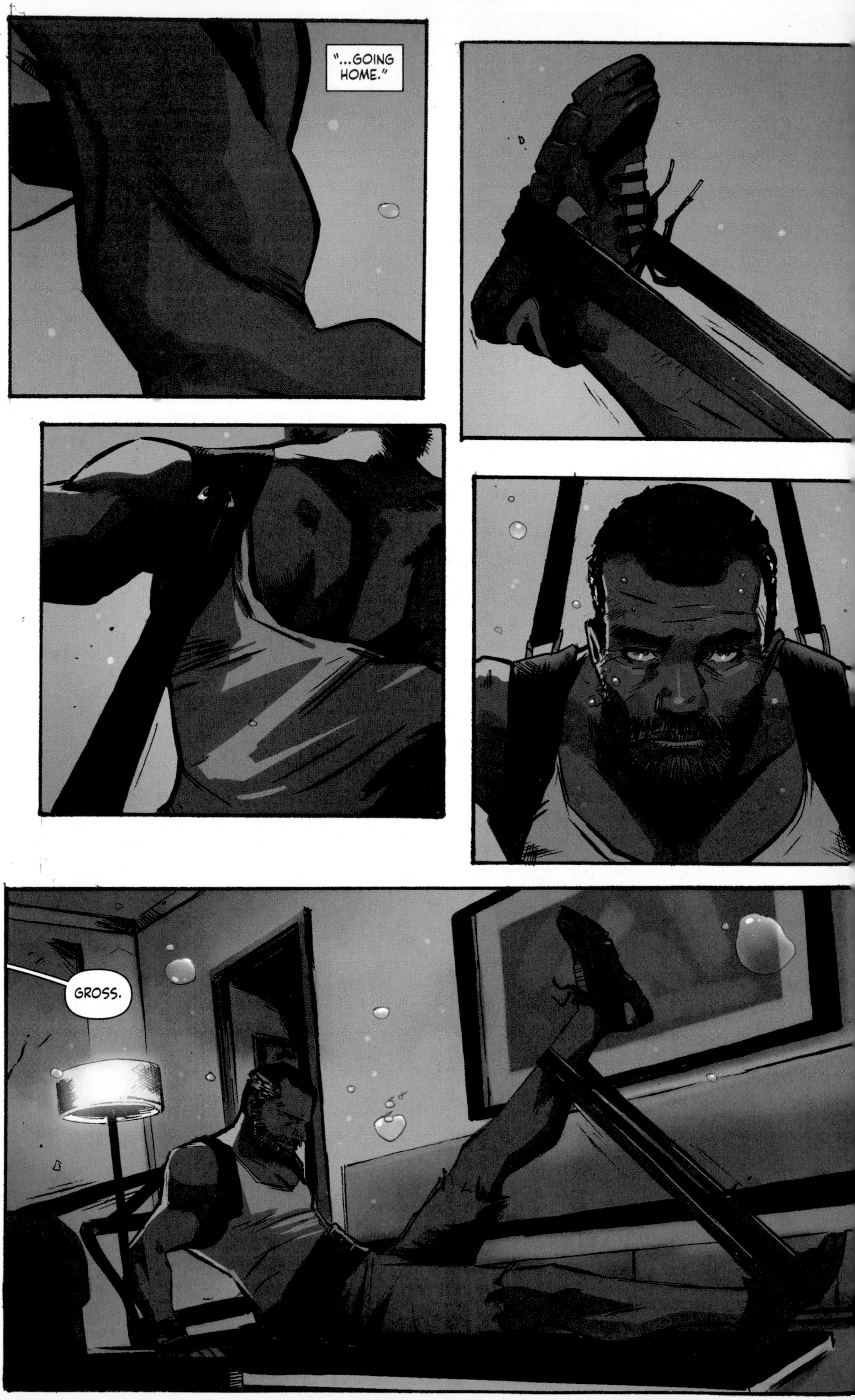
"...GOING HOME."
GROSS.

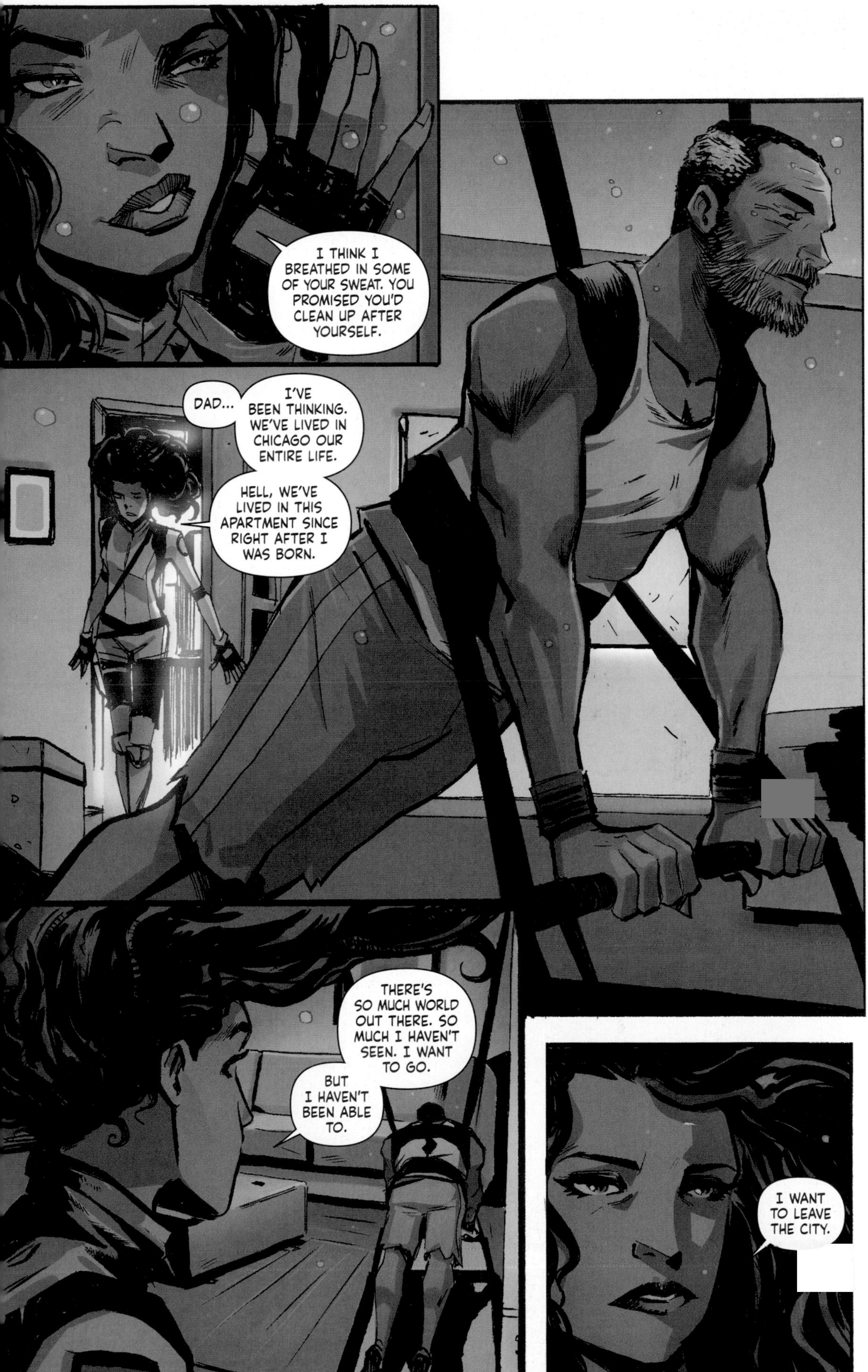
I THINK I BREATHED IN SOME OF YOUR SWEAT. YOU PROMISED YOU'D CLEAN UP AFTER YOURSELF.
DAD...
I'VE BEEN THINKING. WE'VE LIVED IN CHICAGO OUR ENTIRE LIFE.
HELL, WE'VE LIVED IN THIS APARTMENT SINCE RIGHT AFTER I WAS BORN.
THERE'S SO MUCH WORLD OUT THERE. SO MUCH I HAVEN'T SEEN. I WANT TO GO.
BUT I HAVEN'T BEEN ABLE TO.
I WANT TO LEAVE THE CITY.

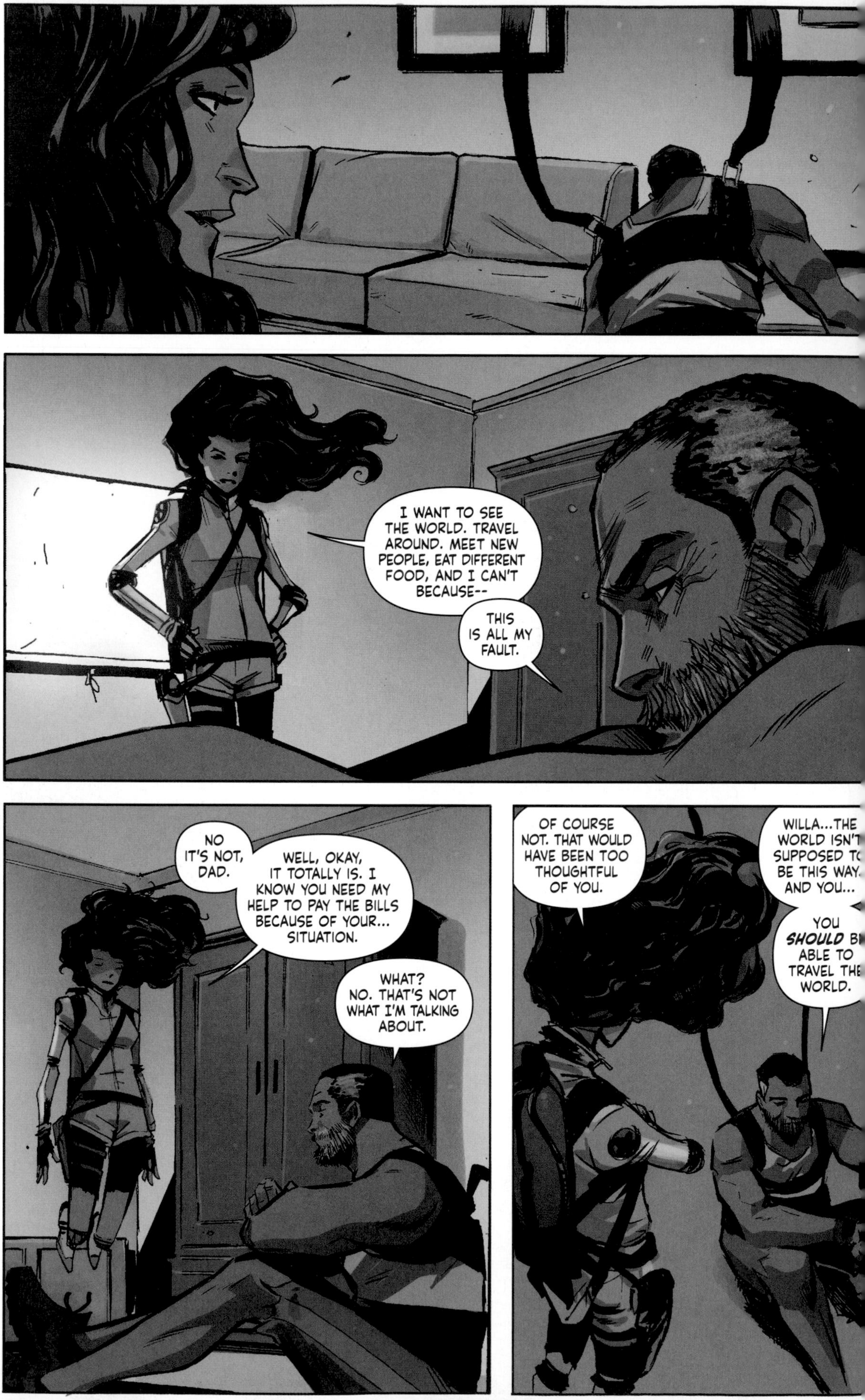
I WANT TO SEE THE WORLD. TRAVEL AROUND. MEET NEW PEOPLE, EAT DIFFERENT FOOD, AND I CAN'T BECAUSE--
THIS IS ALL MY FAULT.
NO IT'S NOT, DAD.
WELL, OKAY, IT TOTALLY IS. I KNOW YOU NEED MY HELP TO PAY THE BILLS BECAUSE OF YOUR... SITUATION.
WHAT? NO. THAT'S NOT WHAT I'M TALKING ABOUT.
OF COURSE NOT. THAT WOULD HAVE BEEN TOO THOUGHTFUL OF YOU.
WILLA...THE WORLD ISN'T SUPPOSED TO BE THIS WAY. AND YOU...
YOU **SHOULD** BE ABLE TO TRAVEL THE WORLD.

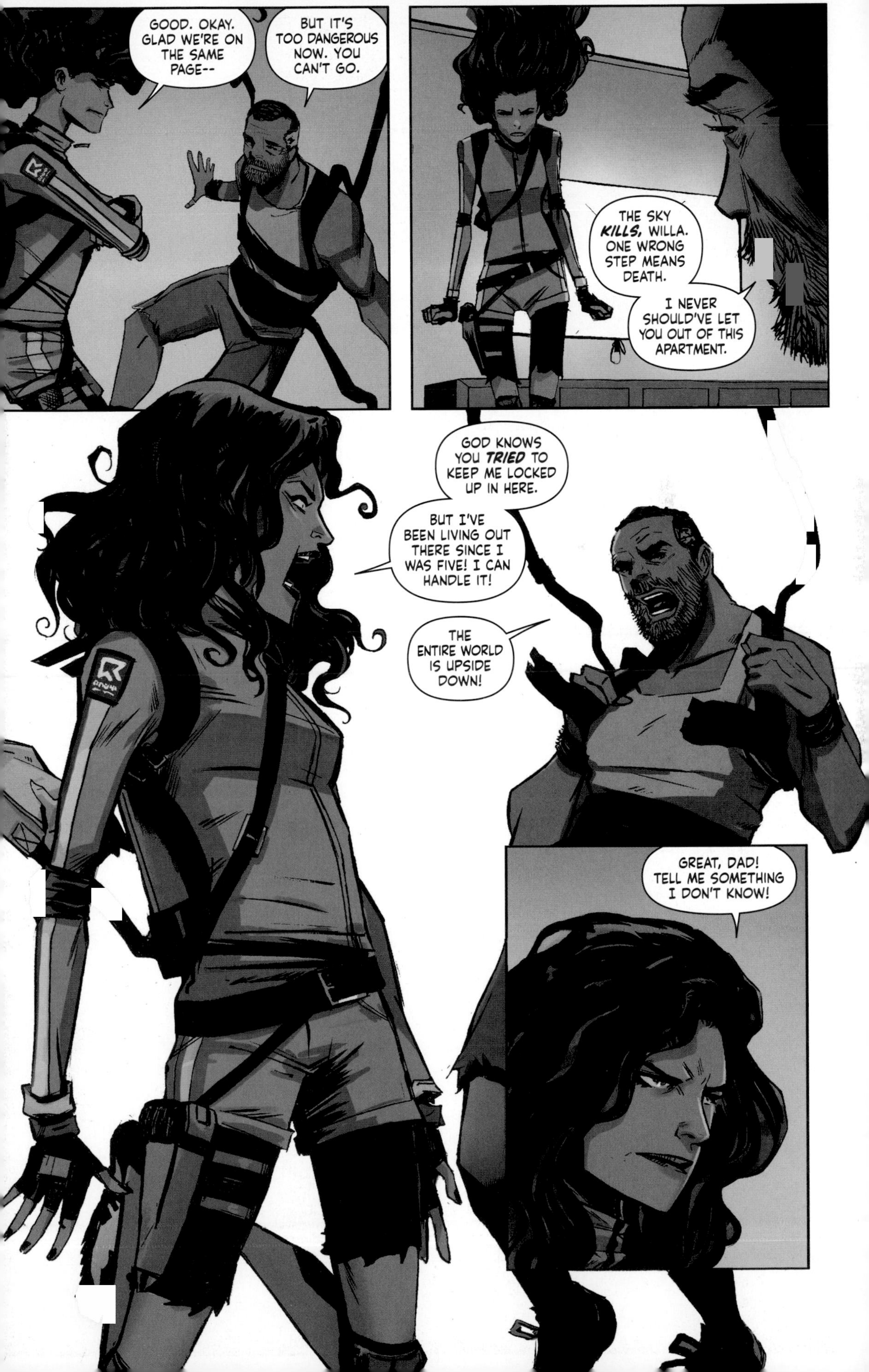
GOOD. OKAY. GLAD WE'RE ON THE SAME PAGE--
BUT IT'S TOO DANGEROUS NOW. YOU CAN'T GO.
THE SKY KILLS, WILLA. ONE WRONG STEP MEANS DEATH.
I NEVER SHOULD'VE LET YOU OUT OF THIS APARTMENT.
GOD KNOWS YOU TRIED TO KEEP ME LOCKED UP IN HERE.
BUT I'VE BEEN LIVING OUT THERE SINCE I WAS FIVE! I CAN HANDLE IT!
THE ENTIRE WORLD IS UPSIDE DOWN!
GREAT, DAD! TELL ME SOMETHING I DON'T KNOW!

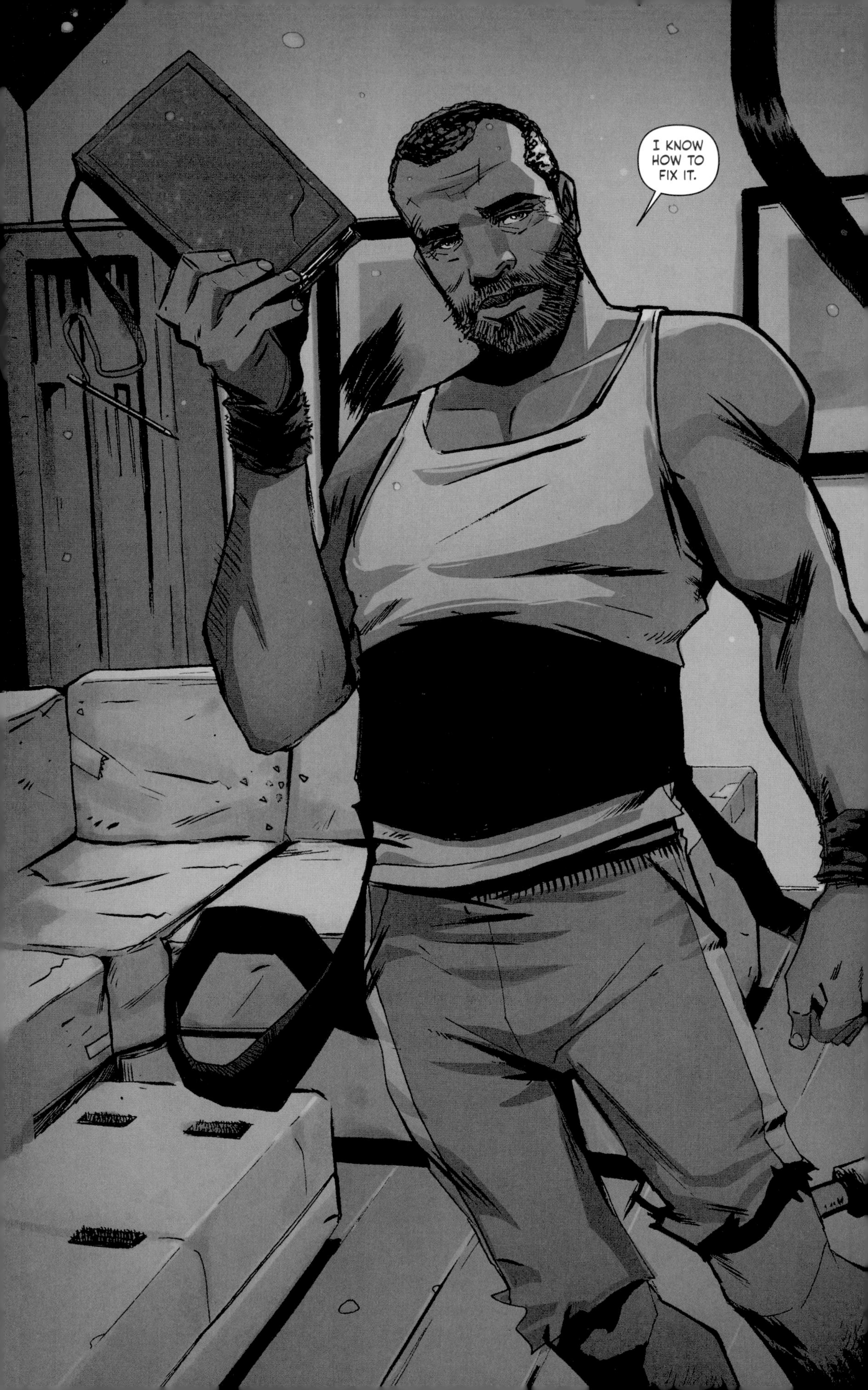
I KNOW HOW TO FIX IT.

END CHAPTER ONE

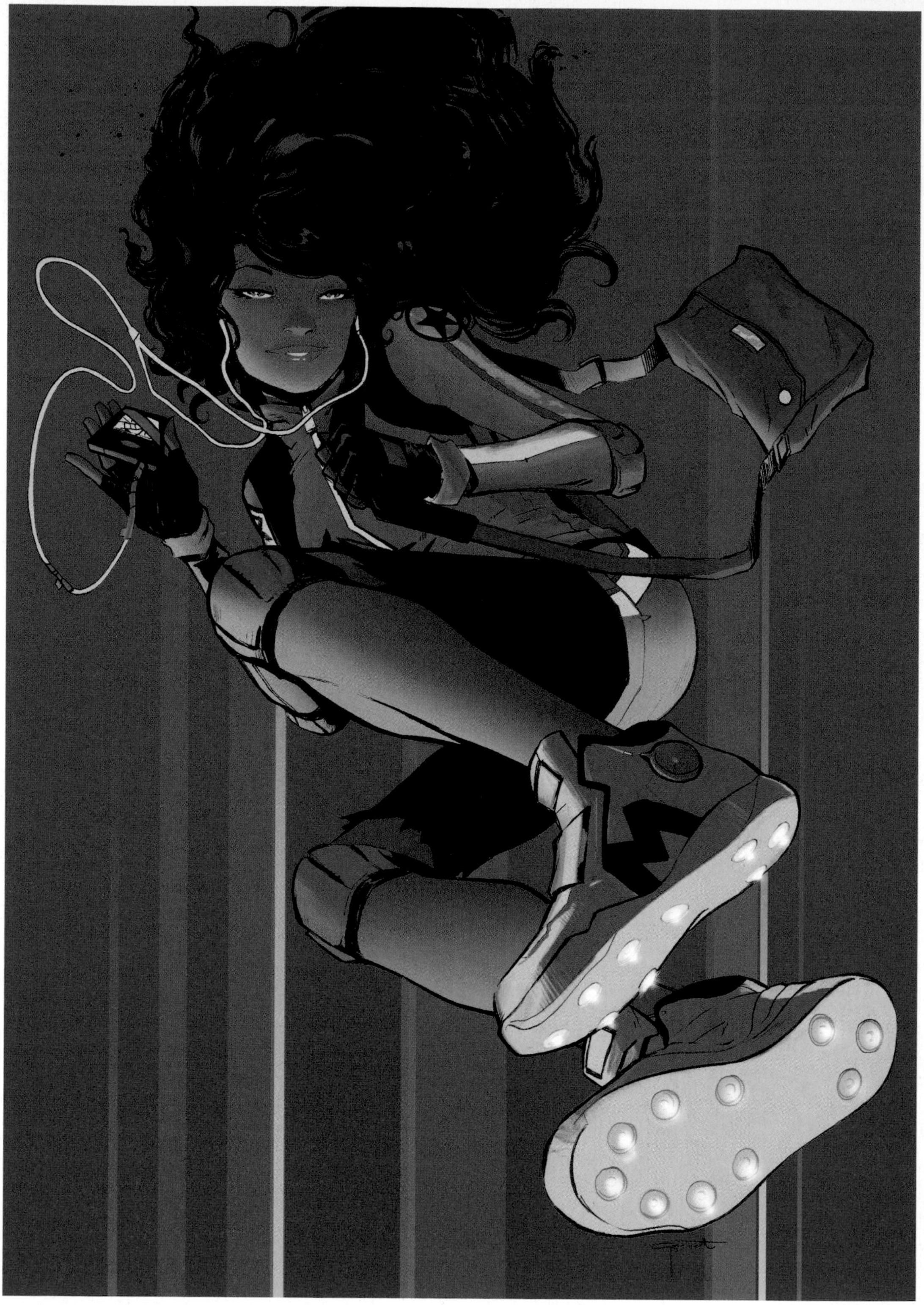

CHAPTER TWO

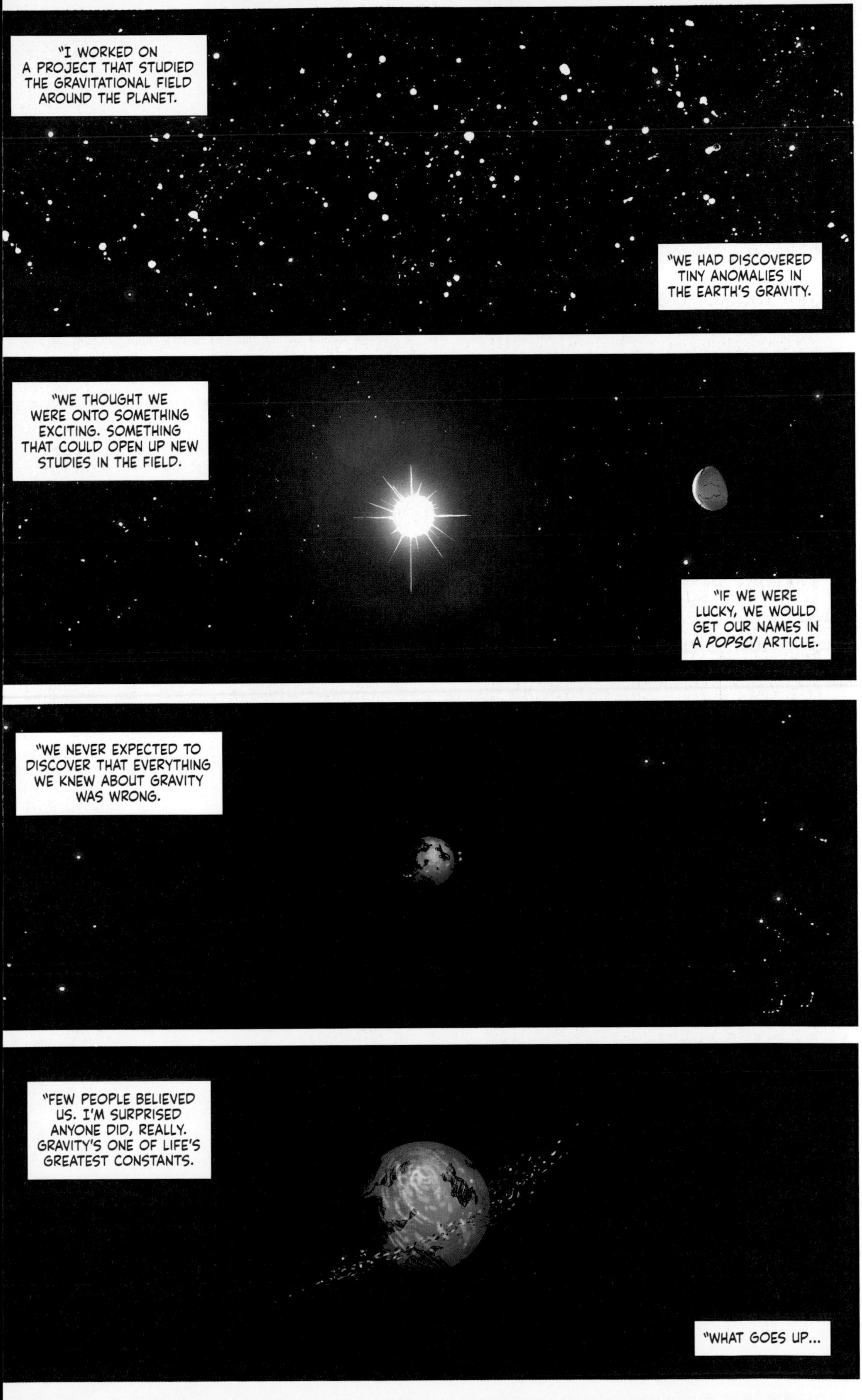

"I WORKED ON A PROJECT THAT STUDIED THE GRAVITATIONAL FIELD AROUND THE PLANET.
"WE HAD DISCOVERED TINY ANOMALIES IN THE EARTH'S GRAVITY.
"WE THOUGHT WE WERE ONTO SOMETHING EXCITING. SOMETHING THAT COULD OPEN UP NEW STUDIES IN THE FIELD.
"IF WE WERE LUCKY, WE WOULD GET OUR NAMES IN A *POPSCI* ARTICLE.
"WE NEVER EXPECTED TO DISCOVER THAT EVERYTHING WE KNEW ABOUT GRAVITY WAS WRONG.
"FEW PEOPLE BELIEVED US. I'M SURPRISED ANYONE DID, REALLY. GRAVITY'S ONE OF LIFE'S GREATEST CONSTANTS.
"WHAT GOES UP...

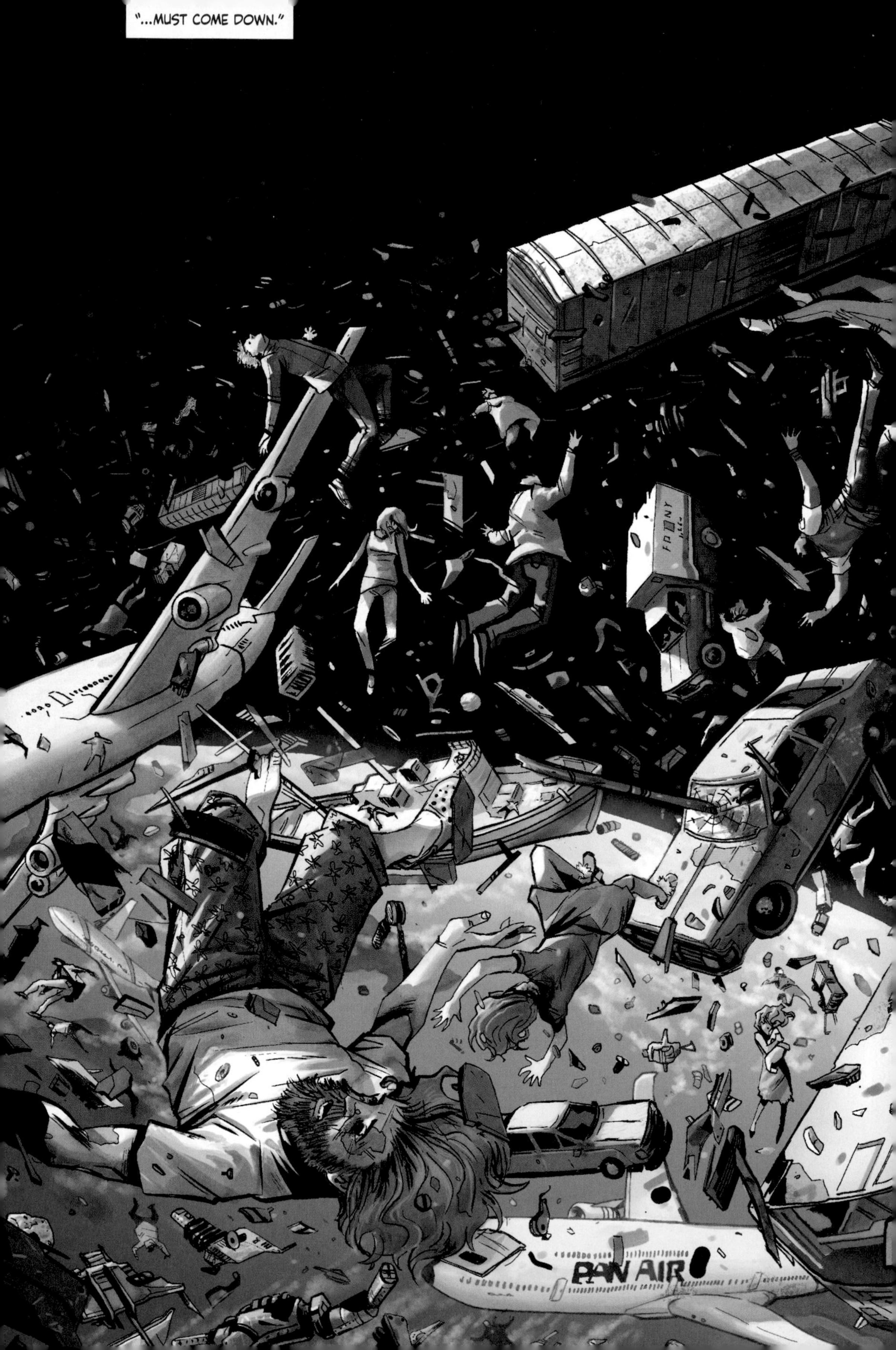
"...MUST COME DOWN."
PAN AIR

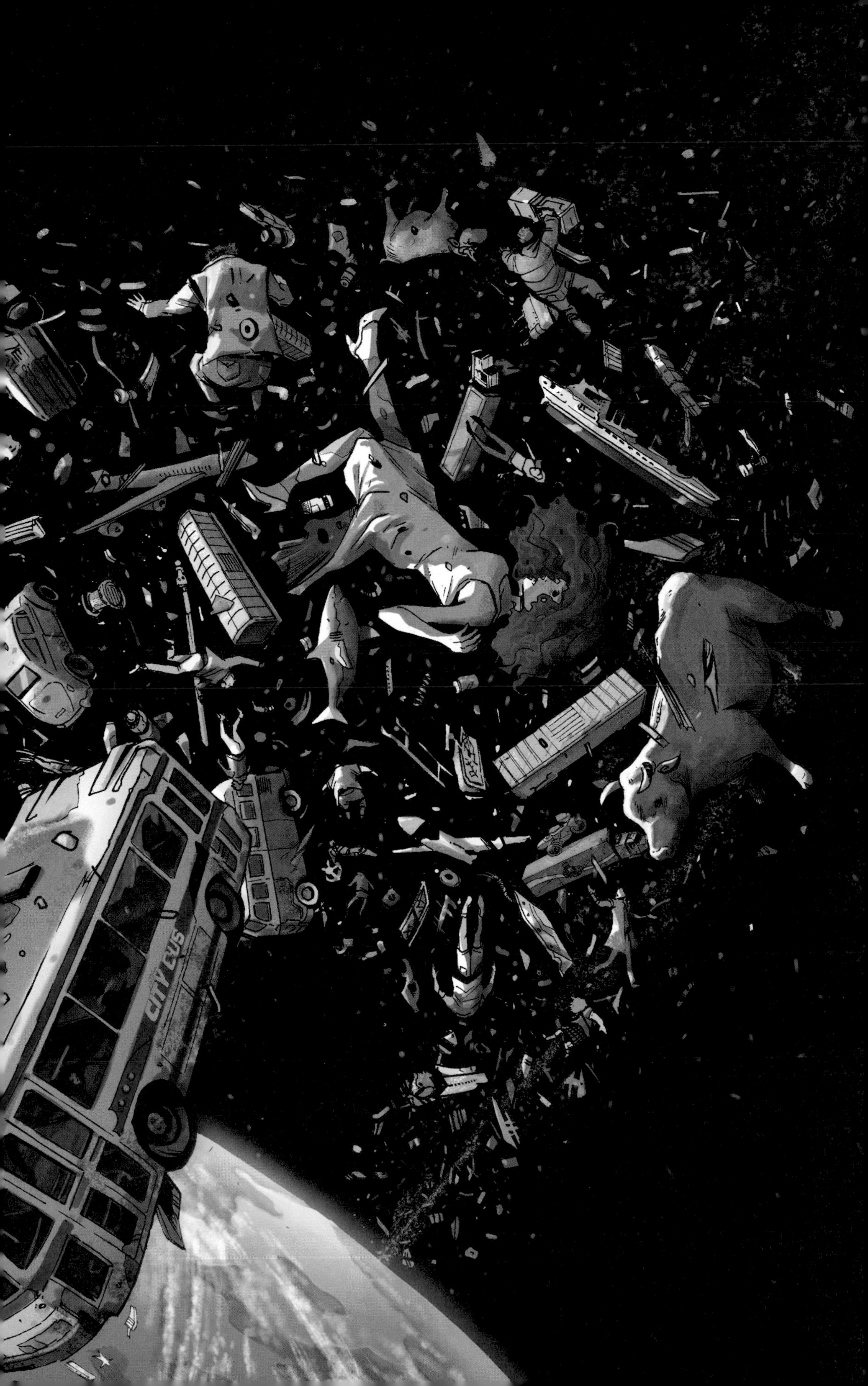
CITY BUS

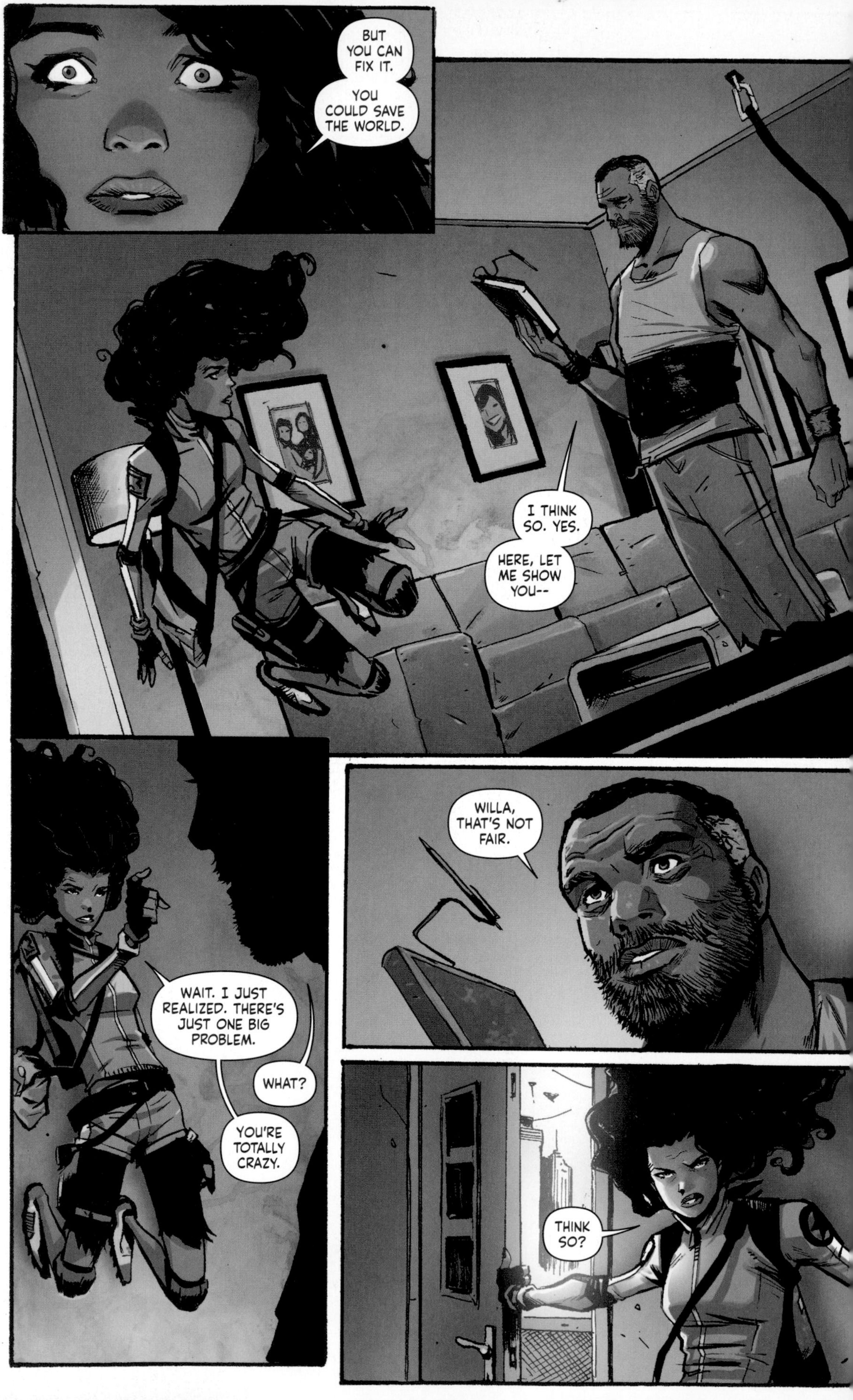
BUT YOU CAN FIX IT.
YOU COULD SAVE THE WORLD.
I THINK SO. YES.
HERE, LET ME SHOW YOU--
WAIT. I JUST REALIZED. THERE'S JUST ONE BIG PROBLEM.
WHAT?
YOU'RE TOTALLY CRAZY.
WILLA, THAT'S NOT FAIR.
THINK SO?

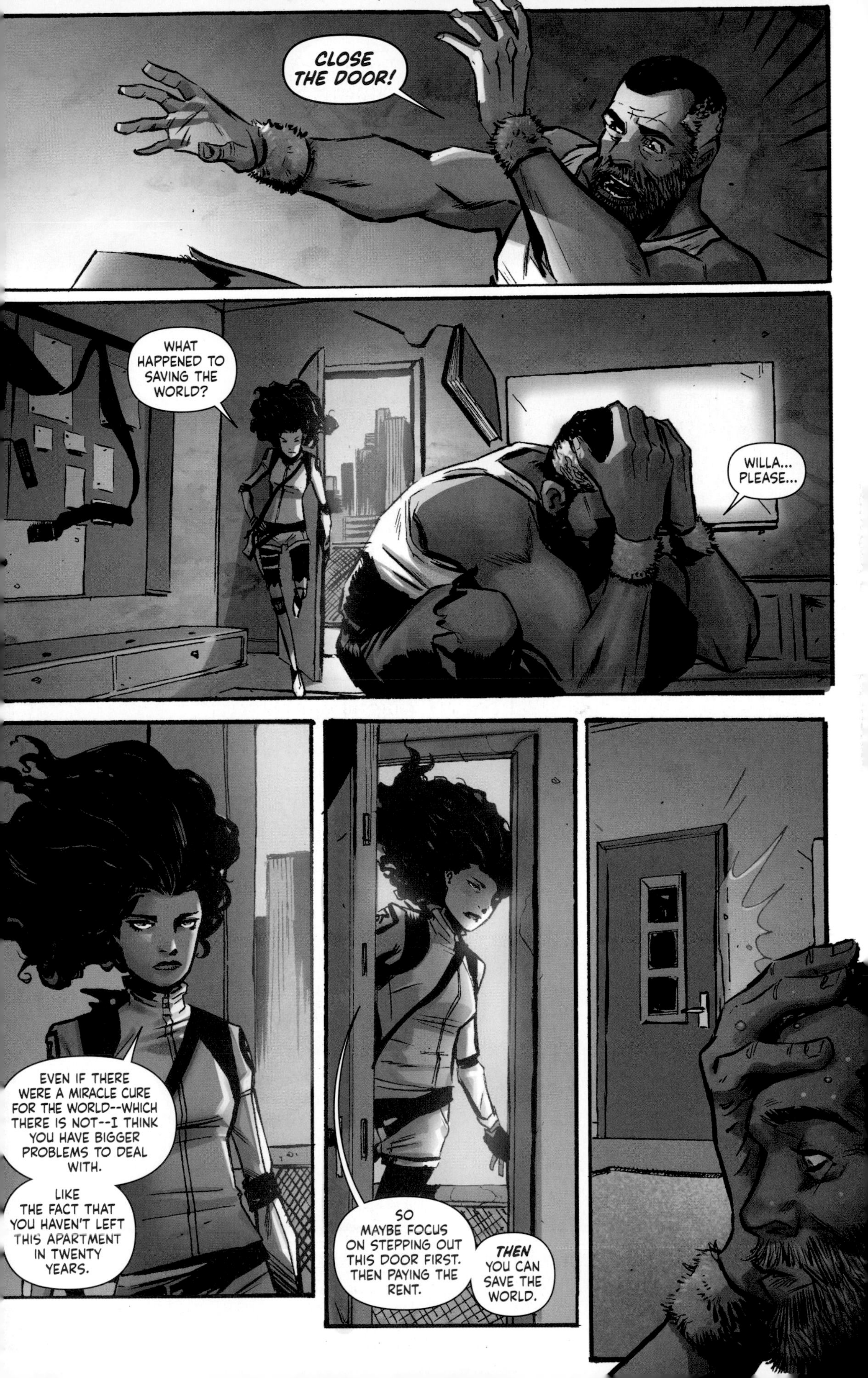
CLOSE THE DOOR!
WHAT HAPPENED TO SAVING THE WORLD?
WILLA... PLEASE...
EVEN IF THERE WERE A MIRACLE CURE FOR THE WORLD--WHICH THERE IS NOT--I THINK YOU HAVE BIGGER PROBLEMS TO DEAL WITH.
LIKE THE FACT THAT YOU HAVEN'T LEFT THIS APARTMENT IN TWENTY YEARS.
SO MAYBE FOCUS ON STEPPING OUT THIS DOOR FIRST. THEN PAYING THE RENT.
THEN YOU CAN SAVE THE WORLD.

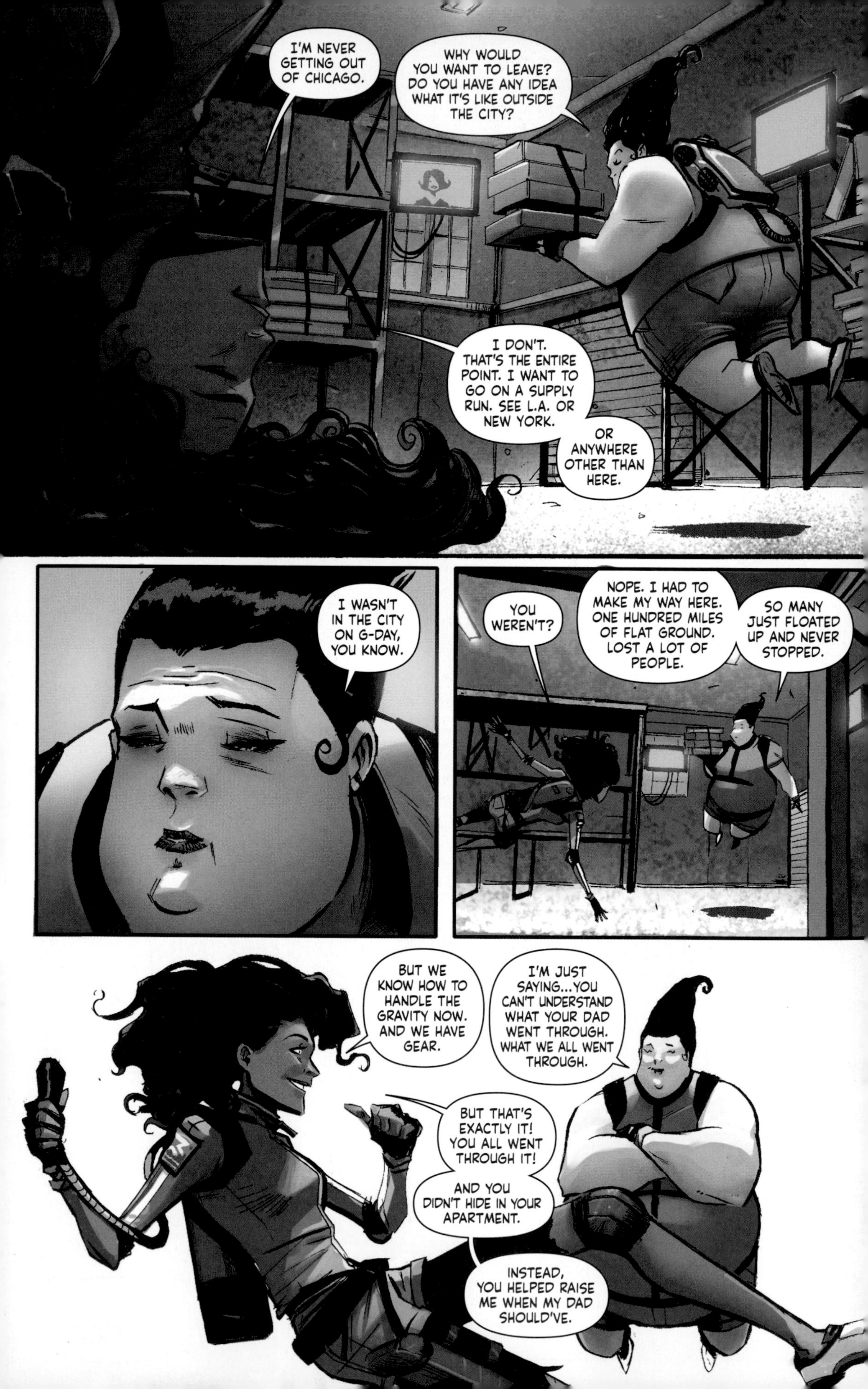
I'M NEVER GETTING OUT OF CHICAGO.
WHY WOULD YOU WANT TO LEAVE? DO YOU HAVE ANY IDEA WHAT IT'S LIKE OUTSIDE THE CITY?
I DON'T. THAT'S THE ENTIRE POINT. I WANT TO GO ON A SUPPLY RUN. SEE L.A. OR NEW YORK.
OR ANYWHERE OTHER THAN HERE.
I WASN'T IN THE CITY ON G-DAY, YOU KNOW.
YOU WEREN'T?
NOPE. I HAD TO MAKE MY WAY HERE. ONE HUNDRED MILES OF FLAT GROUND. LOST A LOT OF PEOPLE.
SO MANY JUST FLOATED UP AND NEVER STOPPED.
BUT WE KNOW HOW TO HANDLE THE GRAVITY NOW. AND WE HAVE GEAR.
I'M JUST SAYING...YOU CAN'T UNDERSTAND WHAT YOUR DAD WENT THROUGH. WHAT WE ALL WENT THROUGH.
BUT THAT'S EXACTLY IT! YOU ALL WENT THROUGH IT!
AND YOU DIDN'T HIDE IN YOUR APARTMENT.
INSTEAD, YOU HELPED RAISE ME WHEN MY DAD SHOULD'VE.

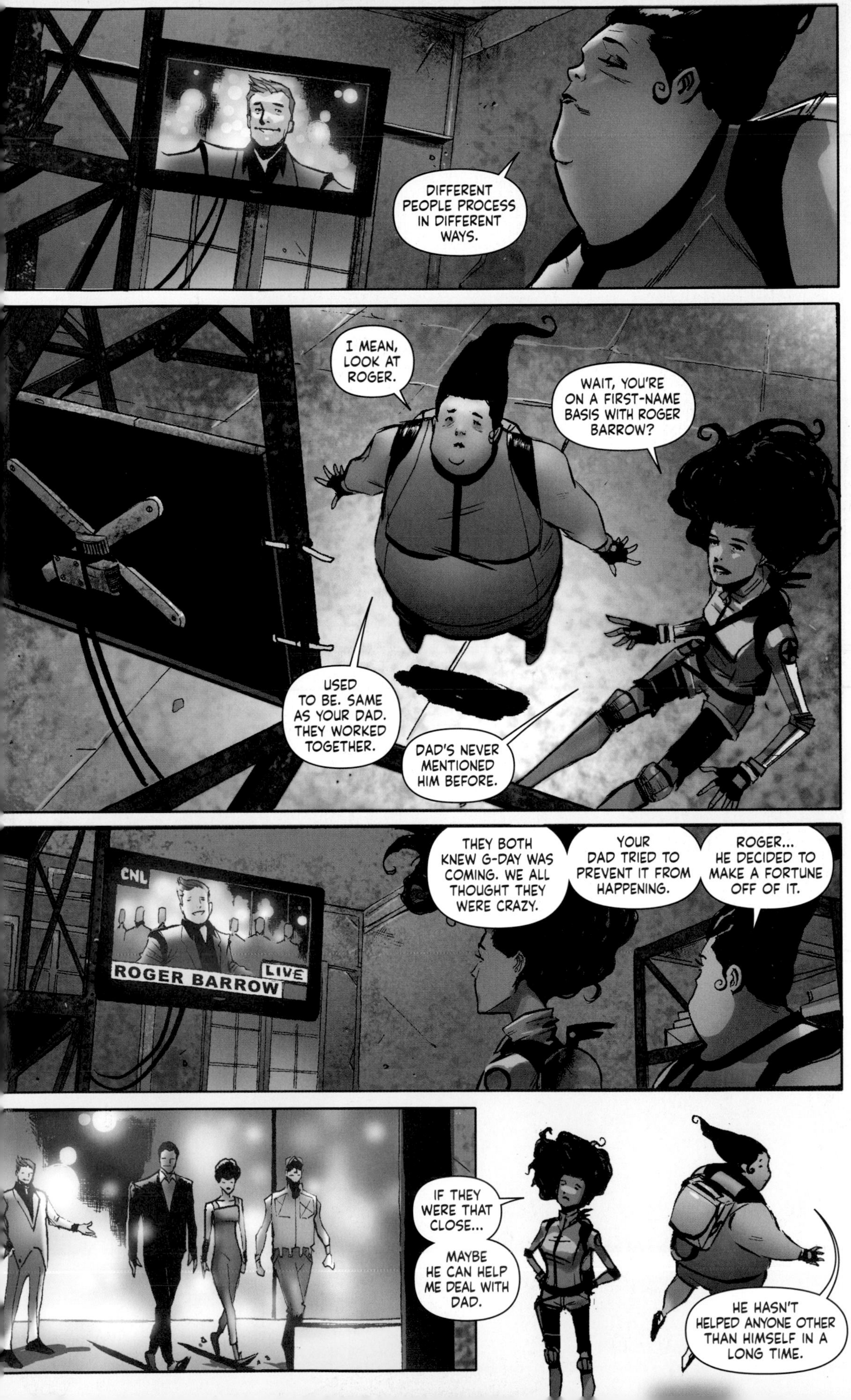
DIFFERENT PEOPLE PROCESS IN DIFFERENT WAYS.
I MEAN, LOOK AT ROGER.
WAIT, YOU'RE ON A FIRST-NAME BASIS WITH ROGER BARROW?
USED TO BE. SAME AS YOUR DAD. THEY WORKED TOGETHER.
DAD'S NEVER MENTIONED HIM BEFORE.
CNL
ROGER BARROW
LIVE
THEY BOTH KNEW G-DAY WAS COMING. WE ALL THOUGHT THEY WERE CRAZY.
YOUR DAD TRIED TO PREVENT IT FROM HAPPENING.
ROGER... HE DECIDED TO MAKE A FORTUNE OFF OF IT.
IF THEY WERE THAT CLOSE...
MAYBE HE CAN HELP ME DEAL WITH DAD.
HE HASN'T HELPED ANYONE OTHER THAN HIMSELF IN A LONG TIME.

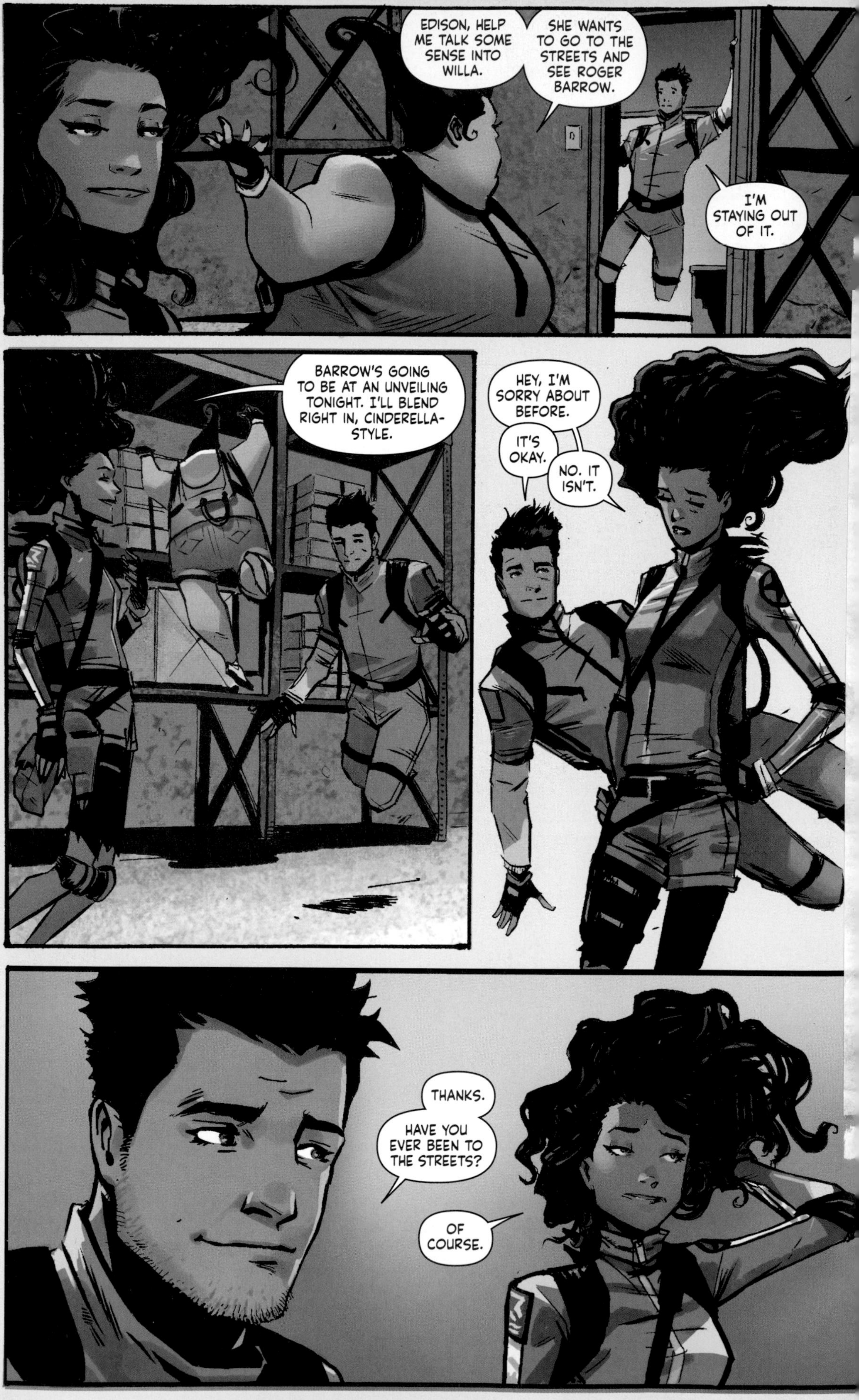
EDISON, HELP ME TALK SOME SENSE INTO WILLA.
SHE WANTS TO GO TO THE STREETS AND SEE ROGER BARROW.
I'M STAYING OUT OF IT.
BARROW'S GOING TO BE AT AN UNVEILING TONIGHT. I'LL BLEND RIGHT IN, CINDERELLA-STYLE.
HEY, I'M SORRY ABOUT BEFORE.
IT'S OKAY.
NO. IT ISN'T.
THANKS.
HAVE YOU EVER BEEN TO THE STREETS?
OF COURSE.

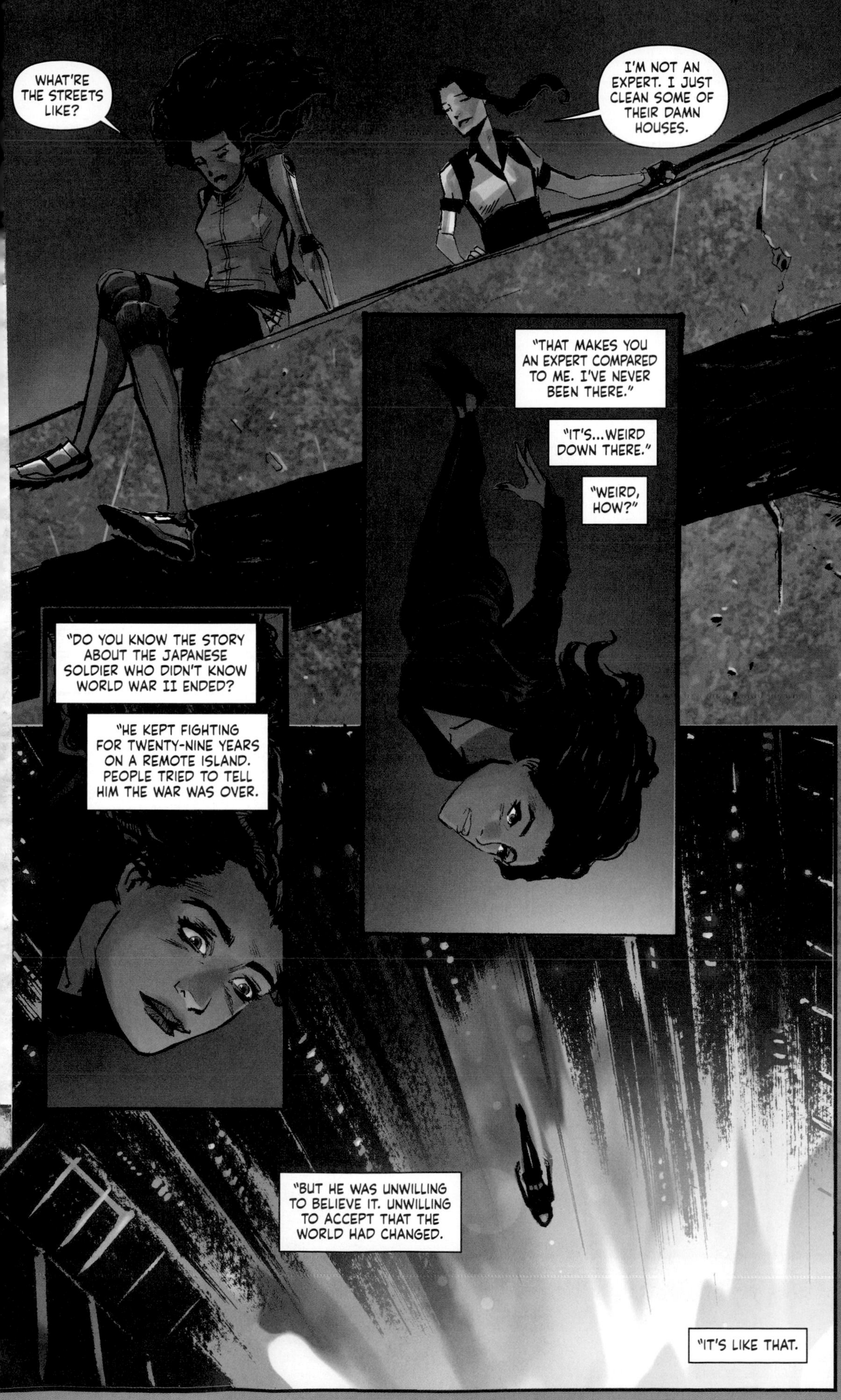
WHAT'RE THE STREETS LIKE?
I'M NOT AN EXPERT. I JUST CLEAN SOME OF THEIR DAMN HOUSES.
"THAT MAKES YOU AN EXPERT COMPARED TO ME. I'VE NEVER BEEN THERE."
"IT'S...WEIRD DOWN THERE."
"WEIRD, HOW?"
"DO YOU KNOW THE STORY ABOUT THE JAPANESE SOLDIER WHO DIDN'T KNOW WORLD WAR II ENDED?
"HE KEPT FIGHTING FOR TWENTY-NINE YEARS ON A REMOTE ISLAND. PEOPLE TRIED TO TELL HIM THE WAR WAS OVER.
"BUT HE WAS UNWILLING TO BELIEVE IT. UNWILLING TO ACCEPT THAT THE WORLD HAD CHANGED.
"IT'S LIKE THAT.

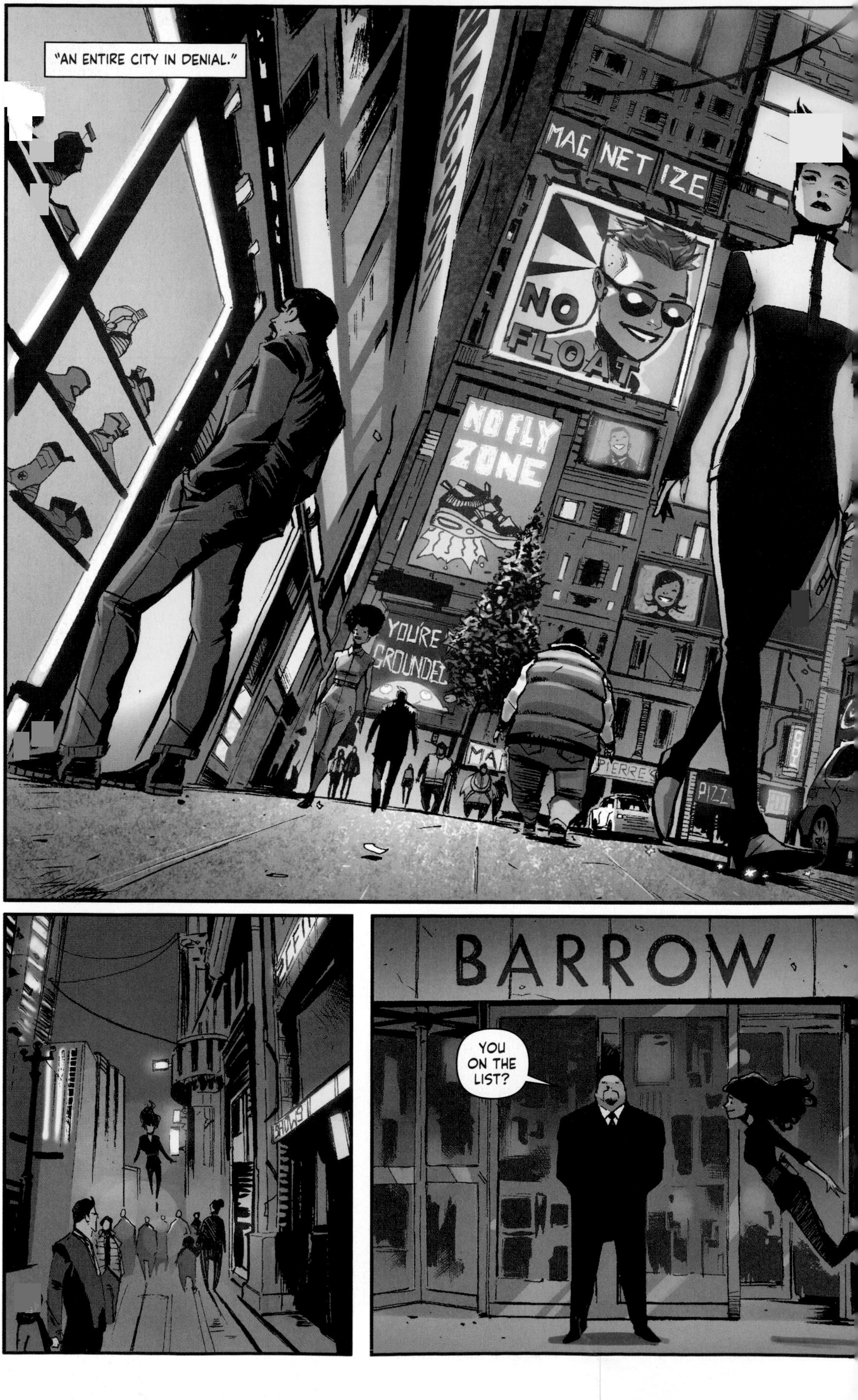
"AN ENTIRE CITY IN DENIAL."
MAGNETIZE
NO FLOAT
NO FLY ZONE
YOU'RE
PIERRE'S
BARROW
YOU ON THE LIST?

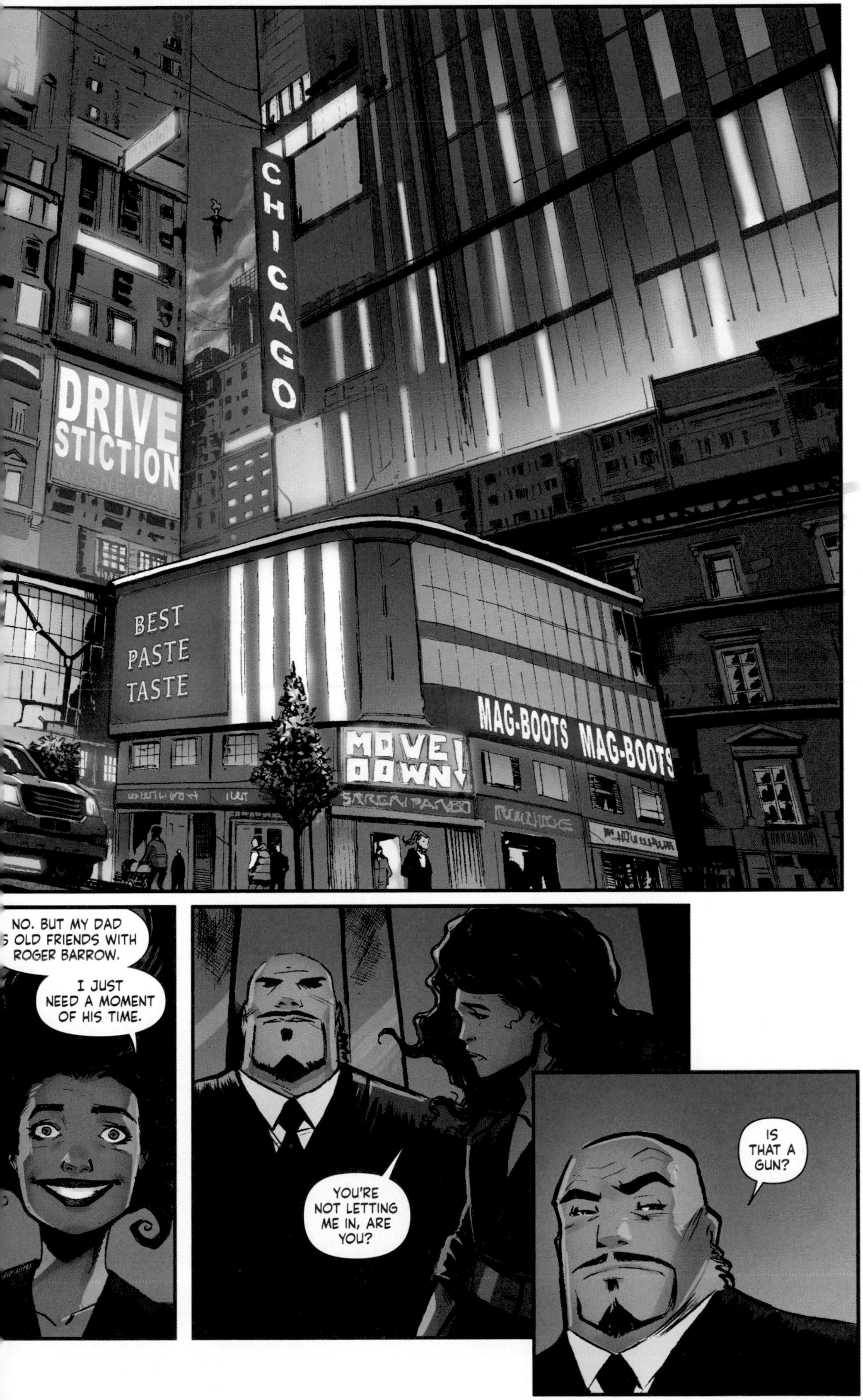
CHICAGO
DRIVE STICTION
BEST PASTE TASTE
MOVE DOWN
MAG-BOOTS MAG-BOOTS
NO. BUT MY DAD S OLD FRIENDS WITH ROGER BARROW.
I JUST NEED A MOMENT OF HIS TIME.
YOU'RE NOT LETTING ME IN, ARE YOU?
IS THAT A GUN?

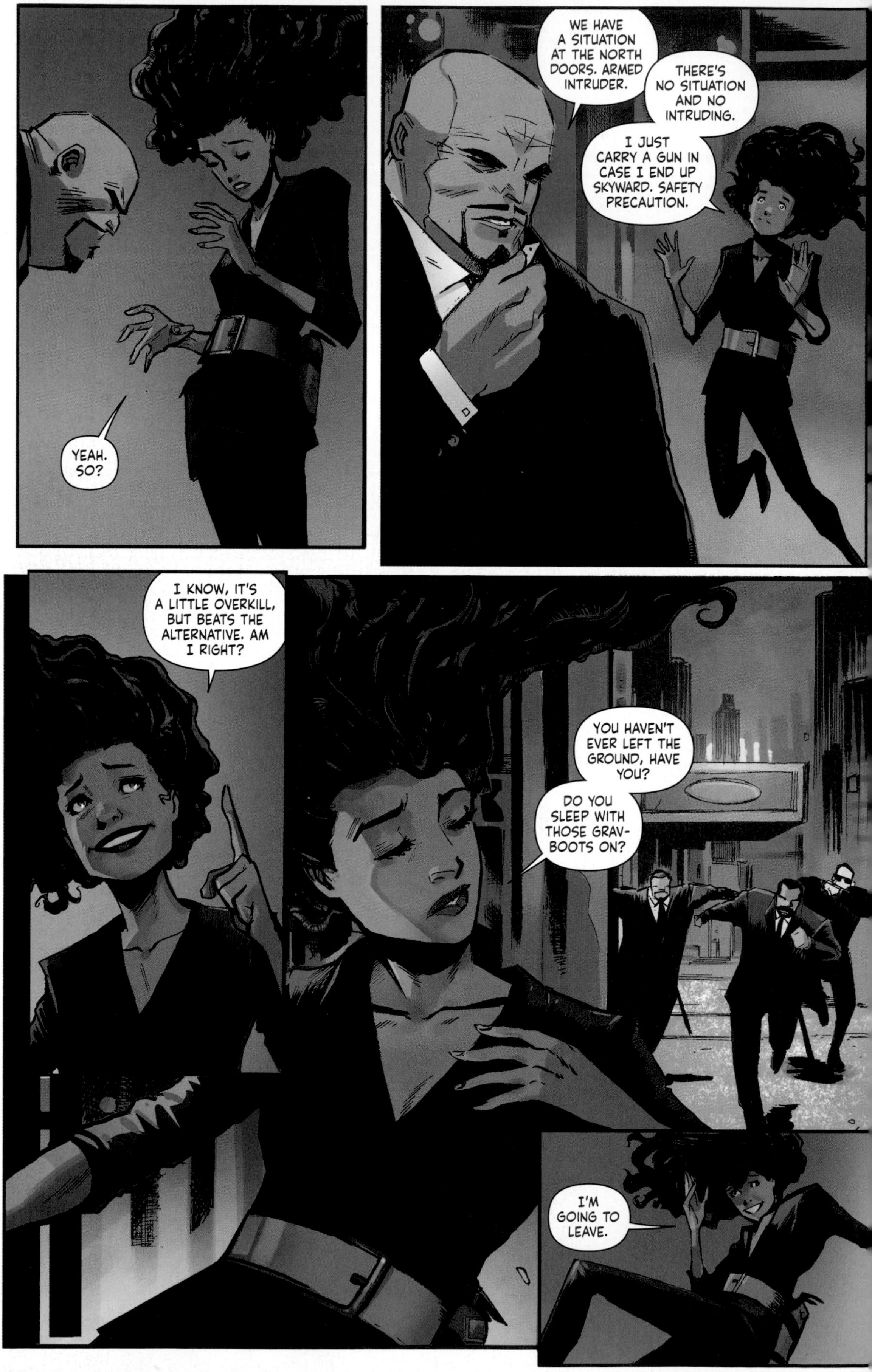
YEAH. SO?
WE HAVE A SITUATION AT THE NORTH DOORS. ARMED INTRUDER.
THERE'S NO SITUATION AND NO INTRUDING.
I JUST CARRY A GUN IN CASE I END UP SKYWARD. SAFETY PRECAUTION.
I KNOW, IT'S A LITTLE OVERKILL, BUT BEATS THE ALTERNATIVE. AM I RIGHT?
YOU HAVEN'T EVER LEFT THE GROUND, HAVE YOU?
DO YOU SLEEP WITH THOSE GRAV-BOOTS ON?
I'M GOING TO LEAVE.

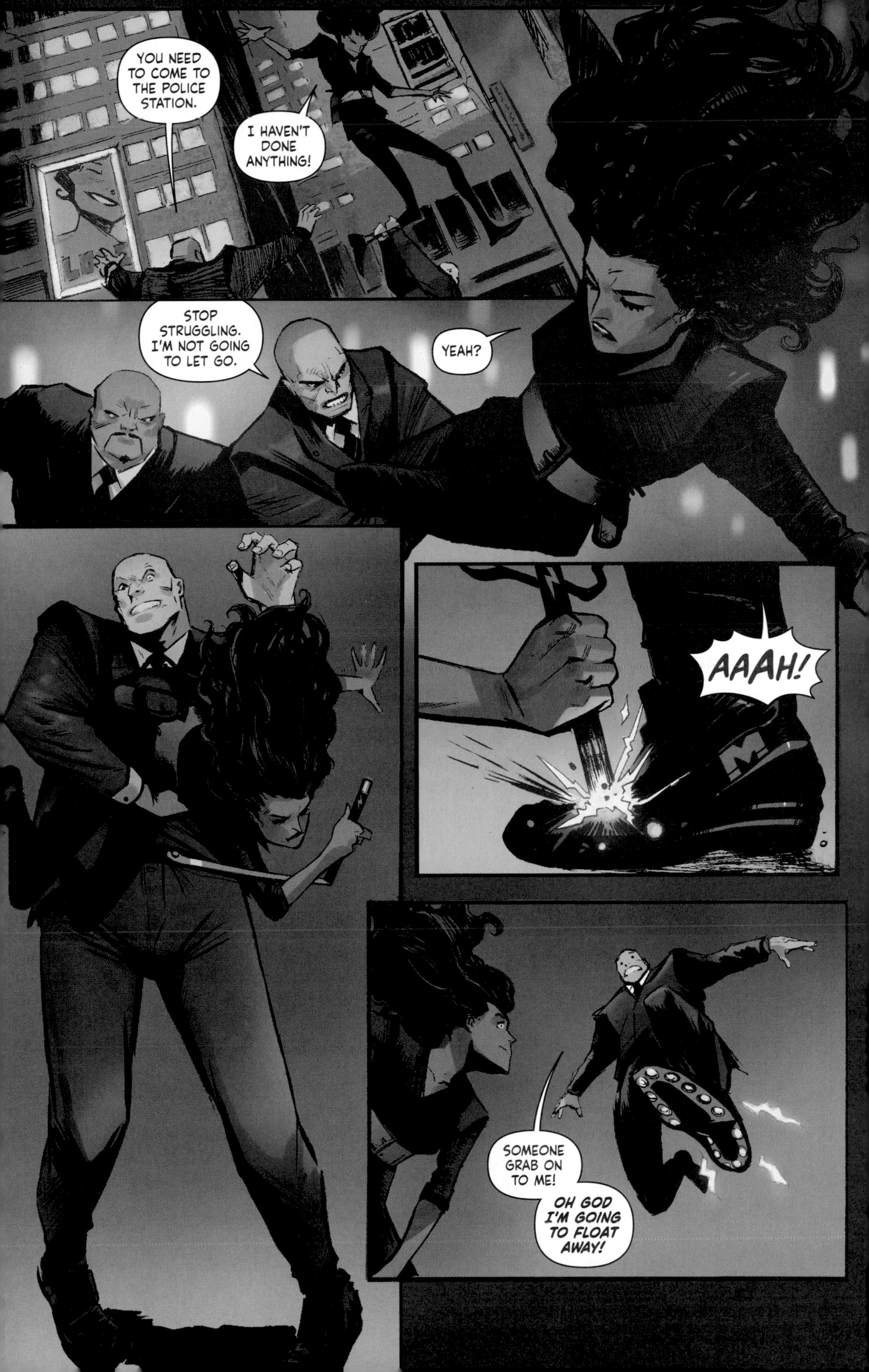
YOU NEED TO COME TO THE POLICE STATION.
I HAVEN'T DONE ANYTHING!
STOP STRUGGLING. I'M NOT GOING TO LET GO.
YEAH?
AAAH!
SOMEONE GRAB ON TO ME!
OH GOD I'M GOING TO FLOAT AWAY!

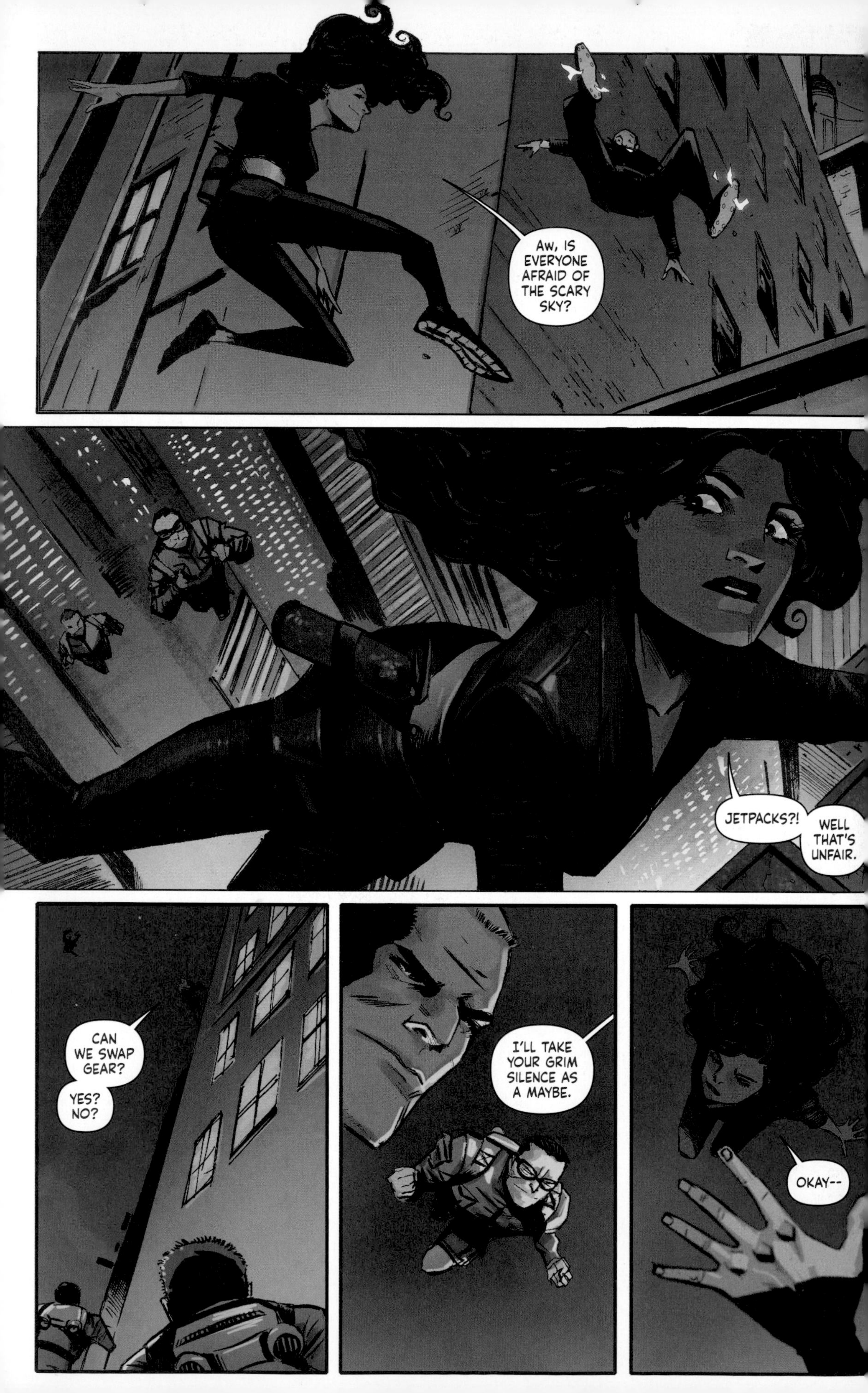
AW, IS EVERYONE AFRAID OF THE SCARY SKY?
JETPACKS?!
WELL THAT'S UNFAIR.
CAN WE SWAP GEAR?
YES? NO?
I'LL TAKE YOUR GRIM SILENCE AS A MAYBE.
OKAY--

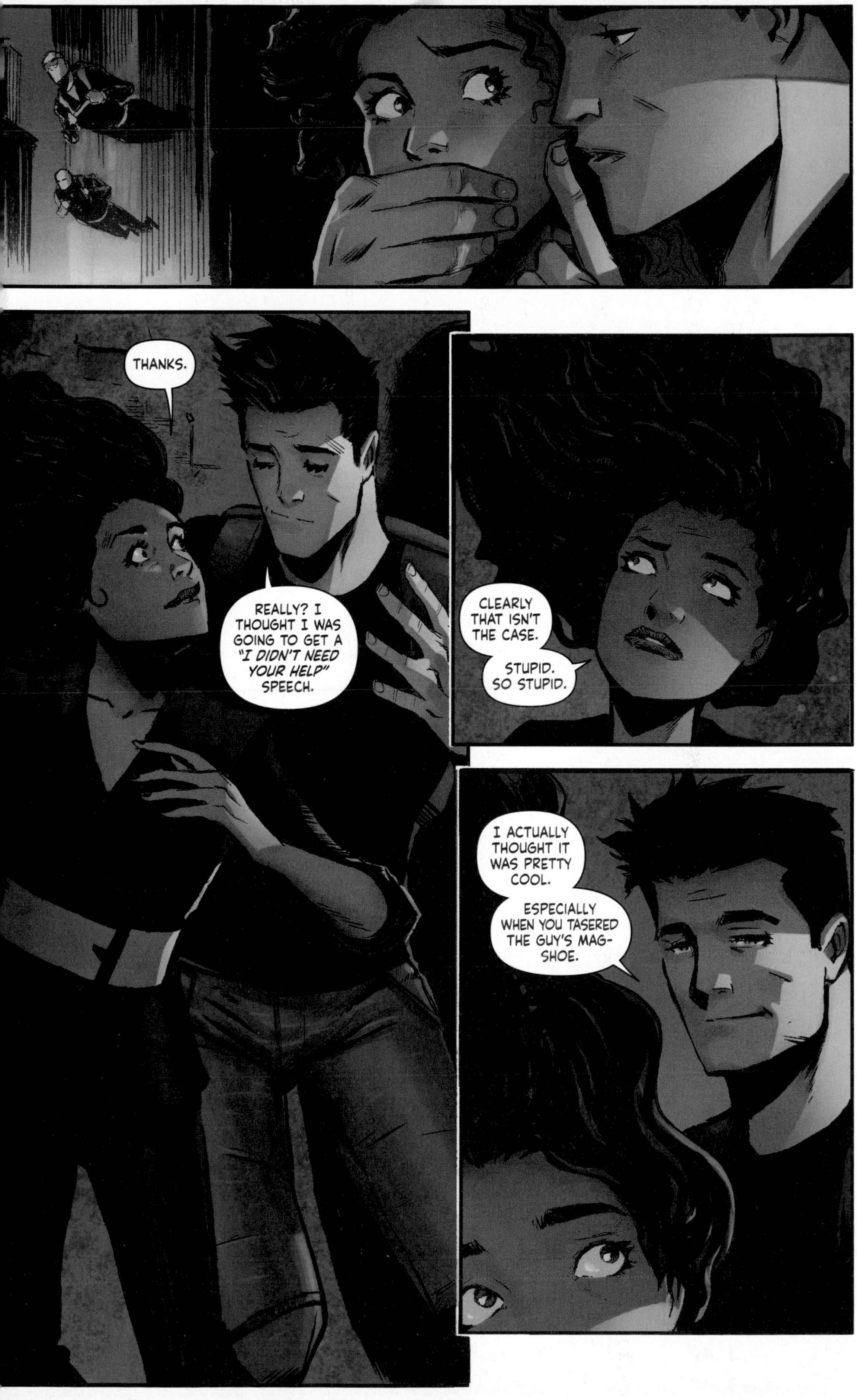
THANKS.
REALLY? I THOUGHT I WAS GOING TO GET A *"I DIDN'T NEED YOUR HELP"* SPEECH.
CLEARLY THAT ISN'T THE CASE.
STUPID. SO STUPID.
I ACTUALLY THOUGHT IT WAS PRETTY COOL.
ESPECIALLY WHEN YOU TASERED THE GUY'S MAG-SHOE.

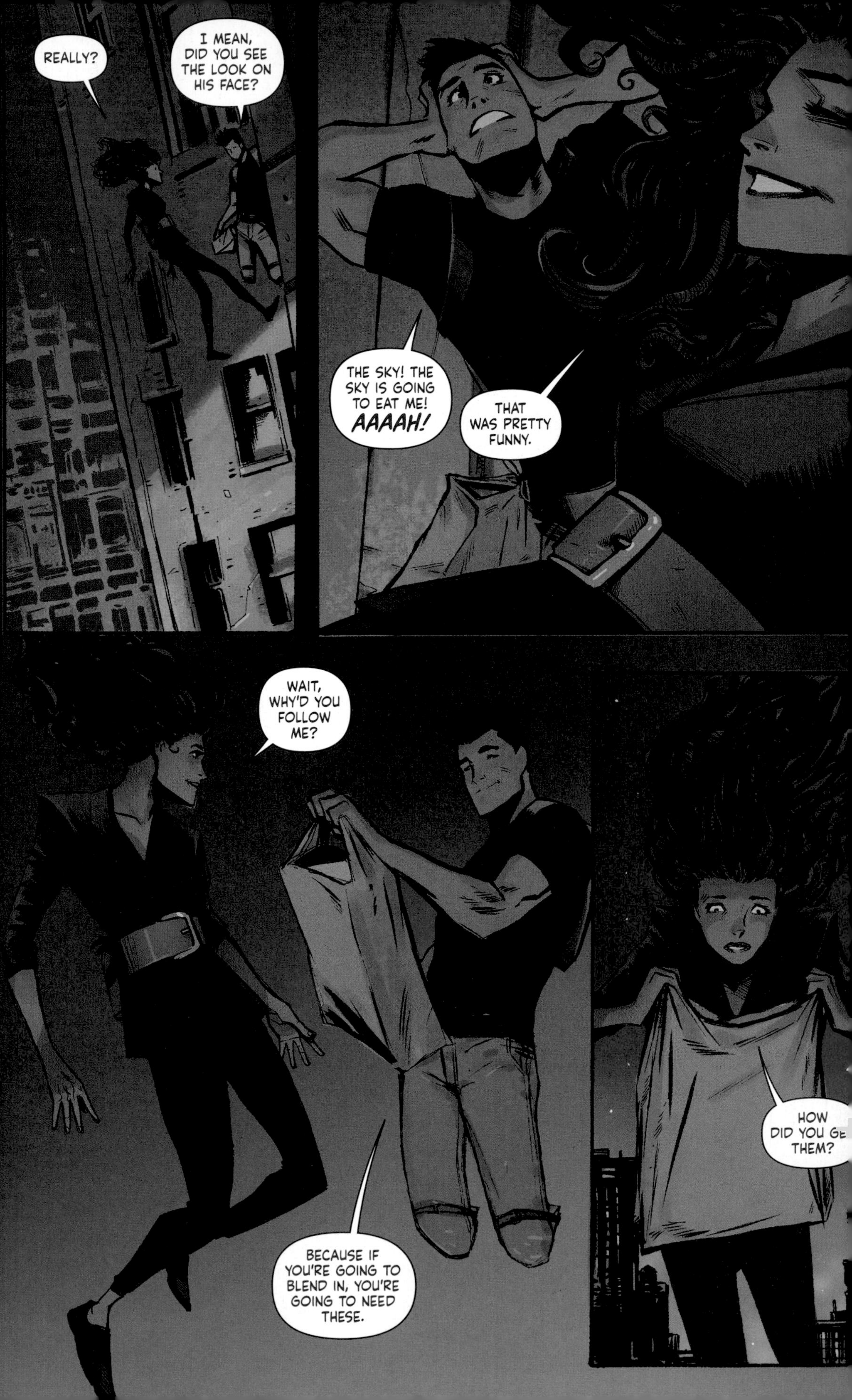
REALLY?
I MEAN, DID YOU SEE THE LOOK ON HIS FACE?
THE SKY! THE SKY IS GOING TO EAT ME! AAAAH!
THAT WAS PRETTY FUNNY.
WAIT, WHY'D YOU FOLLOW ME?
BECAUSE IF YOU'RE GOING TO BLEND IN, YOU'RE GOING TO NEED THESE.
HOW DID YOU GE
THEM?

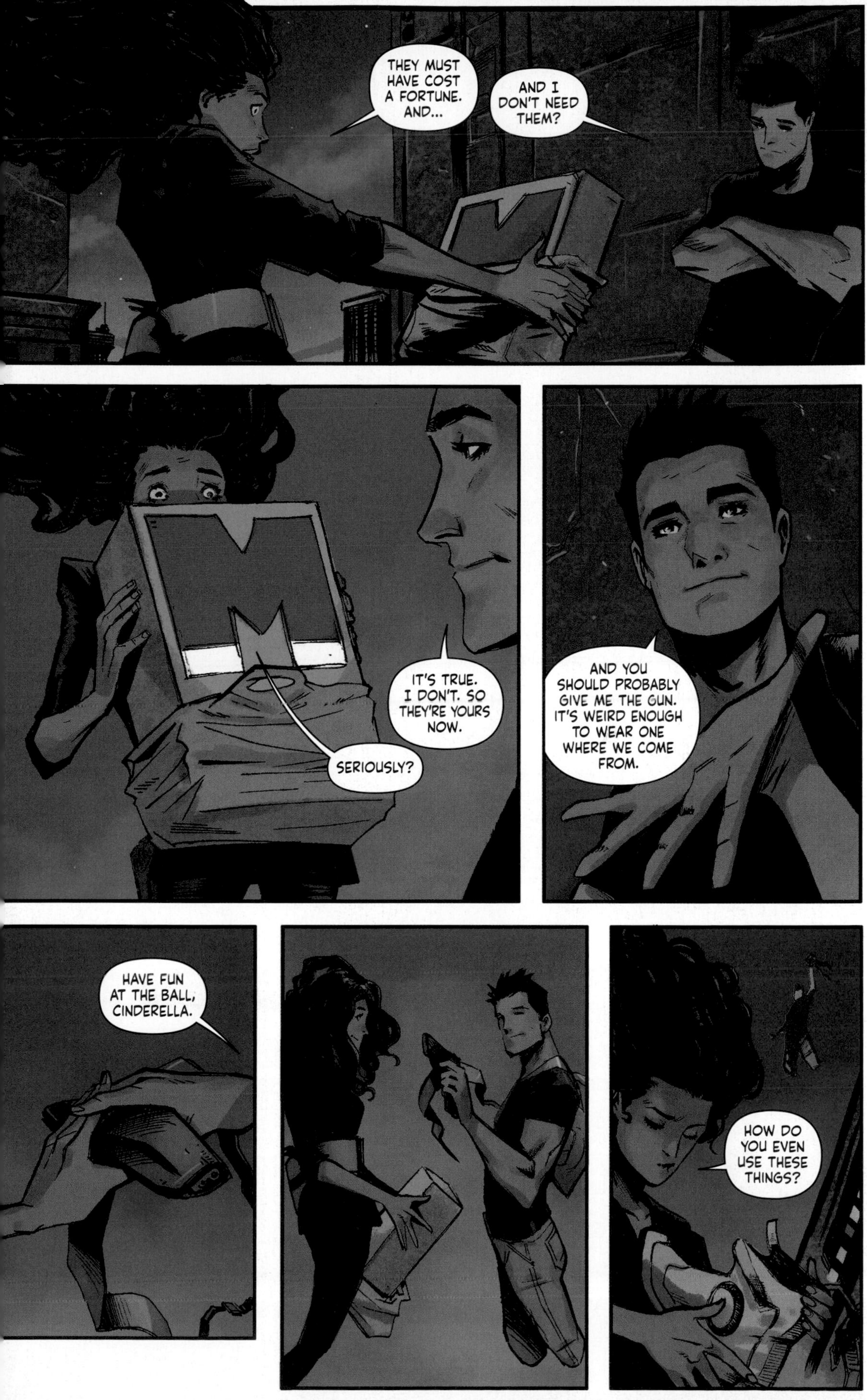
THEY MUST HAVE COST A FORTUNE. AND...
AND I DON'T NEED THEM?
IT'S TRUE. I DON'T. SO THEY'RE YOURS NOW.
SERIOUSLY?
AND YOU SHOULD PROBABLY GIVE ME THE GUN. IT'S WEIRD ENOUGH TO WEAR ONE WHERE WE COME FROM.
HAVE FUN AT THE BALL, CINDERELLA.
HOW DO YOU EVEN USE THESE THINGS?

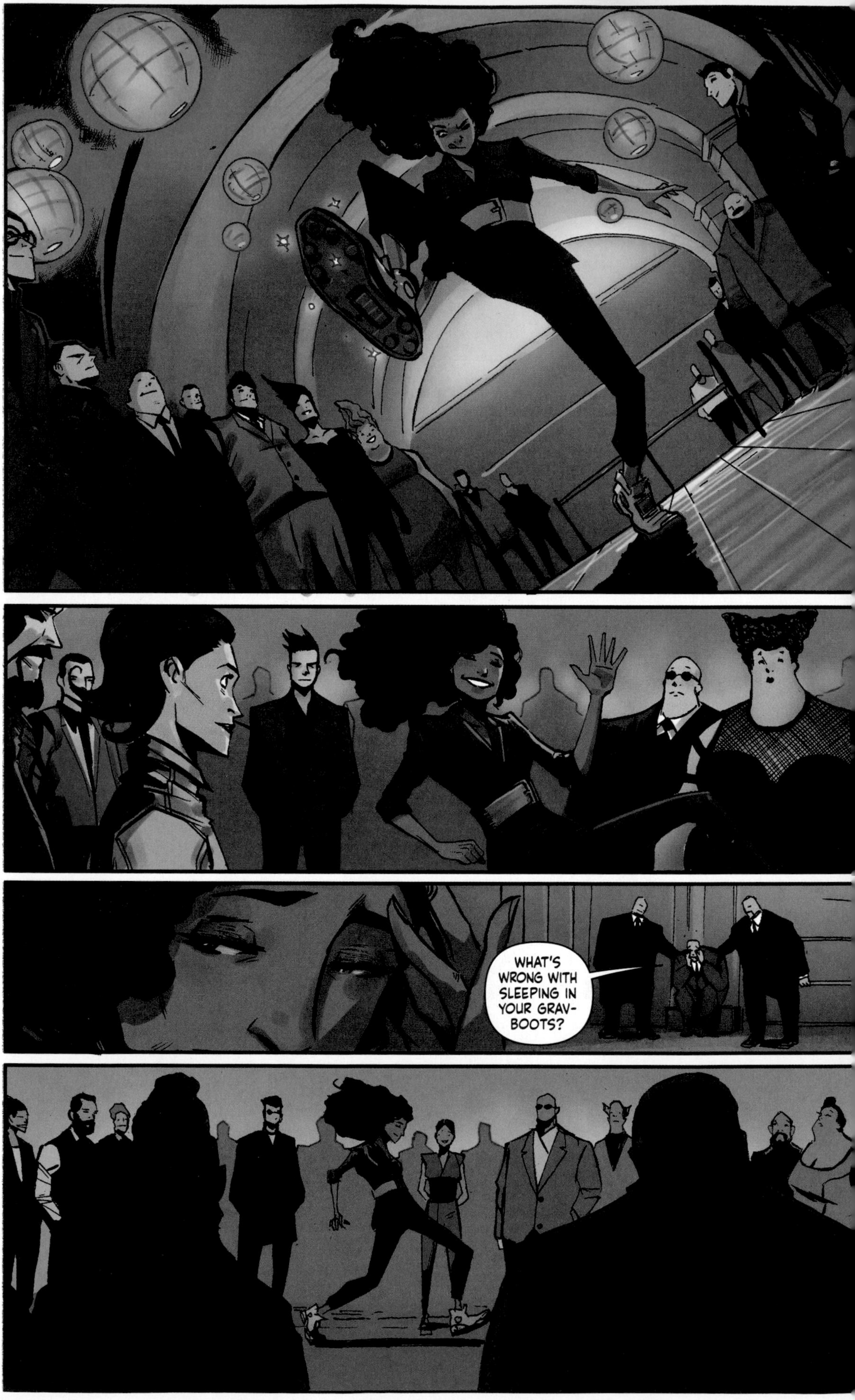
WHAT'S WRONG WITH SLEEPING IN YOUR GRAV-BOOTS?

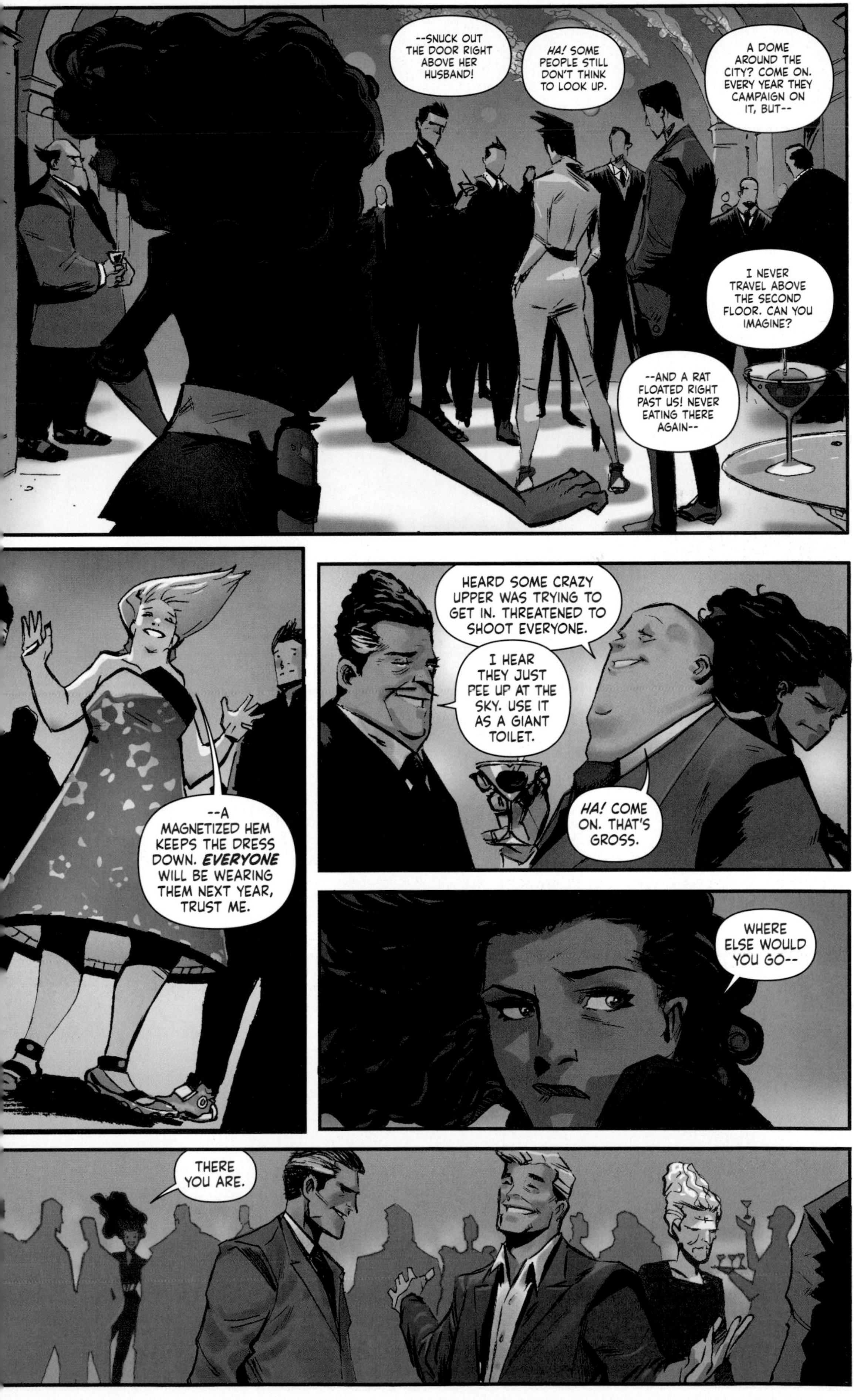
--SNUCK OUT THE DOOR RIGHT ABOVE HER HUSBAND!
HA! SOME PEOPLE STILL DON'T THINK TO LOOK UP.
A DOME AROUND THE CITY? COME ON. EVERY YEAR THEY CAMPAIGN ON IT, BUT--
I NEVER TRAVEL ABOVE THE SECOND FLOOR. CAN YOU IMAGINE?
--AND A RAT FLOATED RIGHT PAST US! NEVER EATING THERE AGAIN--
--A MAGNETIZED HEM KEEPS THE DRESS DOWN. EVERYONE WILL BE WEARING THEM NEXT YEAR, TRUST ME.
HEARD SOME CRAZY UPPER WAS TRYING TO GET IN. THREATENED TO SHOOT EVERYONE.
I HEAR THEY JUST PEE UP AT THE SKY. USE IT AS A GIANT TOILET.
HA! COME ON. THAT'S GROSS.
WHERE ELSE WOULD YOU GO--
THERE YOU ARE.

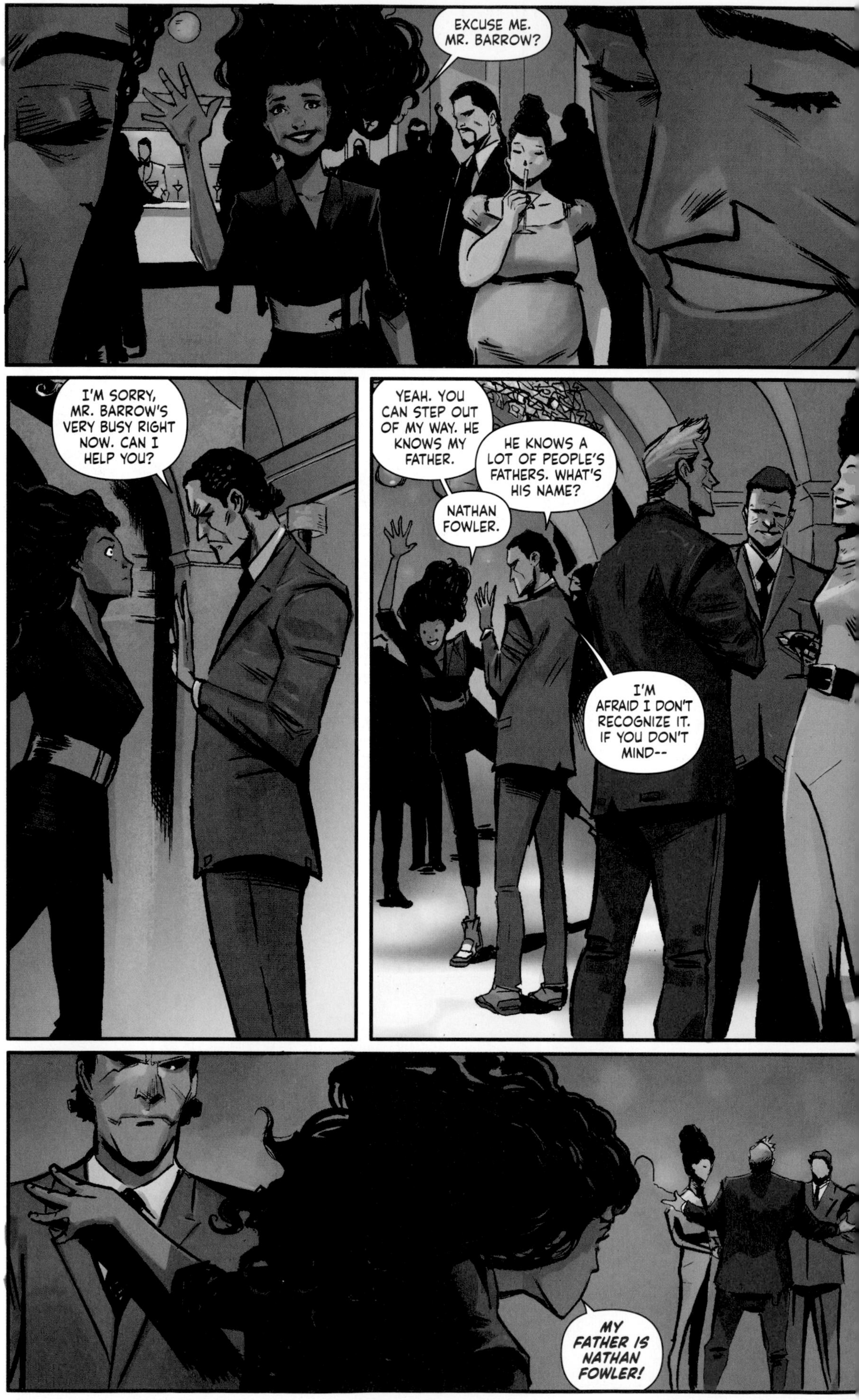
EXCUSE ME. MR. BARROW?
I'M SORRY, MR. BARROW'S VERY BUSY RIGHT NOW. CAN I HELP YOU?
YEAH. YOU CAN STEP OUT OF MY WAY. HE KNOWS MY FATHER.
HE KNOWS A LOT OF PEOPLE'S FATHERS. WHAT'S HIS NAME?
NATHAN FOWLER.
I'M AFRAID I DON'T RECOGNIZE IT. IF YOU DON'T MIND--
MY FATHER IS NATHAN FOWLER!

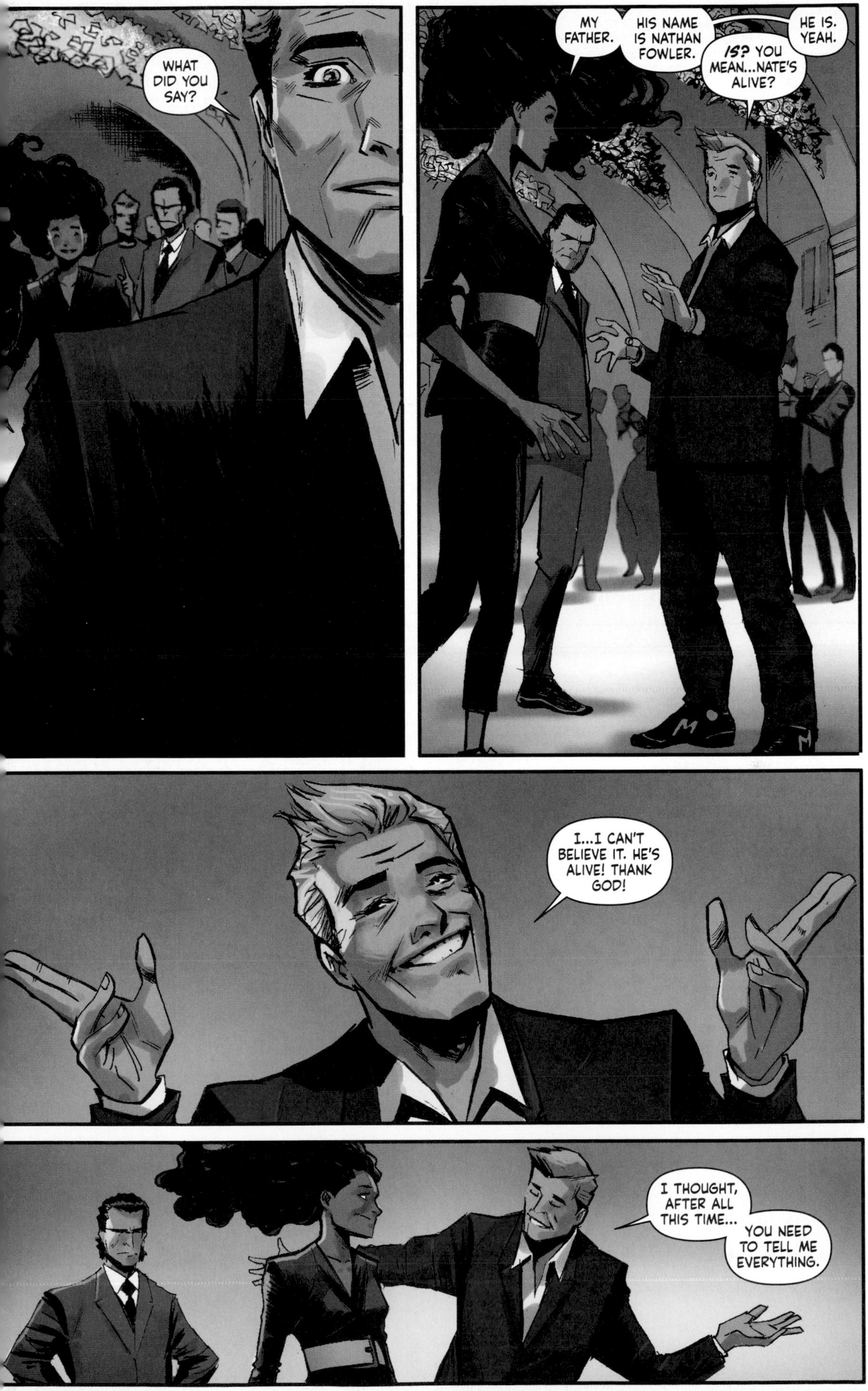
WHAT DID YOU SAY?
MY FATHER.
HIS NAME IS NATHAN FOWLER.
IS? YOU MEAN...NATE'S ALIVE?
HE IS. YEAH.
I...I CAN'T BELIEVE IT. HE'S ALIVE! THANK GOD!
I THOUGHT, AFTER ALL THIS TIME...
YOU NEED TO TELL ME EVERYTHING.

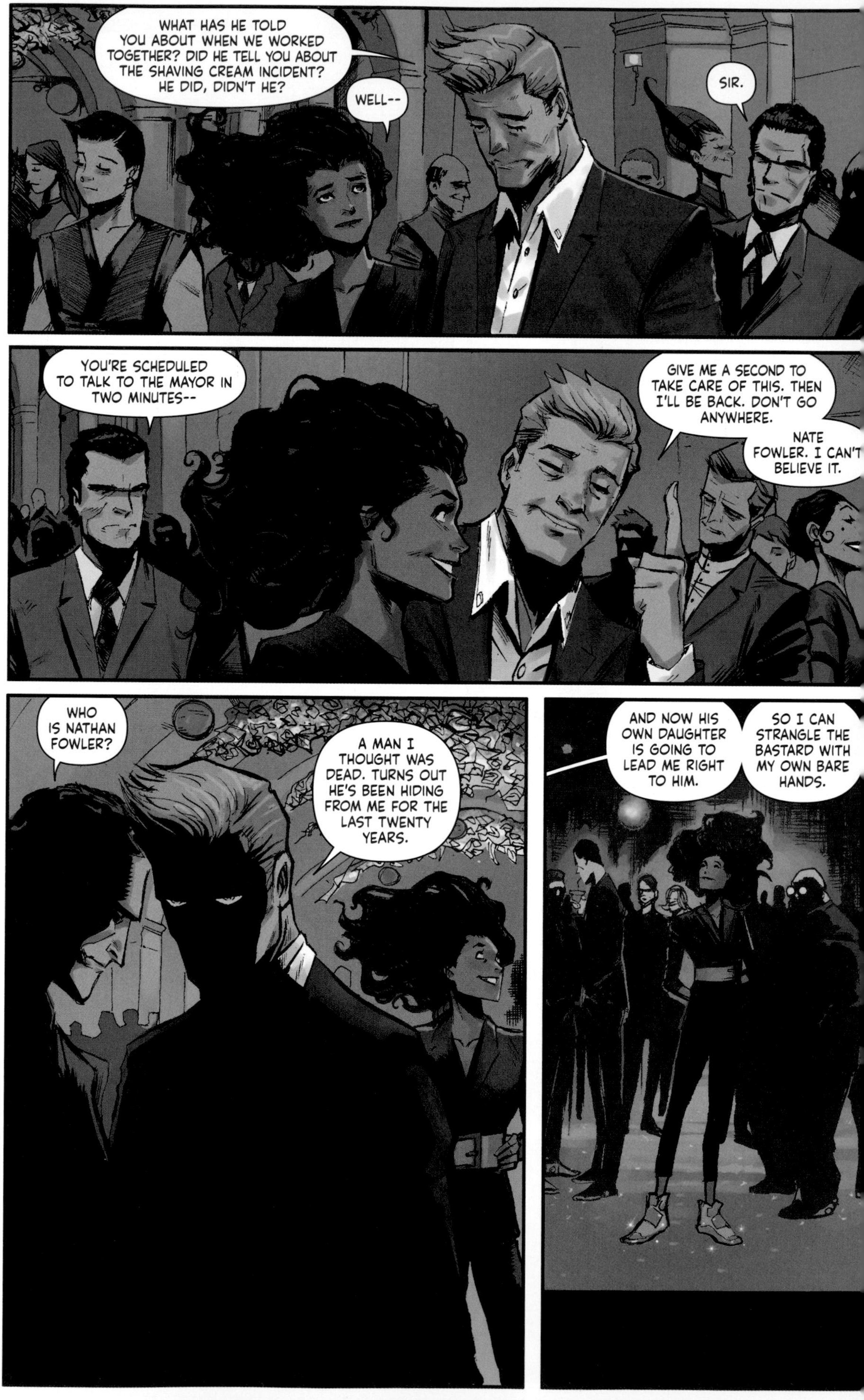
WHAT HAS HE TOLD YOU ABOUT WHEN WE WORKED TOGETHER? DID HE TELL YOU ABOUT THE SHAVING CREAM INCIDENT? HE DID, DIDN'T HE?
WELL--
SIR.
YOU'RE SCHEDULED TO TALK TO THE MAYOR IN TWO MINUTES--
GIVE ME A SECOND TO TAKE CARE OF THIS. THEN I'LL BE BACK. DON'T GO ANYWHERE.
NATE FOWLER. I CAN'T BELIEVE IT.
WHO IS NATHAN FOWLER?
A MAN I THOUGHT WAS DEAD. TURNS OUT HE'S BEEN HIDING FROM ME FOR THE LAST TWENTY YEARS.
AND NOW HIS OWN DAUGHTER IS GOING TO LEAD ME RIGHT TO HIM.
SO I CAN STRANGLE THE BASTARD WITH MY OWN BARE HANDS.

END CHAPTER TWO

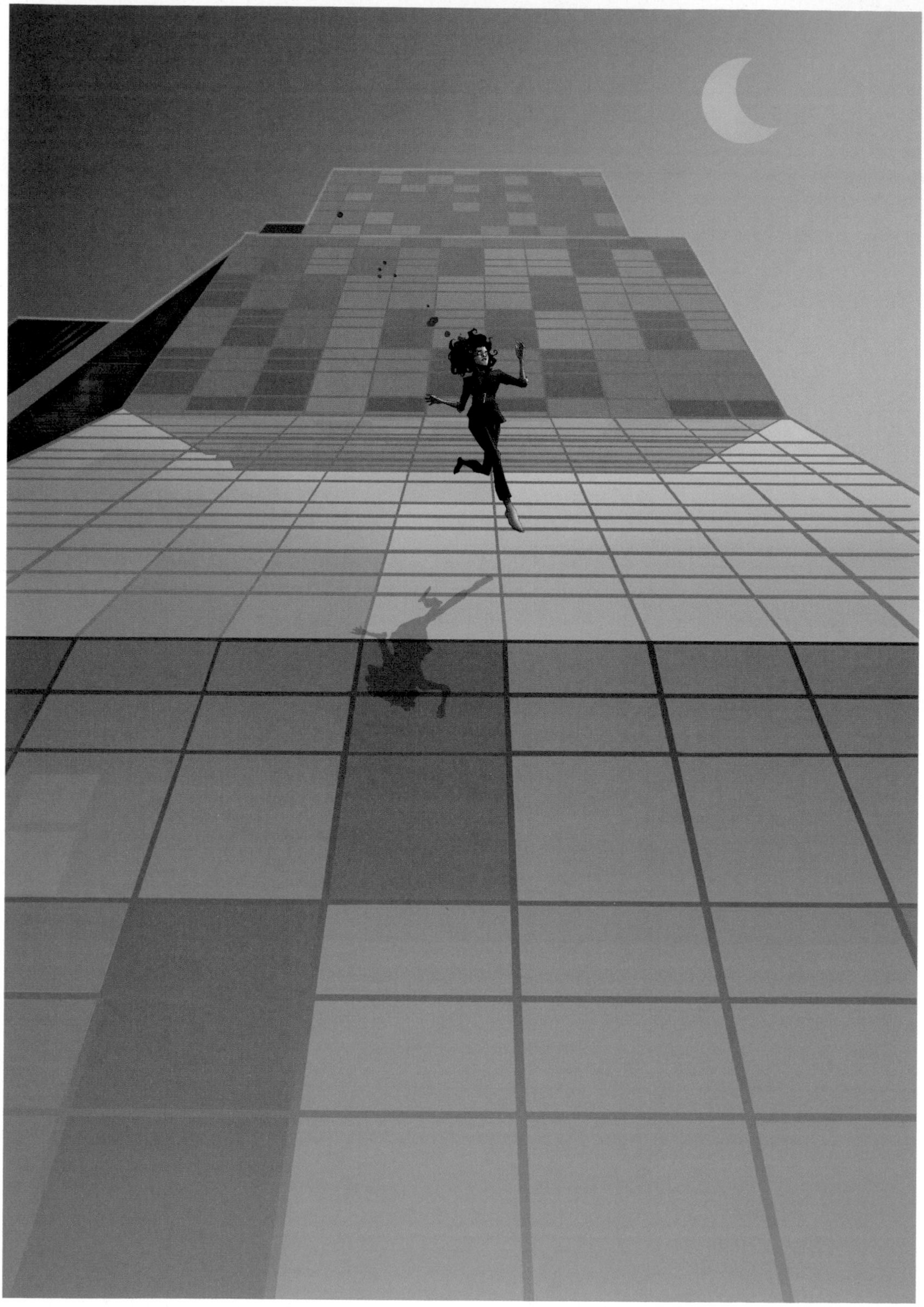

CHAPTER THREE

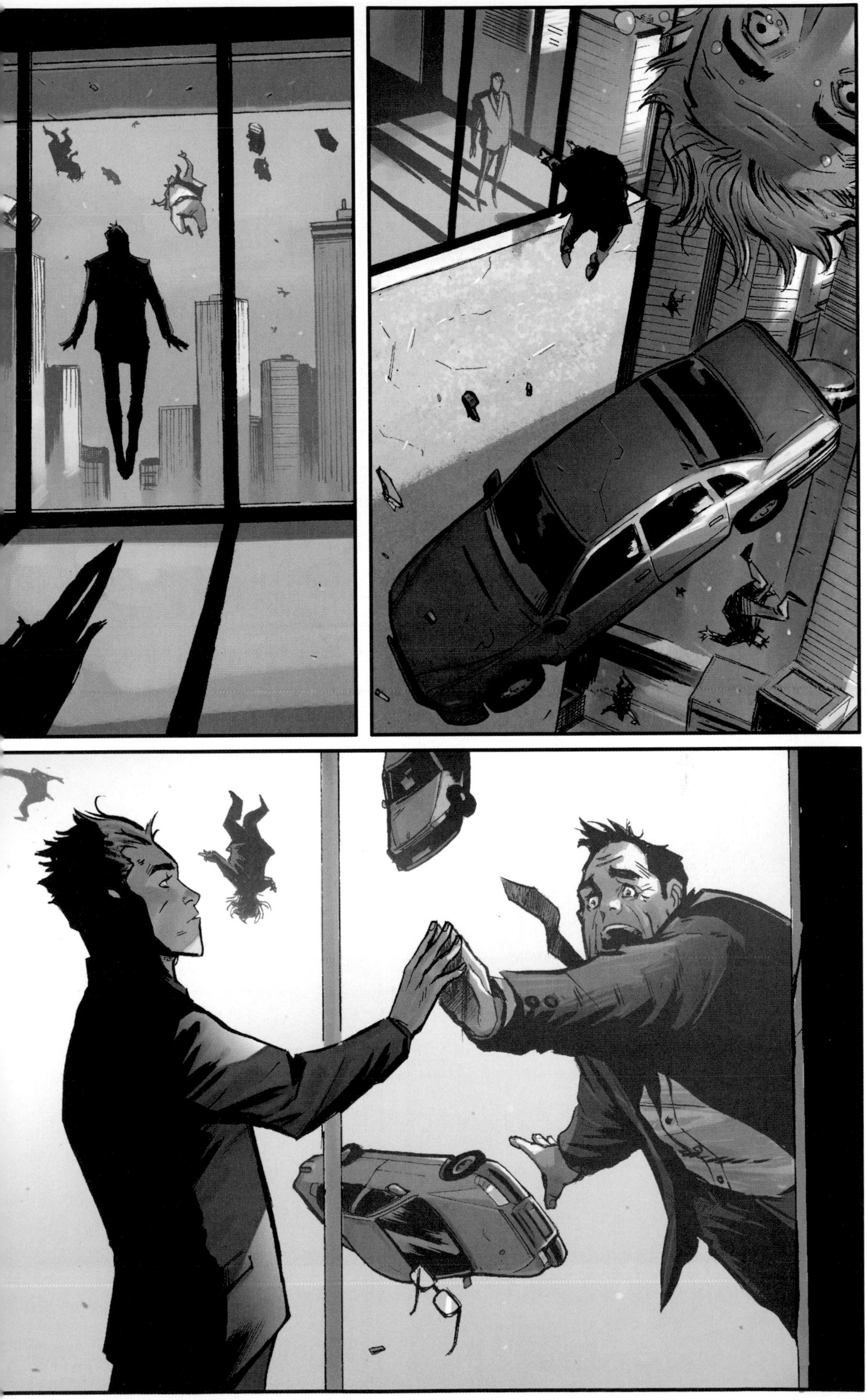

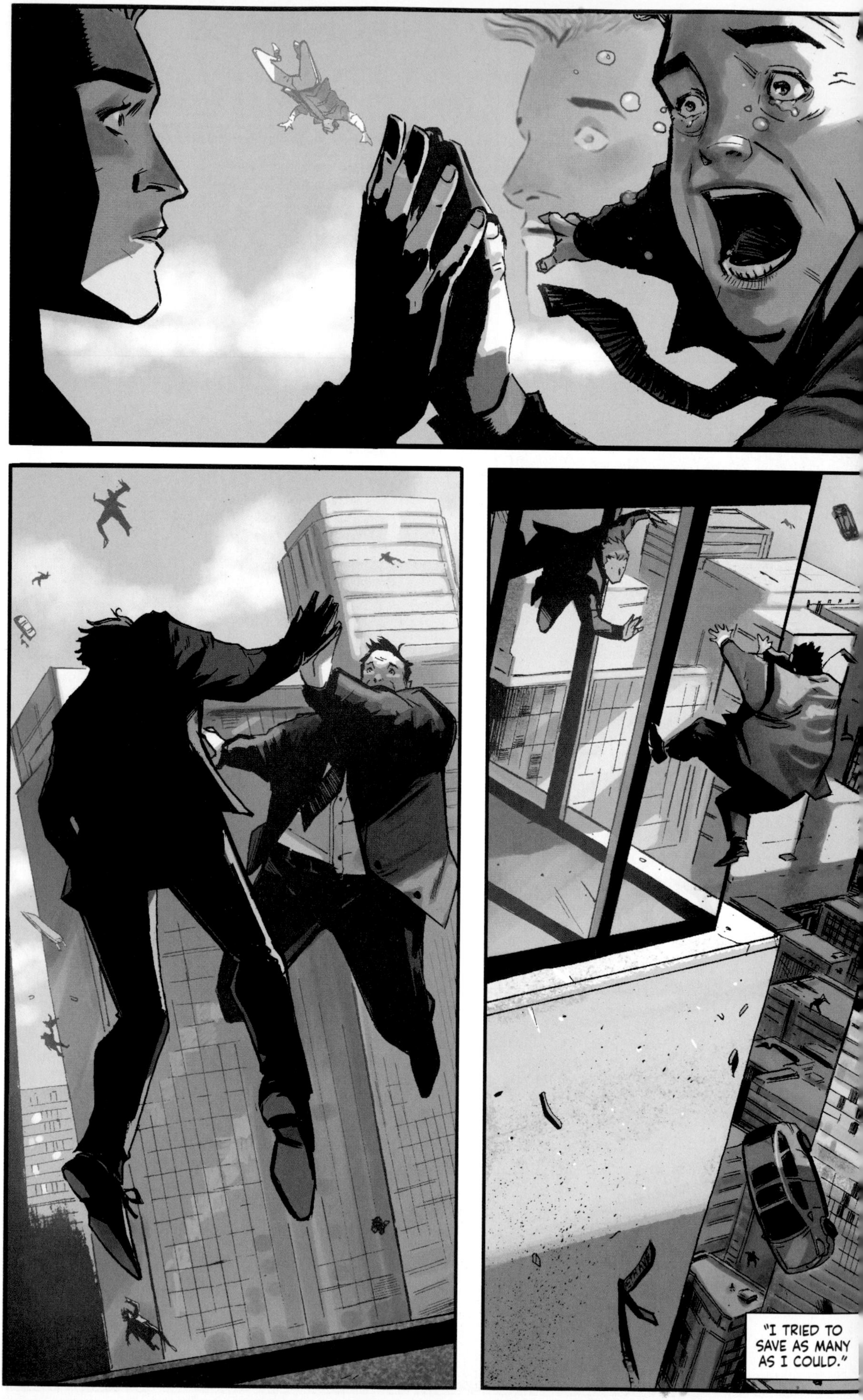
"I TRIED TO SAVE AS MANY AS I COULD."

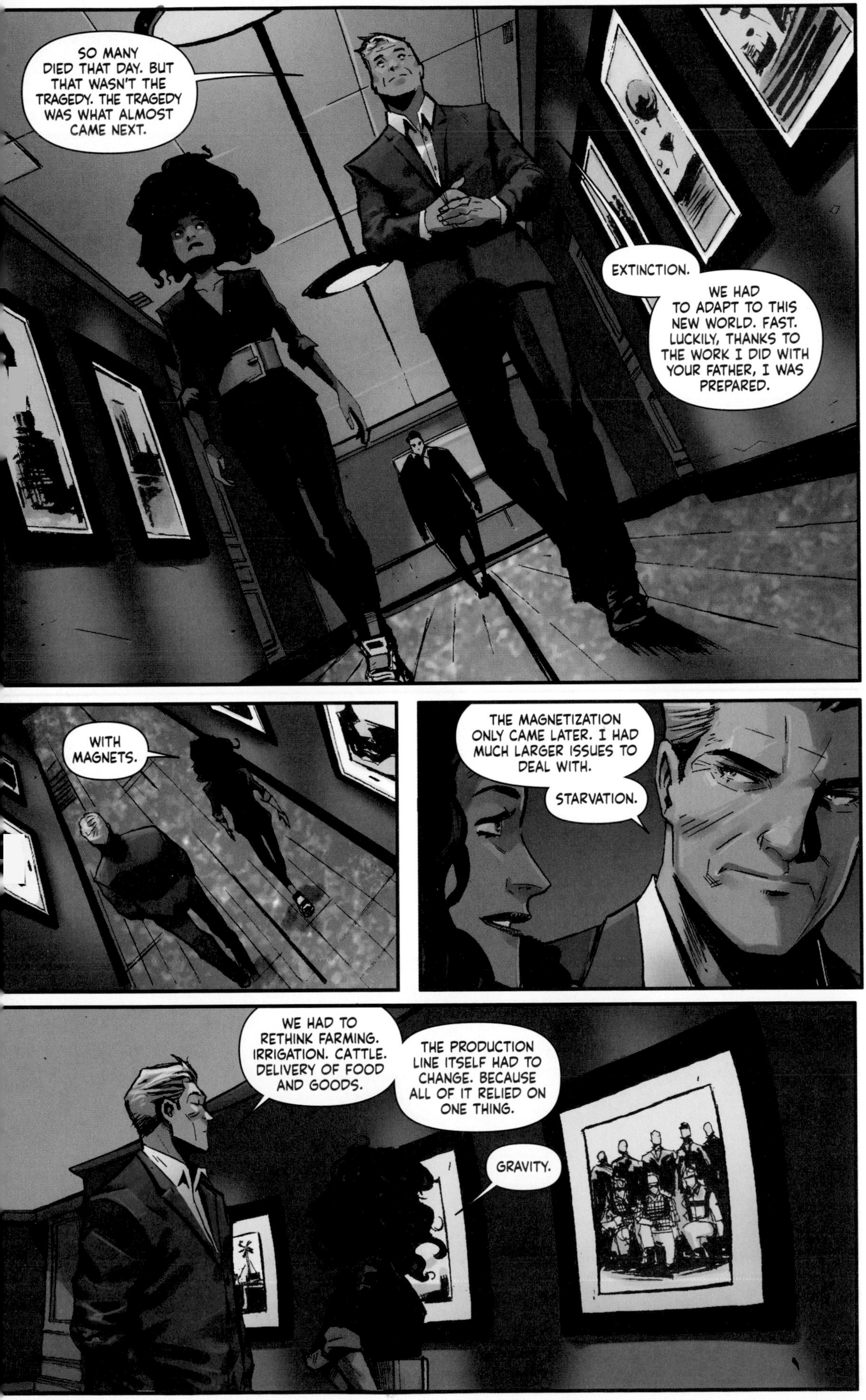
SO MANY DIED THAT DAY. BUT THAT WASN'T THE TRAGEDY. THE TRAGEDY WAS WHAT ALMOST CAME NEXT.
EXTINCTION.
WE HAD TO ADAPT TO THIS NEW WORLD. FAST. LUCKILY, THANKS TO THE WORK I DID WITH YOUR FATHER, I WAS PREPARED.
WITH MAGNETS.
THE MAGNETIZATION ONLY CAME LATER. I HAD MUCH LARGER ISSUES TO DEAL WITH.
STARVATION.
WE HAD TO RETHINK FARMING. IRRIGATION. CATTLE. DELIVERY OF FOOD AND GOODS.
THE PRODUCTION LINE ITSELF HAD TO CHANGE. BECAUSE ALL OF IT RELIED ON ONE THING.
GRAVITY.

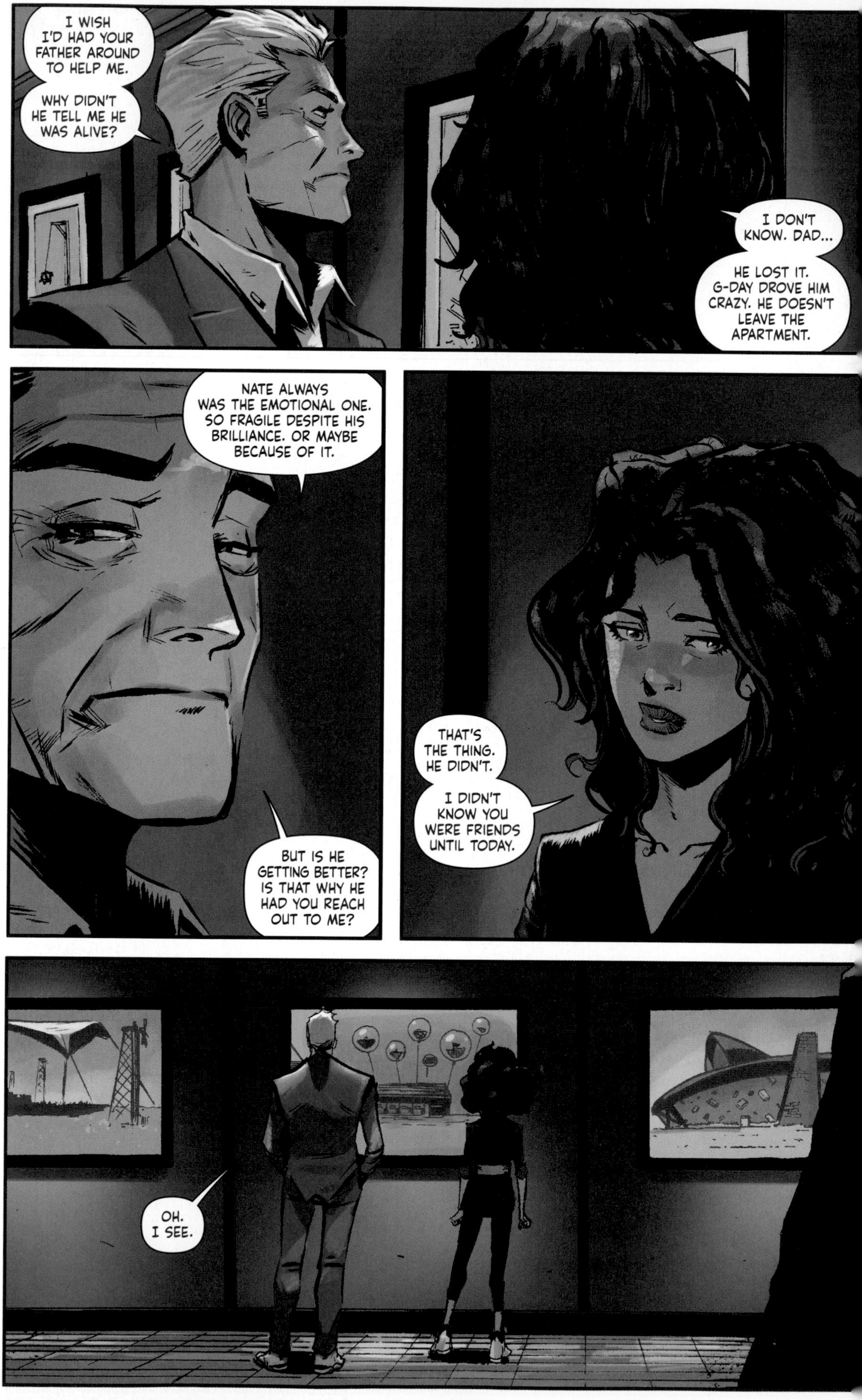
I WISH I'D HAD YOUR FATHER AROUND TO HELP ME.
WHY DIDN'T HE TELL ME HE WAS ALIVE?
I DON'T KNOW. DAD...
HE LOST IT. G-DAY DROVE HIM CRAZY. HE DOESN'T LEAVE THE APARTMENT.
NATE ALWAYS WAS THE EMOTIONAL ONE. SO FRAGILE DESPITE HIS BRILLIANCE. OR MAYBE BECAUSE OF IT.
BUT IS HE GETTING BETTER? IS THAT WHY HE HAD YOU REACH OUT TO ME?
THAT'S THE THING. HE DIDN'T.
I DIDN'T KNOW YOU WERE FRIENDS UNTIL TODAY.
OH. I SEE.

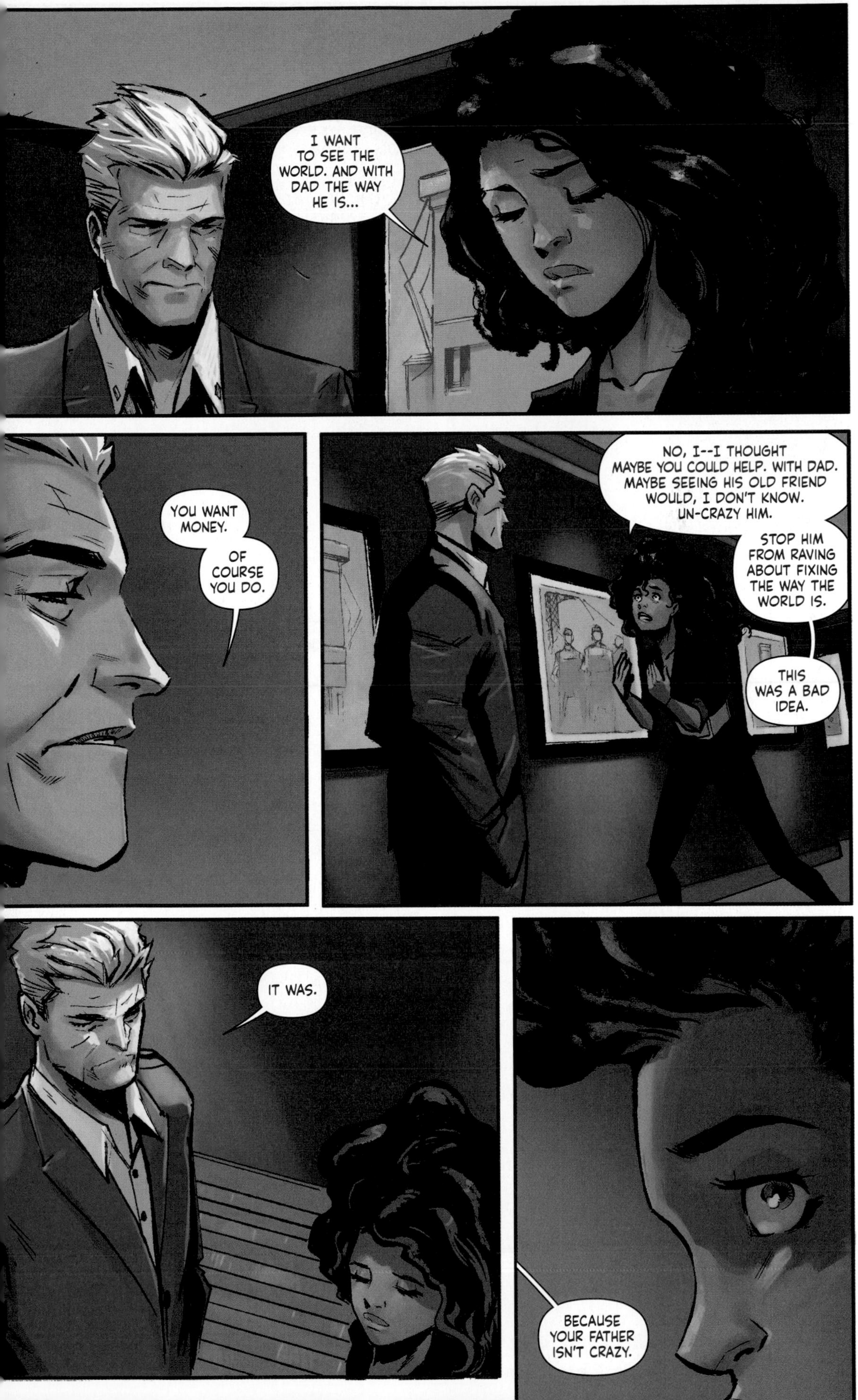
I WANT TO SEE THE WORLD. AND WITH DAD THE WAY HE IS...
YOU WANT MONEY.
OF COURSE YOU DO.
NO, I--I THOUGHT MAYBE YOU COULD HELP. WITH DAD. MAYBE SEEING HIS OLD FRIEND WOULD, I DON'T KNOW. UN-CRAZY HIM.
STOP HIM FROM RAVING ABOUT FIXING THE WAY THE WORLD IS.
THIS WAS A BAD IDEA.
IT WAS.
BECAUSE YOUR FATHER ISN'T CRAZY.

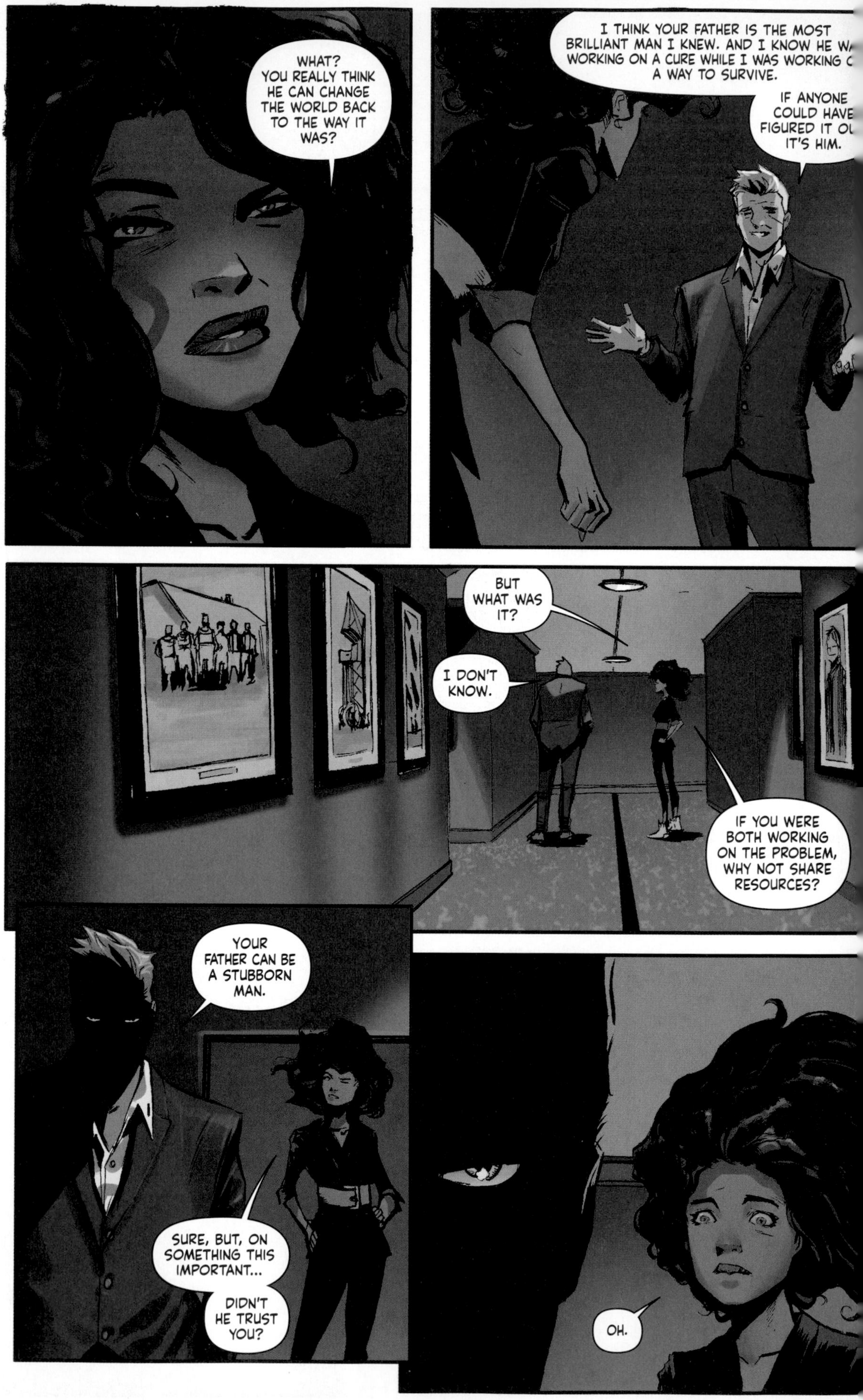
WHAT? YOU REALLY THINK HE CAN CHANGE THE WORLD BACK TO THE WAY IT WAS?
I THINK YOUR FATHER IS THE MOST BRILLIANT MAN I KNEW. AND I KNOW HE WA
WORKING ON A CURE WHILE I WAS WORKING O
A WAY TO SURVIVE.
IF ANYONE COULD HAVE FIGURED IT OU
IT'S HIM.
BUT WHAT WAS IT?
I DON'T KNOW.
IF YOU WERE BOTH WORKING ON THE PROBLEM, WHY NOT SHARE RESOURCES?
YOUR FATHER CAN BE A STUBBORN MAN.
SURE, BUT, ON SOMETHING THIS IMPORTANT...
DIDN'T HE TRUST YOU?
OH.

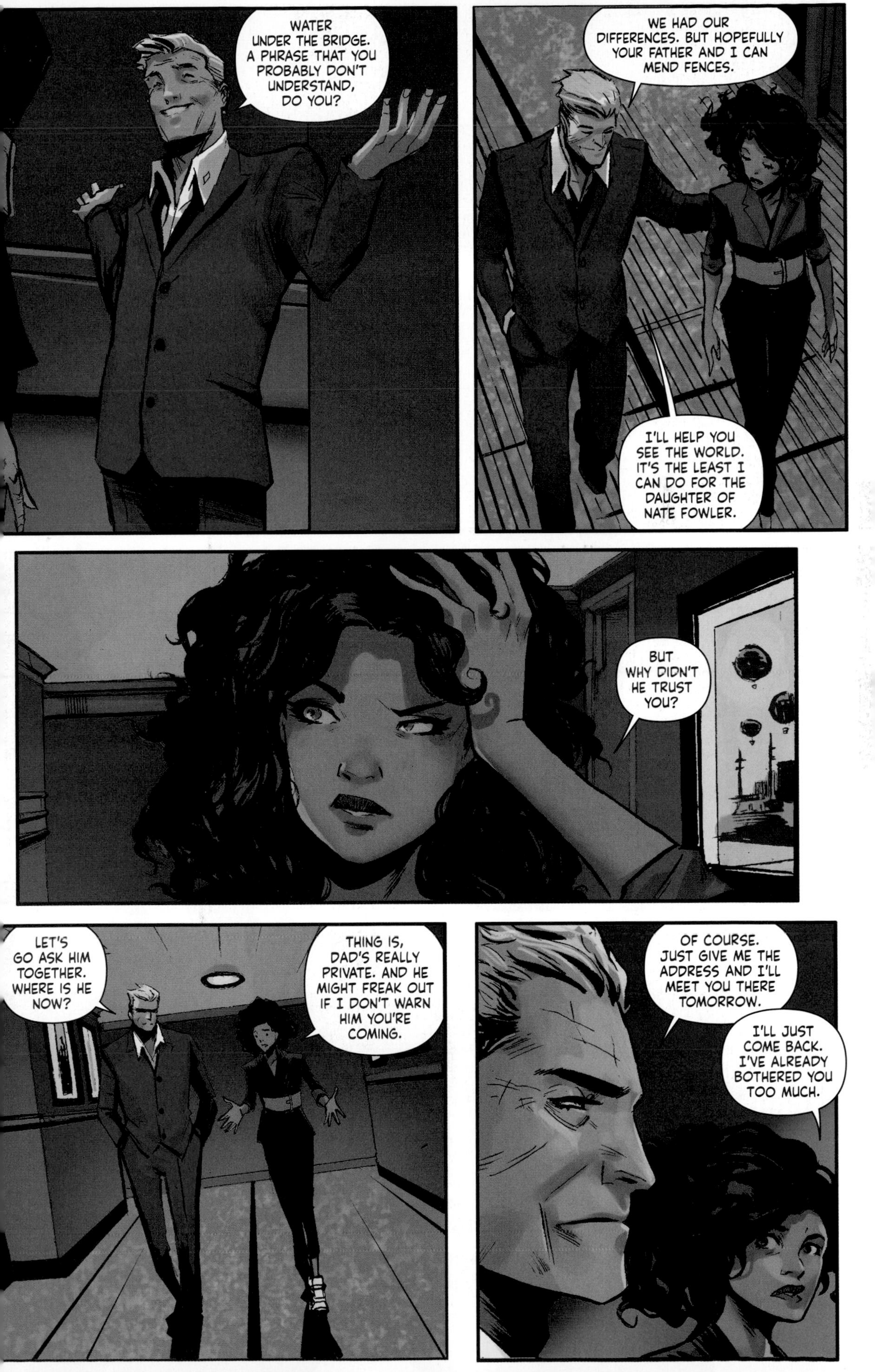
WATER UNDER THE BRIDGE. A PHRASE THAT YOU PROBABLY DON'T UNDERSTAND, DO YOU?
WE HAD OUR DIFFERENCES. BUT HOPEFULLY YOUR FATHER AND I CAN MEND FENCES.
I'LL HELP YOU SEE THE WORLD. IT'S THE LEAST I CAN DO FOR THE DAUGHTER OF NATE FOWLER.
BUT WHY DIDN'T HE TRUST YOU?
LET'S GO ASK HIM TOGETHER. WHERE IS HE NOW?
THING IS, DAD'S REALLY PRIVATE. AND HE MIGHT FREAK OUT IF I DON'T WARN HIM YOU'RE COMING.
OF COURSE. JUST GIVE ME THE ADDRESS AND I'LL MEET YOU THERE TOMORROW.
I'LL JUST COME BACK. I'VE ALREADY BOTHERED YOU TOO MUCH.

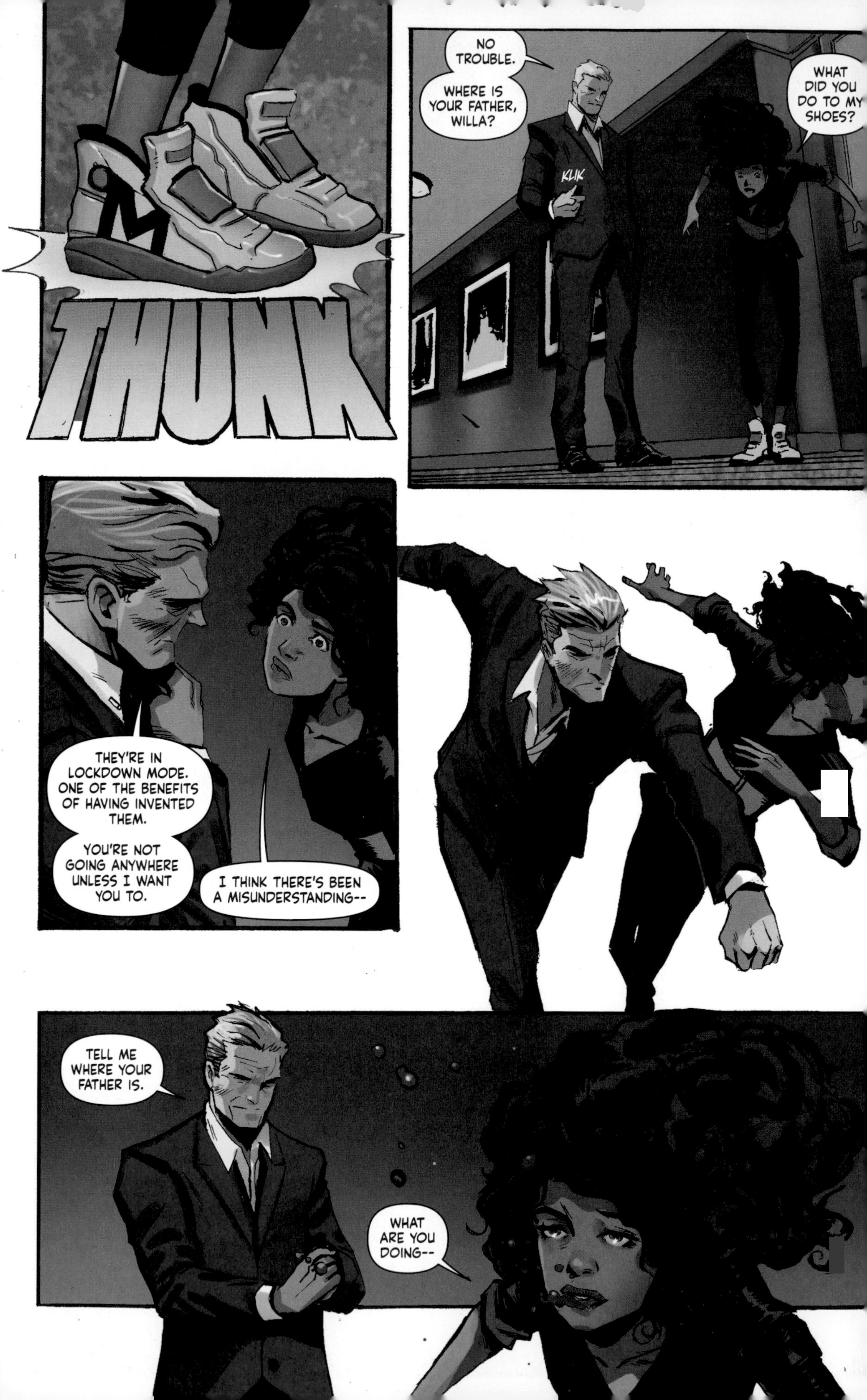
THUNK
NO TROUBLE.
WHERE IS YOUR FATHER, WILLA?
KLIK
WHAT DID YOU DO TO MY SHOES?
THEY'RE IN LOCKDOWN MODE. ONE OF THE BENEFITS OF HAVING INVENTED THEM.
YOU'RE NOT GOING ANYWHERE UNLESS I WANT YOU TO.
I THINK THERE'S BEEN A MISUNDERSTANDING--
TELL ME WHERE YOUR FATHER IS.
WHAT ARE YOU DOING--

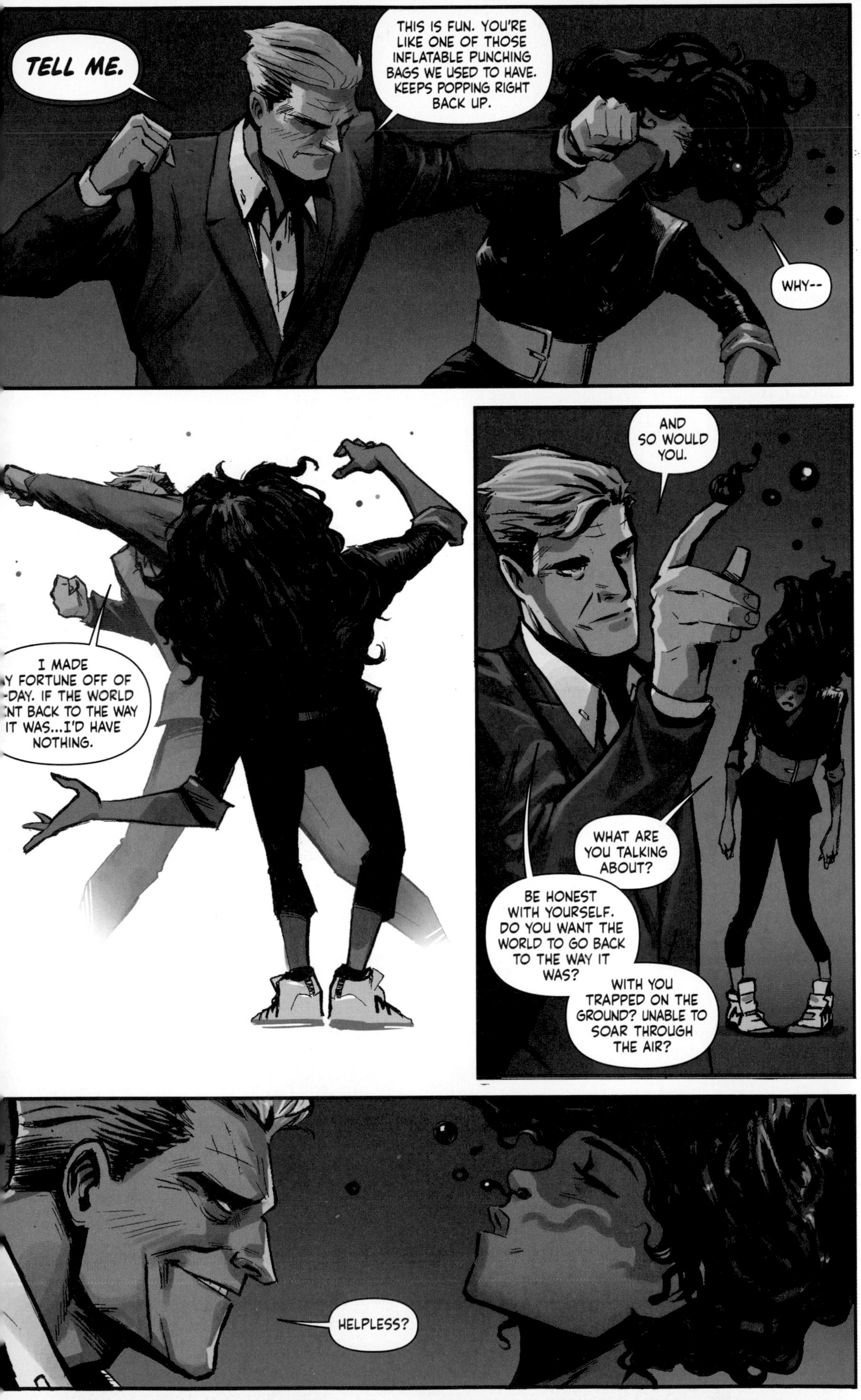
TELL ME.
THIS IS FUN. YOU'RE LIKE ONE OF THOSE INFLATABLE PUNCHING BAGS WE USED TO HAVE. KEEPS POPPING RIGHT BACK UP.
WHY--
I MADE Y FORTUNE OFF OF -DAY. IF THE WORLD NT BACK TO THE WAY IT WAS...I'D HAVE NOTHING.
AND SO WOULD YOU.
WHAT ARE YOU TALKING ABOUT?
BE HONEST WITH YOURSELF. DO YOU WANT THE WORLD TO GO BACK TO THE WAY IT WAS?
WITH YOU TRAPPED ON THE GROUND? UNABLE TO SOAR THROUGH THE AIR?
HELPLESS?

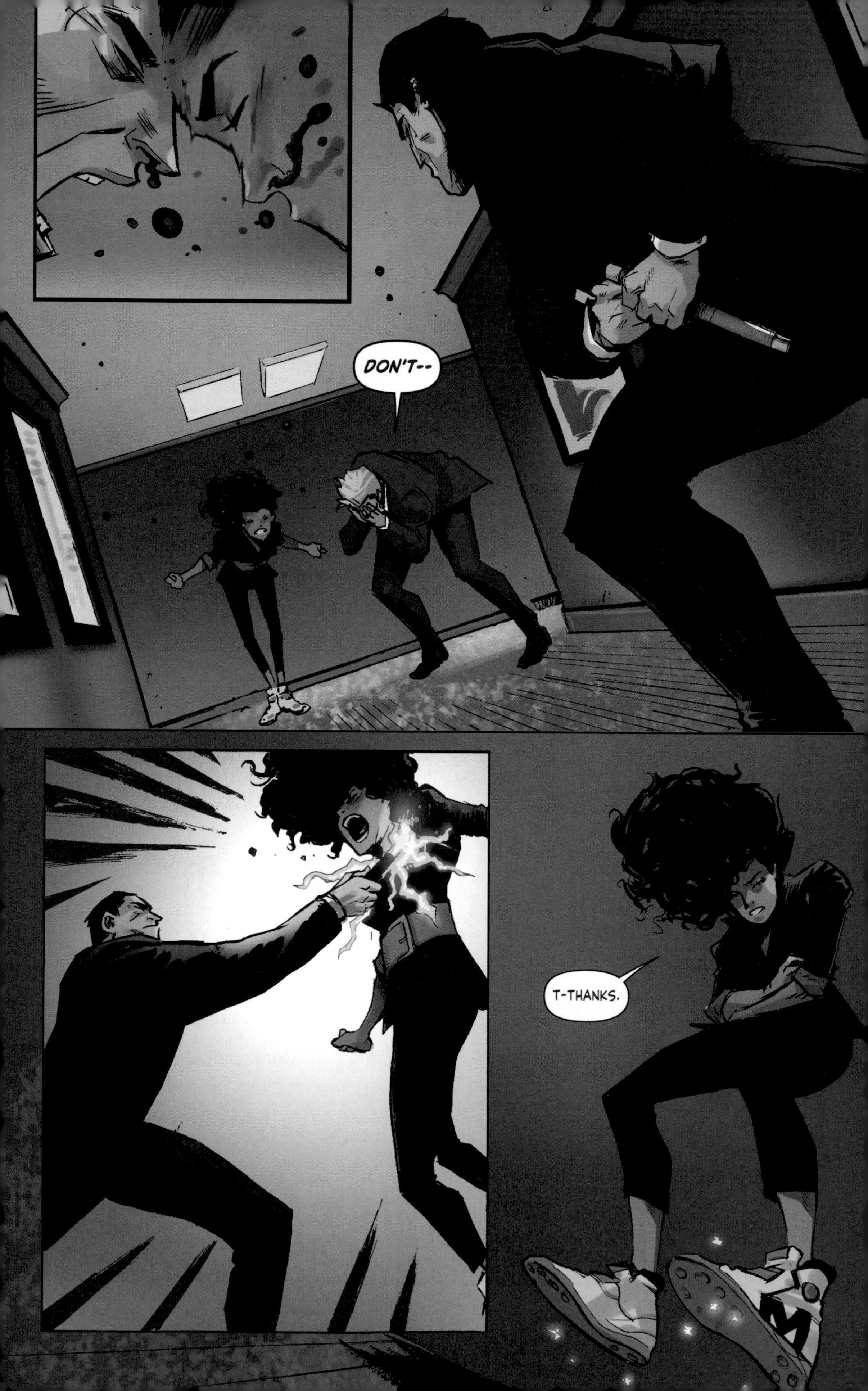
DON'T--
T-THANKS.

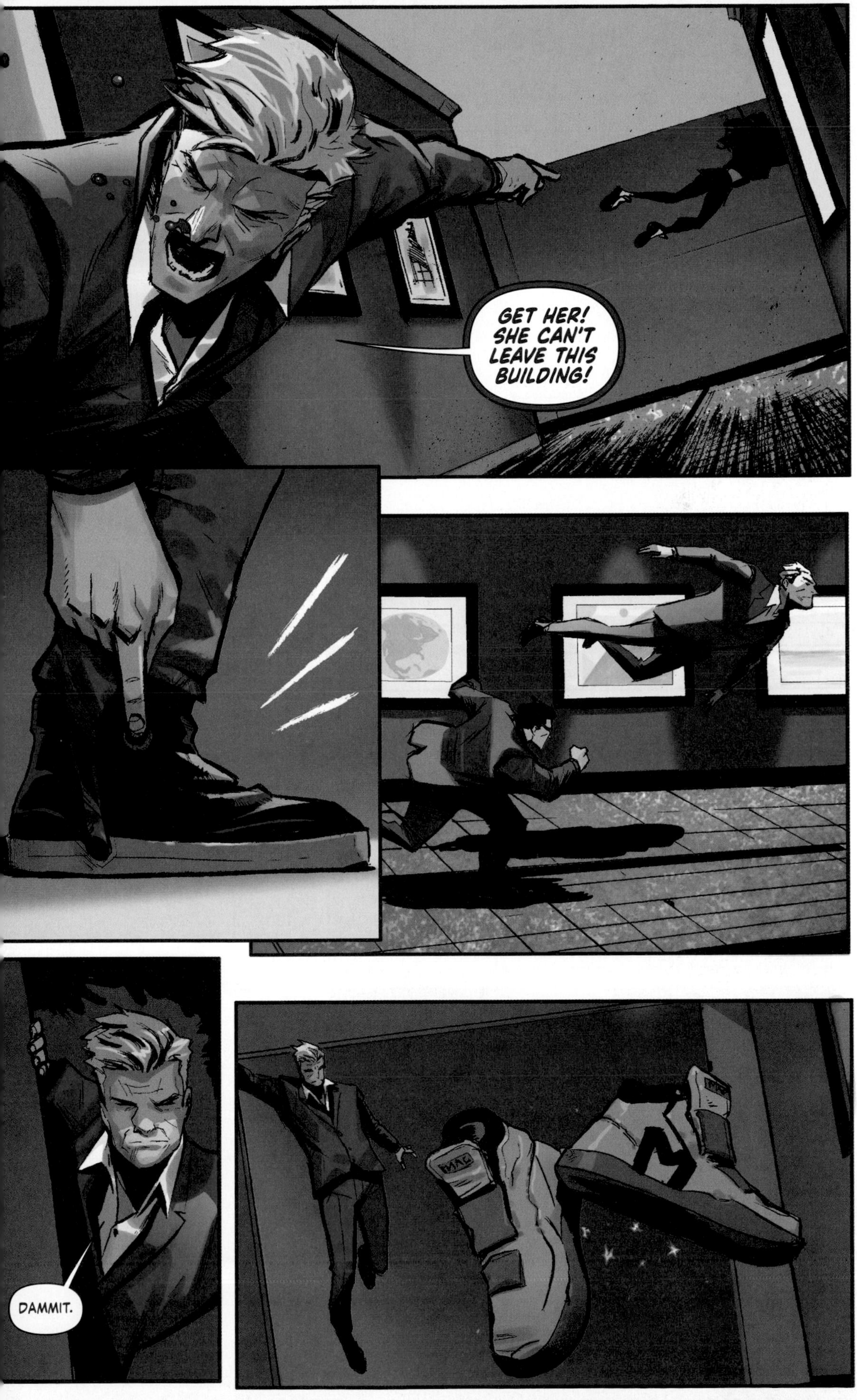
GET HER! SHE CAN'T LEAVE THIS BUILDING!
DAMMIT.

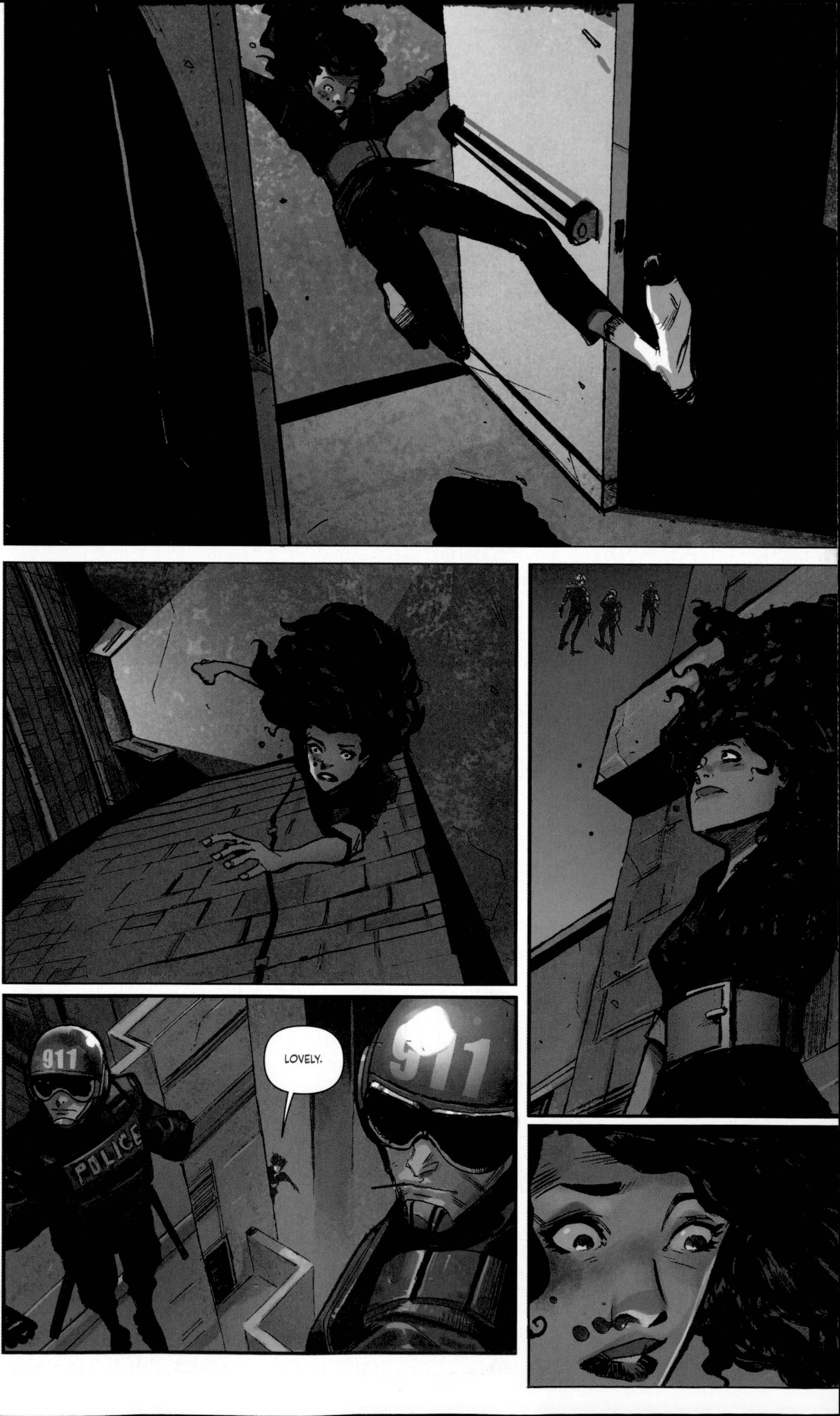
LOVELY.
911
POLICE
911

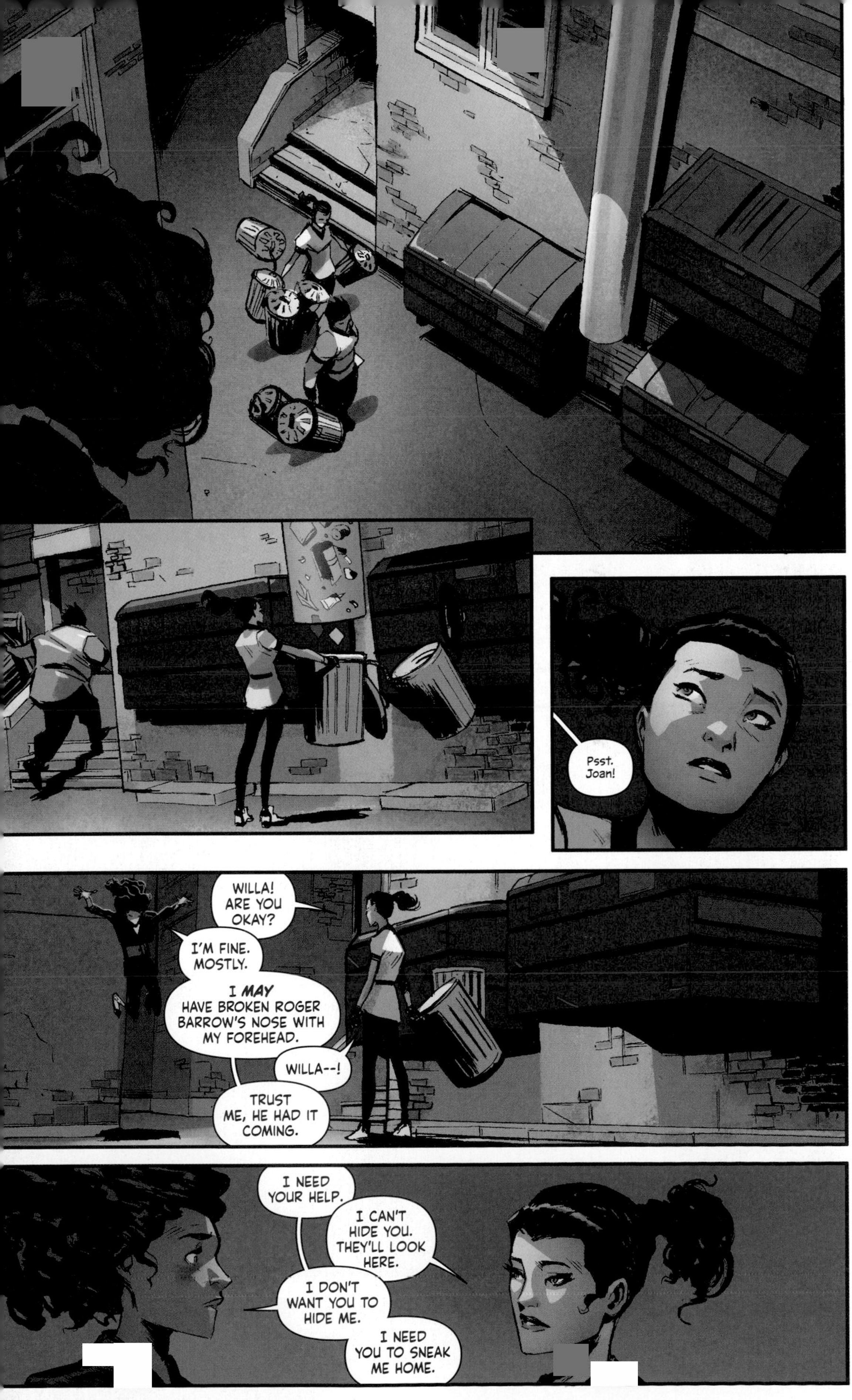
Psst. Joan!
WILLA! ARE YOU OKAY?
I'M FINE. MOSTLY.
I *MAY* HAVE BROKEN ROGER BARROW'S NOSE WITH MY FOREHEAD.
WILLA--!
TRUST ME, HE HAD IT COMING.
I NEED YOUR HELP.
I CAN'T HIDE YOU. THEY'LL LOOK HERE.
I DON'T WANT YOU TO HIDE ME.
I NEED YOU TO SNEAK ME HOME.

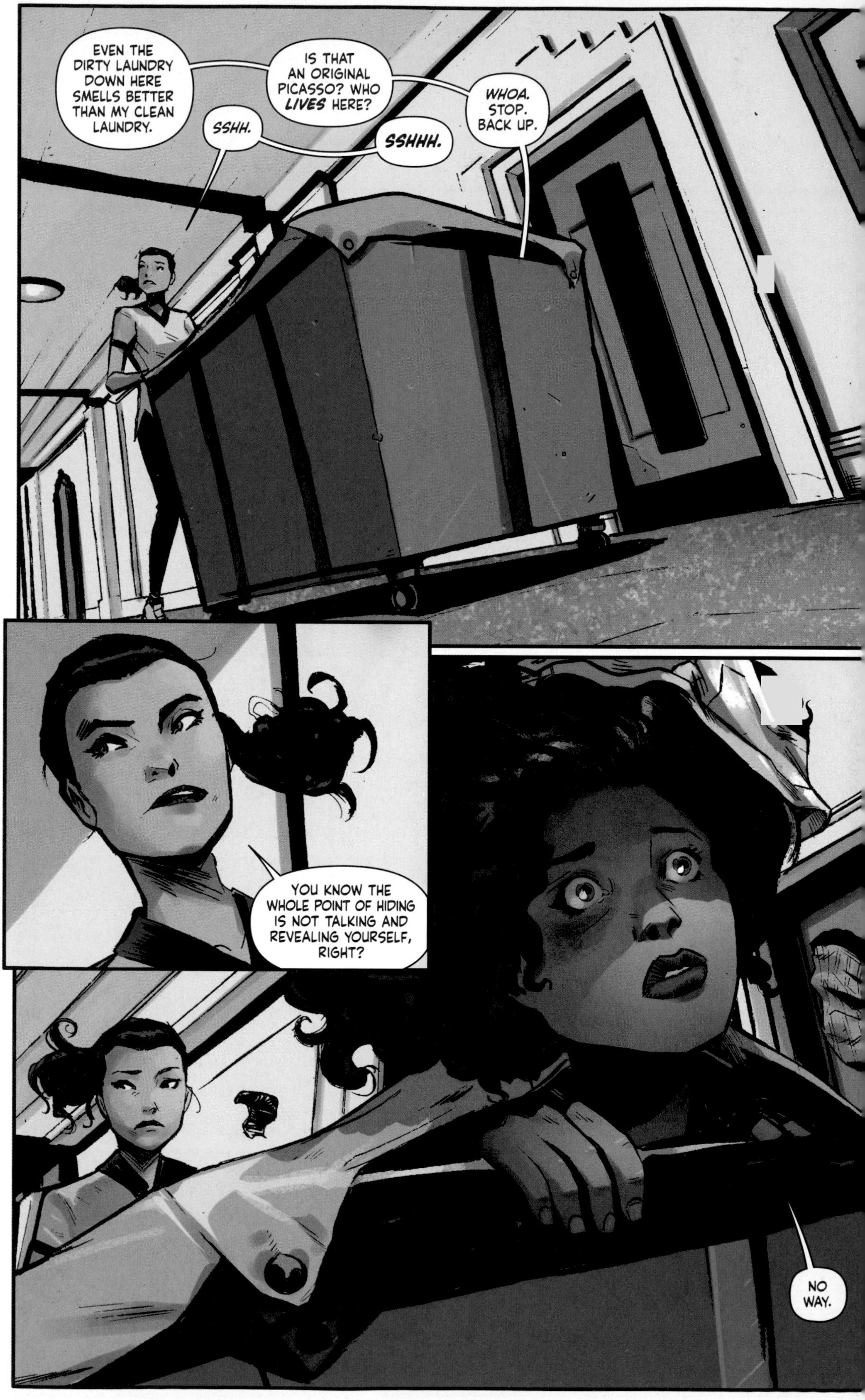
EVEN THE DIRTY LAUNDRY DOWN HERE SMELLS BETTER THAN MY CLEAN LAUNDRY.
IS THAT AN ORIGINAL PICASSO? WHO LIVES HERE?
WHOA. STOP. BACK UP.
SSHH.
SSHHH.
YOU KNOW THE WHOLE POINT OF HIDING IS NOT TALKING AND REVEALING YOURSELF, RIGHT?
NO WAY.

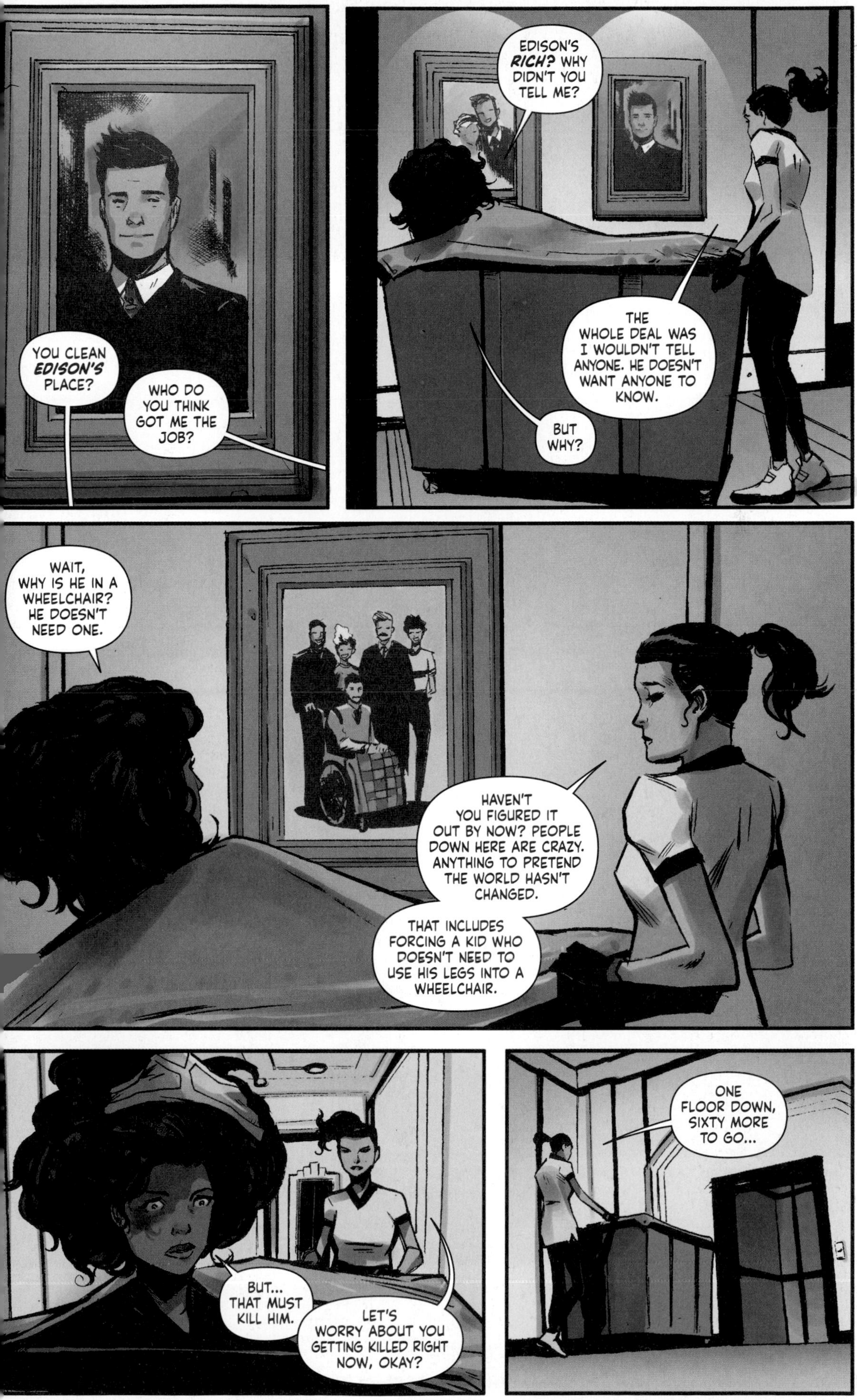
YOU CLEAN EDISON'S PLACE?
WHO DO YOU THINK GOT ME THE JOB?
EDISON'S RICH? WHY DIDN'T YOU TELL ME?
THE WHOLE DEAL WAS I WOULDN'T TELL ANYONE. HE DOESN'T WANT ANYONE TO KNOW.
BUT WHY?
WAIT, WHY IS HE IN A WHEELCHAIR? HE DOESN'T NEED ONE.
HAVEN'T YOU FIGURED IT OUT BY NOW? PEOPLE DOWN HERE ARE CRAZY. ANYTHING TO PRETEND THE WORLD HASN'T CHANGED.
THAT INCLUDES FORCING A KID WHO DOESN'T NEED TO USE HIS LEGS INTO A WHEELCHAIR.
BUT... THAT MUST KILL HIM.
LET'S WORRY ABOUT YOU GETTING KILLED RIGHT NOW, OKAY?
ONE FLOOR DOWN, SIXTY MORE TO GO...

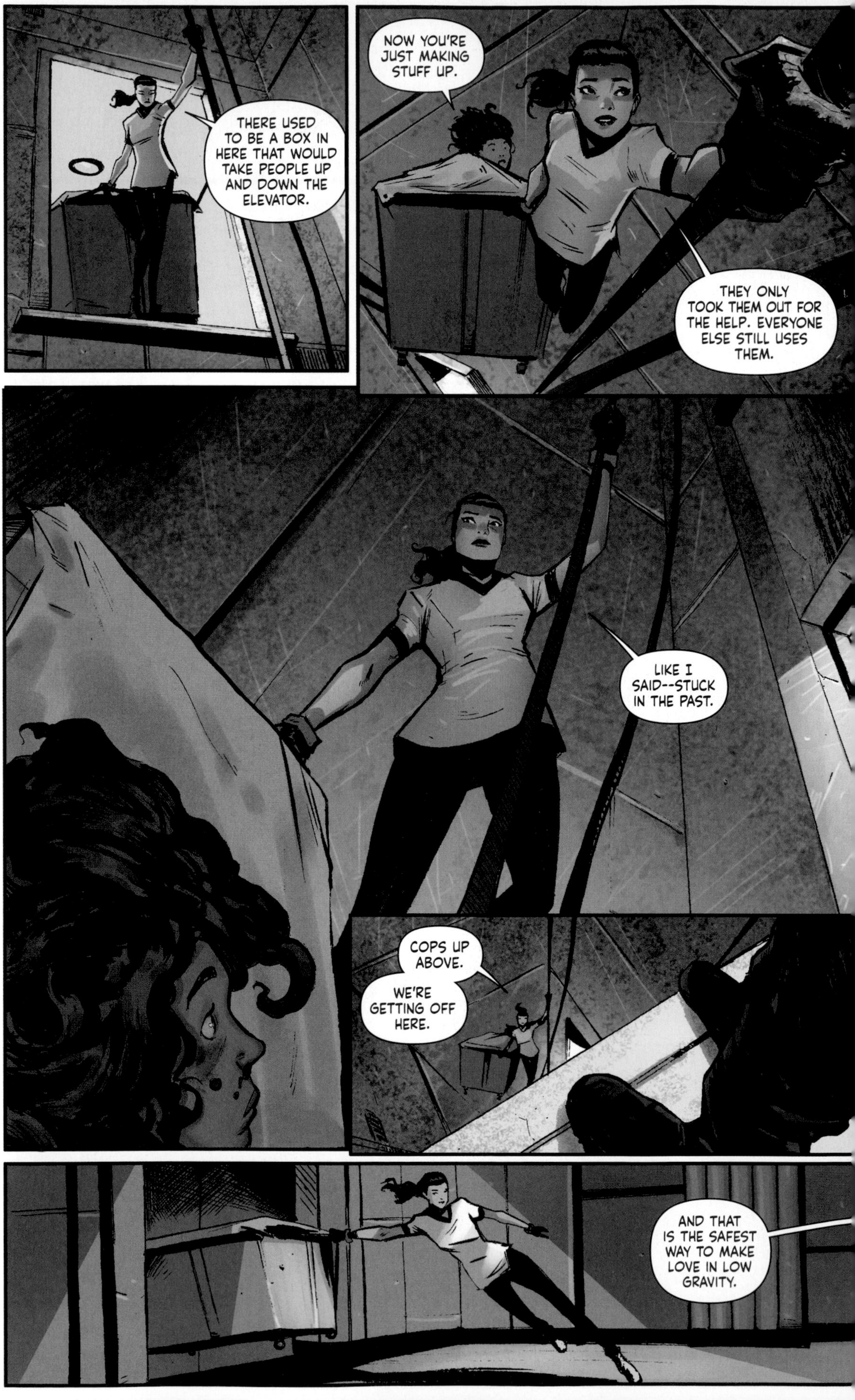
THERE USED TO BE A BOX IN HERE THAT WOULD TAKE PEOPLE UP AND DOWN THE ELEVATOR.
NOW YOU'RE JUST MAKING STUFF UP.
THEY ONLY TOOK THEM OUT FOR THE HELP. EVERYONE ELSE STILL USES THEM.
LIKE I SAID--STUCK IN THE PAST.
COPS UP ABOVE.
WE'RE GETTING OFF HERE.
AND THAT IS THE SAFEST WAY TO MAKE LOVE IN LOW GRAVITY.

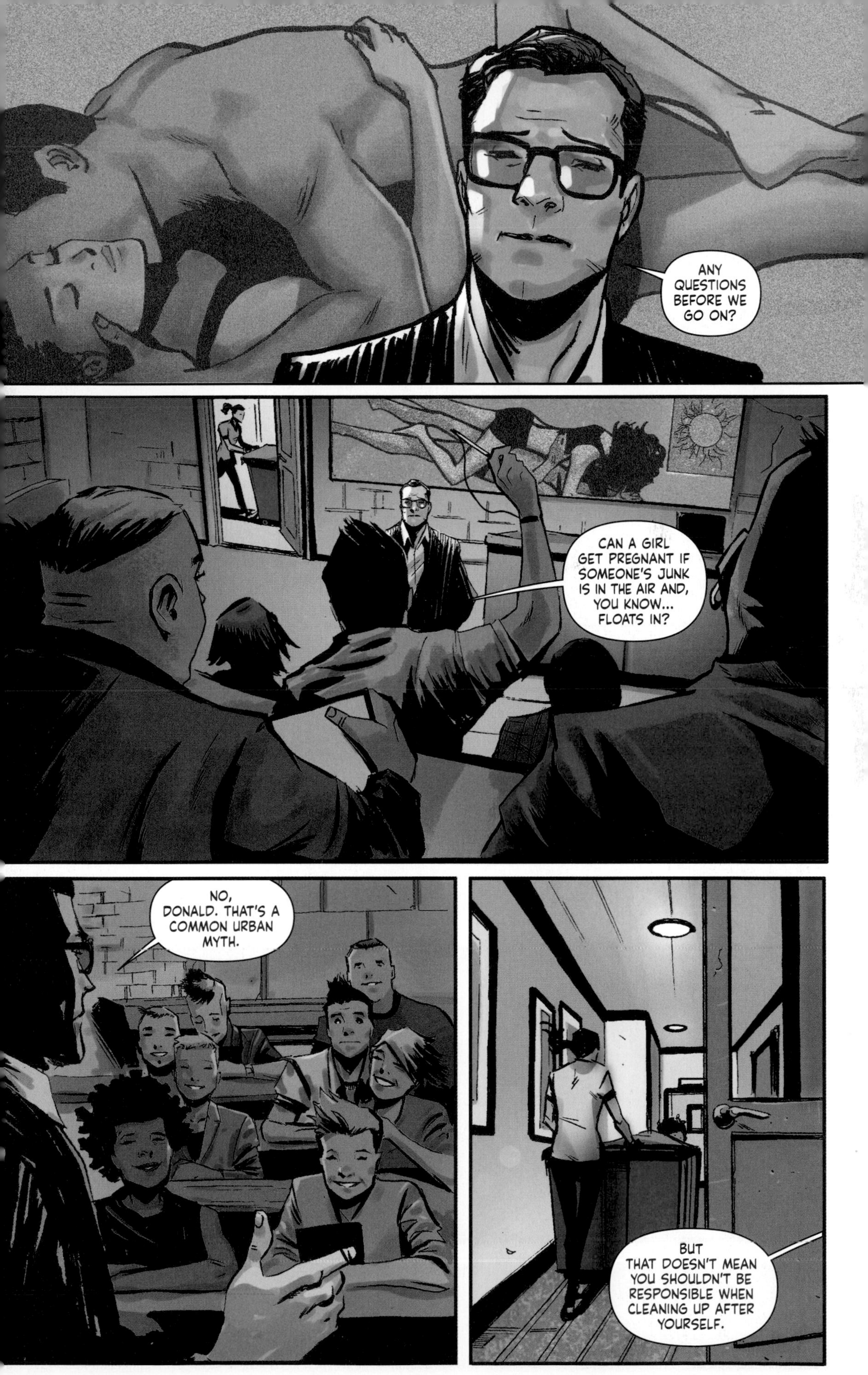
ANY QUESTIONS BEFORE WE GO ON?
CAN A GIRL GET PREGNANT IF SOMEONE'S JUNK IS IN THE AIR AND, YOU KNOW... FLOATS IN?
NO, DONALD. THAT'S A COMMON URBAN MYTH.
BUT THAT DOESN'T MEAN YOU SHOULDN'T BE RESPONSIBLE WHEN CLEANING UP AFTER YOURSELF.

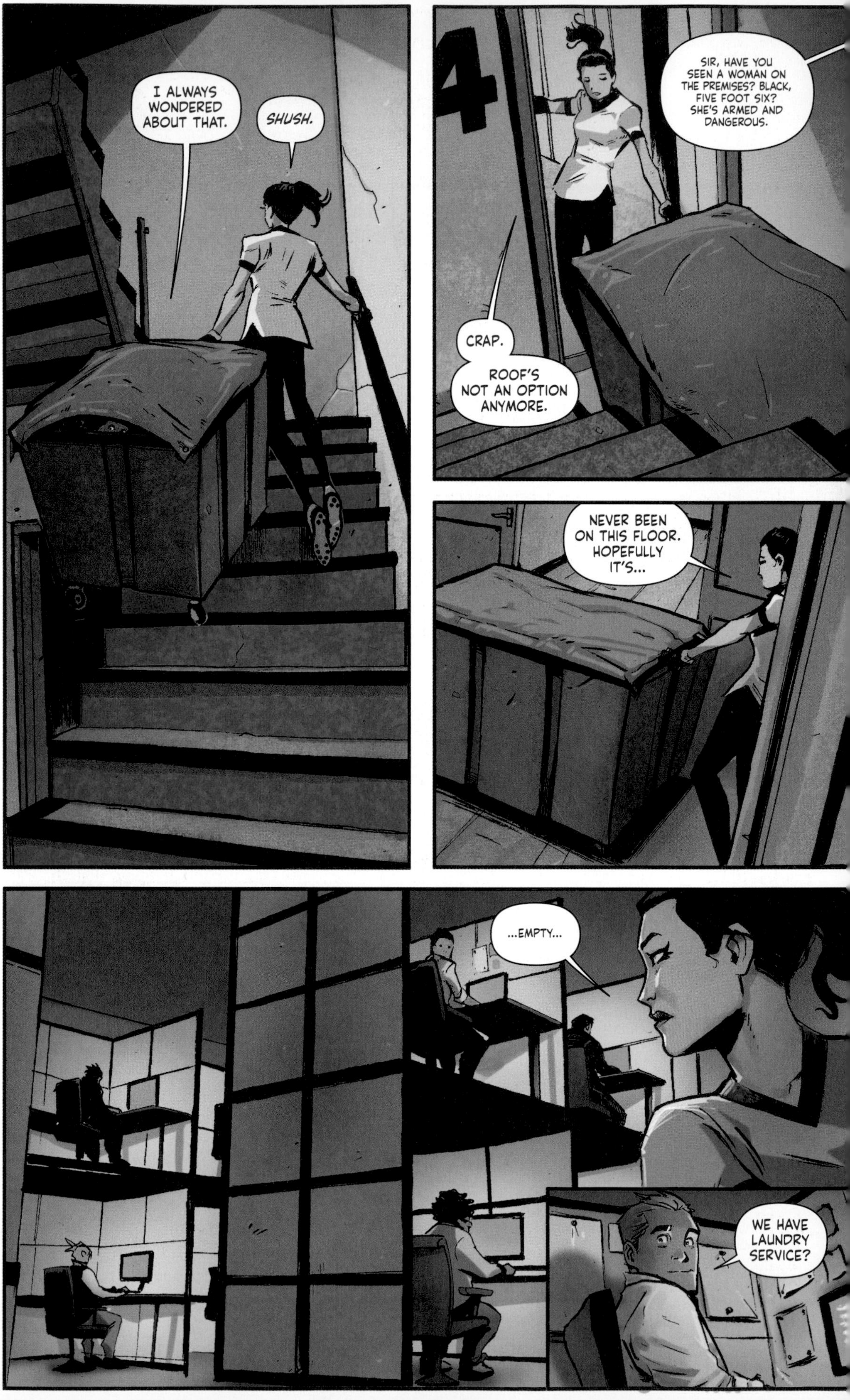
I ALWAYS WONDERED ABOUT THAT.
SHUSH.
SIR, HAVE YOU SEEN A WOMAN ON THE PREMISES? BLACK, FIVE FOOT SIX? SHE'S ARMED AND DANGEROUS.
CRAP.
ROOF'S NOT AN OPTION ANYMORE.
NEVER BEEN ON THIS FLOOR. HOPEFULLY IT'S...
...EMPTY...
WE HAVE LAUNDRY SERVICE?

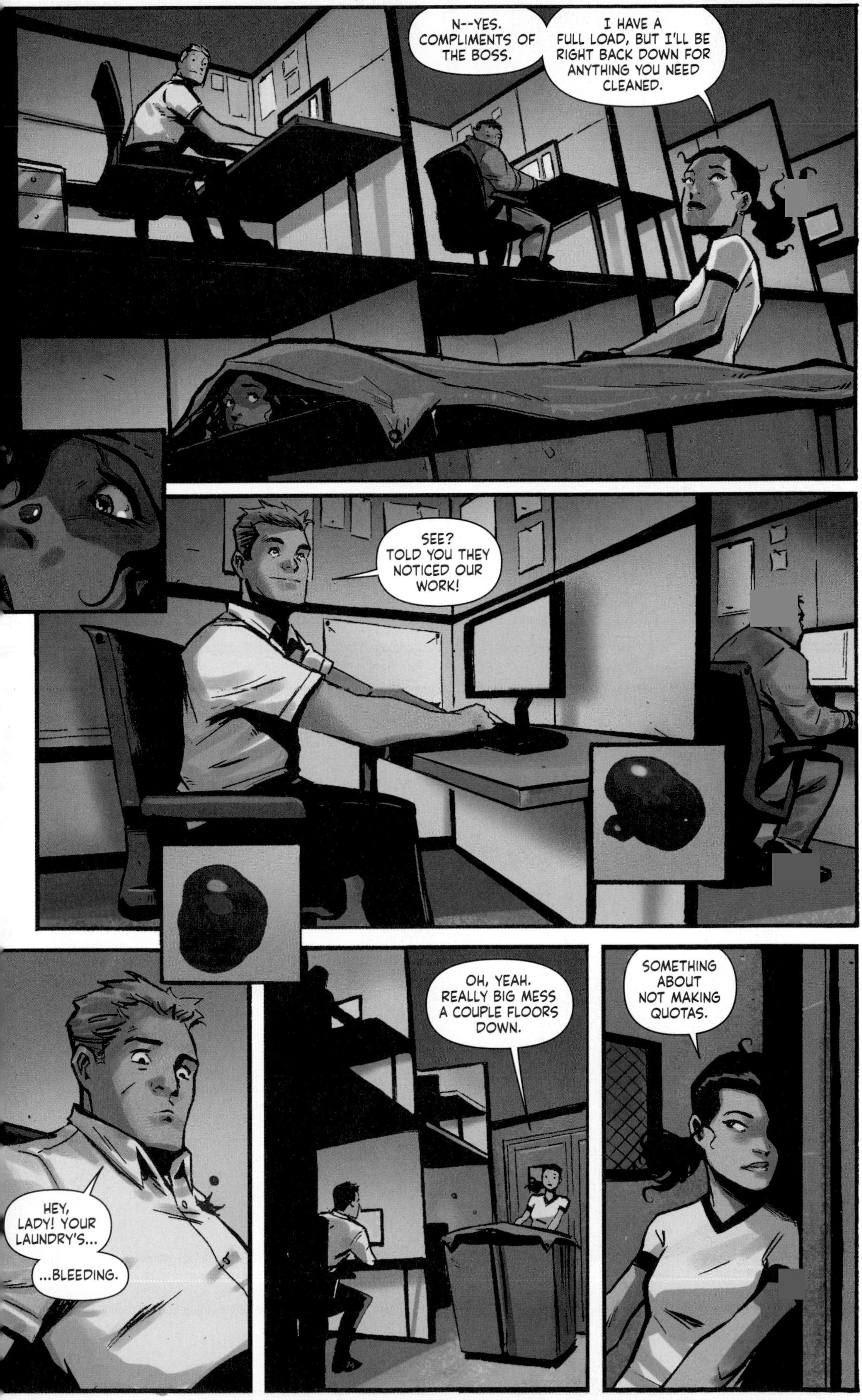
N--YES. COMPLIMENTS OF THE BOSS.
I HAVE A FULL LOAD, BUT I'LL BE RIGHT BACK DOWN FOR ANYTHING YOU NEED CLEANED.
SEE? TOLD YOU THEY NOTICED OUR WORK!
HEY, LADY! YOUR LAUNDRY'S...
...BLEEDING.
OH, YEAH. REALLY BIG MESS A COUPLE FLOORS DOWN.
SOMETHING ABOUT NOT MAKING QUOTAS.

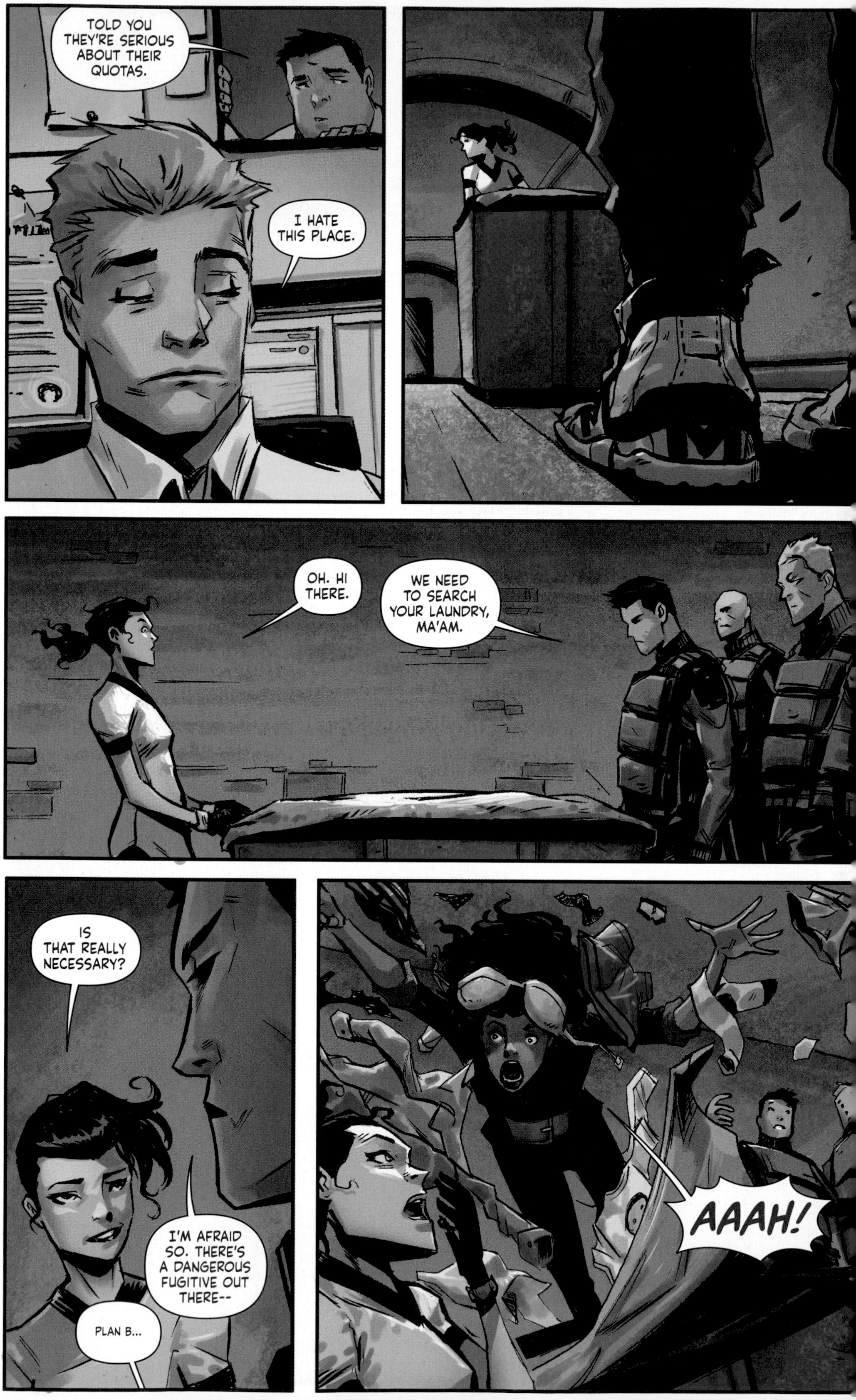
TOLD YOU THEY'RE SERIOUS ABOUT THEIR QUOTAS.
I HATE THIS PLACE.
OH. HI THERE.
WE NEED TO SEARCH YOUR LAUNDRY, MA'AM.
IS THAT REALLY NECESSARY?
I'M AFRAID SO. THERE'S A DANGEROUS FUGITIVE OUT THERE--
PLAN B...
AAAH!

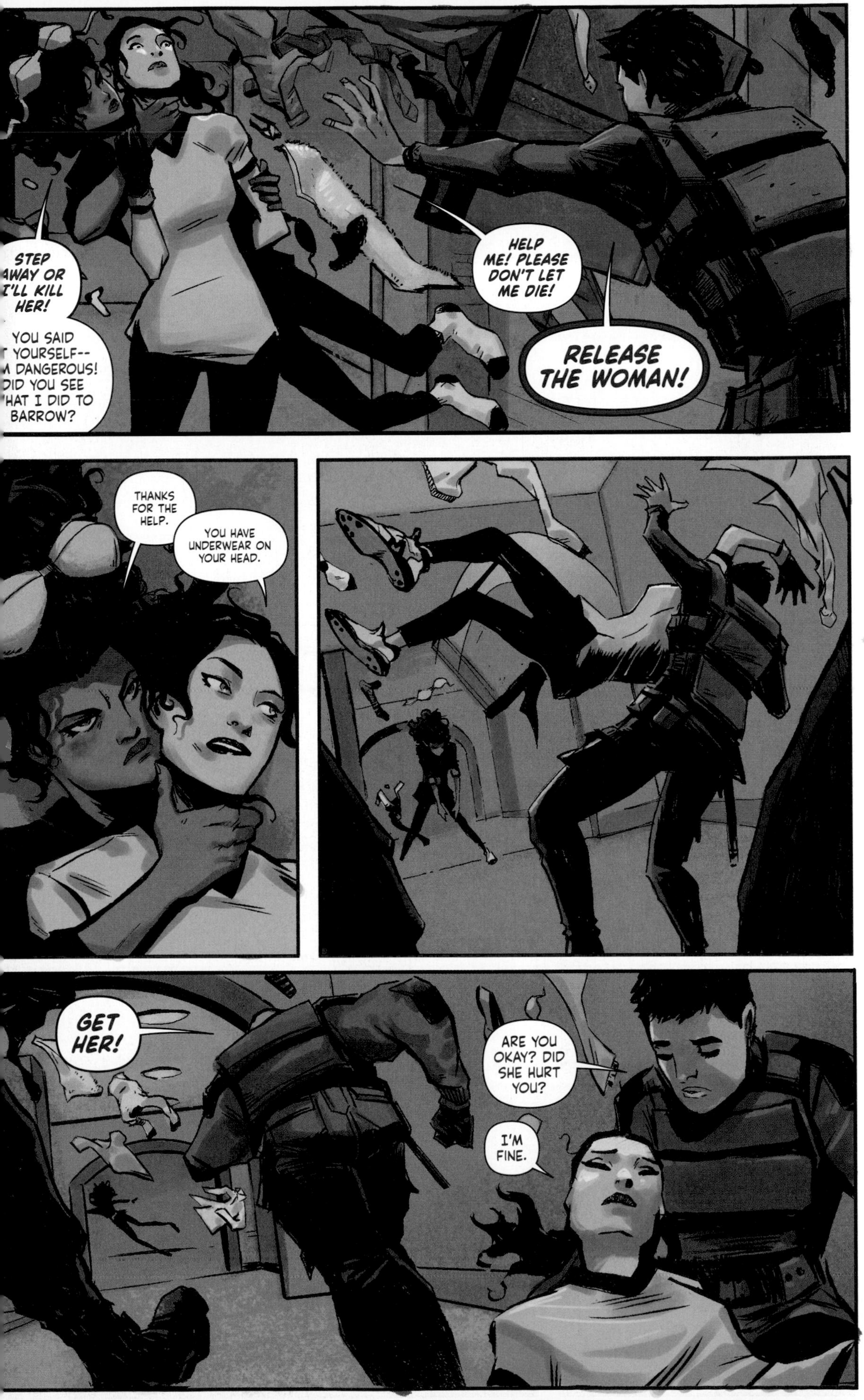
STEP AWAY OR I'LL KILL HER!
YOU SAID T YOURSELF-- M DANGEROUS! DID YOU SEE HAT I DID TO BARROW?
HELP ME! PLEASE DON'T LET ME DIE!
RELEASE THE WOMAN!
THANKS FOR THE HELP.
YOU HAVE UNDERWEAR ON YOUR HEAD.
GET HER!
ARE YOU OKAY? DID SHE HURT YOU?
I'M FINE.

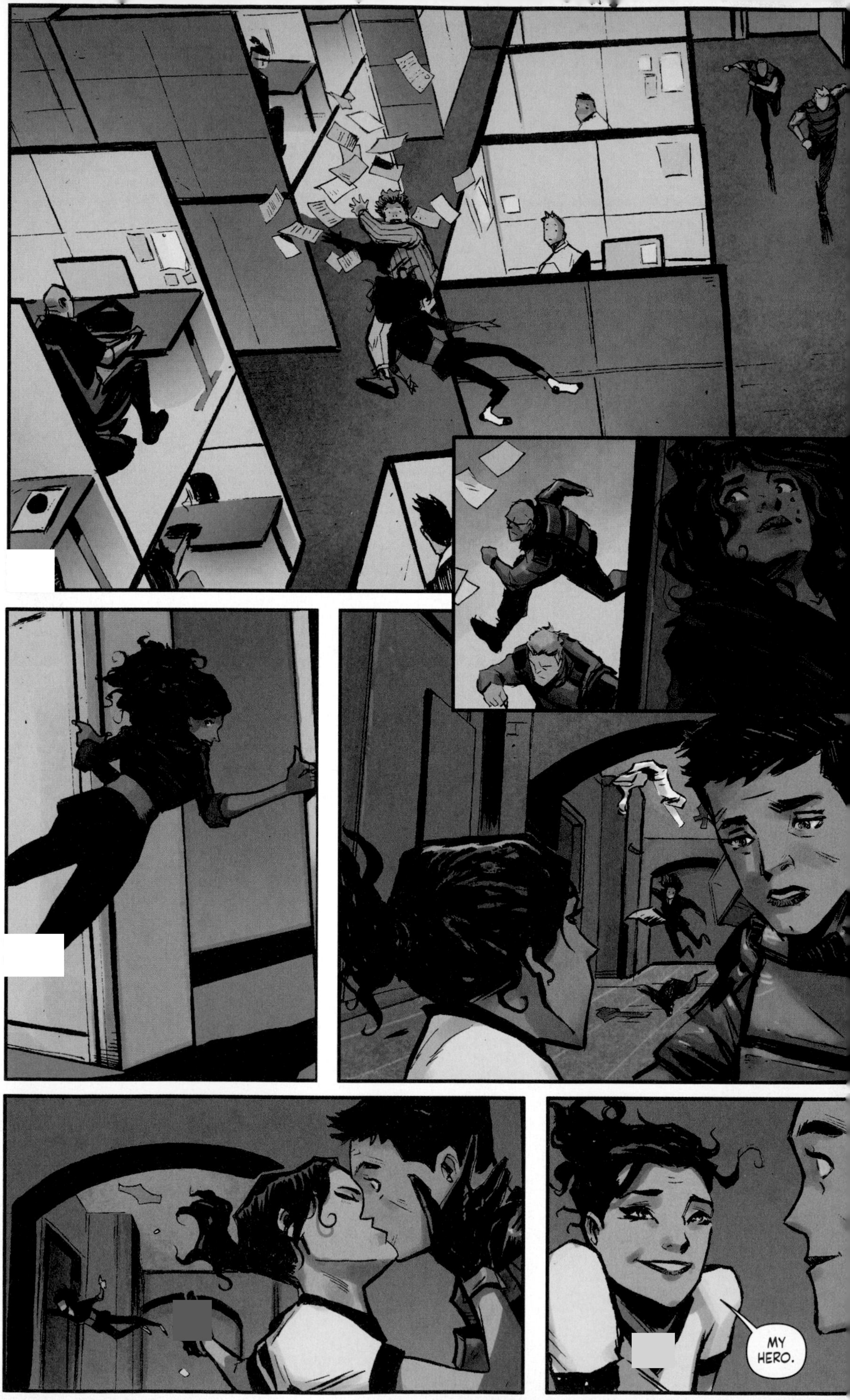
MY HERO.

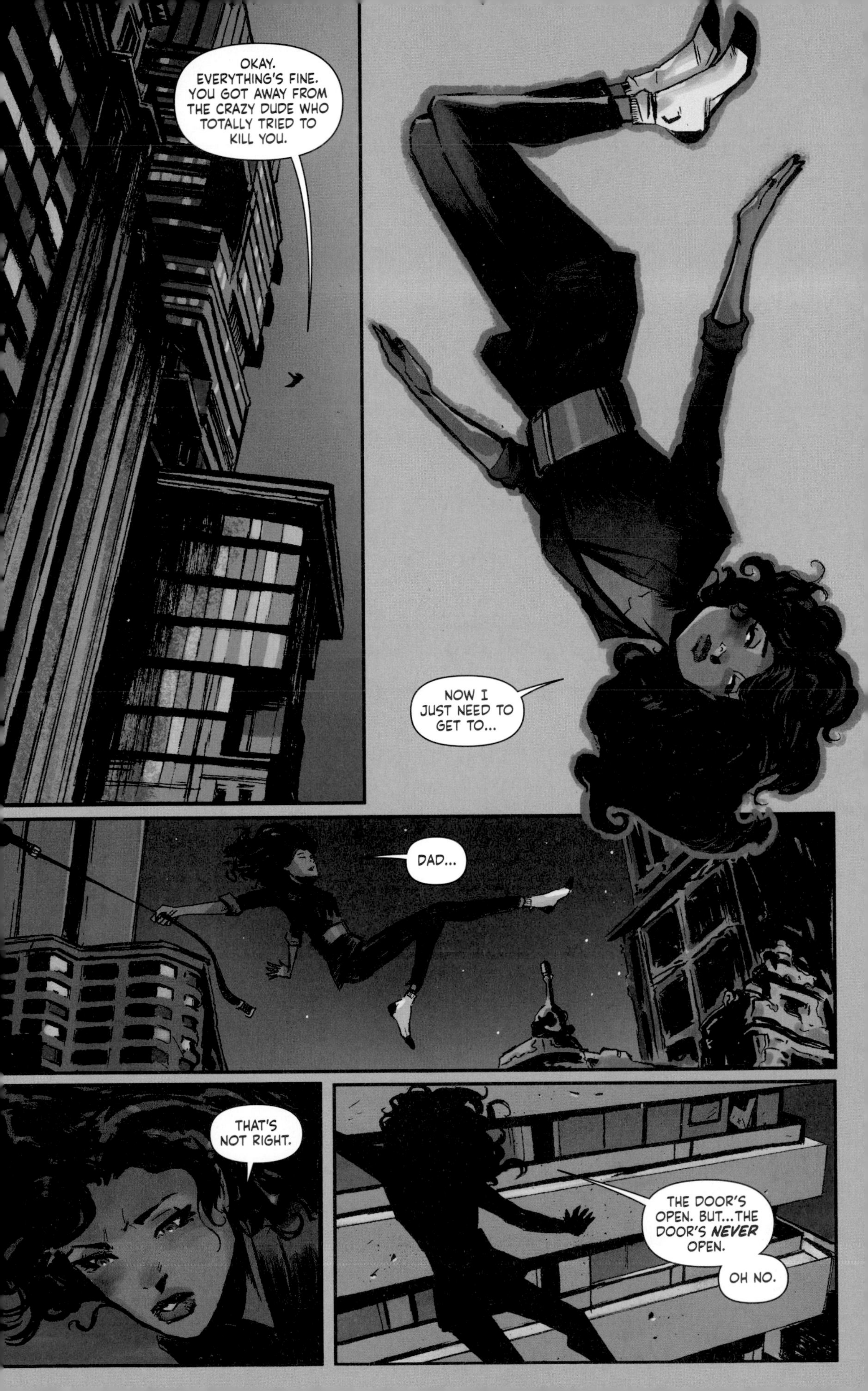
OKAY. EVERYTHING'S FINE. YOU GOT AWAY FROM THE CRAZY DUDE WHO TOTALLY TRIED TO KILL YOU.
NOW I JUST NEED TO GET TO...
DAD...
THAT'S NOT RIGHT.
THE DOOR'S OPEN. BUT...THE DOOR'S ***NEVER*** OPEN.
OH NO.

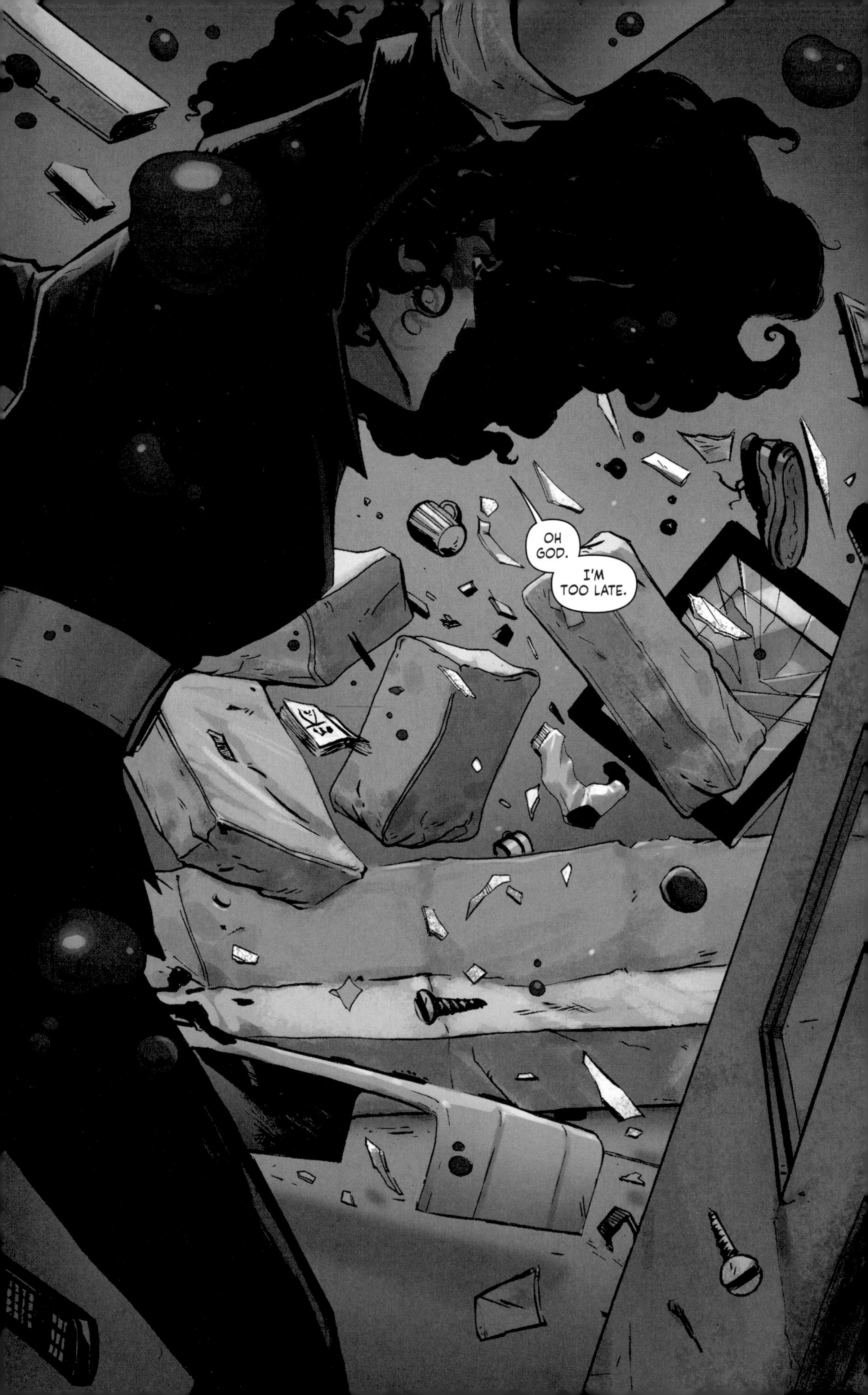
OH GOD.
I'M TOO LATE.

END CHAPTER THREE

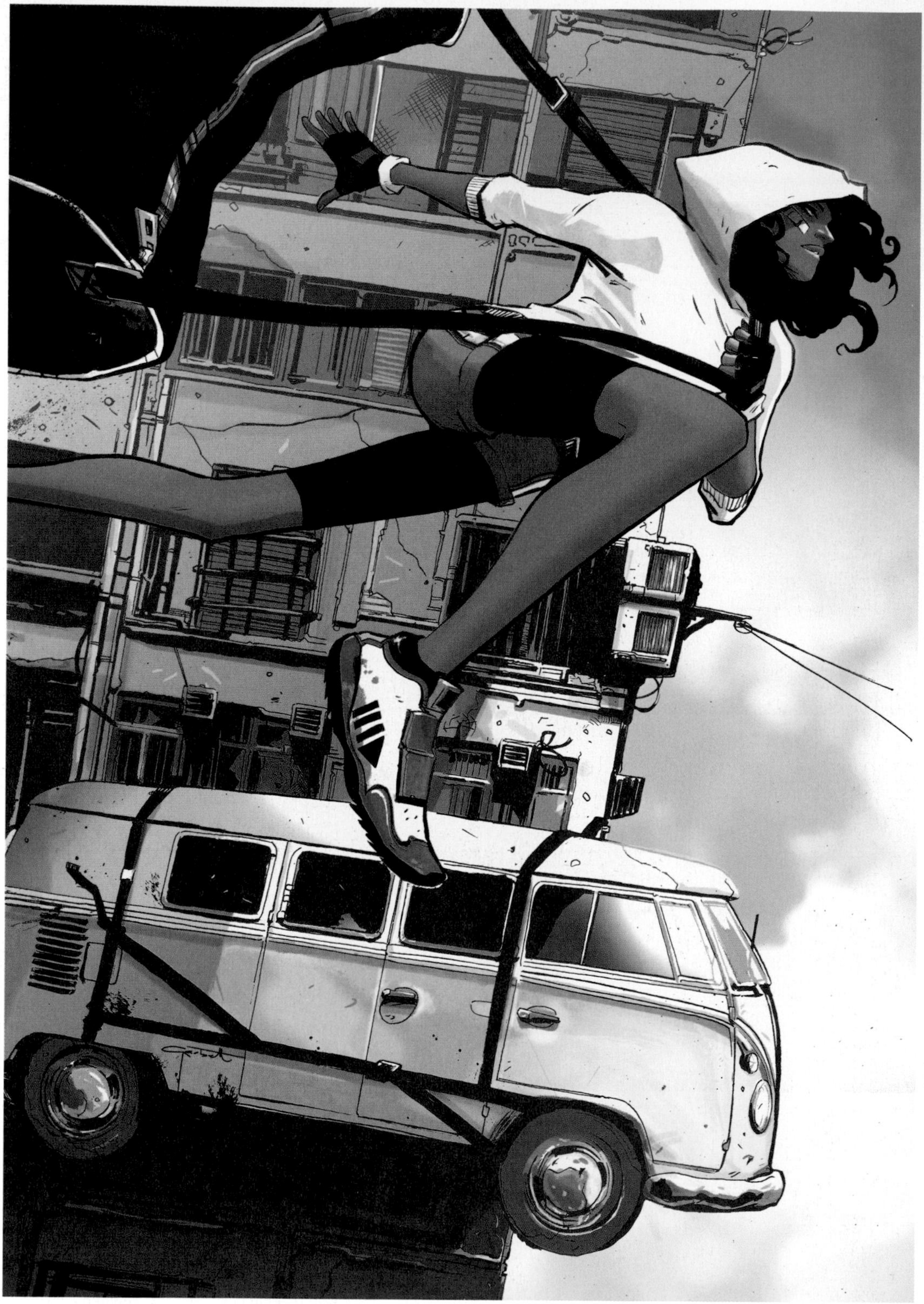

CHAPTER FOUR

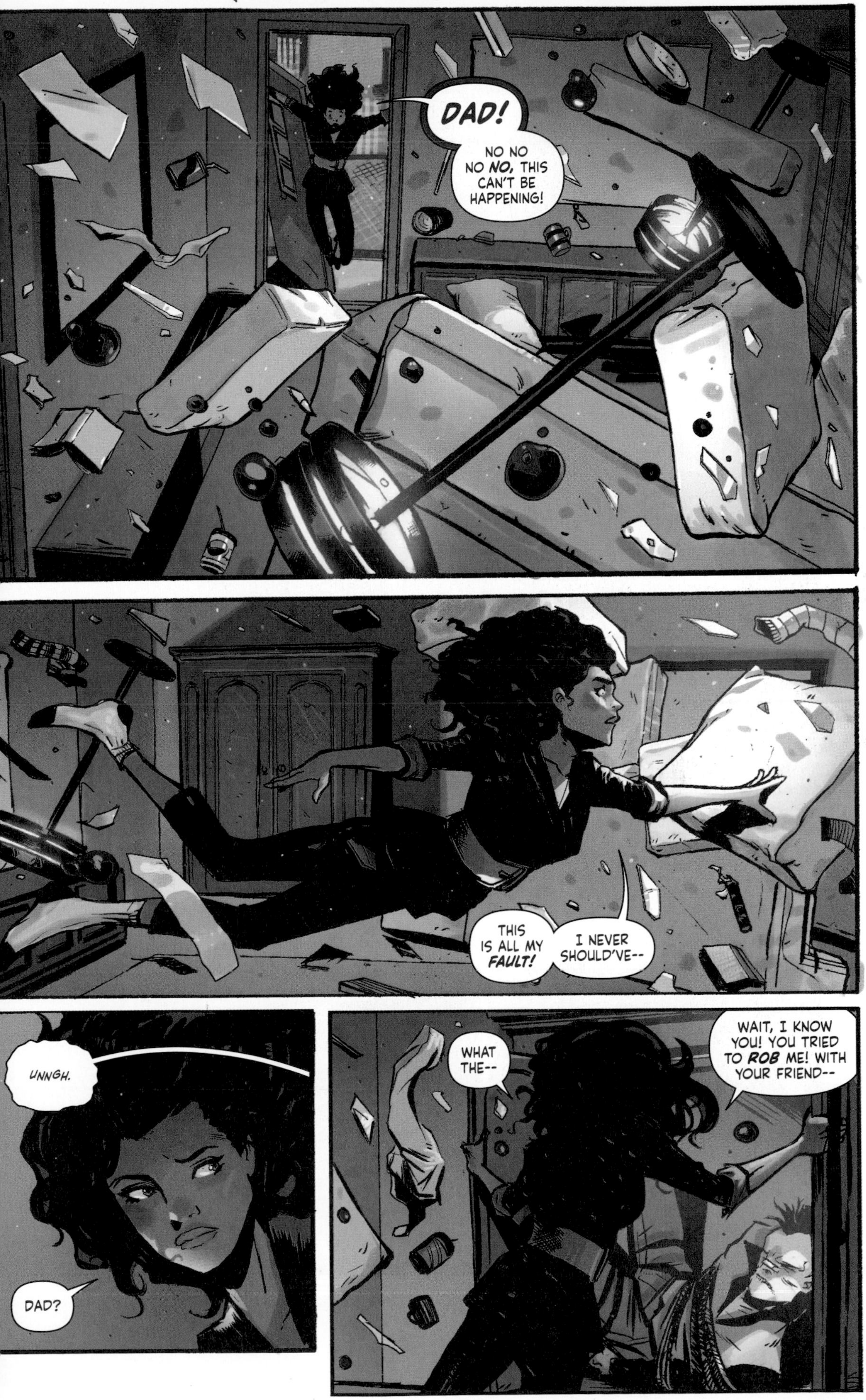
DAD!
NO NO NO NO, THIS CAN'T BE HAPPENING!
THIS IS ALL MY FAULT!
I NEVER SHOULD'VE--
UNNGH.
DAD?
WHAT THE--
WAIT, I KNOW YOU! YOU TRIED TO ROB ME! WITH YOUR FRIEND--

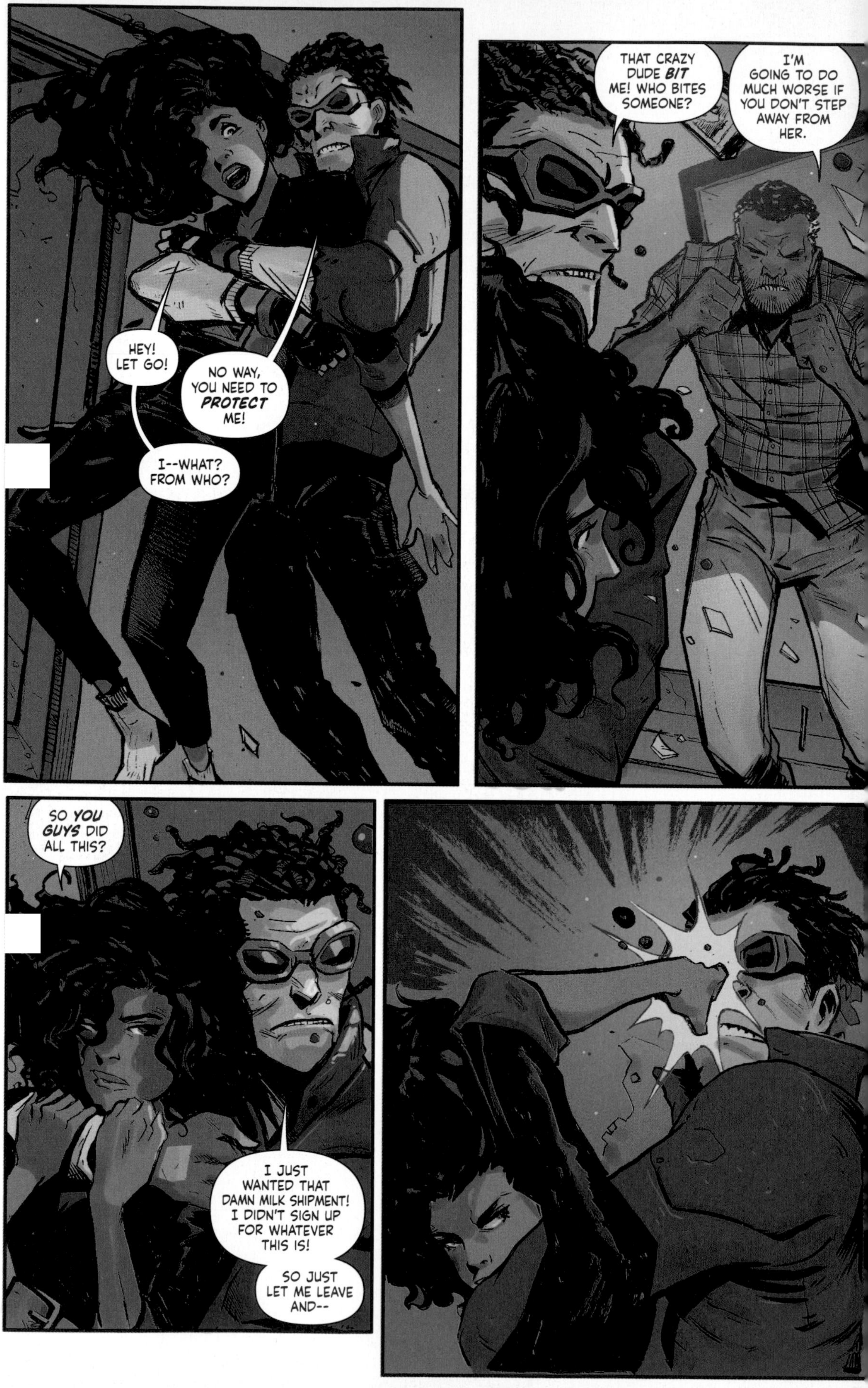
HEY! LET GO!
NO WAY, YOU NEED TO *PROTECT* ME!
I--WHAT? FROM WHO?
THAT CRAZY DUDE *BIT* ME! WHO BITES SOMEONE?
I'M GOING TO DO MUCH WORSE IF YOU DON'T STEP AWAY FROM HER.
SO *YOU GUYS* DID ALL THIS?
I JUST WANTED THAT DAMN MILK SHIPMENT! I DIDN'T SIGN UP FOR WHATEVER THIS IS!
SO JUST LET ME LEAVE AND--

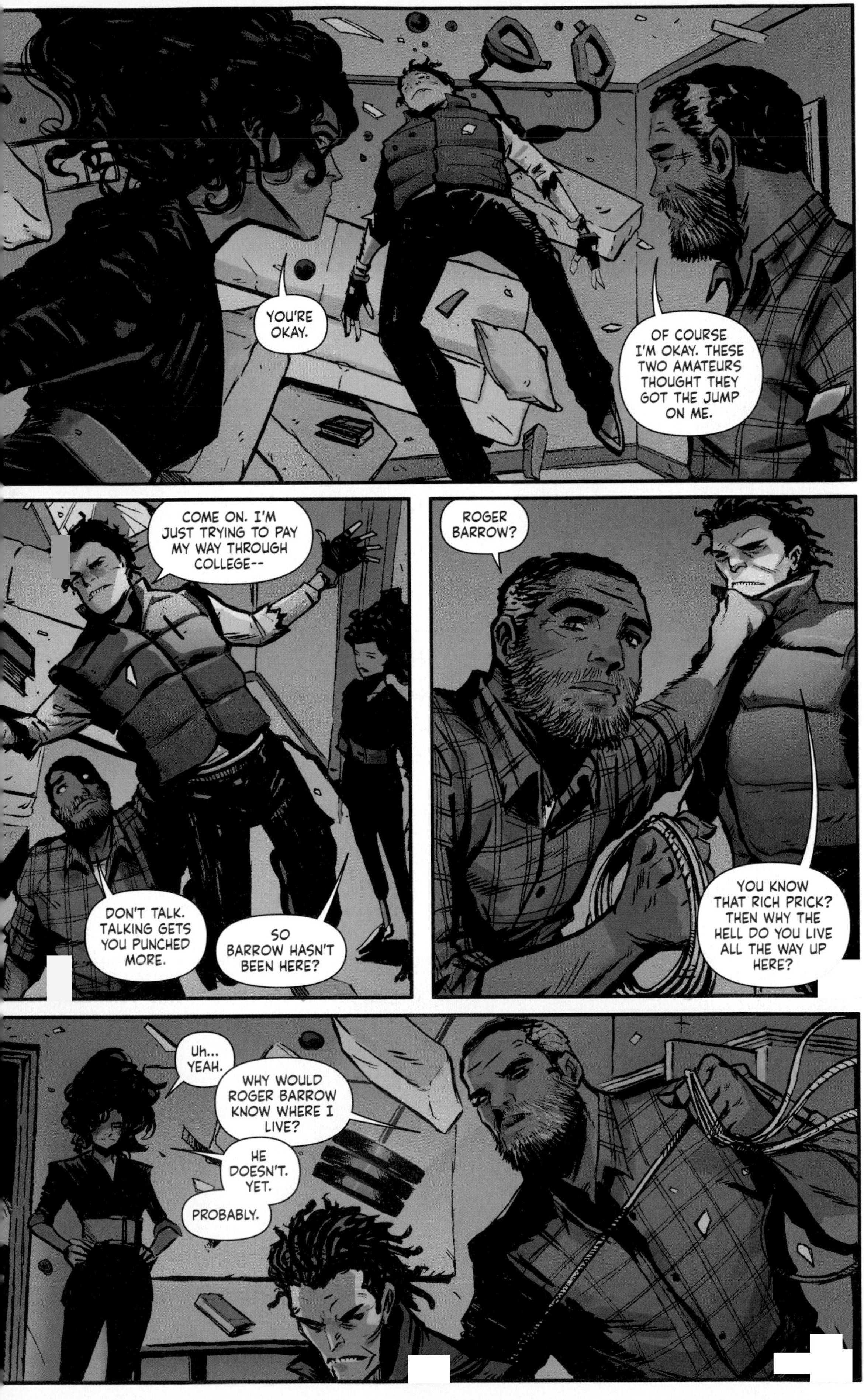
YOU'RE OKAY.
OF COURSE I'M OKAY. THESE TWO AMATEURS THOUGHT THEY GOT THE JUMP ON ME.
COME ON. I'M JUST TRYING TO PAY MY WAY THROUGH COLLEGE--
DON'T TALK. TALKING GETS YOU PUNCHED MORE.
SO BARROW HASN'T BEEN HERE?
ROGER BARROW?
YOU KNOW THAT RICH PRICK? THEN WHY THE HELL DO YOU LIVE ALL THE WAY UP HERE?
Uh... YEAH.
WHY WOULD ROGER BARROW KNOW WHERE I LIVE?
HE DOESN'T. YET.
PROBABLY.

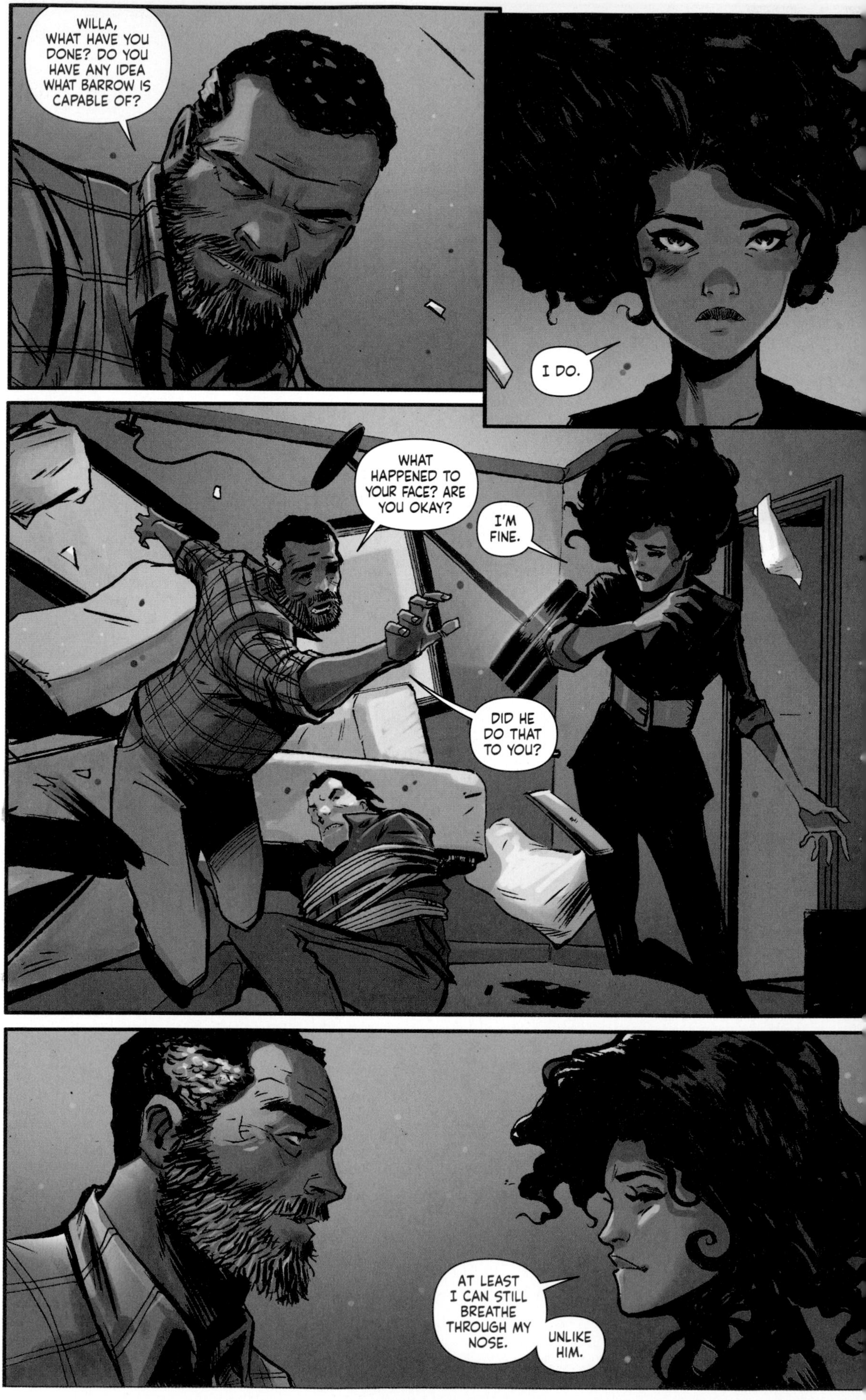
WILLA, WHAT HAVE YOU DONE? DO YOU HAVE ANY IDEA WHAT BARROW IS CAPABLE OF?
I DO.
WHAT HAPPENED TO YOUR FACE? ARE YOU OKAY?
I'M FINE.
DID HE DO THAT TO YOU?
AT LEAST I CAN STILL BREATHE THROUGH MY NOSE.
UNLIKE HIM.

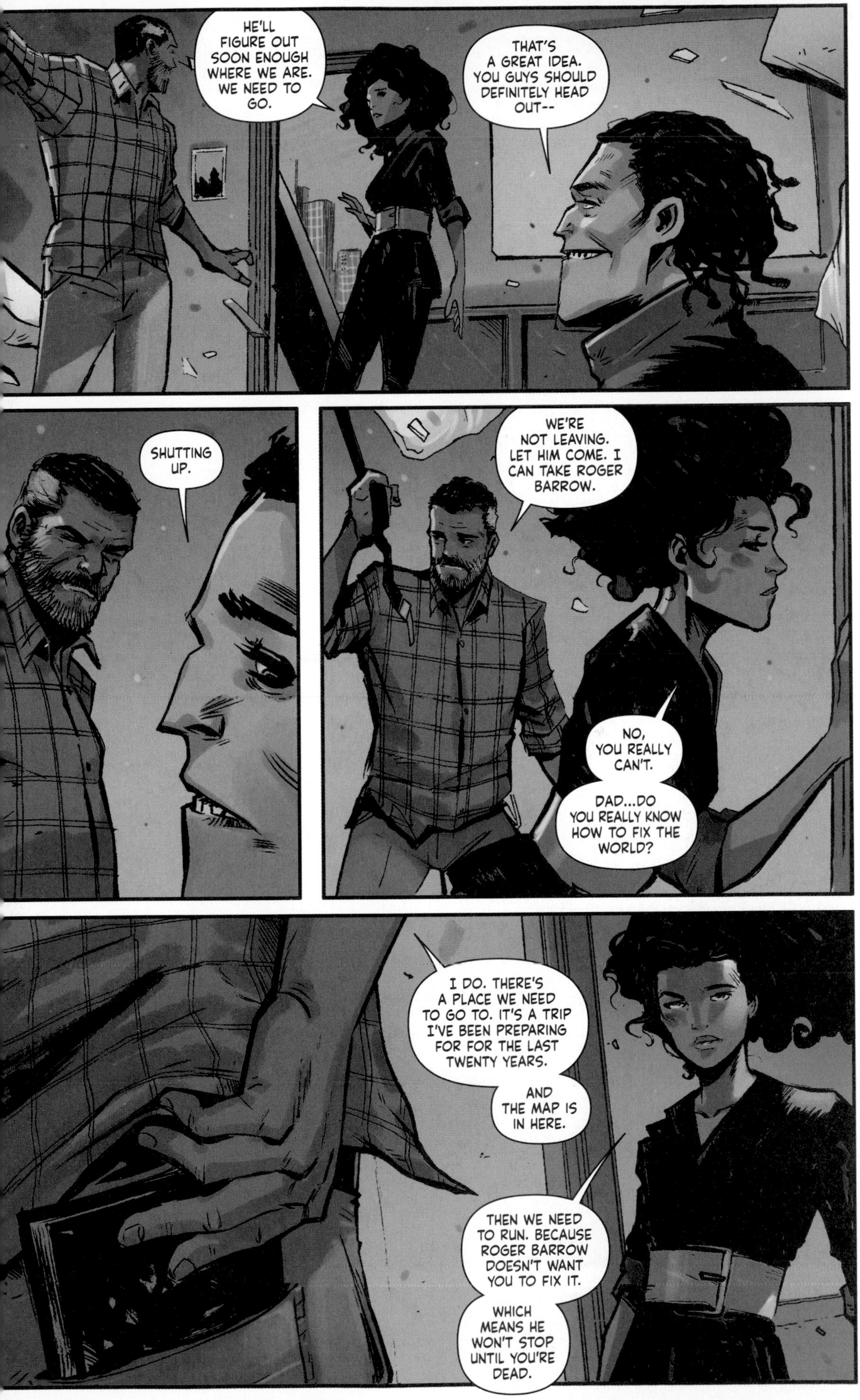
HE'LL FIGURE OUT SOON ENOUGH WHERE WE ARE. WE NEED TO GO.
THAT'S A GREAT IDEA. YOU GUYS SHOULD DEFINITELY HEAD OUT--
SHUTTING UP.
WE'RE NOT LEAVING. LET HIM COME. I CAN TAKE ROGER BARROW.
NO, YOU REALLY CAN'T.
DAD...DO YOU REALLY KNOW HOW TO FIX THE WORLD?
I DO. THERE'S A PLACE WE NEED TO GO TO. IT'S A TRIP I'VE BEEN PREPARING FOR FOR THE LAST TWENTY YEARS.
AND THE MAP IS IN HERE.
THEN WE NEED TO RUN. BECAUSE ROGER BARROW DOESN'T WANT YOU TO FIX IT.
WHICH MEANS HE WON'T STOP UNTIL YOU'RE DEAD.

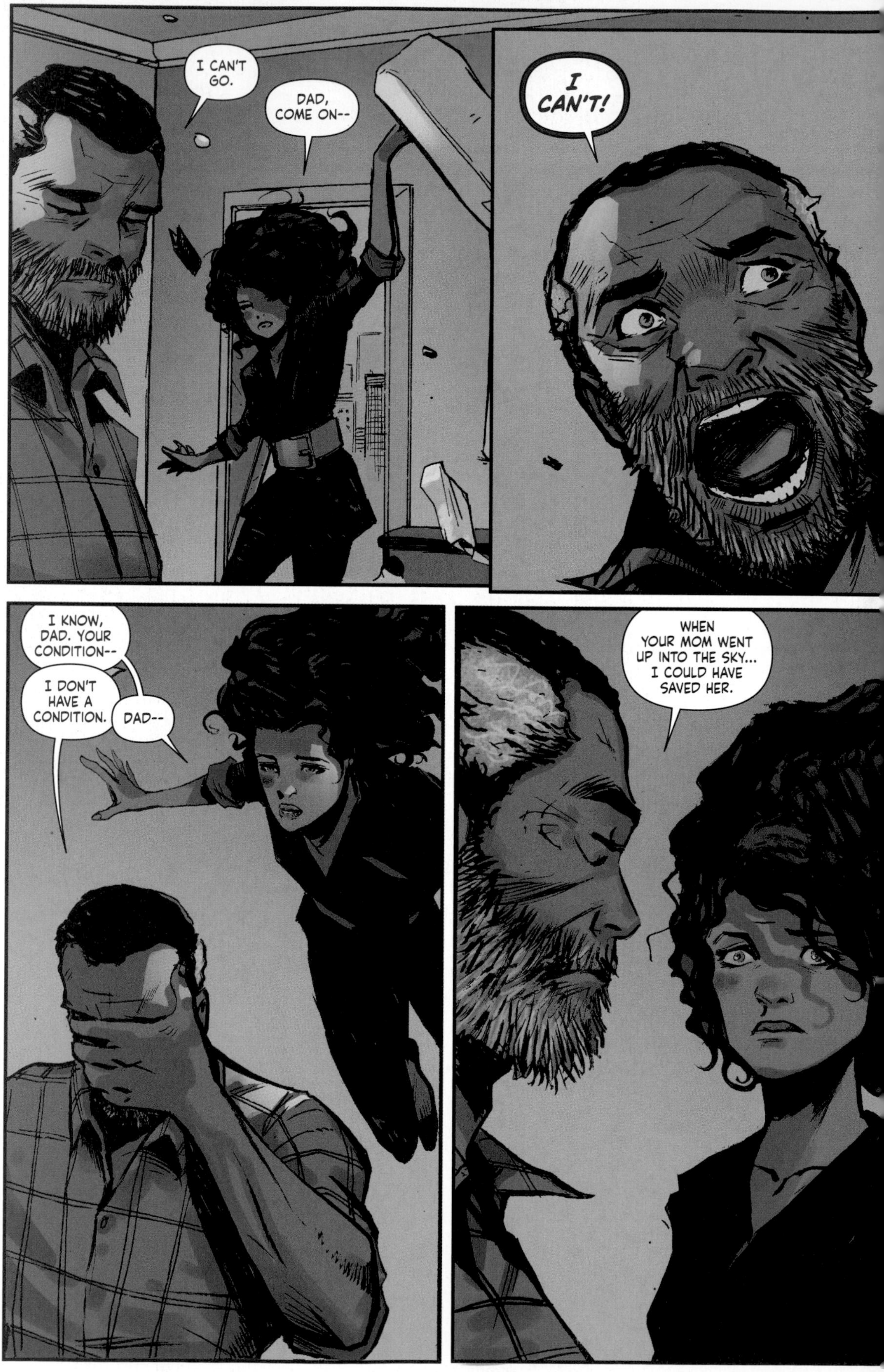
I CAN'T GO.
DAD, COME ON--
I CAN'T!
I KNOW, DAD. YOUR CONDITION--
I DON'T HAVE A CONDITION.
DAD--
WHEN YOUR MOM WENT UP INTO THE SKY... I COULD HAVE SAVED HER.

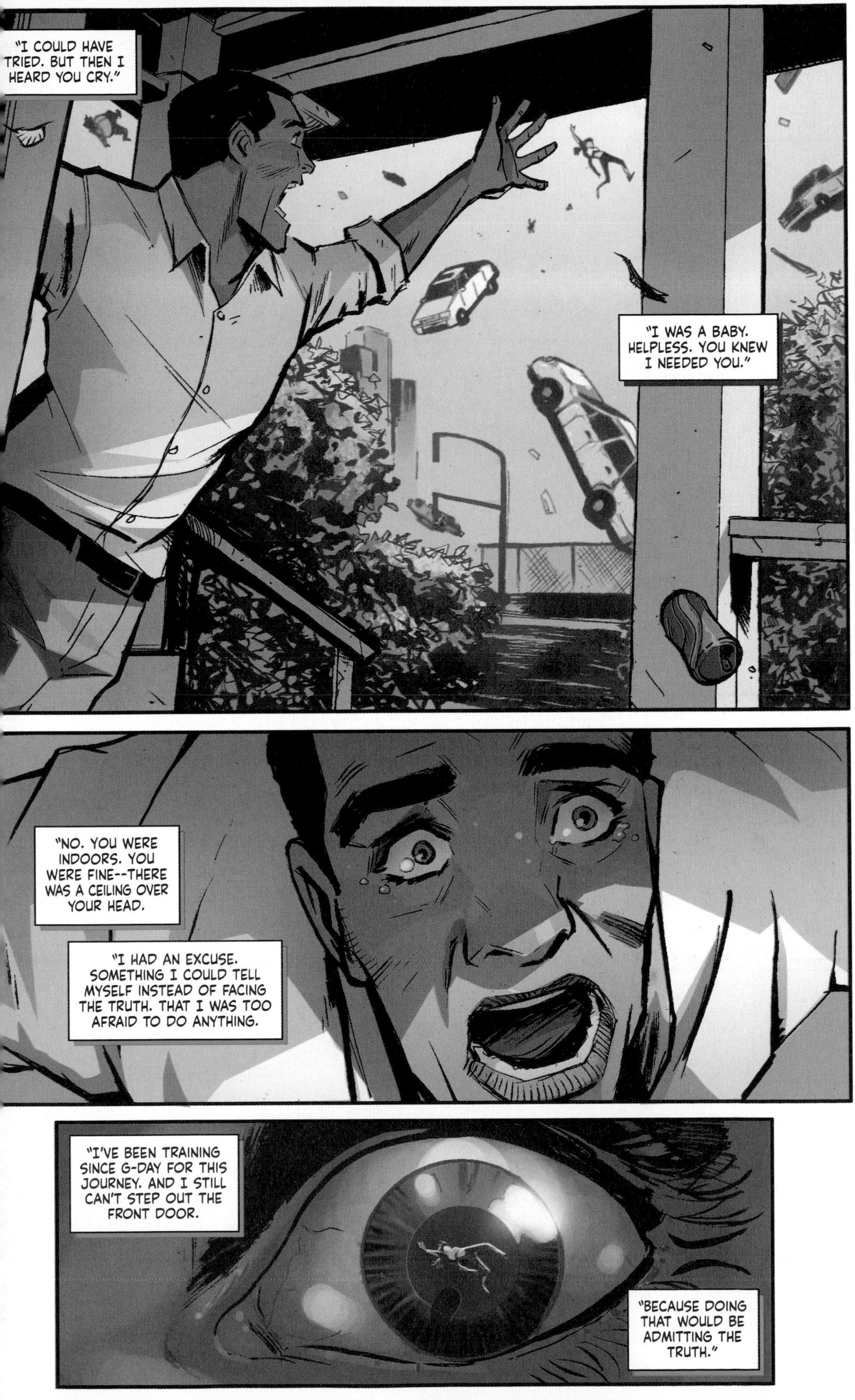
"I COULD HAVE TRIED. BUT THEN I HEARD YOU CRY."
"I WAS A BABY. HELPLESS. YOU KNEW I NEEDED YOU."
"NO. YOU WERE INDOORS. YOU WERE FINE--THERE WAS A CEILING OVER YOUR HEAD.
"I HAD AN EXCUSE. SOMETHING I COULD TELL MYSELF INSTEAD OF FACING THE TRUTH. THAT I WAS TOO AFRAID TO DO ANYTHING.
"I'VE BEEN TRAINING SINCE G-DAY FOR THIS JOURNEY. AND I STILL CAN'T STEP OUT THE FRONT DOOR.
"BECAUSE DOING THAT WOULD BE ADMITTING THE TRUTH."

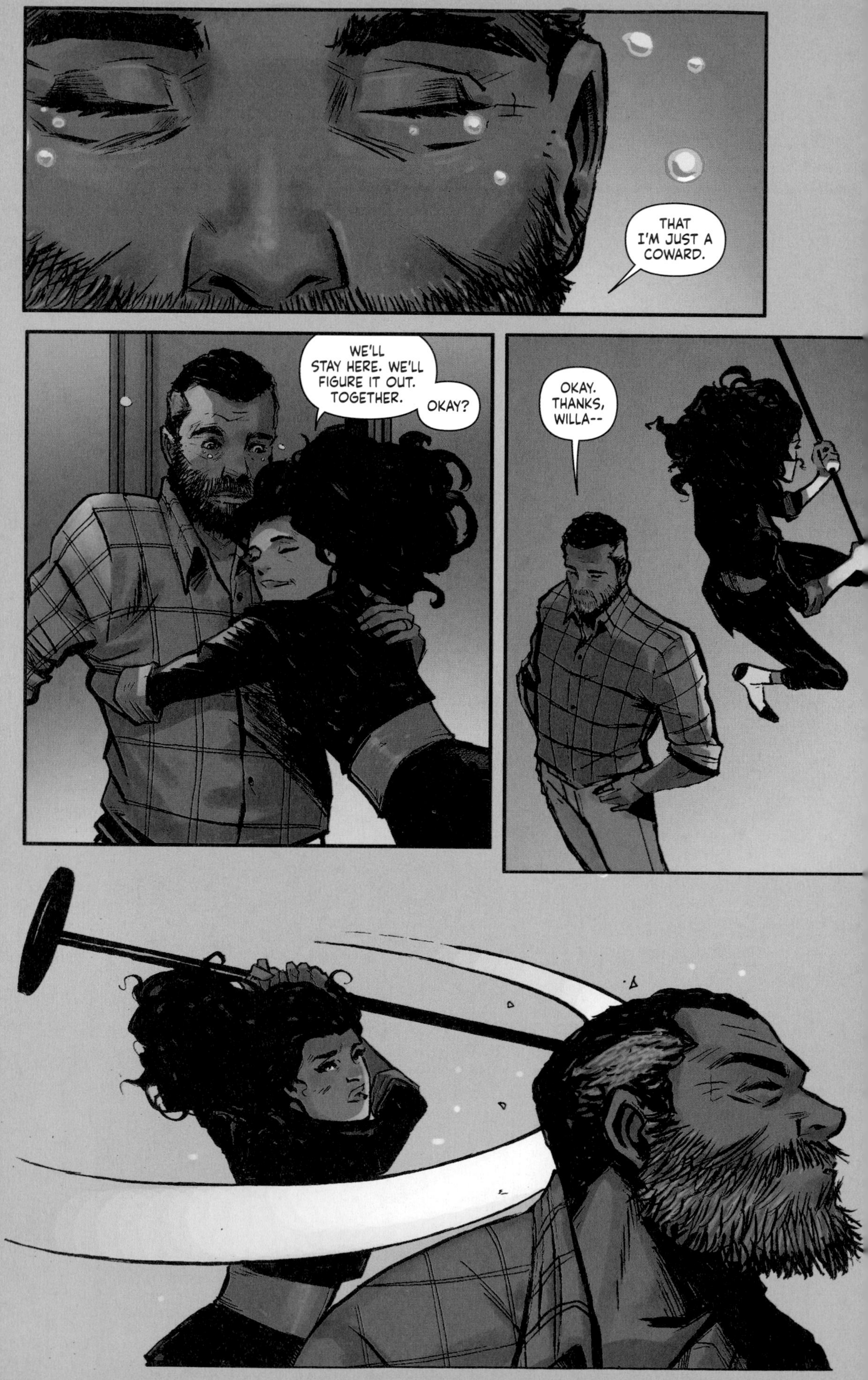
THAT I'M JUST A COWARD.
WE'LL STAY HERE. WE'LL FIGURE IT OUT. TOGETHER.
OKAY?
OKAY. THANKS, WILLA--

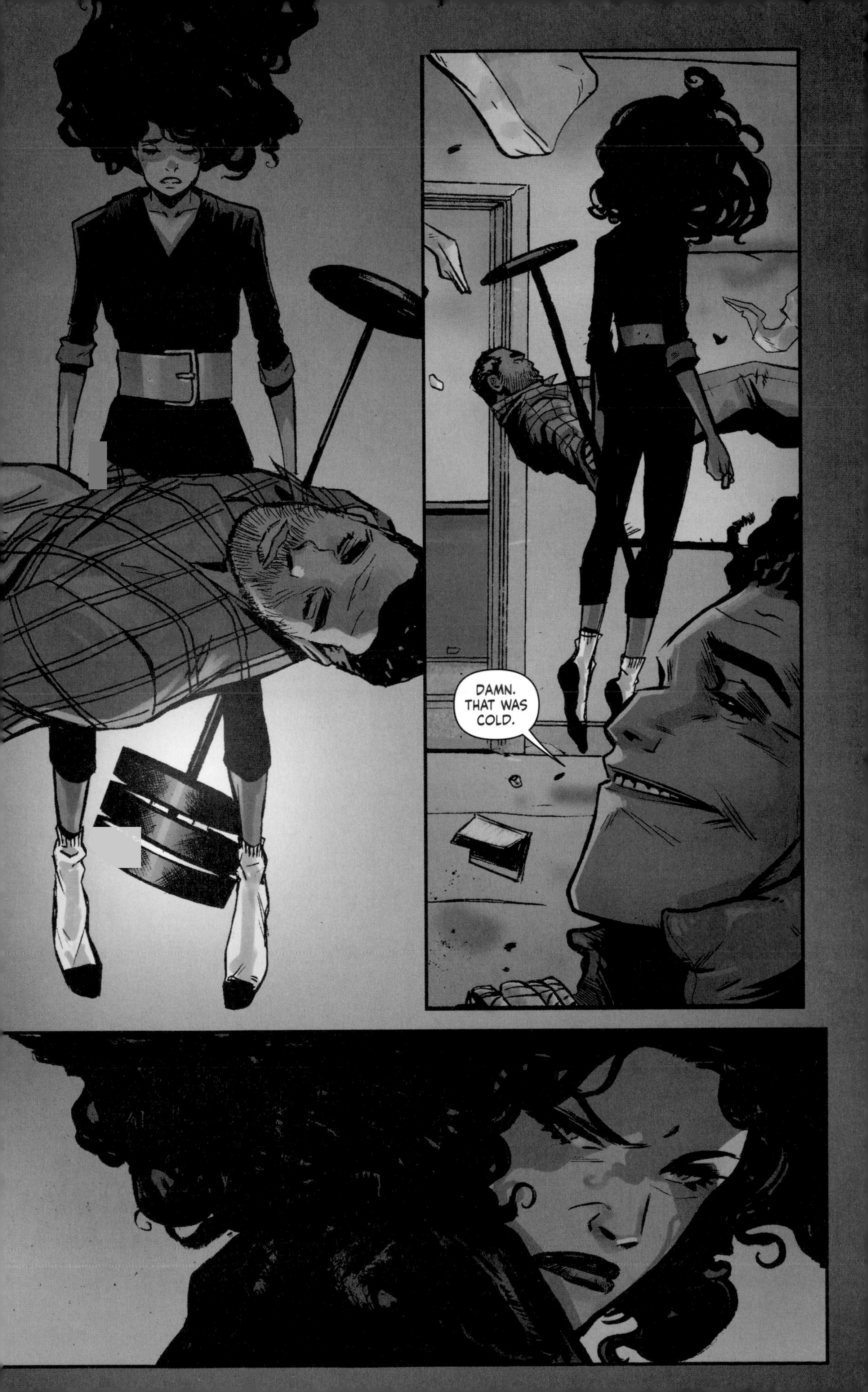
DAMN. THAT WAS COLD.

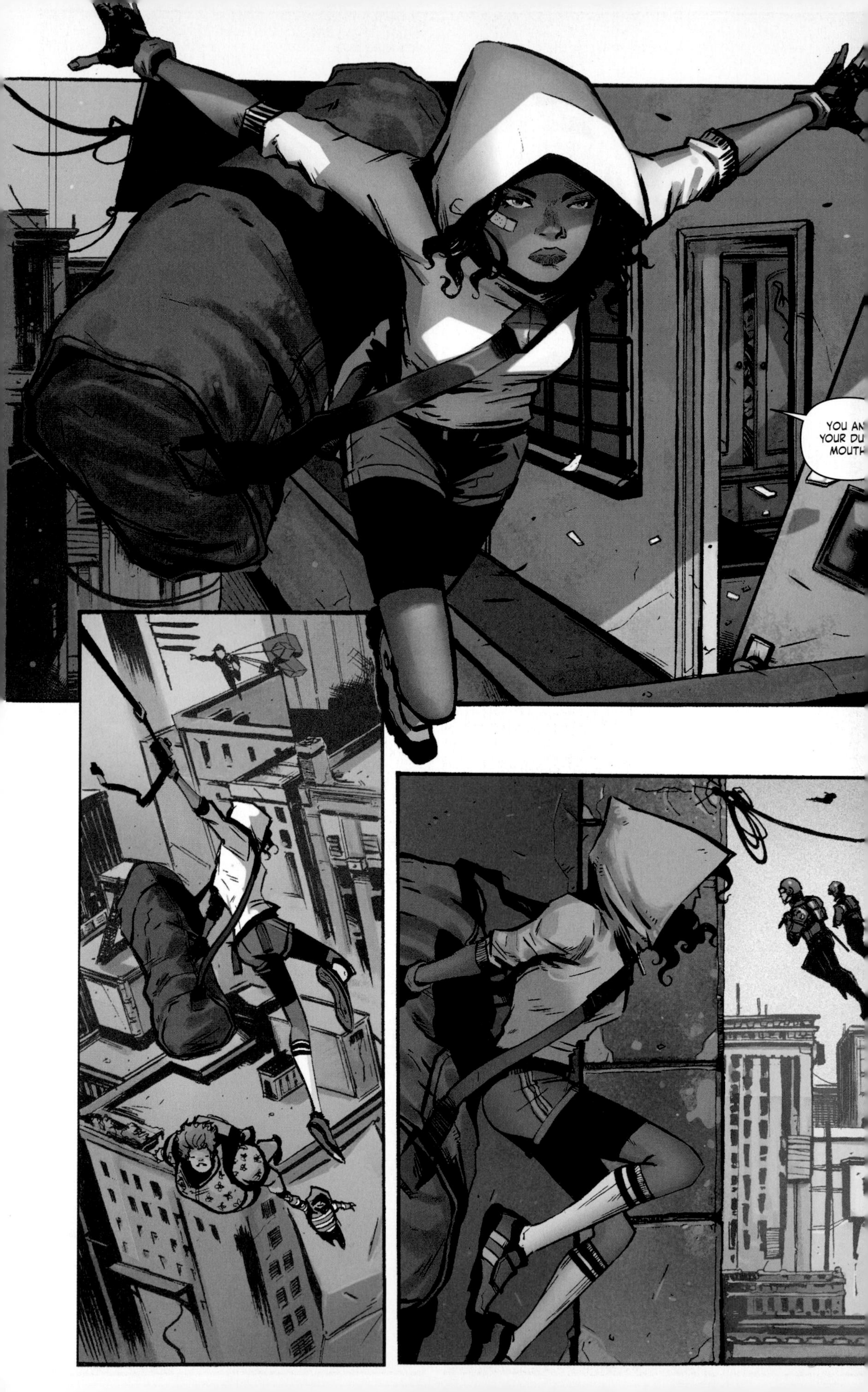
YOU AN
YOUR DU
MOUTH

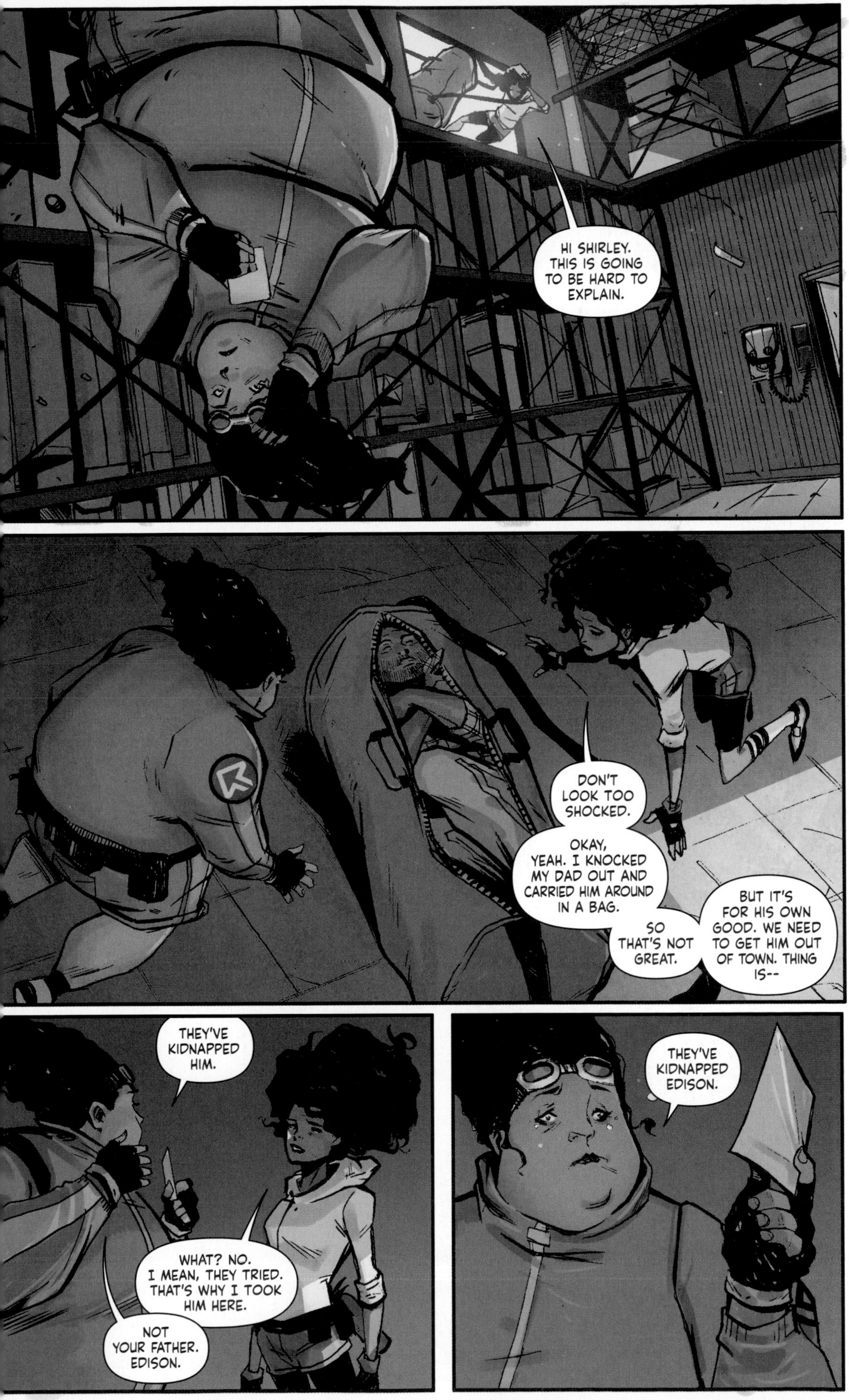
HI SHIRLEY. THIS IS GOING TO BE HARD TO EXPLAIN.
DON'T LOOK TOO SHOCKED.
OKAY, YEAH. I KNOCKED MY DAD OUT AND CARRIED HIM AROUND IN A BAG.
SO THAT'S NOT GREAT.
BUT IT'S FOR HIS OWN GOOD. WE NEED TO GET HIM OUT OF TOWN. THING IS--
THEY'VE KIDNAPPED HIM.
WHAT? NO. I MEAN, THEY TRIED. THAT'S WHY I TOOK HIM HERE.
NOT YOUR FATHER. EDISON.
THEY'VE KIDNAPPED EDISON.

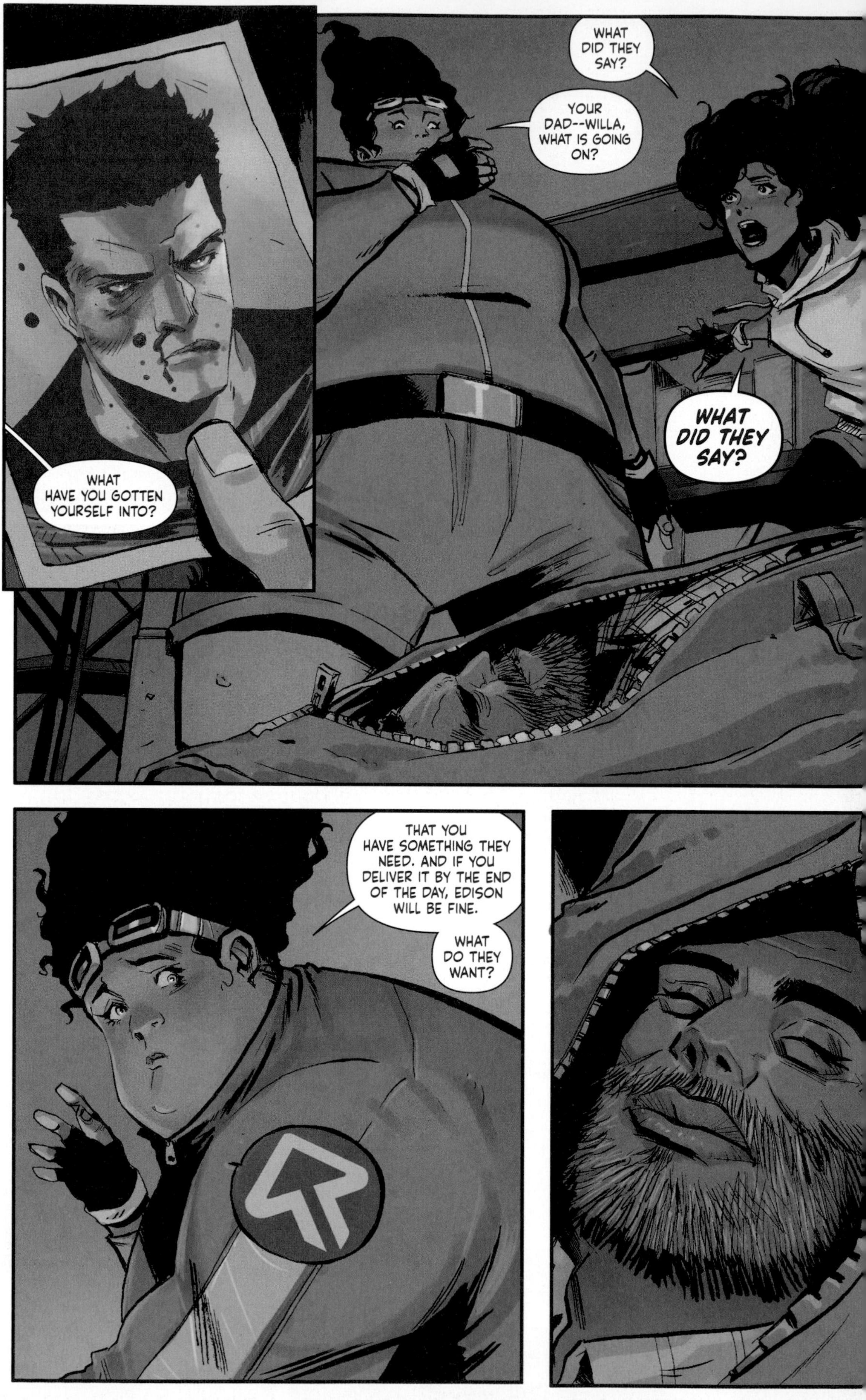
WHAT HAVE YOU GOTTEN YOURSELF INTO?
WHAT DID THEY SAY?
YOUR DAD--WILLA, WHAT IS GOING ON?
WHAT DID THEY SAY?
THAT YOU HAVE SOMETHING THEY NEED. AND IF YOU DELIVER IT BY THE END OF THE DAY, EDISON WILL BE FINE.
WHAT DO THEY WANT?

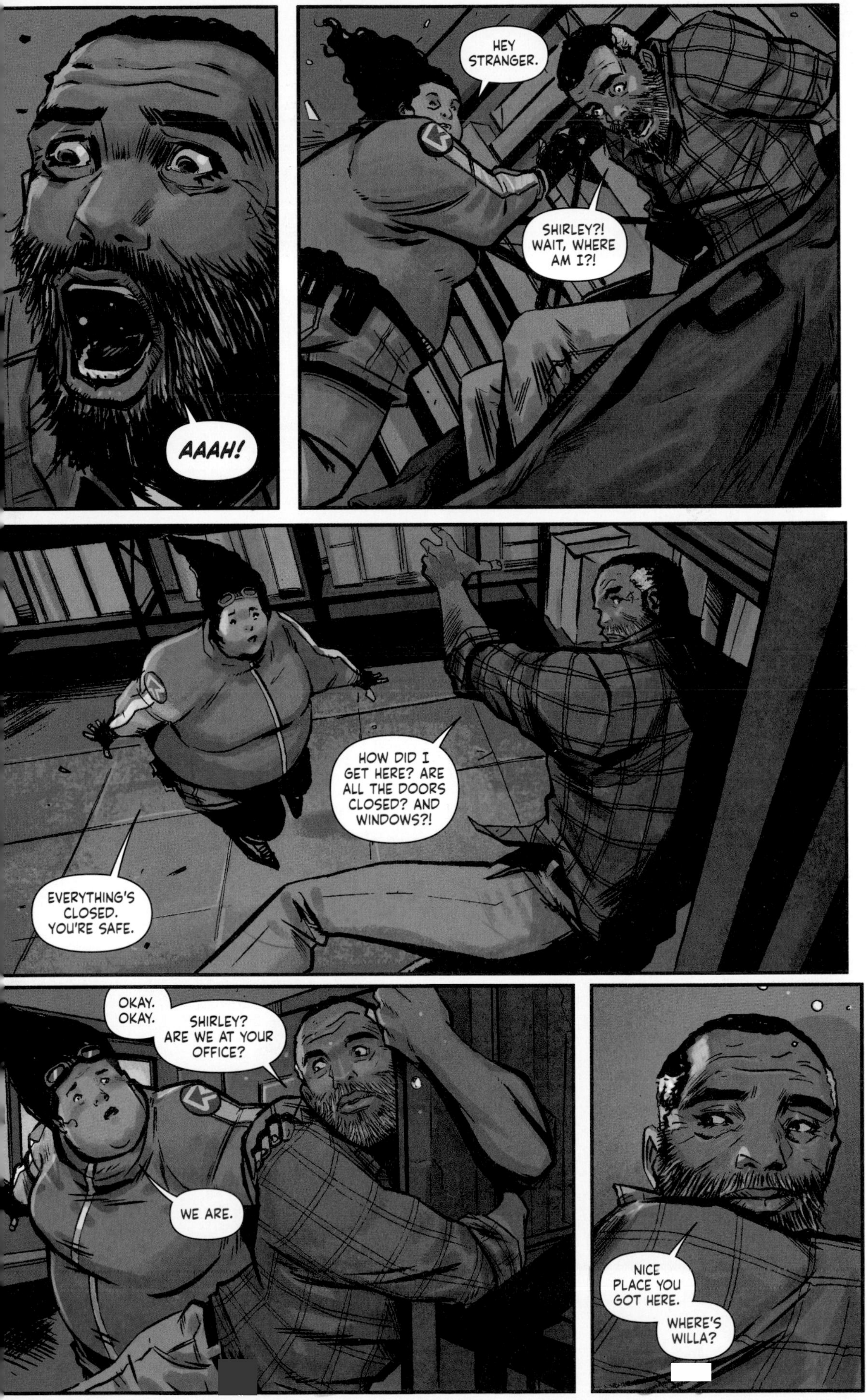
AAAH!
HEY STRANGER.
SHIRLEY?! WAIT, WHERE AM I?!
HOW DID I GET HERE? ARE ALL THE DOORS CLOSED? AND WINDOWS?!
EVERYTHING'S CLOSED. YOU'RE SAFE.
OKAY. OKAY.
SHIRLEY? ARE WE AT YOUR OFFICE?
WE ARE.
NICE PLACE YOU GOT HERE.
WHERE'S WILLA?

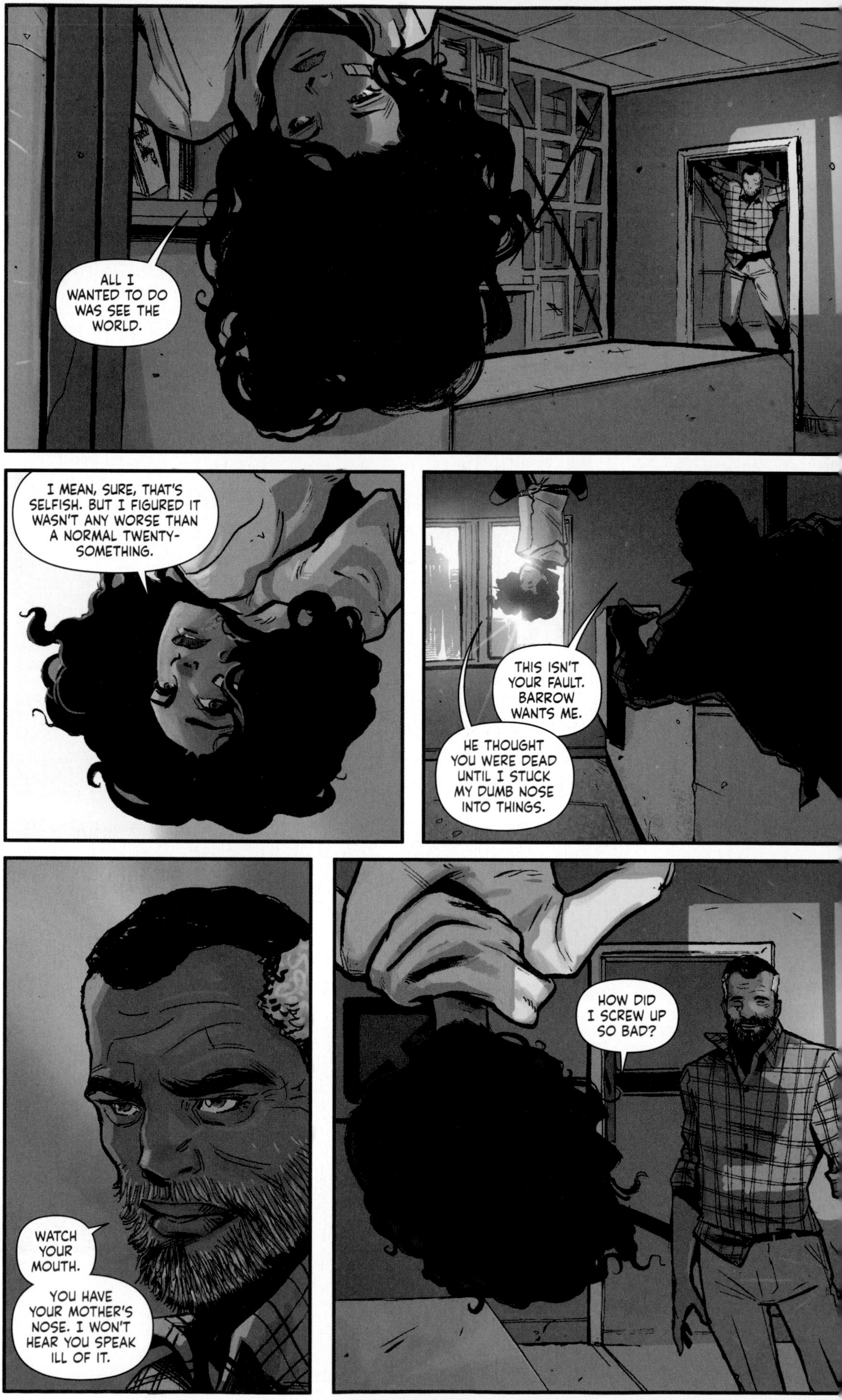
ALL I WANTED TO DO WAS SEE THE WORLD.
I MEAN, SURE, THAT'S SELFISH. BUT I FIGURED IT WASN'T ANY WORSE THAN A NORMAL TWENTY-SOMETHING.
THIS ISN'T YOUR FAULT. BARROW WANTS ME.
HE THOUGHT YOU WERE DEAD UNTIL I STUCK MY DUMB NOSE INTO THINGS.
WATCH YOUR MOUTH.
YOU HAVE YOUR MOTHER'S NOSE. I WON'T HEAR YOU SPEAK ILL OF IT.
HOW DID I SCREW UP SO BAD?

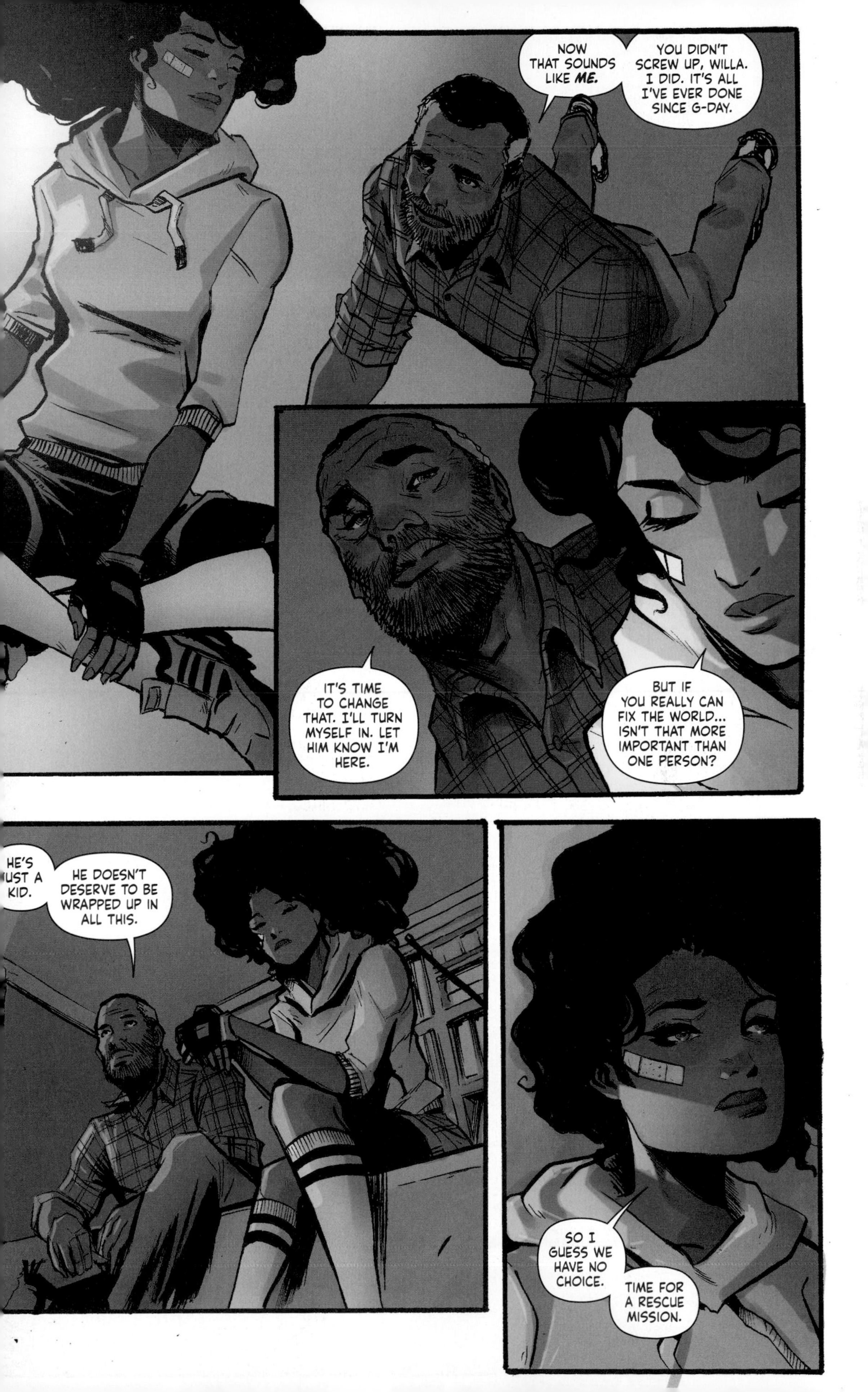
NOW THAT SOUNDS LIKE *ME.*
YOU DIDN'T SCREW UP, WILLA. I DID. IT'S ALL I'VE EVER DONE SINCE G-DAY.
IT'S TIME TO CHANGE THAT. I'LL TURN MYSELF IN. LET HIM KNOW I'M HERE.
BUT IF YOU REALLY CAN FIX THE WORLD... ISN'T THAT MORE IMPORTANT THAN ONE PERSON?
HE'S JUST A KID.
HE DOESN'T DESERVE TO BE WRAPPED UP IN ALL THIS.
SO I GUESS WE HAVE NO CHOICE.
TIME FOR A RESCUE MISSION.

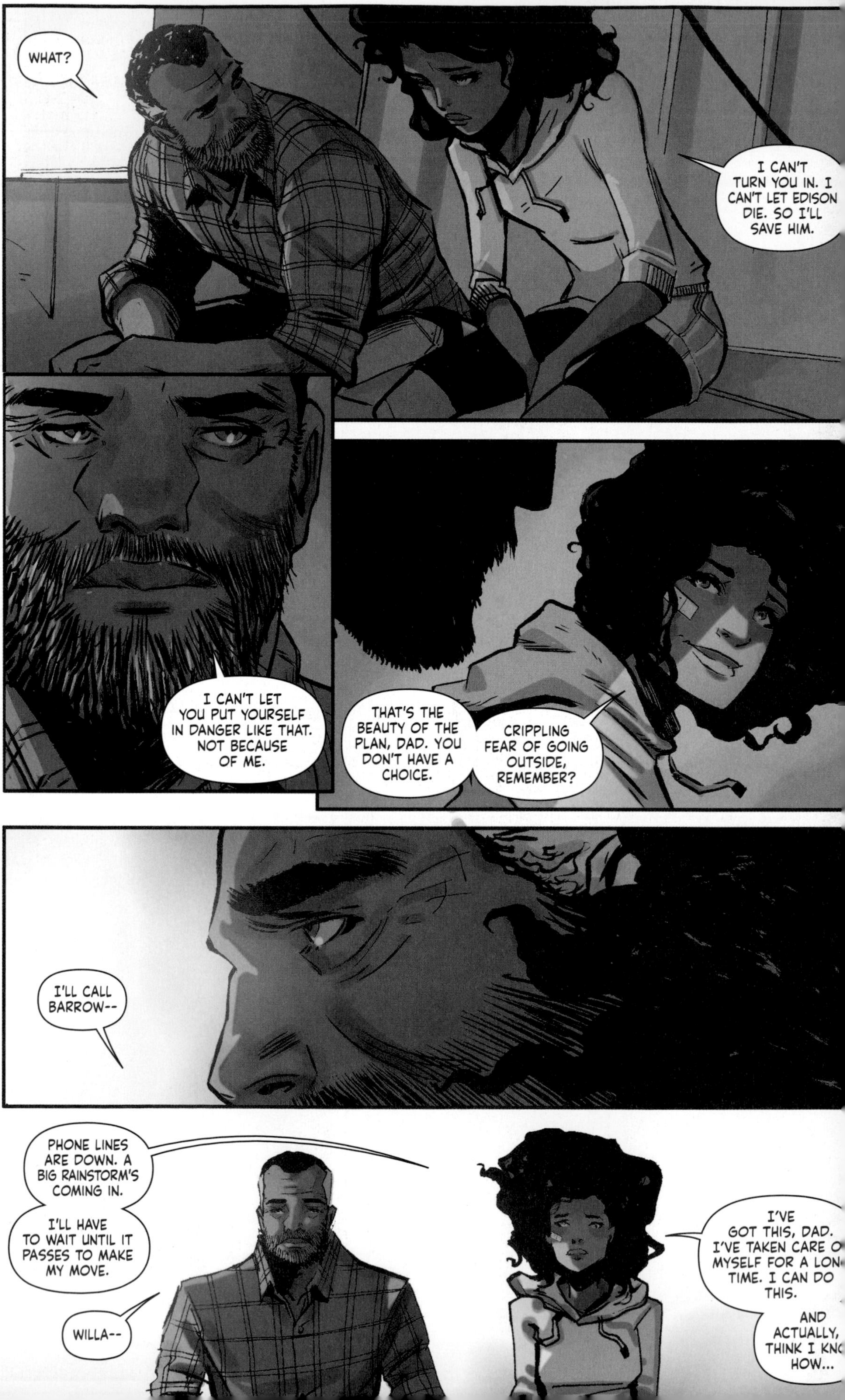
WHAT?
I CAN'T TURN YOU IN. I CAN'T LET EDISON DIE. SO I'LL SAVE HIM.
I CAN'T LET YOU PUT YOURSELF IN DANGER LIKE THAT. NOT BECAUSE OF ME.
THAT'S THE BEAUTY OF THE PLAN, DAD. YOU DON'T HAVE A CHOICE.
CRIPPLING FEAR OF GOING OUTSIDE, REMEMBER?
I'LL CALL BARROW--
PHONE LINES ARE DOWN. A BIG RAINSTORM'S COMING IN.
I'LL HAVE TO WAIT UNTIL IT PASSES TO MAKE MY MOVE.
WILLA--
I'VE GOT THIS, DAD. I'VE TAKEN CARE O MYSELF FOR A LON TIME. I CAN DO THIS.
AND ACTUALLY, THINK I KN HOW...

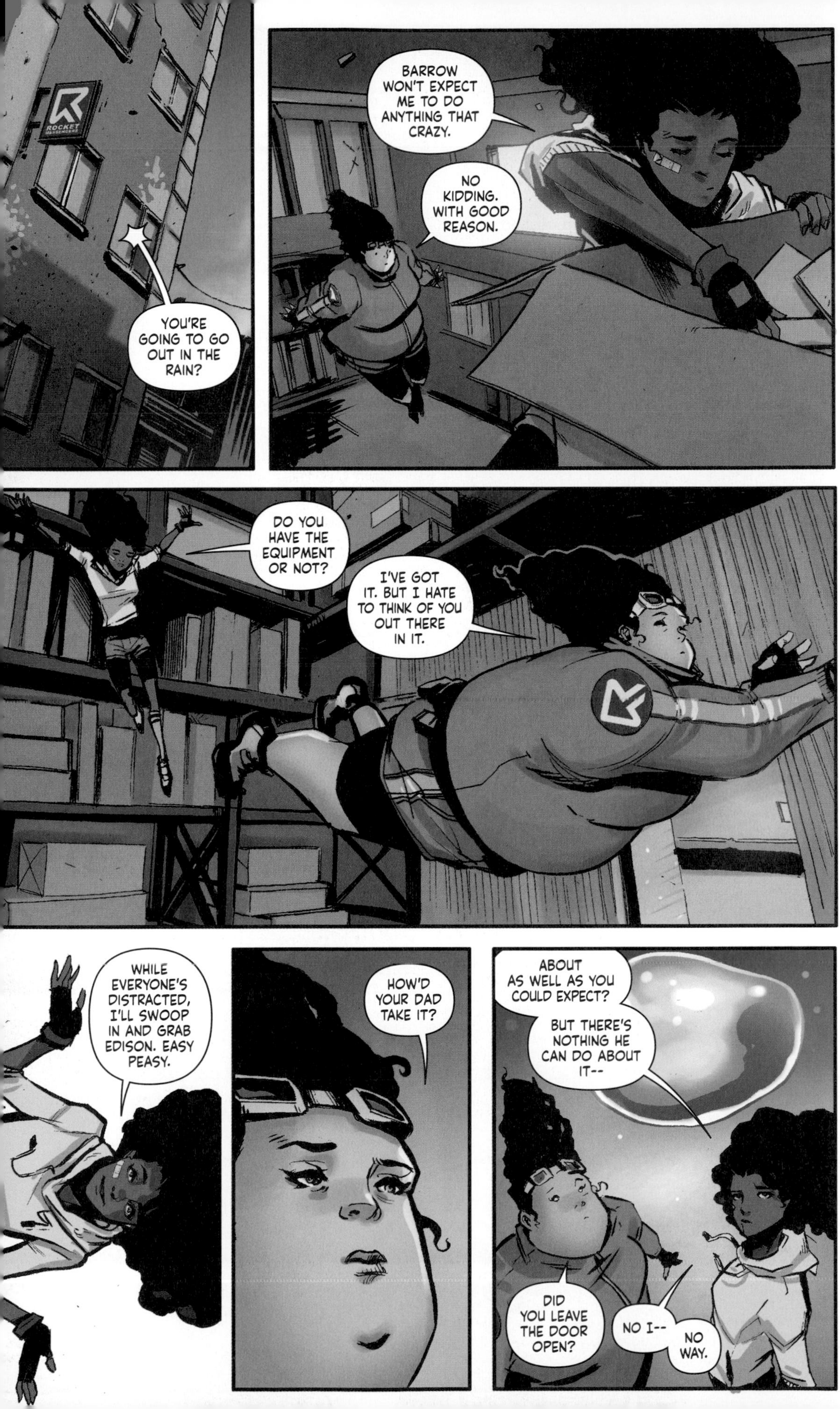
YOU'RE GOING TO GO OUT IN THE RAIN?
BARROW WON'T EXPECT ME TO DO ANYTHING THAT CRAZY.
NO KIDDING. WITH GOOD REASON.
DO YOU HAVE THE EQUIPMENT OR NOT?
I'VE GOT IT. BUT I HATE TO THINK OF YOU OUT THERE IN IT.
WHILE EVERYONE'S DISTRACTED, I'LL SWOOP IN AND GRAB EDISON. EASY PEASY.
HOW'D YOUR DAD TAKE IT?
ABOUT AS WELL AS YOU COULD EXPECT?
BUT THERE'S NOTHING HE CAN DO ABOUT IT--
DID YOU LEAVE THE DOOR OPEN?
NO I--
NO WAY.

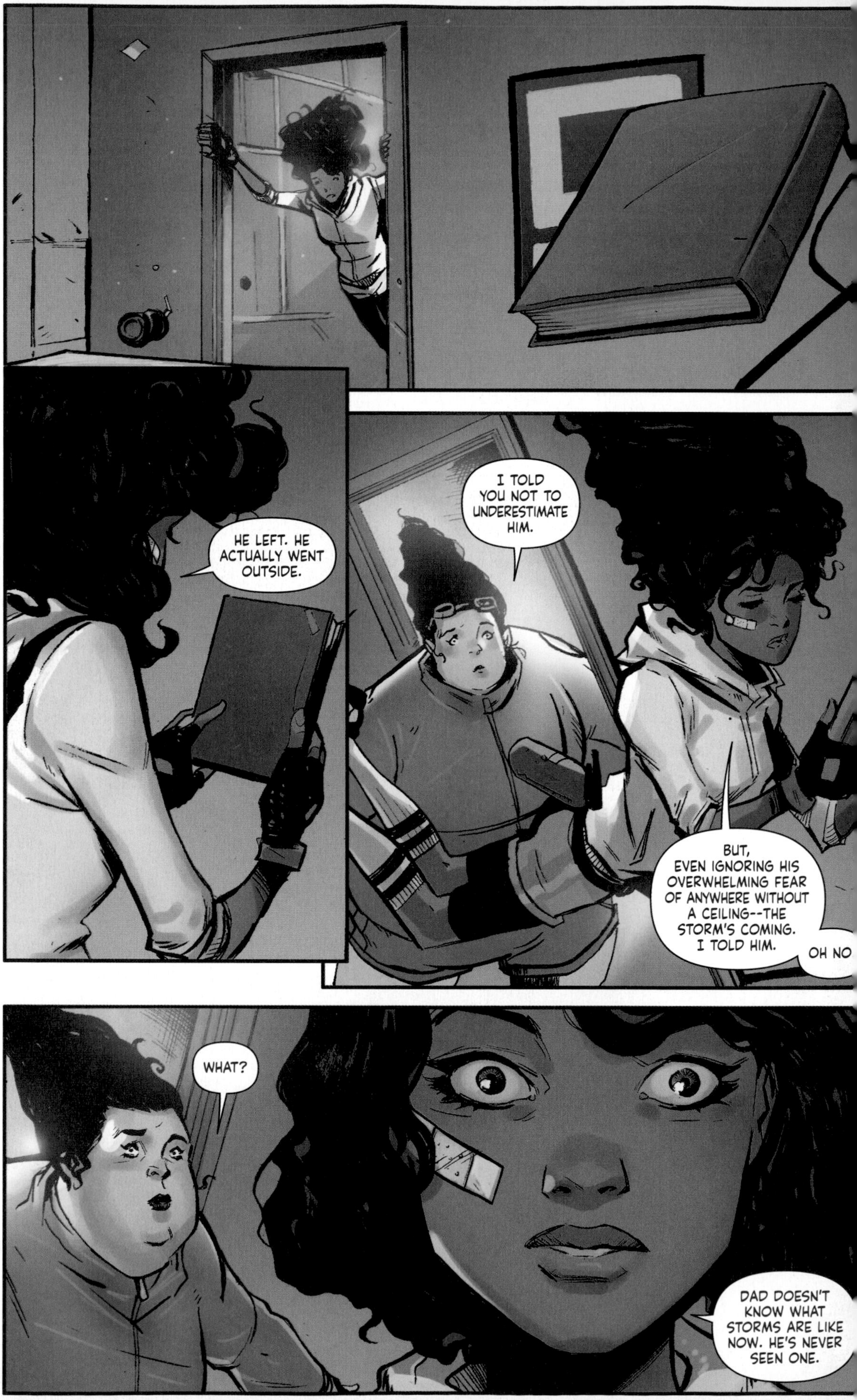
HE LEFT. HE ACTUALLY WENT OUTSIDE.
I TOLD YOU NOT TO UNDERESTIMATE HIM.
BUT, EVEN IGNORING HIS OVERWHELMING FEAR OF ANYWHERE WITHOUT A CEILING--THE STORM'S COMING. I TOLD HIM.
OH NO
WHAT?
DAD DOESN'T KNOW WHAT STORMS ARE LIKE NOW. HE'S NEVER SEEN ONE.

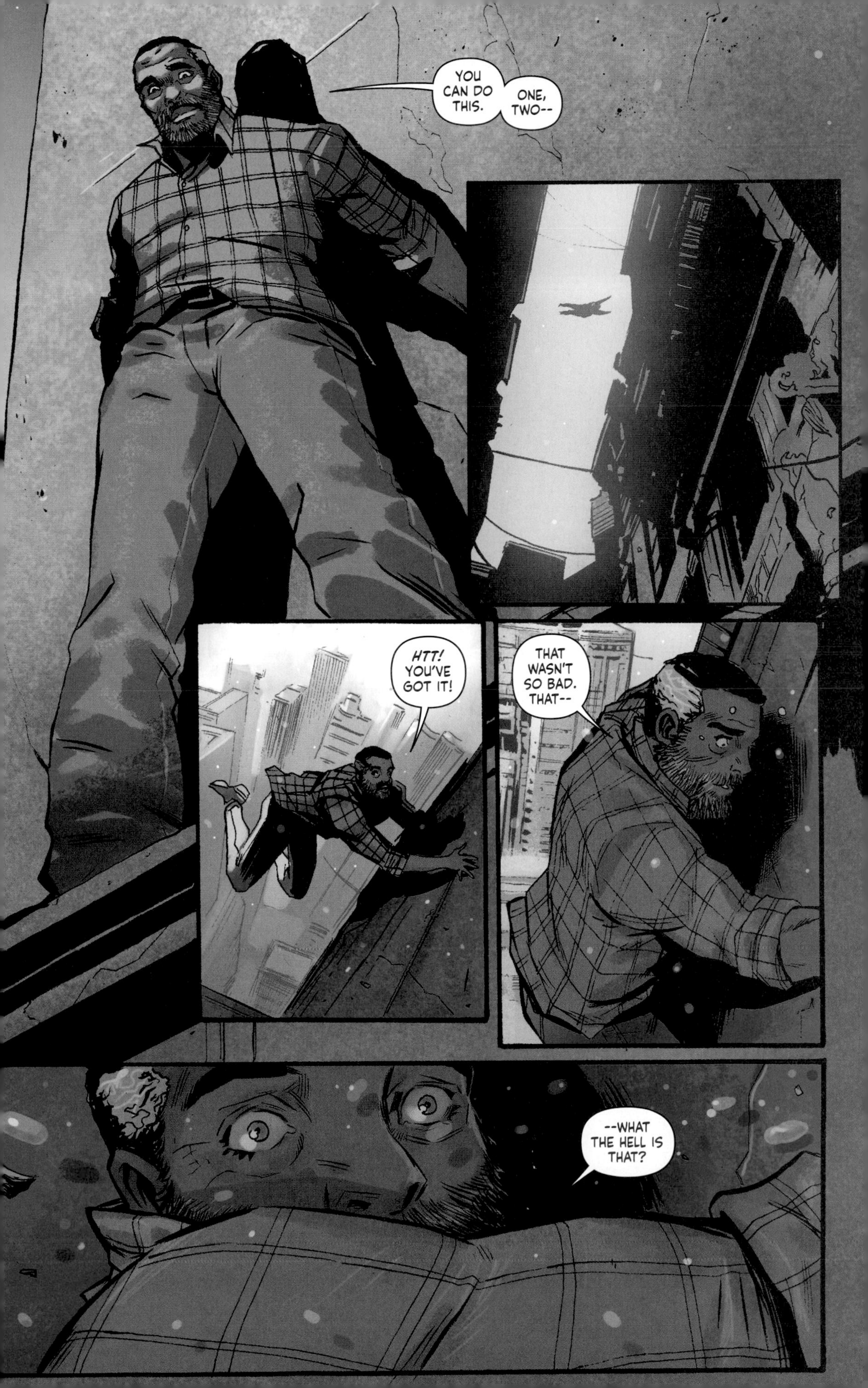
YOU CAN DO THIS.
ONE, TWO--
HTT! YOU'VE GOT IT!
THAT WASN'T SO BAD. THAT--
--WHAT THE HELL IS THAT?

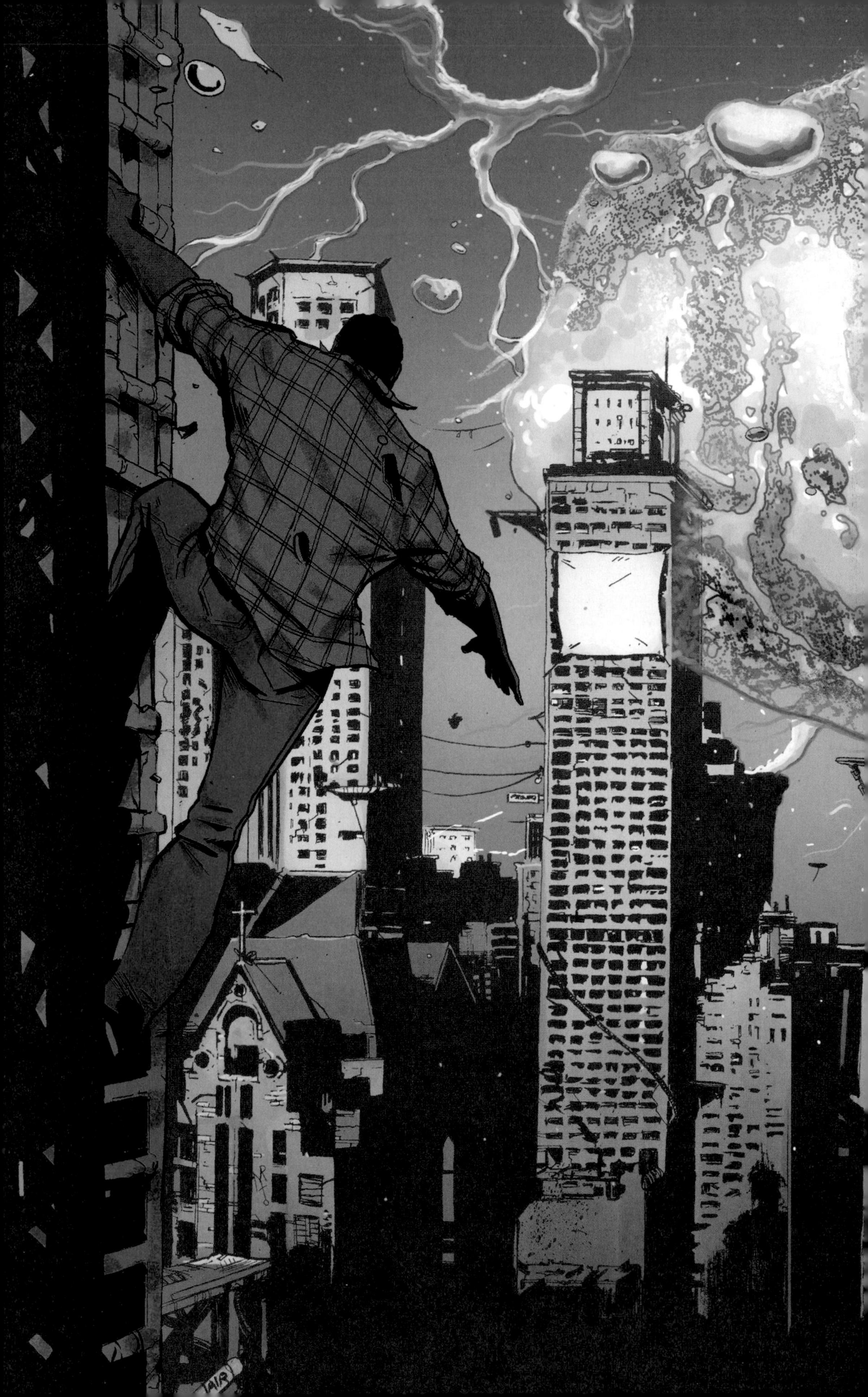

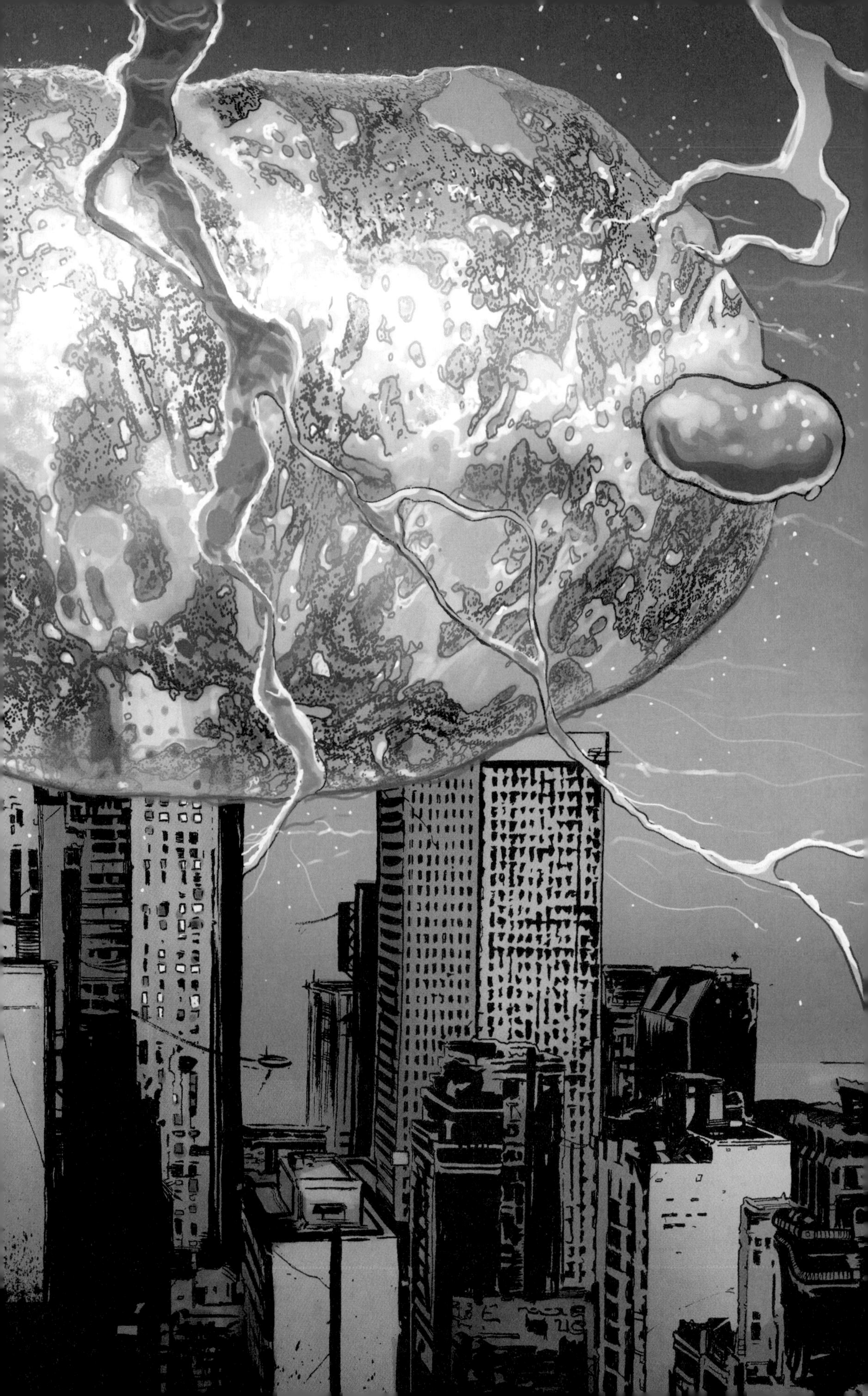

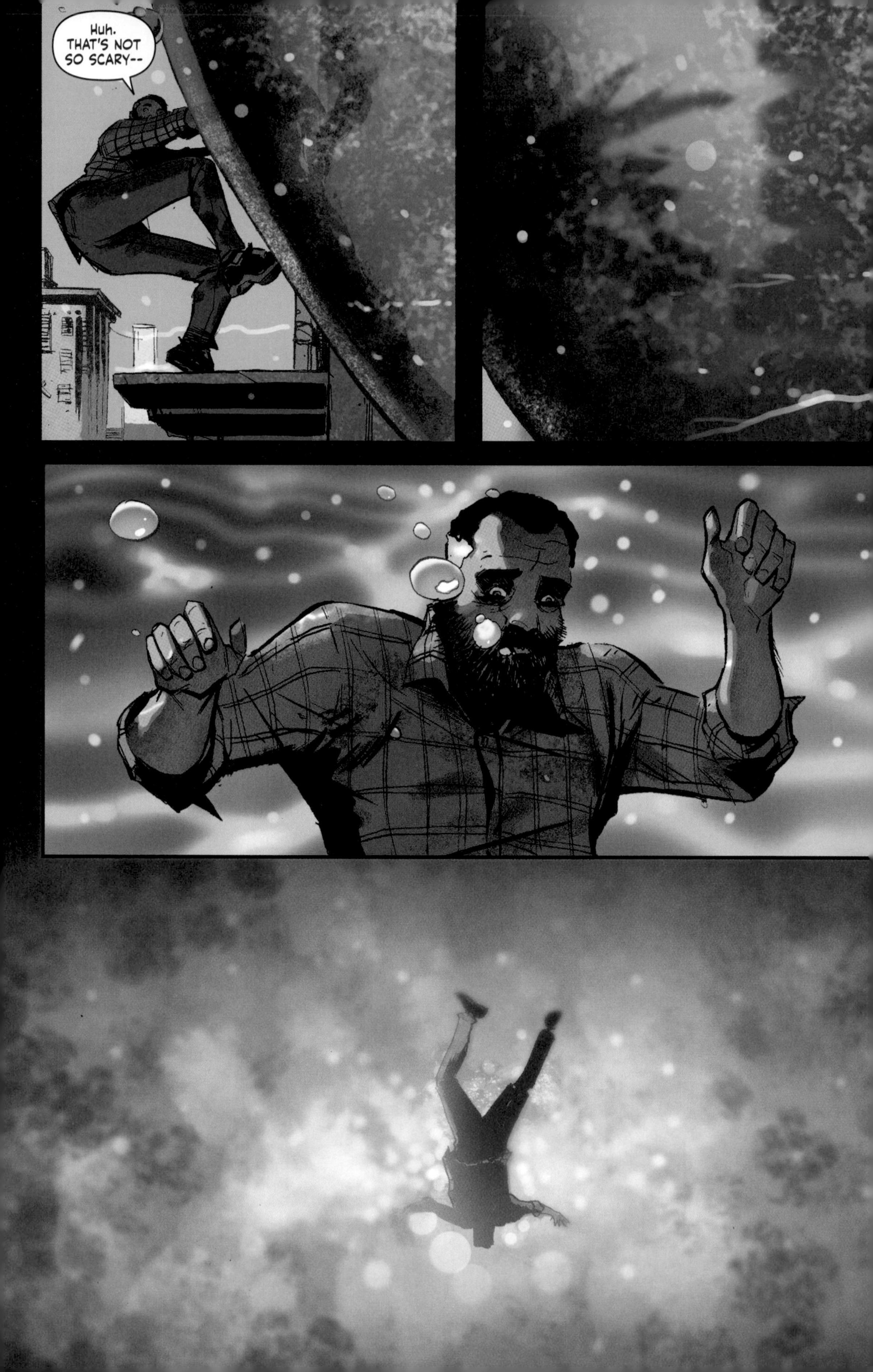
Huh. THAT'S NOT SO SCARY--

END CHAPTER FOUR

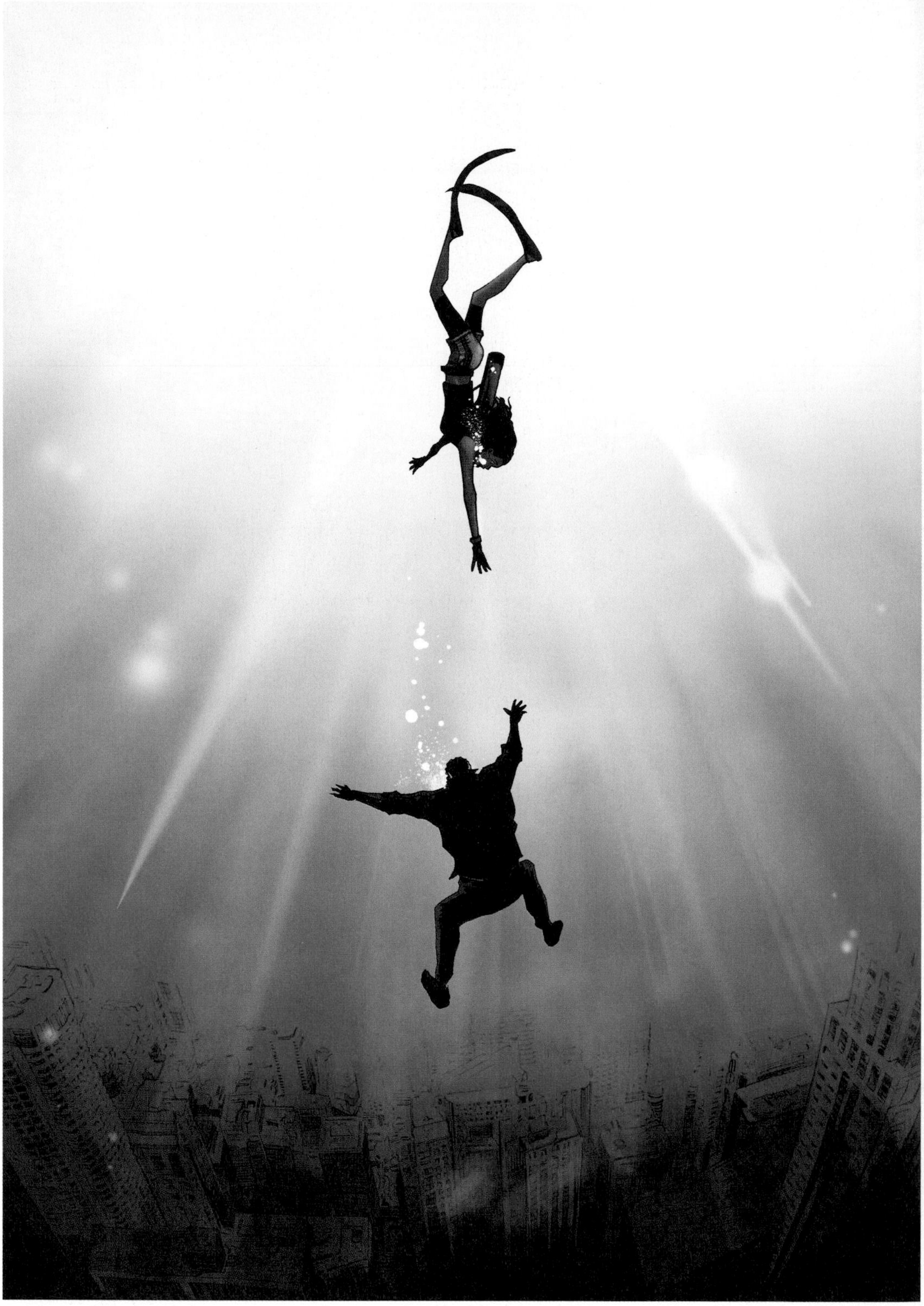

CHAPTER FIVE

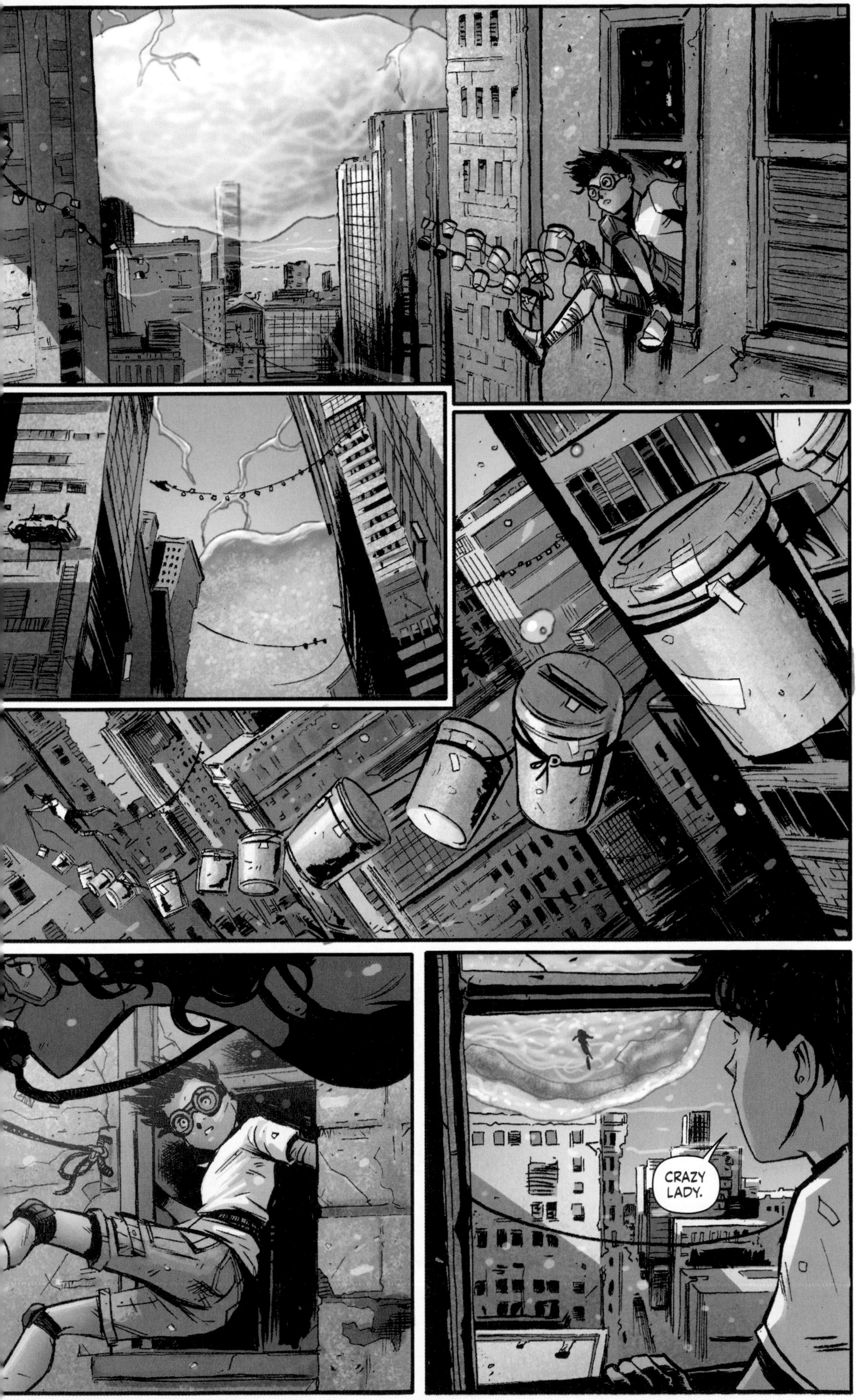
CRAZY
LADY.

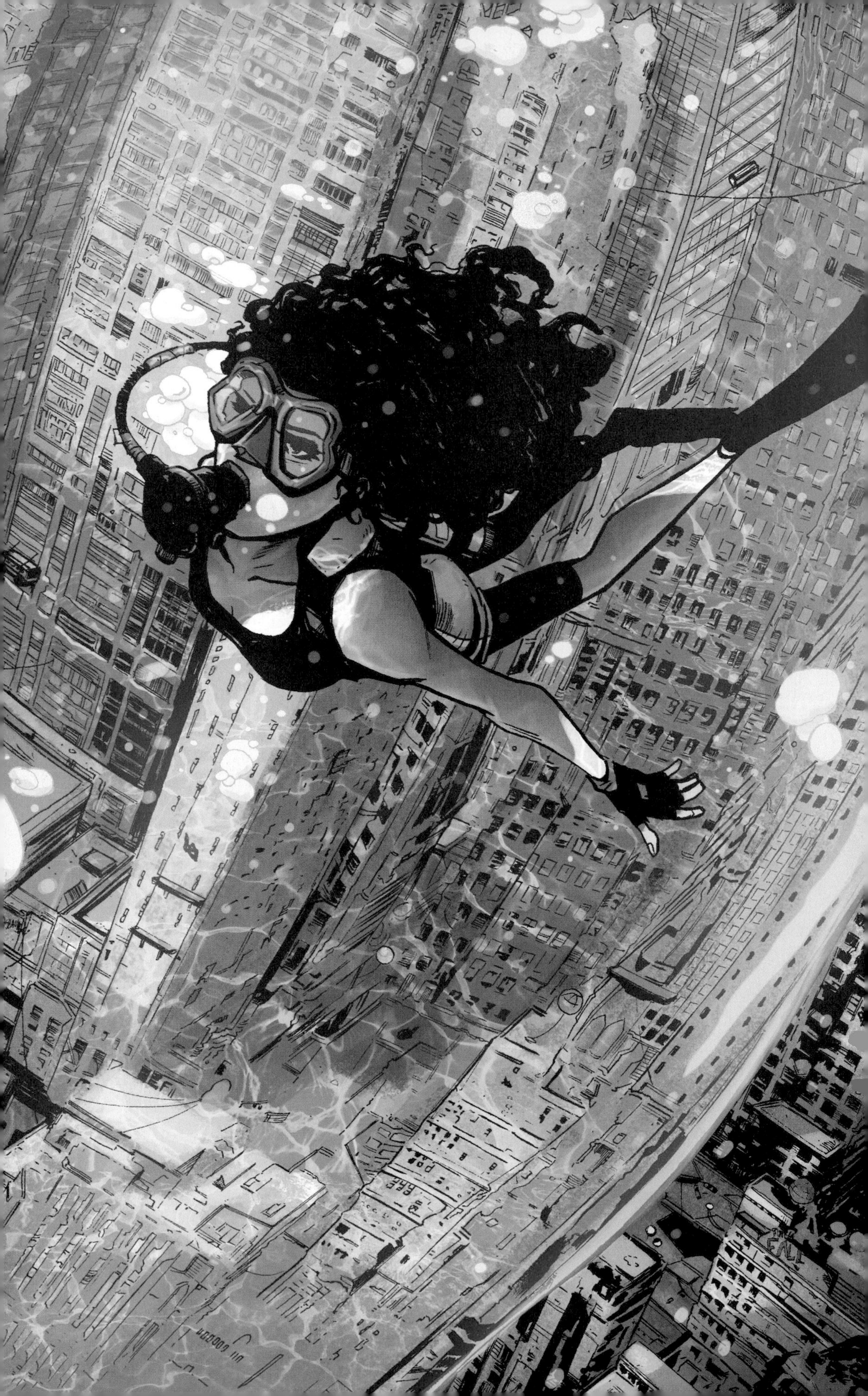

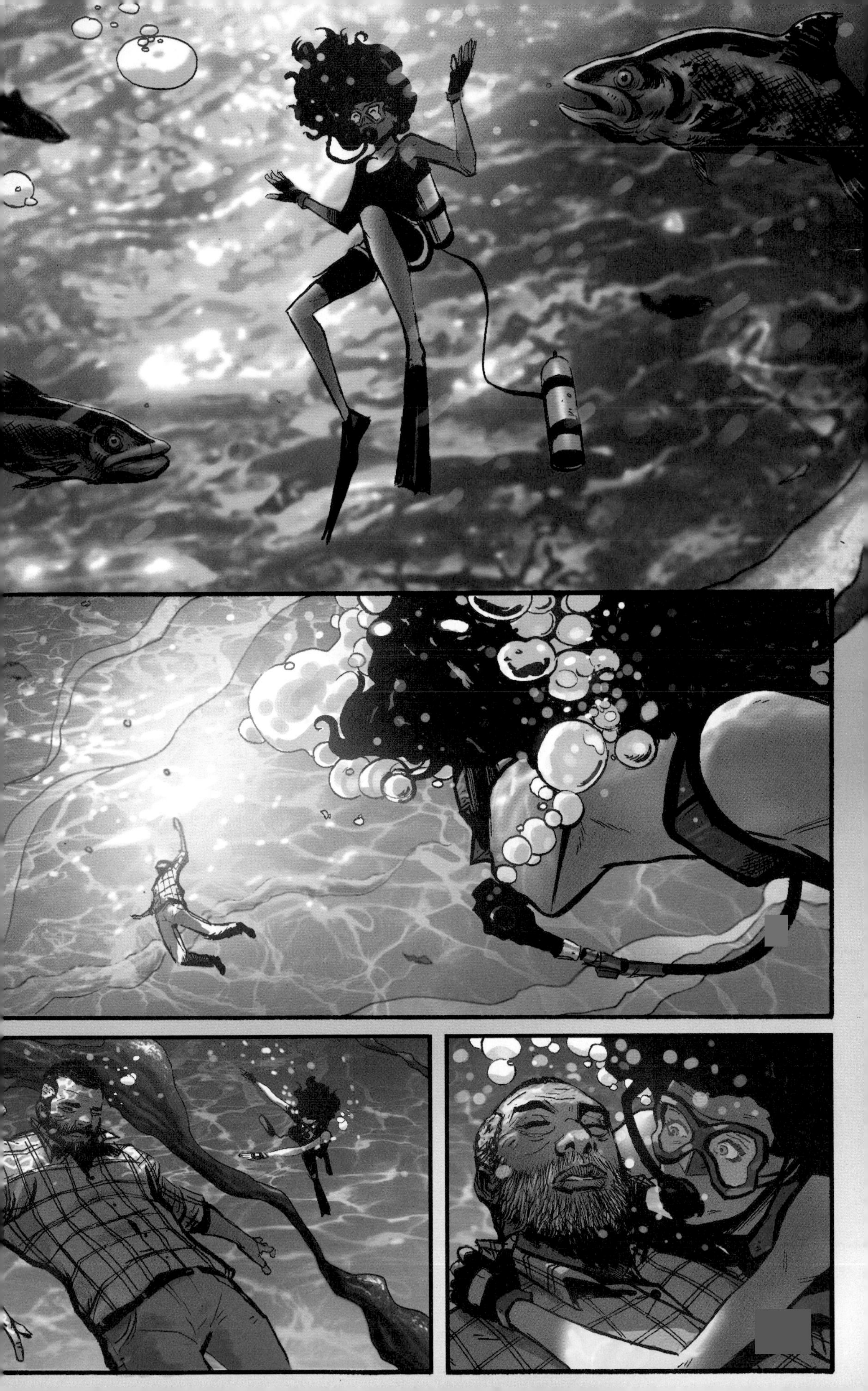

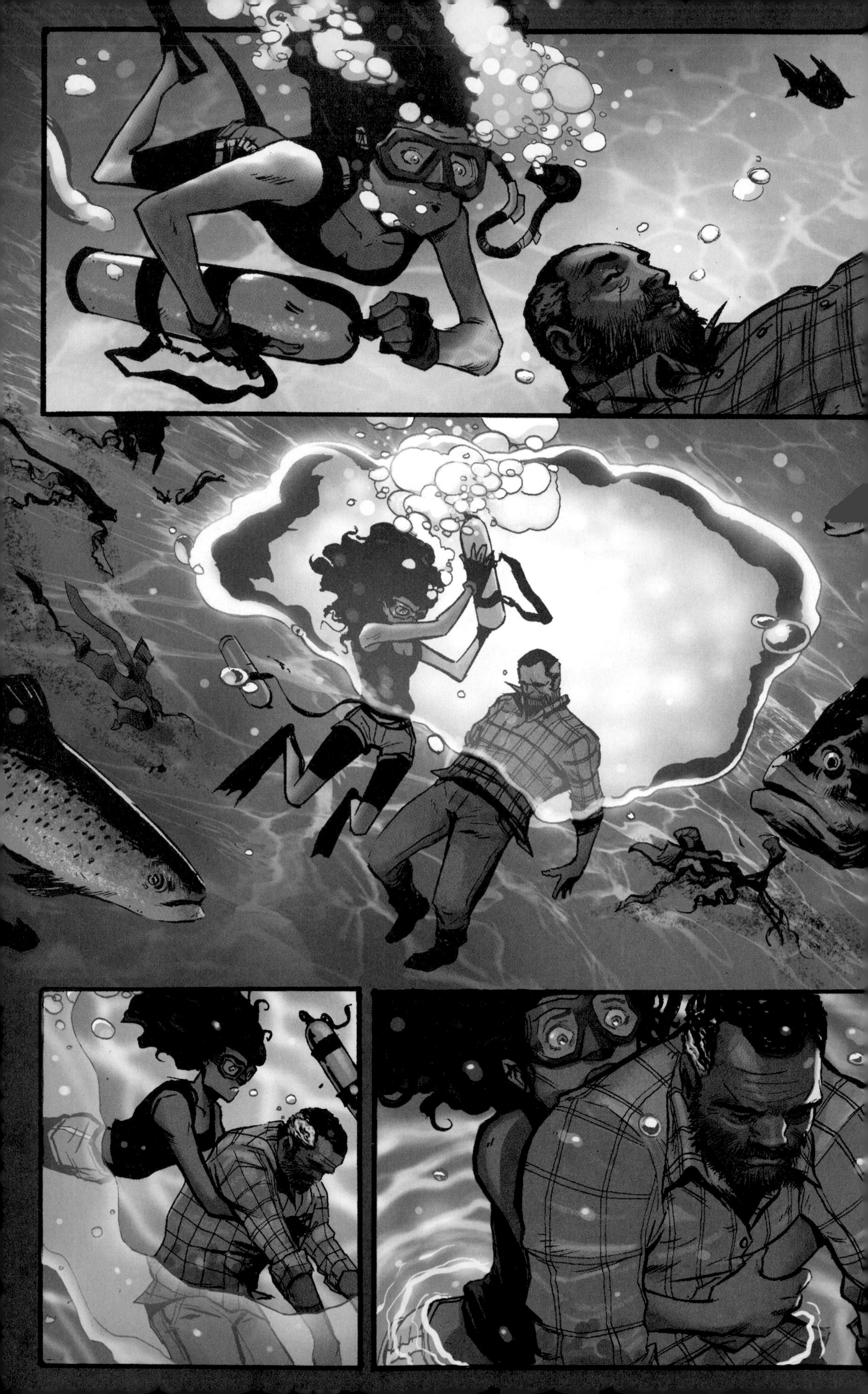

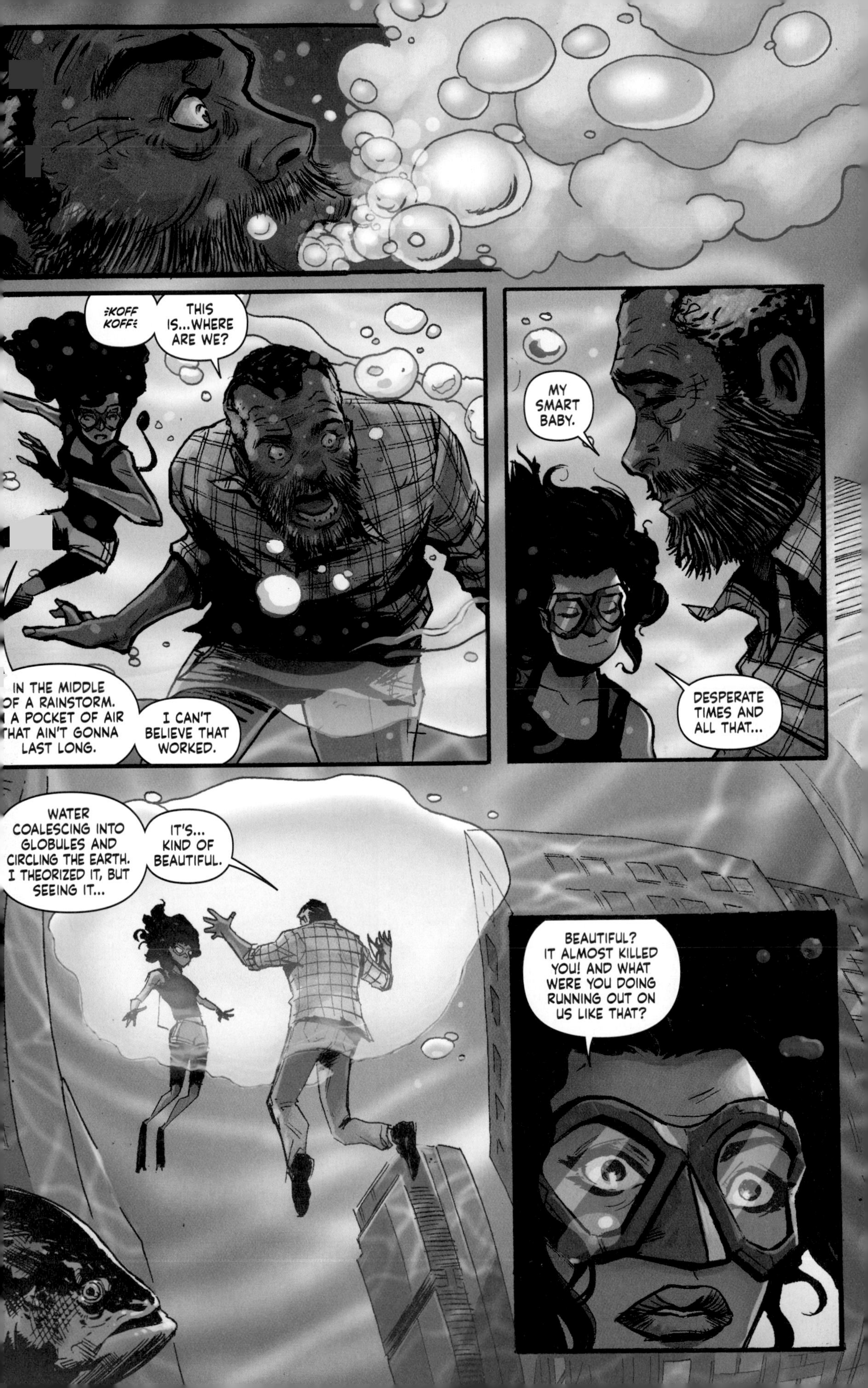
KOFF KOFF
THIS IS...WHERE ARE WE?
MY SMART BABY.
IN THE MIDDLE OF A RAINSTORM. A POCKET OF AIR THAT AIN'T GONNA LAST LONG.
I CAN'T BELIEVE THAT WORKED.
DESPERATE TIMES AND ALL THAT...
WATER COALESCING INTO GLOBULES AND CIRCLING THE EARTH. I THEORIZED IT, BUT SEEING IT...
IT'S... KIND OF BEAUTIFUL.
BEAUTIFUL? IT ALMOST KILLED YOU! AND WHAT WERE YOU DOING RUNNING OUT ON US LIKE THAT?

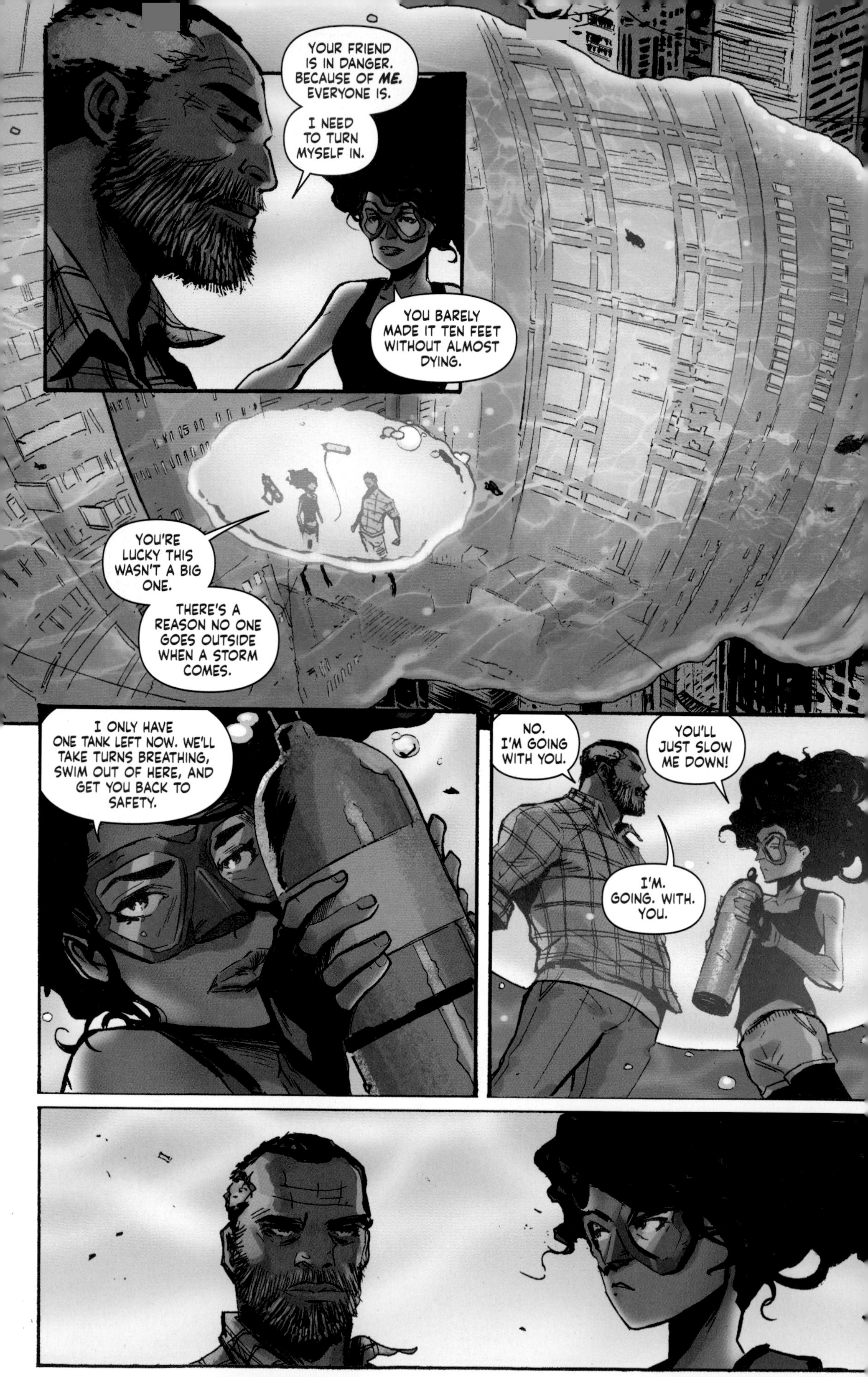
YOUR FRIEND IS IN DANGER. BECAUSE OF **ME.** EVERYONE IS.
I NEED TO TURN MYSELF IN.
YOU BARELY MADE IT TEN FEET WITHOUT ALMOST DYING.
YOU'RE LUCKY THIS WASN'T A BIG ONE.
THERE'S A REASON NO ONE GOES OUTSIDE WHEN A STORM COMES.
I ONLY HAVE ONE TANK LEFT NOW. WE'LL TAKE TURNS BREATHING, SWIM OUT OF HERE, AND GET YOU BACK TO SAFETY.
NO. I'M GOING WITH YOU.
YOU'LL JUST SLOW ME DOWN!
I'M. GOING. WITH. YOU.

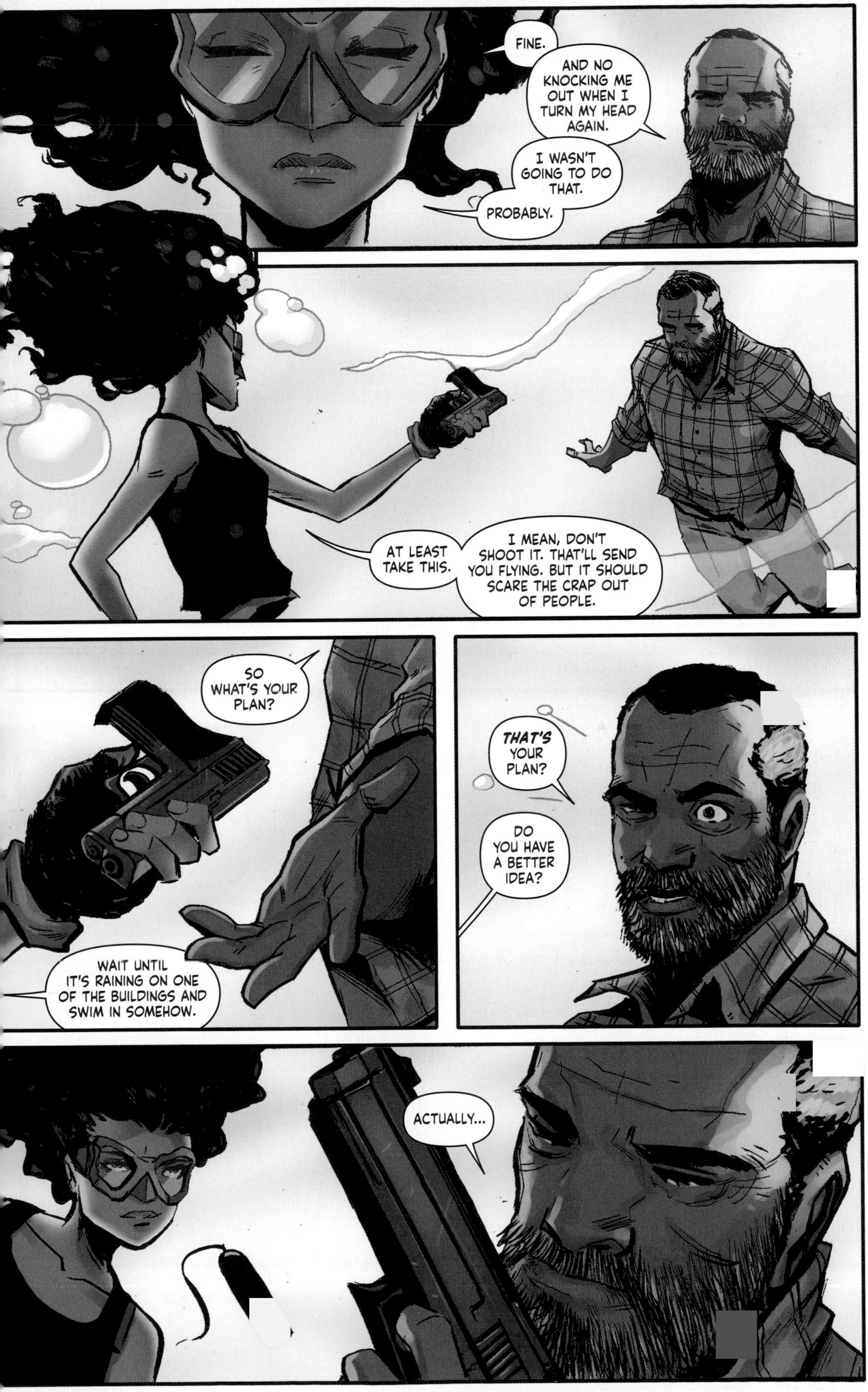
FINE.
AND NO KNOCKING ME OUT WHEN I TURN MY HEAD AGAIN.
I WASN'T GOING TO DO THAT.
PROBABLY.
AT LEAST TAKE THIS.
I MEAN, DON'T SHOOT IT. THAT'LL SEND YOU FLYING. BUT IT SHOULD SCARE THE CRAP OUT OF PEOPLE.
SO WHAT'S YOUR PLAN?
WAIT UNTIL IT'S RAINING ON ONE OF THE BUILDINGS AND SWIM IN SOMEHOW.
THAT'S YOUR PLAN?
DO YOU HAVE A BETTER IDEA?
ACTUALLY...

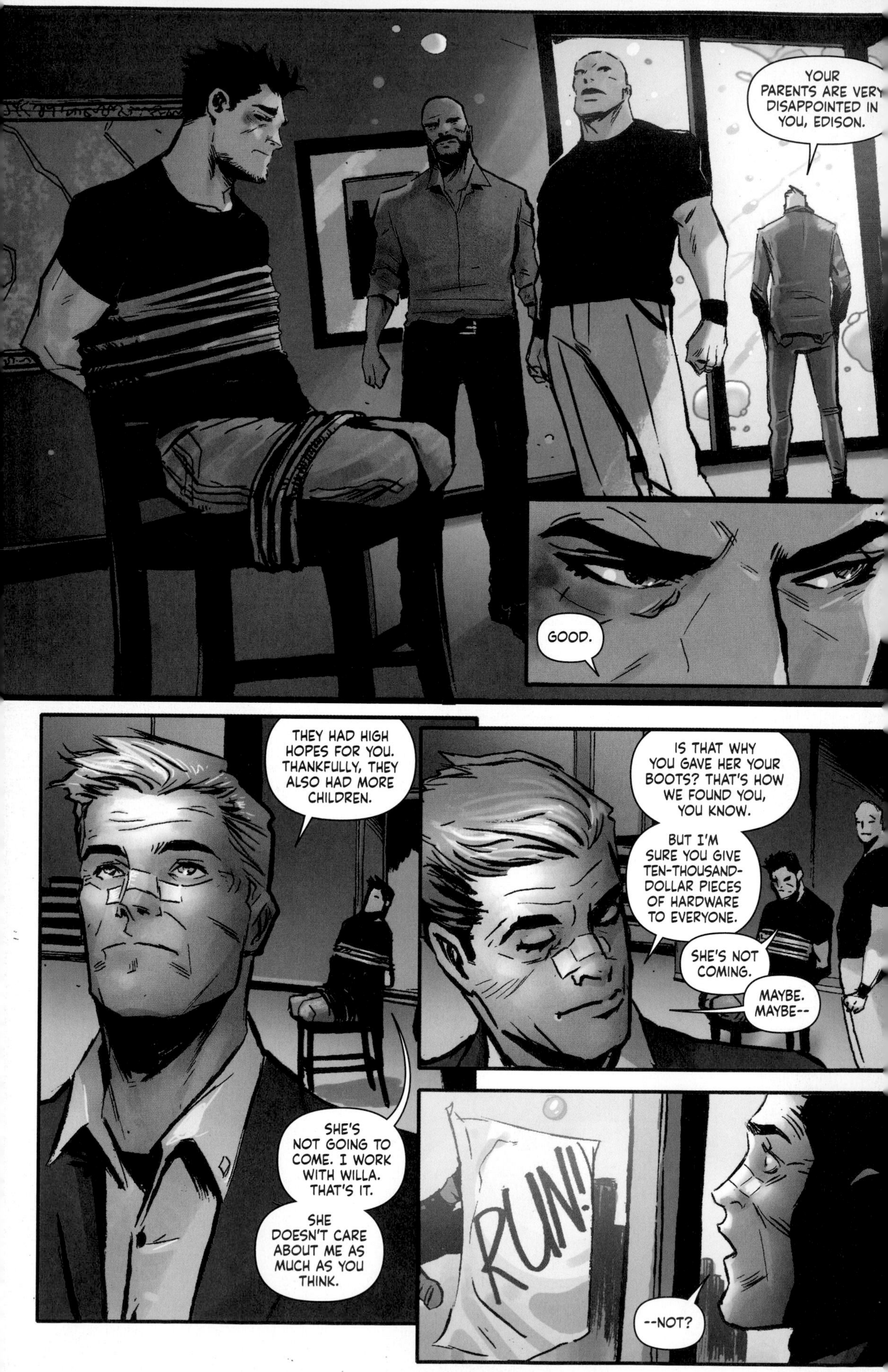
YOUR PARENTS ARE VERY DISAPPOINTED IN YOU, EDISON.
GOOD.
THEY HAD HIGH HOPES FOR YOU. THANKFULLY, THEY ALSO HAD MORE CHILDREN.
SHE'S NOT GOING TO COME. I WORK WITH WILLA. THAT'S IT.
SHE DOESN'T CARE ABOUT ME AS MUCH AS YOU THINK.
IS THAT WHY YOU GAVE HER YOUR BOOTS? THAT'S HOW WE FOUND YOU, YOU KNOW.
BUT I'M SURE YOU GIVE TEN-THOUSAND-DOLLAR PIECES OF HARDWARE TO EVERYONE.
SHE'S NOT COMING.
MAYBE. MAYBE--
RUN!
--NOT?

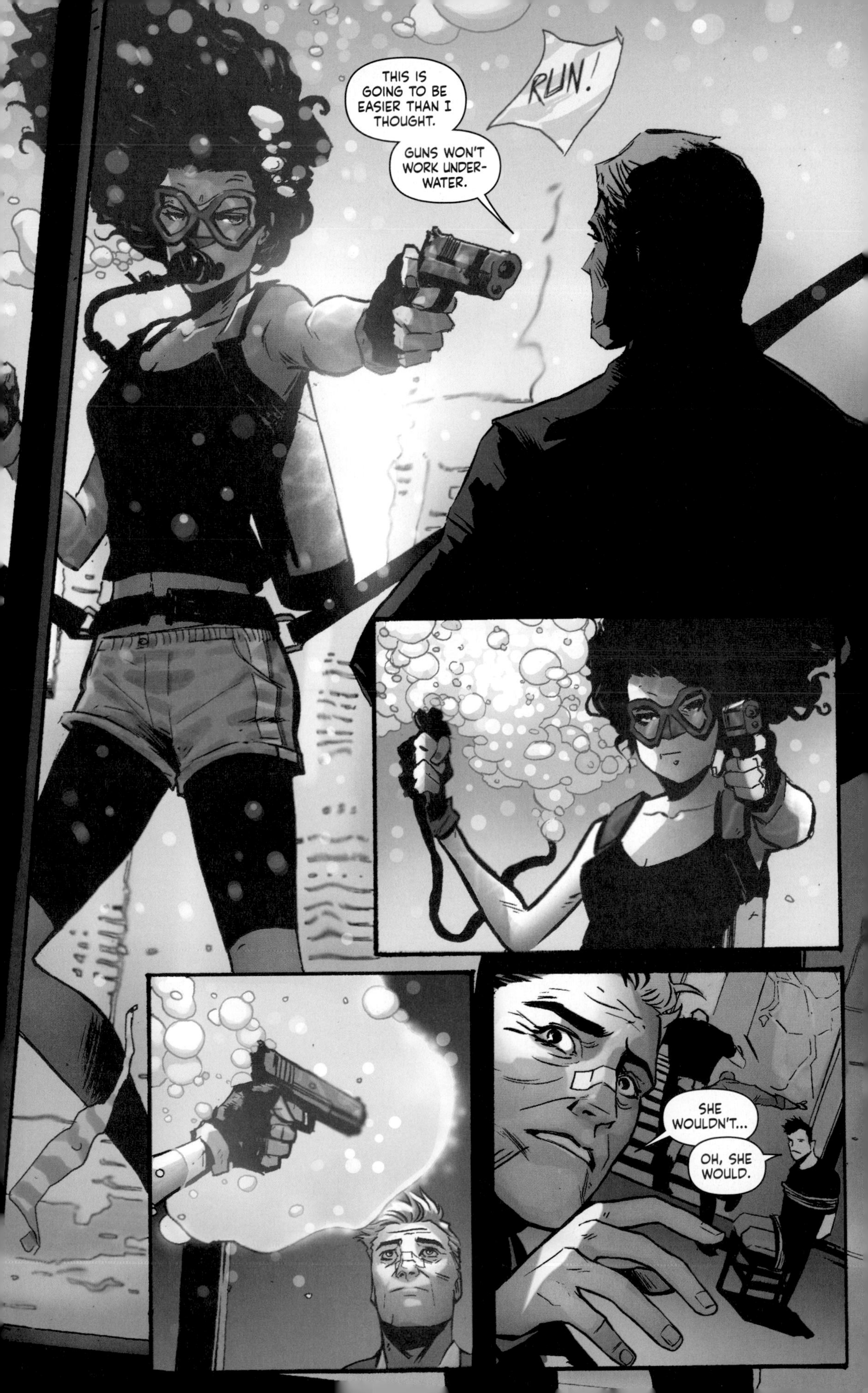
THIS IS GOING TO BE EASIER THAN I THOUGHT.
GUNS WON'T WORK UNDER-WATER.
RUN!
SHE WOULDN'T...
OH, SHE WOULD.

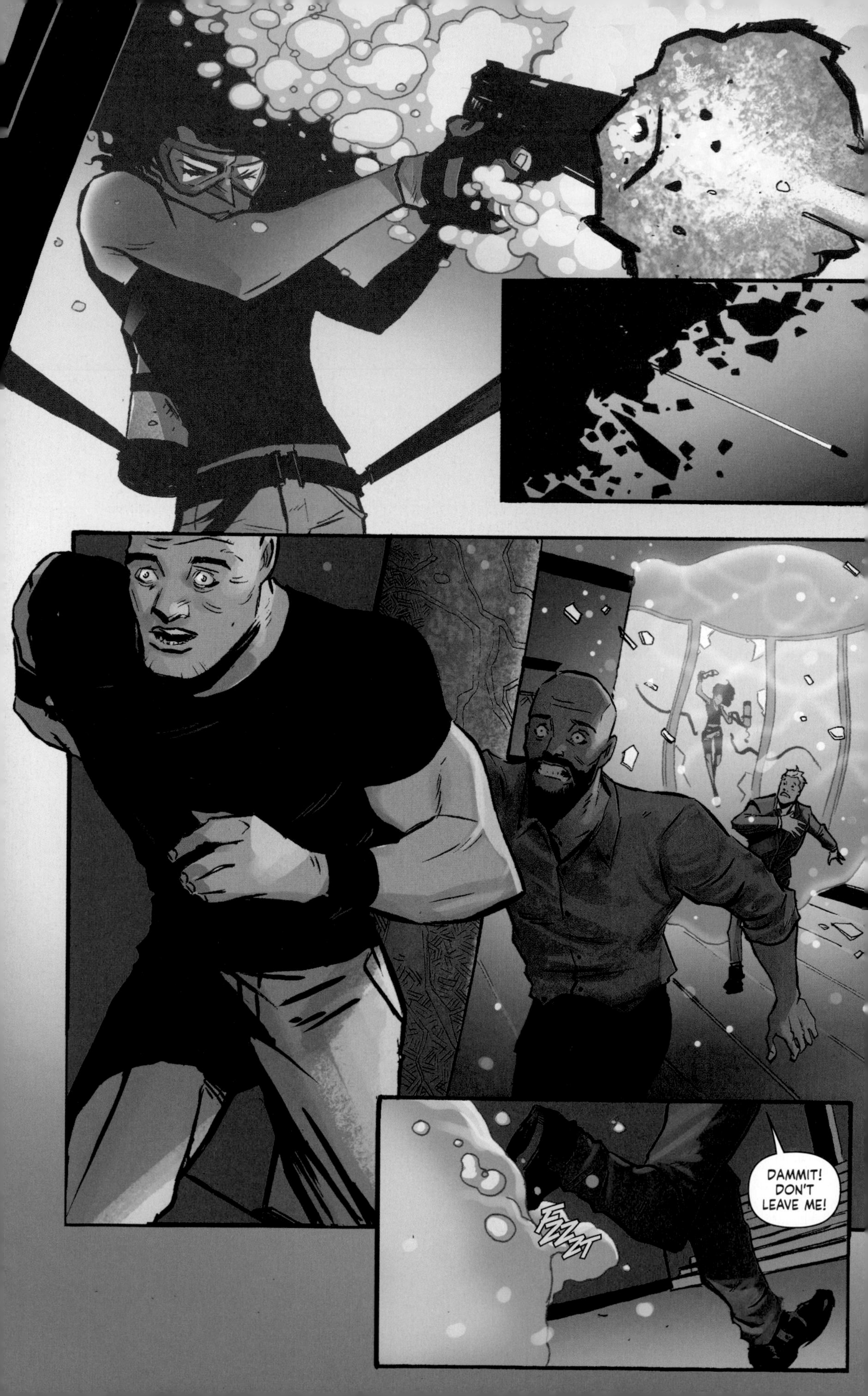
DAMMIT! DON'T LEAVE ME!
FZZZT

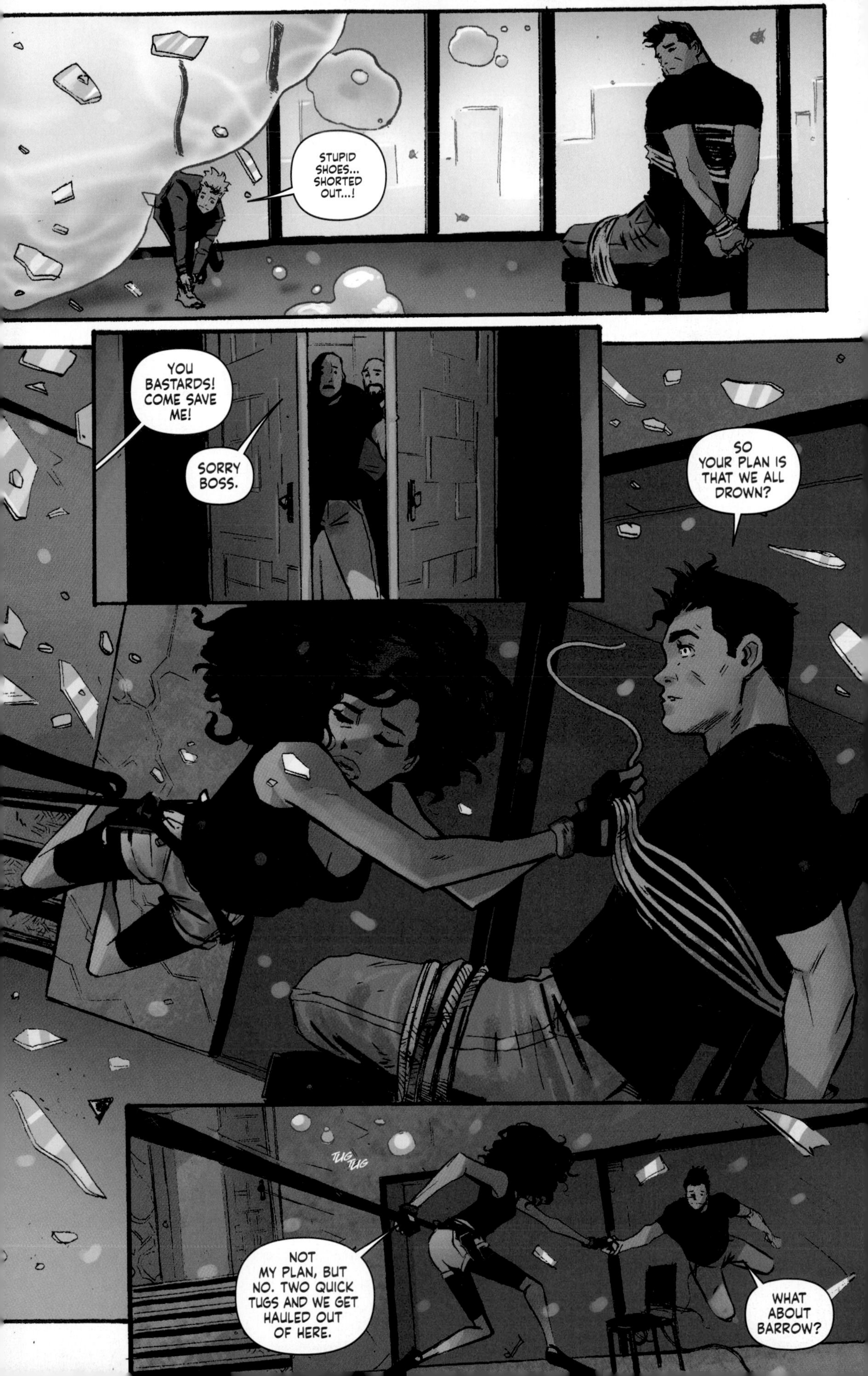
STUPID SHOES... SHORTED OUT...!
YOU BASTARDS! COME SAVE ME!
SORRY BOSS.
SO YOUR PLAN IS THAT WE ALL DROWN?
TUG TUG
NOT MY PLAN, BUT NO. TWO QUICK TUGS AND WE GET HAULED OUT OF HERE.
WHAT ABOUT BARROW?

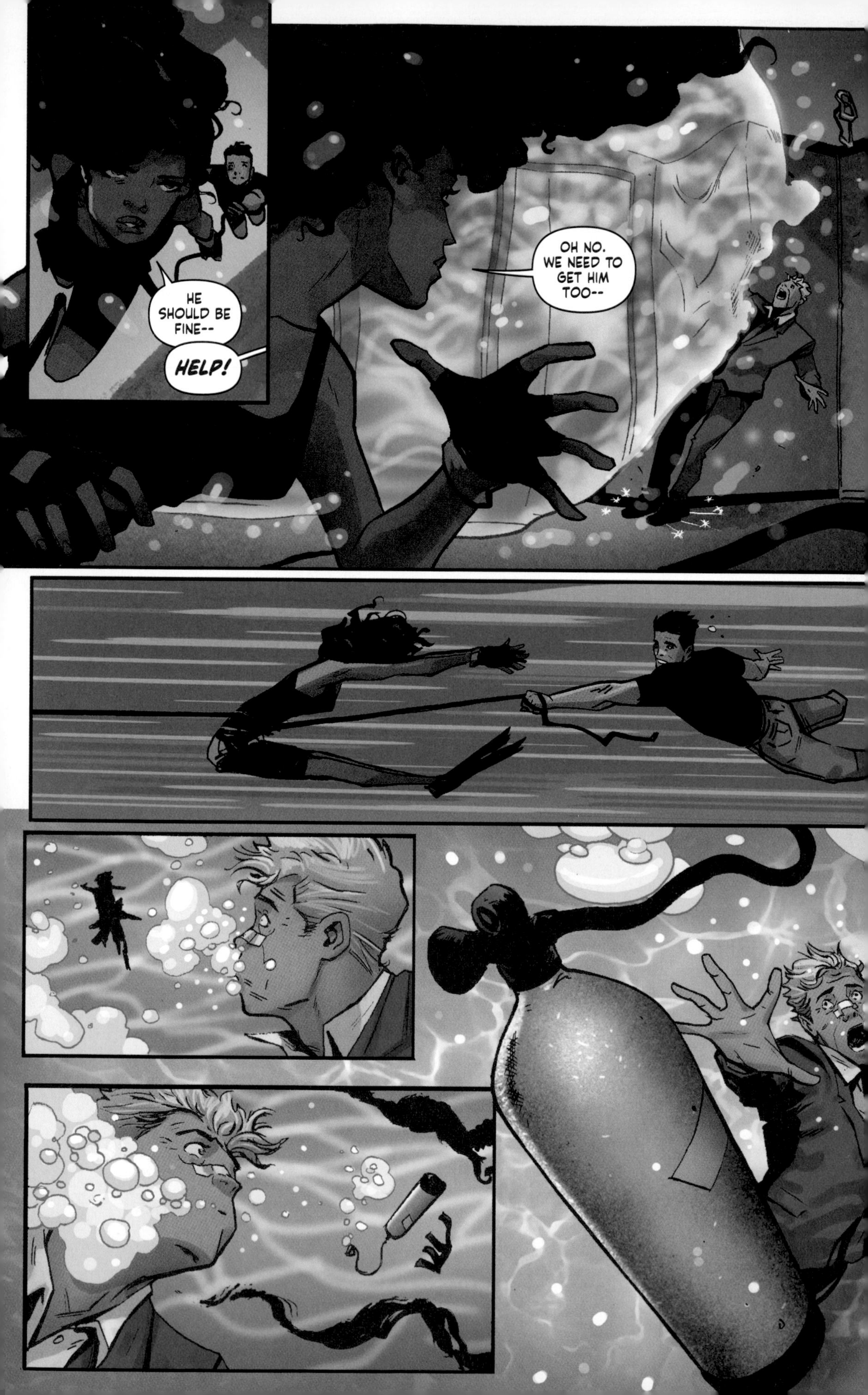
HE SHOULD BE FINE--
HELP!
OH NO. WE NEED TO GET HIM TOO--

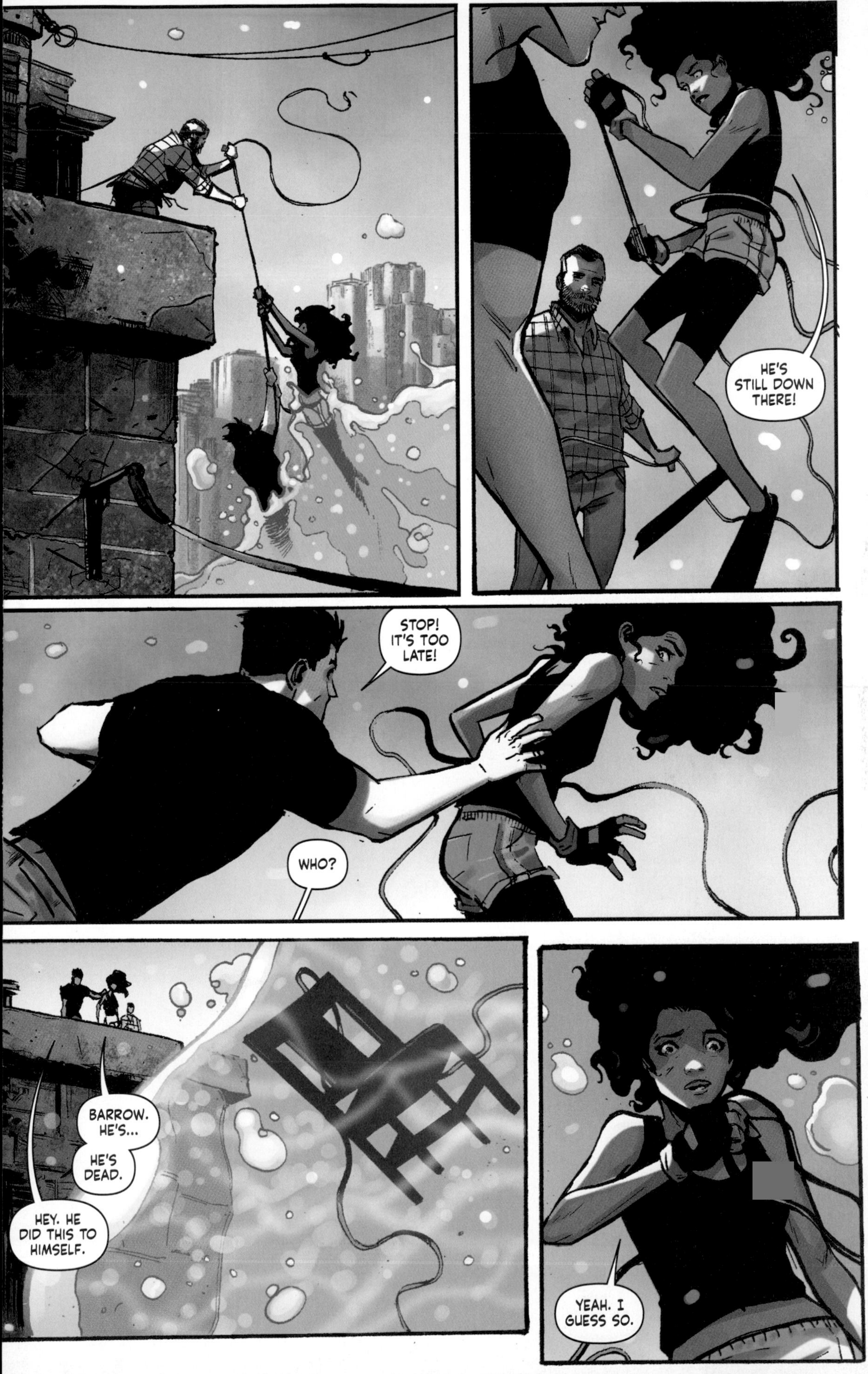
HE'S STILL DOWN THERE!
STOP! IT'S TOO LATE!
WHO?
BARROW. HE'S...
HE'S DEAD.
HEY. HE DID THIS TO HIMSELF.
YEAH. I GUESS SO.

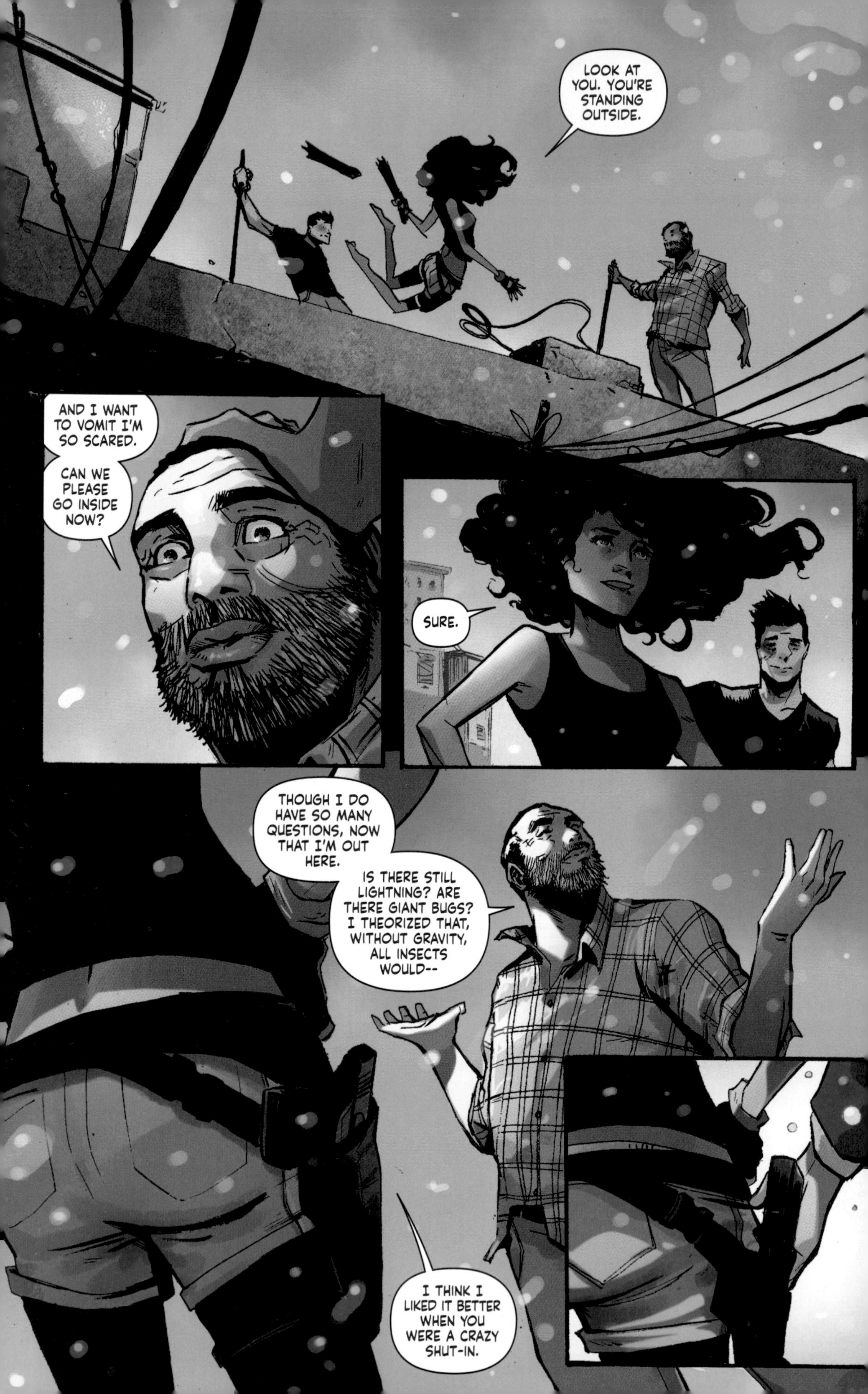
LOOK AT YOU. YOU'RE STANDING OUTSIDE.
AND I WANT TO VOMIT I'M SO SCARED.
CAN WE PLEASE GO INSIDE NOW?
SURE.
THOUGH I DO HAVE SO MANY QUESTIONS, NOW THAT I'M OUT HERE.
IS THERE STILL LIGHTNING? ARE THERE GIANT BUGS? I THEORIZED THAT, WITHOUT GRAVITY, ALL INSECTS WOULD--
I THINK I LIKED IT BETTER WHEN YOU WERE A CRAZY SHUT-IN.

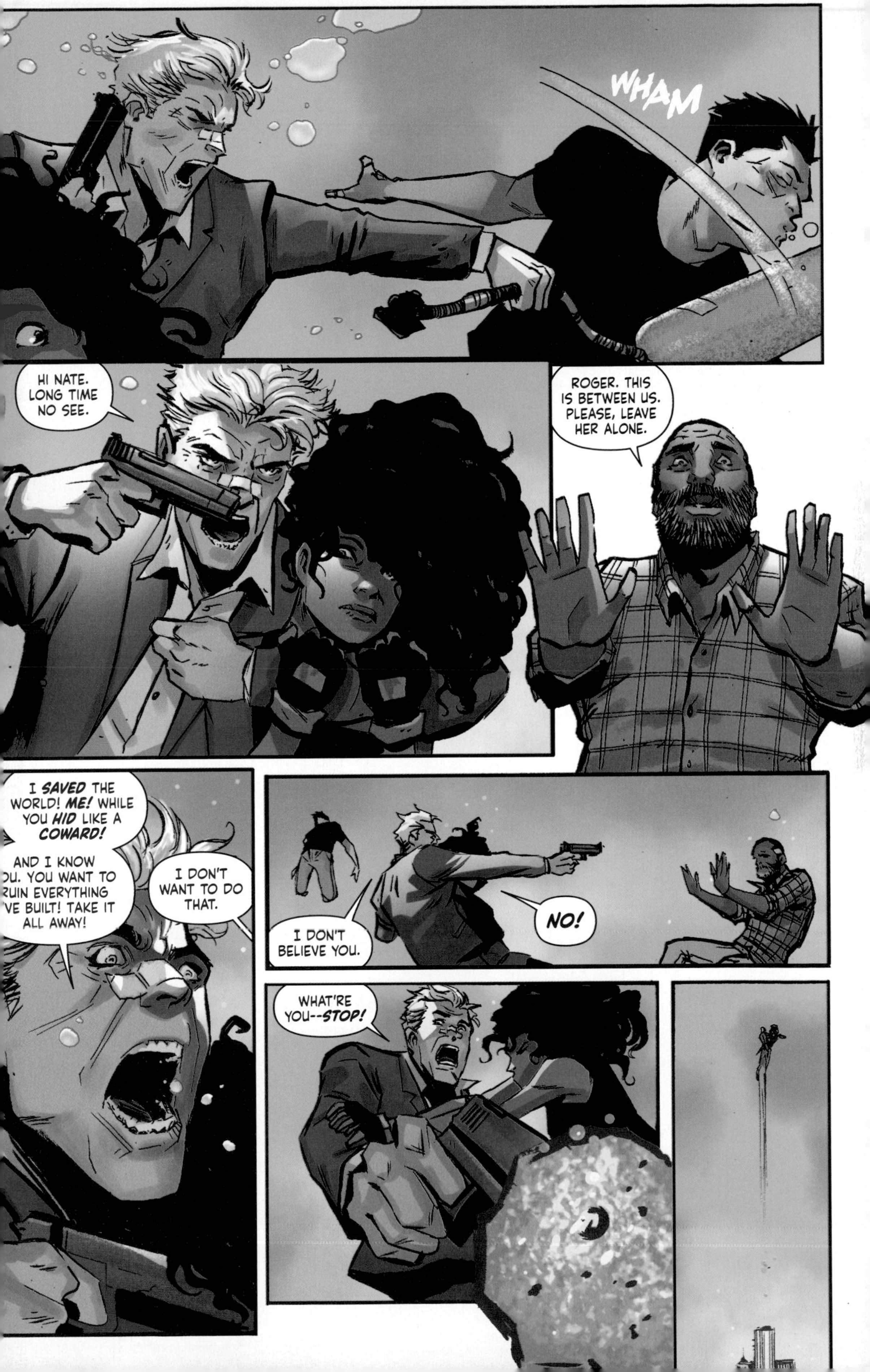
WHAM
HI NATE. LONG TIME NO SEE.
ROGER. THIS IS BETWEEN US. PLEASE, LEAVE HER ALONE.
I SAVED THE WORLD! ME! WHILE YOU HID LIKE A COWARD!
AND I KNOW OU. YOU WANT TO RUIN EVERYTHING VE BUILT! TAKE IT ALL AWAY!
I DON'T WANT TO DO THAT.
I DON'T BELIEVE YOU.
NO!
WHAT'RE YOU--STOP!

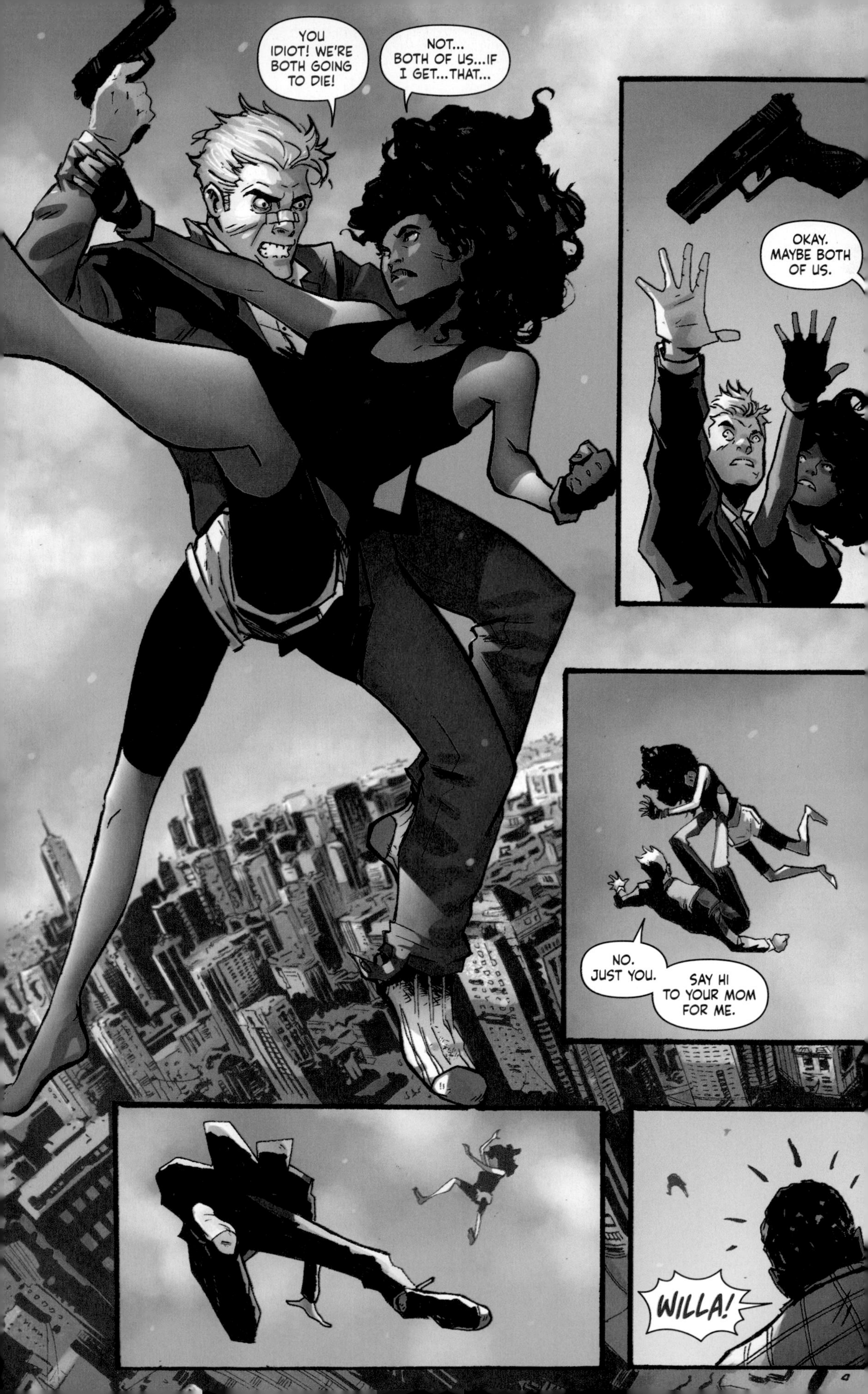
YOU IDIOT! WE'RE BOTH GOING TO DIE!
NOT... BOTH OF US...IF I GET...THAT...
OKAY. MAYBE BOTH OF US.
NO. JUST YOU.
SAY HI TO YOUR MOM FOR ME.
WILLA!

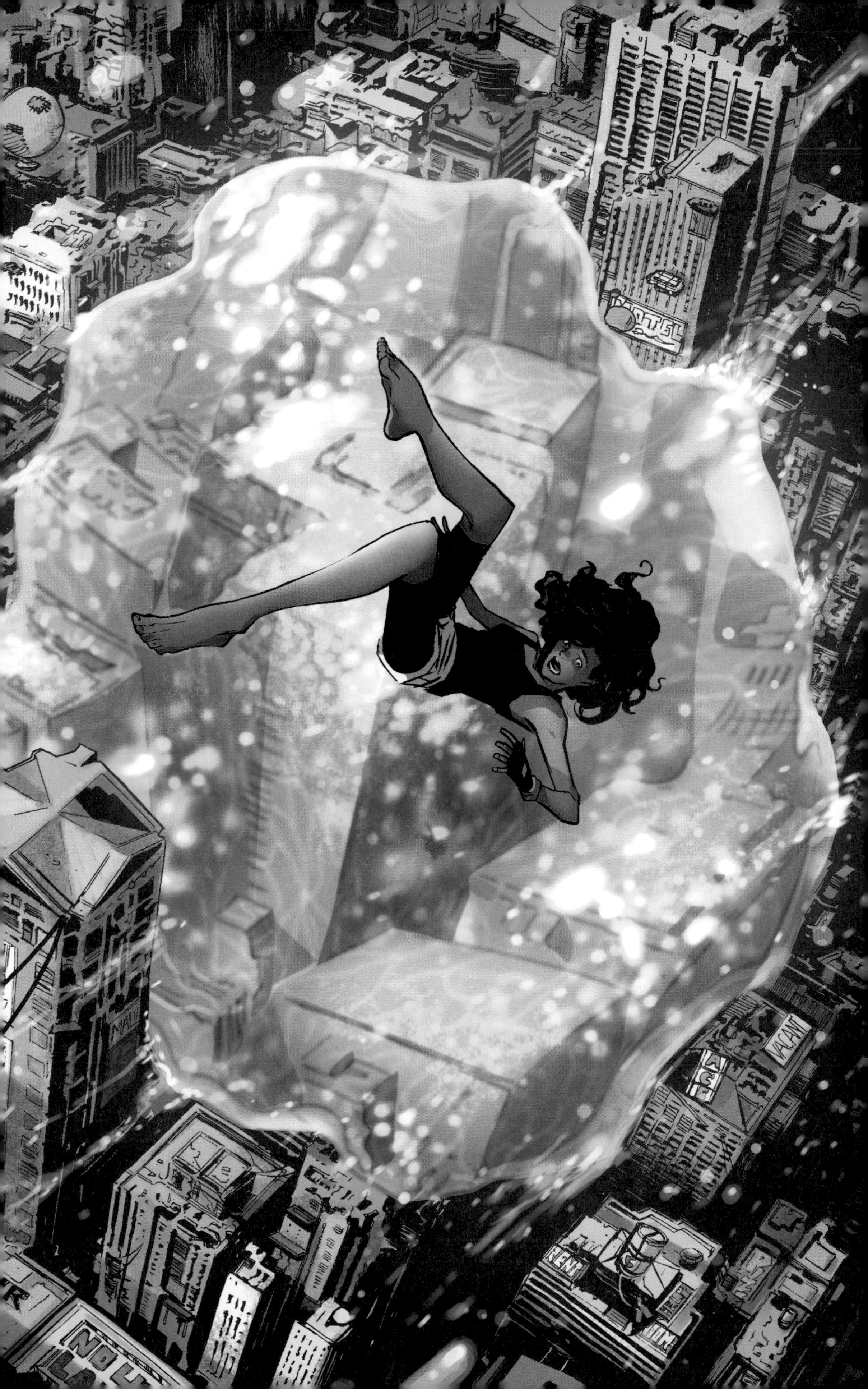
VACANT
RENT

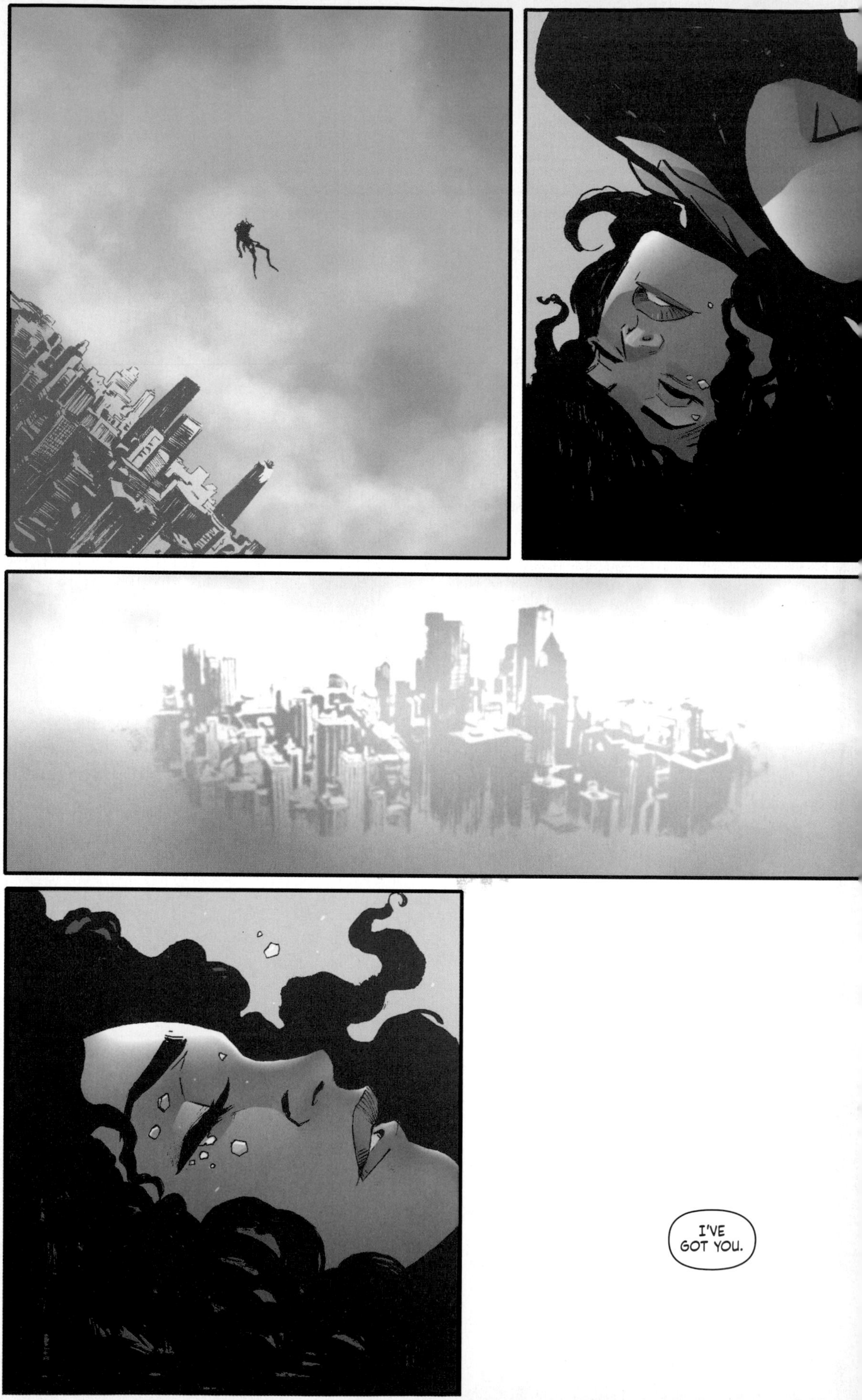
I'VE GOT YOU.

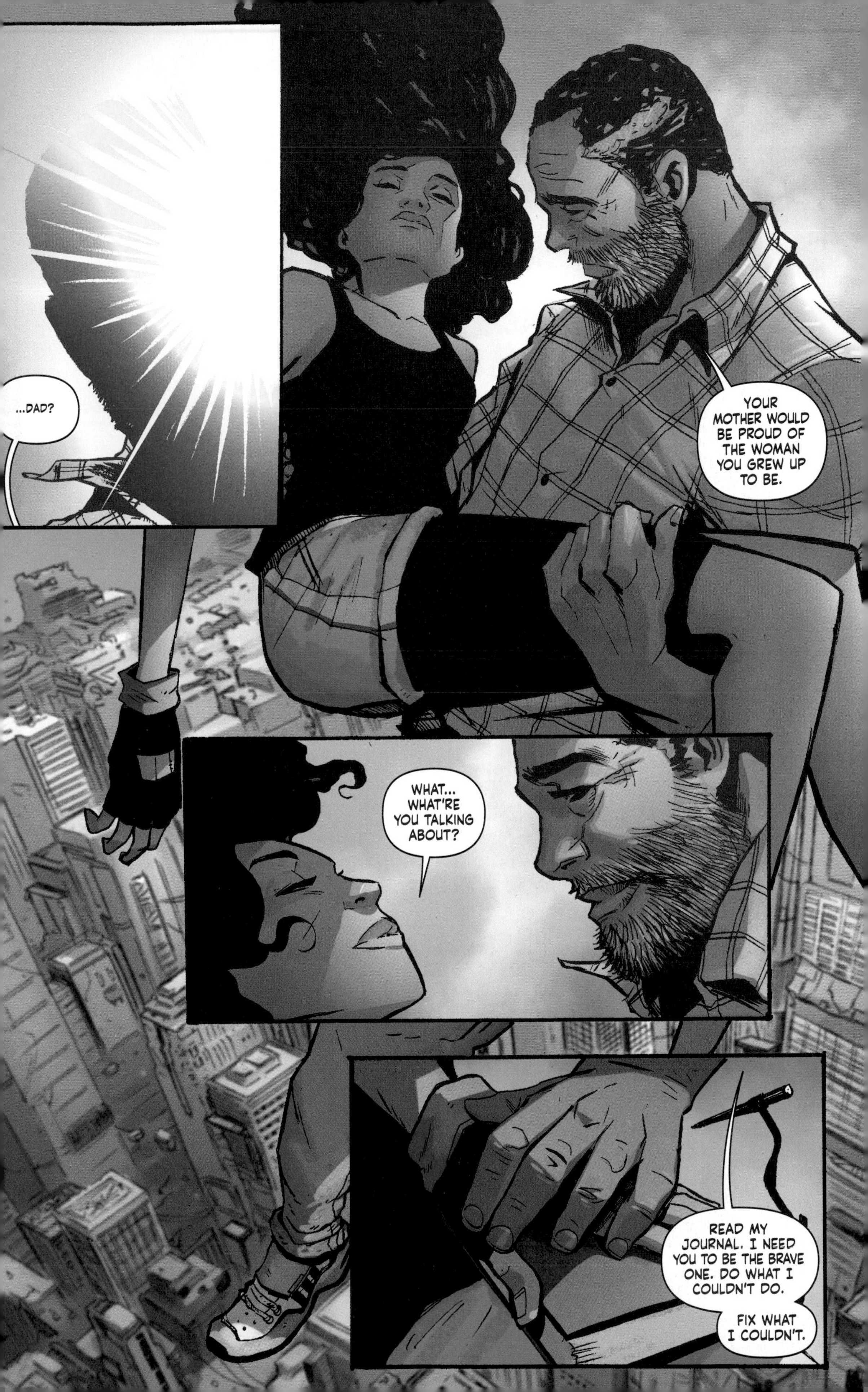
...DAD?
YOUR MOTHER WOULD BE PROUD OF THE WOMAN YOU GREW UP TO BE.
WHAT... WHAT'RE YOU TALKING ABOUT?
READ MY JOURNAL. I NEED YOU TO BE THE BRAVE ONE. DO WHAT I COULDN'T DO.
FIX WHAT I COULDN'T.

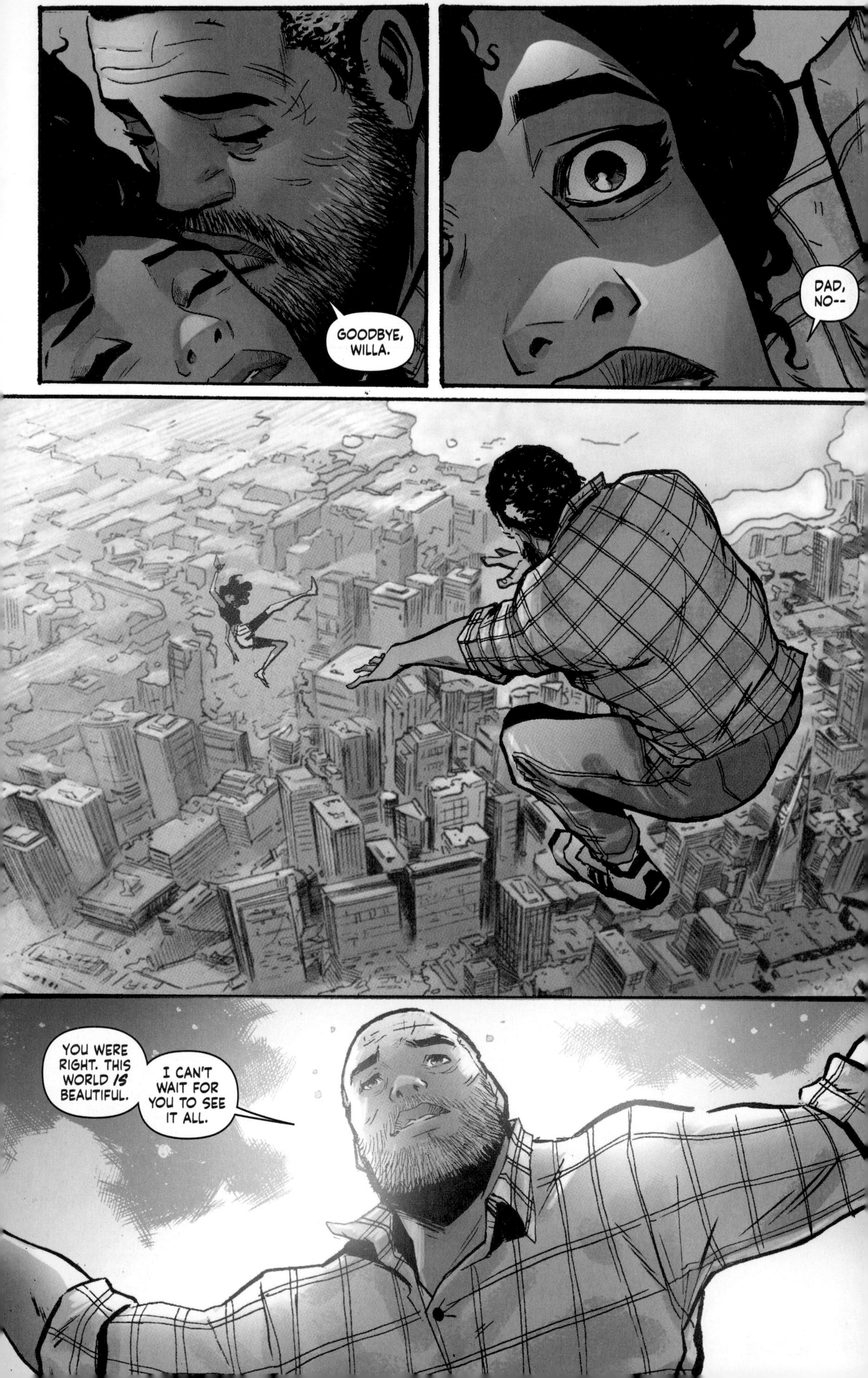
GOODBYE, WILLA.
DAD, NO--
YOU WERE RIGHT. THIS WORLD *IS* BEAUTIFUL.
I CAN'T WAIT FOR YOU TO SEE IT ALL.

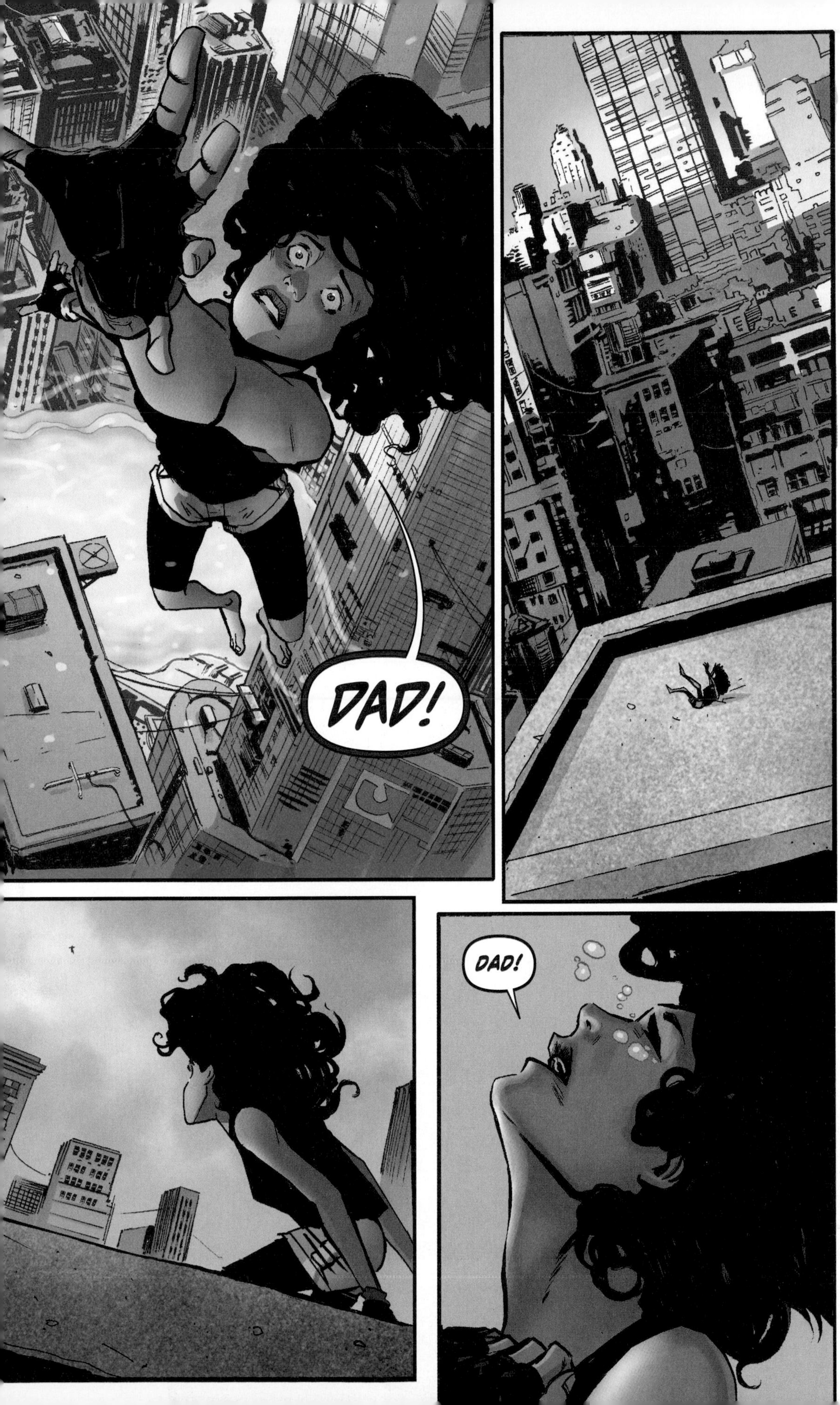
DAD!
DAD!

UNION STATION

PENNSYLVANIA RR   BURLINGTON ROUTE   G.M. & O. RR   MILWAUKEE ROAD

I WANTED
TO SEE THE
WORLD.

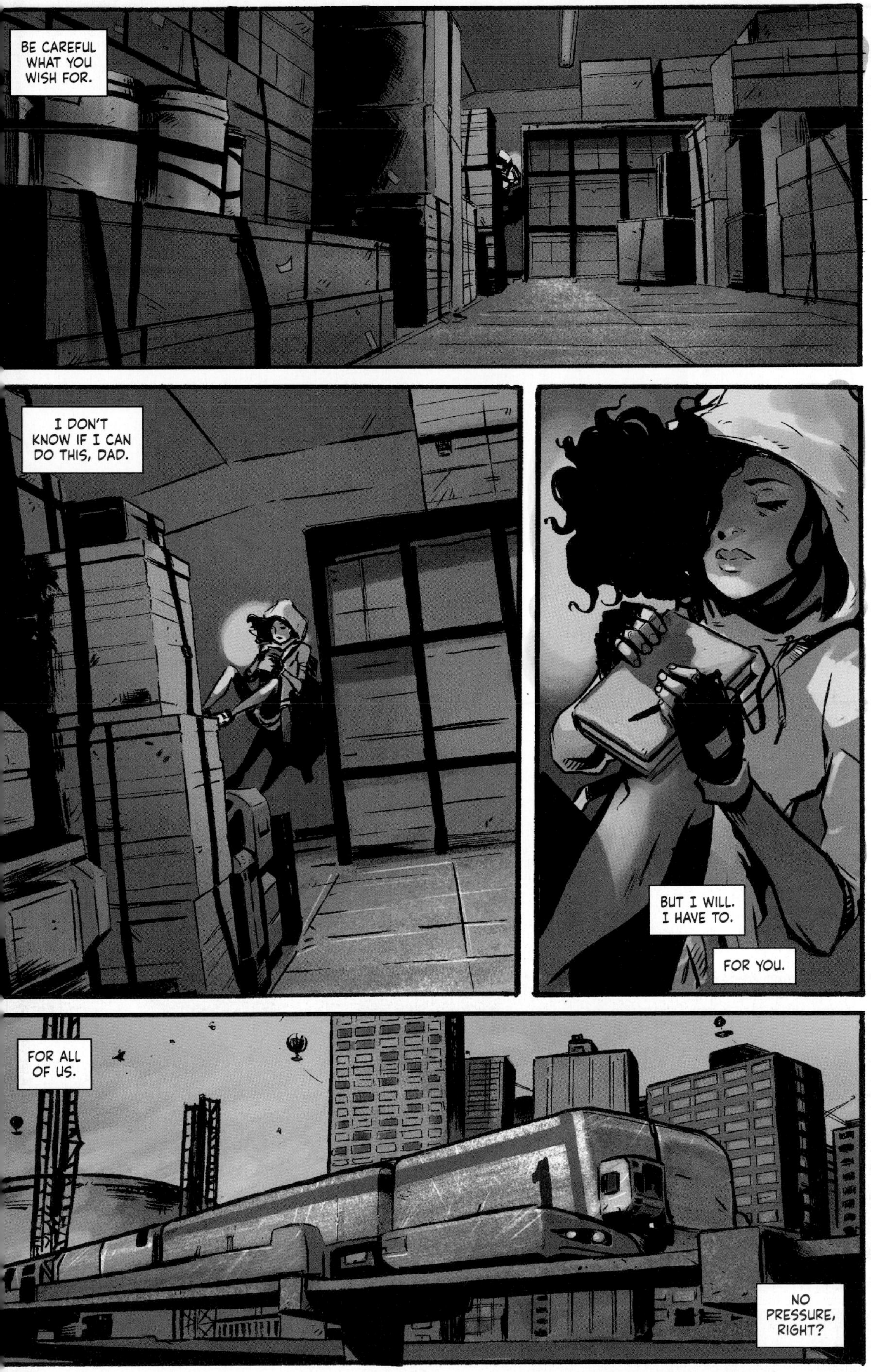
BE CAREFUL WHAT YOU WISH FOR.
I DON'T KNOW IF I CAN DO THIS, DAD.
BUT I WILL. I HAVE TO.
FOR YOU.
FOR ALL OF US.
NO PRESSURE, RIGHT?

TO BE CONTINUED

Jock's concept for Issue 1 second printing cover

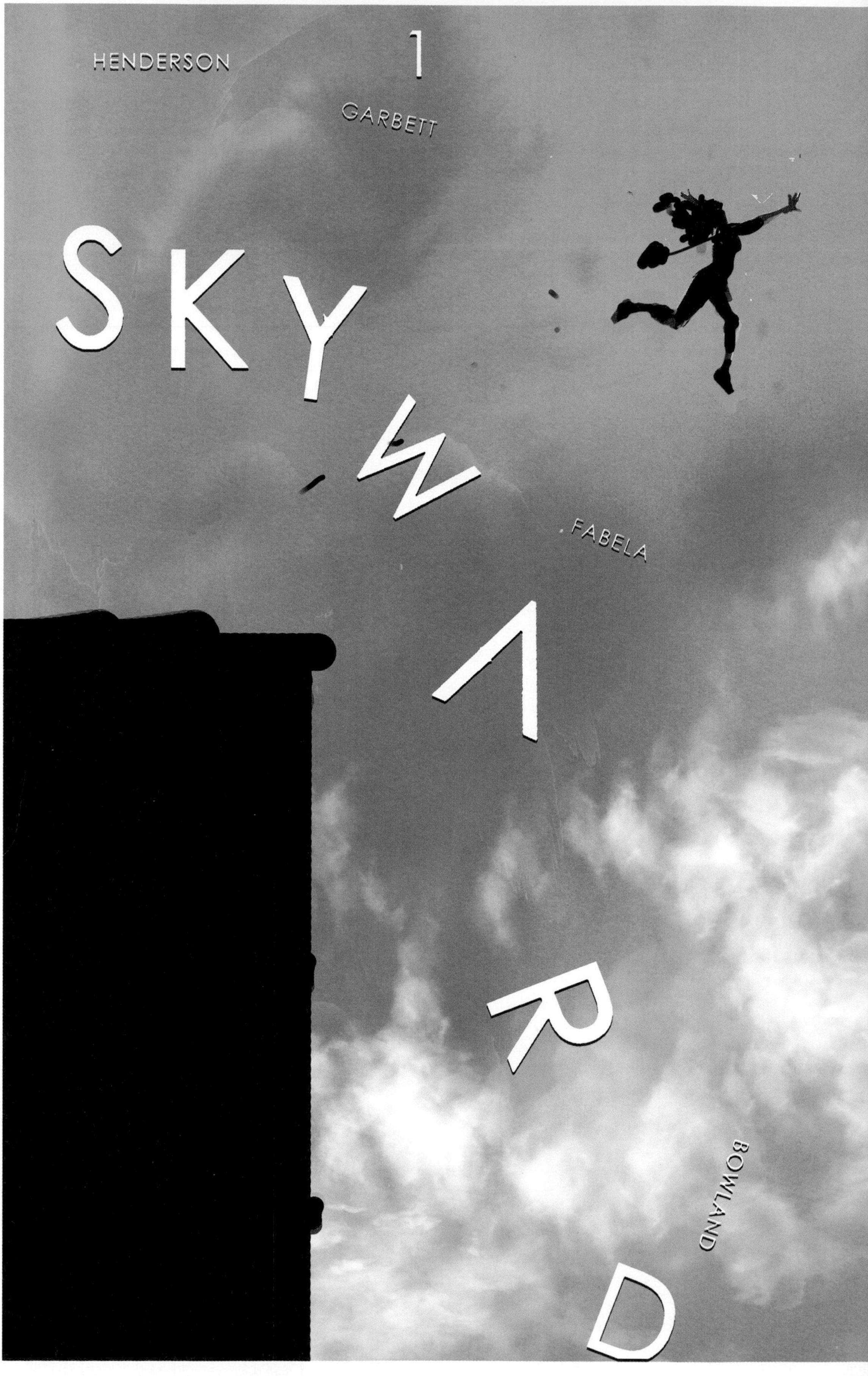
HENDERSON
1
GARBETT
SKYWARD
FABELA
BOWLAND

Jock's line art for Issue 1 second printing cover

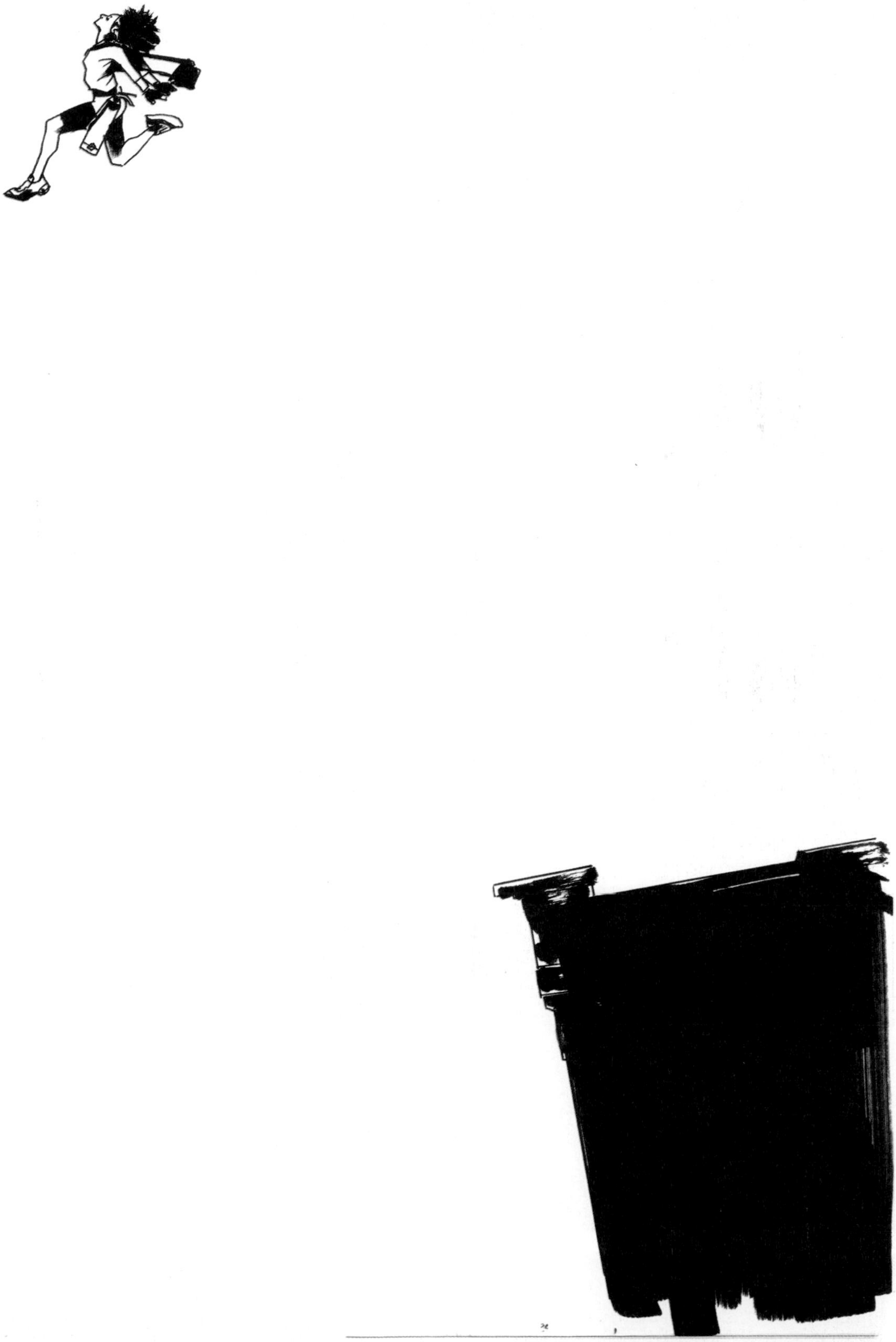

Jock's Issue 1 second printing cover

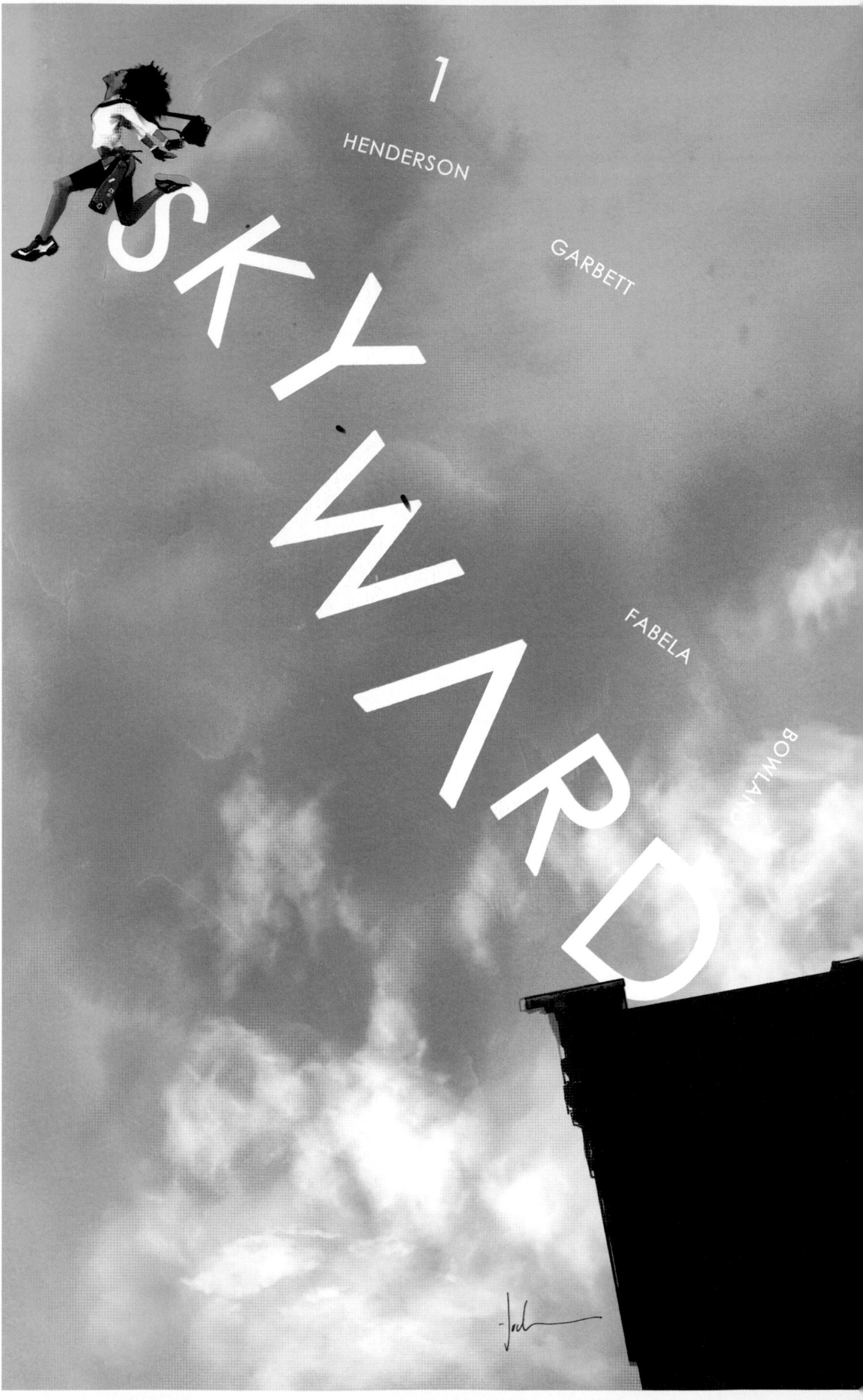
1
HENDERSON
GARBETT
FABELA
BOWLAND
SKYWARD